THE BOOK OF DESTINY

THE LAST ORACLE, BOOK NINE

MELISSA MCSHANE

Night Harbor Publishing

This book,
and the Last Oracle series,
are dedicated to Hallie O'Donovan, wonderful friend
and Abernathy's first fan

I pushed open the door to Abernathy's office with more effort than usual. It wasn't a heavy door, but today it felt like something was pushing back against me. I checked to see if there was anything behind it, but saw nothing but a box half-full of Abernathy's catalogues, minor divination tools for answering simple questions like "Where should I eat lunch?" or "Where did I leave my keys?" The box was about five feet away from the door, not in a position to block it. I shut the door behind me and deposited my purse on the melamine desk, next to the computer monitor.

Silas Abernathy's picture caught my eye, and I took a moment to look him over, captured frozen for eternity in his three-piece suit and hat. He had his hands tucked into his pockets and his smile was carefree, not the smile of someone who knew what the future held. Silas had been the first custodian of Abernathy's ever to abdicate his position in favor of becoming a magus, and he'd taken a lot of heat for it. I'd wondered, once I knew Silas's full story, why later custodians had kept his picture on the wall if so many people believed he was a traitor to his calling. Sure, it hid the wall safe, but any large framed image could do that. But Silas had brought the store from London to Portland, a huge undertaking, and maybe those other custodians honored that.

I sighed. "I wish I had your advice," I told Silas. "You'd understand, though I don't know if you ever knew the oracle was a living creature. I don't know if I'm even doing the right thing."

I polished a smear off the picture glass and straightened the frame. The mail hadn't come yet, or there would be a neat stack of envelopes on the desk, mail-in auguries for me to deal with. When had my job become something I had to "deal with" rather than a joy? That was a stupid question. I knew exactly when that change had occurred: five days shy of four months ago, when I'd walked into the oracle with a burning need for an answer and come out with knowledge I'd never wanted.

I wished Judy was downstairs already so I could talk to her about ordinary things. Usually if she wasn't in the store before me, it was because Mike Conti had spent the night. I didn't resent her love life…well, I resented a little that she wasn't around right now to distract me. And that was foolish and selfish thinking.

I walked through the stacks, straightening books without reading the titles. The room was the perfect temperature, the air smelled of roses, but I felt itchy, like I needed to shed my skin. I checked my watch: 9:17. Too early to open the doors, and when I got to the front of the store there wasn't anyone waiting outside, anyway. I perched on the wobbly metal stool behind the counter and let my eyes go unfocused so I could stare at my reflection in the glass top. I looked normal, just the way I had when I'd left home this morning. I didn't feel normal. I felt haggard, stretched thin, and weary as if I hadn't been getting enough sleep. But I knew that wasn't the problem.

I saw the mail carrier coming down the sun-drenched street and hopped down to open the door. He gave me a cheery smile along with a bundle of mail. "Beautiful day," he said.

"I guess," I replied, returning his smile. He gave me a funny look and proceeded down the street. My smile must have looked strange. It had felt strange and out of place. I really needed to work on smiling like a normal person.

I sorted the augury requests from the bills and tore open the first. *What school should I attend?* That was a nice question. A positive, forward-looking question. Something the oracle shouldn't have any trouble with. I folded the paper back on itself and regarded the bookcases. They ignored me. Well, that made sense; they were made of wood and not alive. Not like the entity they contained, or hosted, or…I was stalling. I let out a deep breath and walked into the timeless silence of the oracle.

The oracle's attention was elsewhere today, something that relieved my mind. I walked the narrow aisles between the laden shelves, looking for the blue glow of a live augury. Until recently, I would have talked to the oracle as I searched, but now I felt like a sneak thief, hoping to get in and out with my treasure without drawing the attention of the dragon guarding it.

No augury presented itself. I knew the oracle hadn't rejected the request, because the light within wasn't red-tinged, but nowhere did it say the oracle was obligated to make it easy on me. And it had become increasingly slow to respond over the last almost four months. I didn't know why, and asking hadn't produced an answer, either in the form of a book or of the oracle communicating through my thoughts. Besides, I didn't want to talk to the oracle, and possibly open up a line of conversation that would end badly.

I circled the entire oracle, checking all the aisles, and saw no spark of blue light anywhere. Time for a more direct approach. I opened the paper and read the question aloud. "Do you have an answer?" I added.

I felt the oracle turn its attention on me and braced myself for it to use my mind as its voice. But it didn't do anything but regard me. Its attention felt like a feather-filled duvet, light and fluffy at first, but slowly and inexorably growing weightier as the minutes passed. I held my tongue. I was *not* going to be drawn into conversation.

Finally, off to the left, a familiar blue glow grew until it made the bookcase it was behind look like it had a sun's corona. "Thank you," I said, and headed in that direction. The oracle went back to whatever it had been doing. I suppressed a sigh of relief and picked up the book, which had a picture of a white pig next to the title *Moo*. Weird, but that described half the books the oracle produced.

I was almost back to the store's front when I thought, **Helena.**

I cringed. I wasn't in the habit of thinking my own name, but I'd have recognized the oracle's "voice" anyway. "Yes?" I said, hoping I sounded polite and not irritated and guilty.

Something comes. Be ready.

Great. Another cryptic warning. Because I needed more of those. "What's coming?"

Something comes. An end. I will end.

I ground my teeth and hurried out of the oracle, clutching the book to my chest like armor. So far, the oracle had never spoken to me, or through me, when I wasn't in its unique space, but I had a feeling that wasn't because it couldn't. I hoped it wouldn't feel compelled to tell me any more, to remind me that it had seen its own death.

That it had seen mine as well.

I set the augury on the counter and stuck the request between its pages. Then I picked up the next envelope. But I didn't open it. I stood at the counter clutching the white envelope and stared sightlessly through the plate glass window with ABERNATHY'S painted on it in reverse. The oracle had told me that it, and I, would die, and it had repeated that warning several times a week for the past almost four months. No elaboration on the theme, no details about how or when it would happen. Just those thoughts reverberating through my head: **I will end. Helena will end.** And I didn't know what to do.

I couldn't even tell anyone. Well, that wasn't strictly true. I always told my husband, Malcolm, everything, and he had suggested I tell Lucia Pontarelli, custodian of the Gunther Node and head of magical law enforcement for the Pacific Northwest. It had been Lucia who'd forbidden me to tell anyone else until I understood the oracle's warning. "If it gets out that the oracle thinks it's going to die, it would be demoralizing as hell," she'd said. "Keep me informed, but don't spread the word." So I'd kept quiet, much as I'd wanted to tell my best friends Judy and Viv. But Lucia was right; people would freak out if they thought the oracle was going away. It was one of the Wardens' best weapons against the creatures trying to destroy our world.

I tore open the next envelope with enough force that the paper inside tore too. Cursing myself, I unfolded it carefully so as not to damage it further. *Where should my team hunt for the next month?* There'd been a lot more augury requests along this line lately, ever since the Wardens had destroyed the traitorous Mercy and struck a powerful blow against the invaders. Malcolm said the victory in Montana had given everyone fresh hope. I tried not to think about Montana and what had come of it. It had been a victory, sure, but it had come at a high personal cost.

Footsteps sounded, echoing through the room, and soon Judy emerged from the stacks. She was dressed in a vividly colored smock and her favorite Mary Janes and looked fresh and alert in a way that made me feel like the Wolfman from a '50s B movie. "Sorry I'm late," she said. "Want me to open the rest of those?" She brandished the letter opener in the direction of the envelopes.

"Sure," I said, handing them over. "And you're not late. I'm early."

"Still, I live just upstairs. It's not like it's a long commute." Judy slit open the next envelope and set it aside. "Are you all right? You look a little down."

"Just tired." I had to be careful not to use the "tired" response too often with Judy or Viv. They'd eventually figure out that something was wrong, and then I'd have to actively lie. I hurried off into the oracle, clutching my torn paper.

To my surprise, the light had gone from a peaceful, calming bluish tint to blood red. "No augury?" I said, feeling relief followed by anxiety. "Are you sure? This could be an important one, directing a team's efforts, I mean."

Two aisles over, a blue star flashed into being. The ambient light didn't change. "I don't understand," I said, making my way over to the augury. "There's an augury, but you're giving me the 'no augury' warning?"

The augury glowed brightly on a lower shelf. I bent to remove it and examined it closely, turning it front to back and over again. It looked like a fantasy novel, an ordinary mass market paperback titled *Old Tin Sorrows*. "Huh," I said, and opened the front cover.

On the title page, in silver ink, was written *Helena Campbell, No Charge*.

My whole body went numb for a few seconds, during which I gripped the augury tightly to keep it from falling, and my heart lurched painfully once before falling back into its normal rhythm, though faster than before. "I see. No augury for this team, just one for me."

I looked the book over again. A fantasy, yes, but a murder-mystery fantasy in which the killer was taking out the members of a household one by one and turning them into zombies or something. I couldn't see any way in which it was relevant to me. I *hoped* it had some sideways meaning, and that the oracle wasn't predicting painful deaths for my friends and family. "Thanks, I guess," I said, and headed for the exit.

Helena. Something comes.

I stopped. "I know that! You told me already! Stop reminding me unless you're going to be more specific. It's driving me crazy!"

The oracle's attention hovered on me, a feeling like having a giant thumb press me like a thumbtack into a wall. Finally, I thought, **They strike. Two are gone. Four remain.**

"That's an improvement. Two of what? Four of what?" I was being testy, but I didn't care.

We remain. Four remain. The guardians fall.

The oracle's attention drifted away, just as if it didn't care about what it had told me. Or maybe it had more faith in my ability to figure things out than I did. I closed my eyes and practiced breathing calmly, in through the nose, out through the mouth. I'd done a lot of calming breathing over the last four months.

When I emerged from the stacks, Judy was gone. I set the torn augury request on the counter and went to the office, where I found her intently staring at the computer screen and typing furiously. "Anything wrong?" she asked.

"I don't know. The oracle gave me an augury." I wasn't sure if I should mention the warning. It didn't seem to have anything to do with its premonition that it would end, but if I was wrong about that, telling Judy would open up all kinds of questions I didn't want to answer.

Judy looked up, her hands pausing. "Did you have a question?"

"Not really. That's what's strange." I showed her the paperback.

She turned it over, read the cover copy, and handed it back. "Weird," she said. "Murders, the undead…you'll have to study it, because nothing's coming to mind. Unless there's another serial killer running around."

"That one belonged to the Mercy. Those guys don't exist anymore." I shoved the book into my capacious purse. "And I don't think the undead are a thing."

Judy went back to typing. "Not that I'm aware. Girls' night tomorrow? Tonight Mike and I are having dinner with my father."

I whistled. "That's brave."

"They have to learn to get along eventually. Mike might be a permanent part of my life now. And if he can be friendly to my father, and vice versa, maybe that means good things for all of magery."

"That's uncharacteristically optimistic of you." Mike was an Ambrosite, and Judy's father William Rasmussen was a

Nicollien—two factions the Wardens had been divided into for the last seventy-odd years. In the time I'd been custodian of Abernathy's, I'd seen the factions' animosity grow from mutual dislike to full-on hatred, and I doubted Judy's hope was reasonable. Even if the Nicolliens stopped using familiars—the sticking point on which the factions' disagreement was based —both sides were so used to seeing each other as the enemy I wasn't sure anything would change.

"They can talk to each other for five minutes at a time without shouting," Judy said, "and if they know what's good for them, they'll manage to be civil for the length of dinner."

Judy's fierce scowl amused me enough that I was able to smile naturally. It had been a long time since I'd done that. "I hope it works out."

Back in the front of the store, I did two more mail-in auguries before I had to open the doors to the waiting Nicolliens. The oracle ignored me both times. I wished I didn't have the tangle of emotions that assailed me every time I entered the oracle: fear of what it might say, guilt and sorrow over losing the closeness with the oracle I'd come to take for granted, anger that it wouldn't just tell me what it meant.

I remembered how it had felt when the oracle had been under the influence of an illusion intended to destroy it, how devastating it had been to watch it effectively descend into madness. This was worse, because the oracle was in its right mind as far as I could tell, and that meant the problem might be me. If *I* was the weakness, and something happened to the oracle because I failed it…I didn't complete that thought.

I opened the door and held it for the first Nicolliens. A breath of warm summer air entered with them, smelling of sunshine and exhaust and hot popcorn from the theater next door. "Welcome to Abernathy's," I said. I managed another very realistic smile. "Please form——"

"Helena," someone called out, and Harry Keller pushed past the Nicolliens filing in, causing a young man to protest. Harry ignored him. He no longer stood as tall as he once had, thanks to an attack that had drained his magic and left him no longer a magus, but his voice was as firm as ever and his hand on his cane was steady. His wife, Harriet, followed in his wake, plump where he was thin. She looked like a stereotypical small-town librarian, down to the glasses perched on her nose, but she'd fought in the Long War years before I was born, and I knew better than to underestimate her.

Now she took my hands in hers and said, "We came as soon as we heard the news. Are you all right, dear?"

Confused, I said, "I'm fine—what news? Has something happened?"

Harry and Harriet looked at each other. "You haven't heard," Harriet said. "Doesn't anyone listen to the news anymore? It was on every channel."

"There was an incident," Harry said, overriding my reply. "In Berryton, Georgia. They're calling it an unexplained phenomenon right now, but that won't last."

All around me, exclamations went up as people stared at their phones, reading about the incident. "So what happened?" I asked.

"Everyone in the town is dead. Illness, the government's saying, but they've got the CDC involved, so I doubt they believe it's as innocuous as simple illness," Harriet said. "Not that they'll figure out the true cause."

"Invaders," I said. "But how could they possibly destroy an entire town?"

"That's a good question, but it's the wrong one," Harry

said. "The real question is, how could they take out a named Neutrality?"

Now I was even more confused. "What are you talking about?"

Harry and Harriet again exchanged glances. "We thought you knew," Harriet said. "Don't all the named Neutralities talk to each other?"

"Of course." There were five named Neutralities, of which Abernathy's was one, and I was in touch with all their custodians via text or email. Claude in Switzerland, Diane in Georgia—

I put a hand on the counter to steady myself. "Diane," I said. "She never said what town the Fountain of Youth is in. It's not—"

"Berryton," Harry said. "It is. Was."

"What happened to Diane?"

Harriet took my hand again. "There are no survivors in Berryton," she said. "Diane Lakin is dead. And the Fountain of Youth has been destroyed."

2

"Destroyed?" I said. It was impossible. Diane had texted me just the other day with her recipe for buttermilk fried chicken. Nobody that down-home could be…

I realized Harriet was saying my name, sounding very far away even though she was standing right next to me. "I'm all right," I said, though I wasn't sure that was true. "It's just…I can't believe it. Even the invaders can't destroy a Neutrality. Something else must have happened. How do you know it was invaders? That wouldn't be on the news."

"We have friends in the Southeast who told us," Harry said. "Somebody went to Berryton early this morning to use the Fountain. They found bodies in the streets, crashed cars, looked like something out of *The Andromeda Strain*. And the trailer park where the Fountain is was wrecked like a hurricane had struck. The Fountain itself was drained and the basin was cracked. The woman got out of there immediately and contacted the Hampton Node—that's the center of the Southeast area. They verified that the Fountain's node was sucked dry."

"But won't it…regenerate, or something? Like the nodes the Mercy drained in South America?"

Harry rested his hand on my shoulder. "The invaders didn't leave anything for the node to regenerate to. The Fountain is lost."

I turned away from him, feeling as if I'd been punched in the stomach. "How?" I whispered. "And why now? They've never been that powerful before. If they could do something like that, why not years or even centuries ago?"

"We don't know, Helena," Harriet said. "But Lucia will. You don't have to be afraid."

"Why—" I shut my mouth. In my grief and confusion I'd missed a key point in this disaster. "You mean they might come here next."

A murmur went up from the listening crowd. "If they do, Lucia will be ready for them," one of my customers said. "They won't catch us by surprise again."

My phone rang. I knew who it was before I looked at the display. "Hi, Lucia."

"You heard the news?" Lucia said, as abrupt as ever.

"The Kellers told me. How did it happen?"

"No idea yet. I'm in touch with Suzuhara at the Hampton Node. They'll figure it out, and she'll tell me. I'm sending someone over to strengthen the wards on the store. The alarm is still active?"

"I guess so. Campbell Security didn't install anything to show whether it's on or off." That struck me as an oversight now. The alarm prevented an invader wearing a human suit from coming through the front door, and the wards blocked everything else. But if something went wrong with the door alarm, I wouldn't know until it was too late. "I'll call Malcolm and get someone to check it."

"Do that. I'll let you know if there's anything else you need to do." She hung up without saying goodbye, as usual.

I let out a deep breath and stuffed my phone into my pocket. I'd finally found a skirt with pockets deep enough to hold a phone. "Someone's coming to check the wards," I said. "Would you all wait while I make a quick call?"

I retreated to the office, where I found Judy mesmerized by the computer screen. "This is unbelievable," she said. "The whole town of Berryton is dead. A *whole town*."

"It was invaders," I said, pulling out my phone again. "The Fountain of Youth has been destroyed, and Diane is dead."

Judy swiveled around to stare at me, her eyes wide. "What?"

"I have to call Malcolm. Harry and Harriet told me. You can get the story from them." I could have told her myself, but the idea of repeating it to Judy and then possibly to Malcolm, if he hadn't heard yet, made me feel exhausted and sick. I was having trouble processing the tragedy myself. A whole named Neutrality destroyed by invaders.

I called Malcolm and got his voice mail. The universe was conspiring against me. I left him a message—*call me immediately* —and put my phone away. Then I leaned on the desk and tried to calm my whirling thoughts, which made a mad cycle from invaders to Diane's death to the town's destruction to the possibility that Abernathy's might be next and around again. I felt dizzy and ill and I wished I could cry, relieve my worries that way, but my eyes ached too much for tears.

Finally I pushed away from the desk and went back to the front of the store. If invaders intended to destroy the oracle, there wasn't anything I could do about it. I had to carry on with my job and hope some of these auguries were part of the solution.

Harry and Harriet were still there, talking to Judy, when I returned. They looked at me with such concern I had to wonder whether my tumultuous emotions finally showed on my face. "Well, line up," I said, at the last minute deciding against trying to sound cheerful. "Until we know more, there's no sense speculating or being afraid."

"That's the spirit," Harry said with a smile. "No sense letting them get to you."

Harriet didn't look nearly so cheerful, but she squeezed my hand and said, "Come for dinner sometime this week, you and Malcolm."

When they were gone, I accepted the first augury slip and said, "I'll try to make this quick."

The bluish light of the oracle comforted me. I hadn't realized I'd been subconsciously expecting the oracle to be gone, which was stupid of me. "Do you know what happened?" I said, feeling my reluctance to speak to the oracle evaporate in the face of this tragedy. "Do you have a connection to the others?"

My skin tightened, and I thought, **Two are gone. Four remain.**

I stopped just around the corner from the blue glow of the augury. "You mean…you were talking about the named Neutralities? But there's only five of them. Four, now. How can *two* be gone?"

Four remain. We remain. Seal the cracks.

"I don't understand."

The pressure on me intensified. **One path. The guardians remain.**

I backed into one of the tall bookcases to support myself, because the oracle's attention had started to bear down on me, crushing me the way it did just before I became the oracle. "I'm sorry, but I don't get it," I cried out. "Two Neutralities— two guardians?—are gone, and four remain to seal something? Block the cracks?"

Abruptly, the pressure vanished, and the oracle's attention went elsewhere. I calmed my breathing and smoothed out the augury slip, which I had crushed. The augury still glowed placidly on a shelf around the corner. I collected it and returned to the store's front to hand it over. Judy gave me a narrow-eyed look when I said she'd take payment, but since taking payment for auguries was one of her jobs, I had to conclude there was something about my appearance deserving of her scrutiny. I took the next augury slip and headed back into the oracle.

By 11:33, there were only three Nicolliens waiting for auguries. I was about to take the next augury slip when the bells over the door jangled. "Welcome to...oh," I said, my voice trailing off as I registered who'd just entered the store. She wore an elegant salmon-colored linen pantsuit with a triple string of pearls, and a matching hat straight out of the '50s perched over her left ear. More pearls in fat clusters hung from both earlobes.

"Helena," Madeleine Campbell said. Her neutral tone put me on edge. As usual.

"Madeleine," I said. "What brings you to Abernathy's? You know this is Nicollien time."

My mother-in-law regarded the three Nicolliens like they were a trio of roaches she expected to see scuttle off into the darkness. "This is beyond the factions," she said, her French accent heavier than usual. "I am here to see to Abernathy's' wards. Lucia Pontarelli insisted."

"She sent *you*?" My surprise was maybe a little too pointed, because Madeleine's smile went wooden. I felt unexpectedly guilty. My relationship with Madeleine was tense at best and actively hostile at worst, given that she'd done everything she could to break me and Malcolm up, but most of the time we managed a superficial politeness. "I mean…this *is* Nicollien time, and I sort of expected her to send one of her own people."

"I am the best," Madeleine said without a trace of modesty.

I didn't know if that were true or not, but I figured Lucia wouldn't have asked Madeleine to come out of some weird desire to force the two of us to overcome our differences.

"Um…okay," I said. "What do you need?"

"Access to your basement, and privacy." Madeleine's attention turned from me to the store. Her casual appraisal of the shelves, as if they didn't meet her standards, irritated me. I caught Judy glancing at me with an expression that said Madeleine had irritated her, too.

I concealed my emotions and gestured to her, nodding at my customers in silent apology. Madeleine followed me through the stacks to the short hallway at the end of which was the staircase leading to the basement. I pulled the string to turn on the bulb lighting the stairs. "Is this good enough?"

"I will return shortly," Madeleine said. She descended the stairs without touching the rail, like she thought it might soil her pantsuit. I wasn't sure why she hadn't dressed down for what I was sure was dirty work, but I'd never seen her less than perfectly turned out, so maybe it was just who she was. I didn't really care.

Sometimes, when I was in a generous mood, I felt sorry for her—how she'd let her grief over her husband's untimely death warp her into a bitter, controlling woman. But that didn't happen often.

The final three auguries went off smoothly. When we were alone in the store again, Judy said, "I guess I shouldn't be surprised Lucia asked Madeleine to come. She was a powerful stone magus before she retired—still is, I guess. I heard she raised a sunken ship, a big one, all by herself off the bottom of the Columbia."

"If she can strengthen the store's wards, I can put up with her rudeness. At least she's stopped hinting that Malcolm and I should have kids already."

Judy whistled. "That's a major attitude shift."

"Yeah, well, I might have hinted back that nagging me on the subject might delay the blessed event indefinitely. I don't know. She might have moved on to nagging Ewan and Cathy about it." Malcolm's brother and his wife were on better terms with Madeleine than I was, mainly because Ewan had married the woman his mother had picked out for him. That they were genuinely in love was a nice bonus.

My phone rang. It was Malcolm. "I'm sorry I couldn't return your call sooner, love," he said. "Are you all right? We've been deluged with calls all morning, from people wanting their wards checked or strengthened."

"I'm fine. Just shaken. Have you heard any more about what happened? *How* it happened?"

"Nothing more than what everyone now knows—that the invaders were able to overcome the wards on the Fountain of Youth. We still don't know how they managed that, but I suspect, purely for your ears, that the intelligent invaders were behind it."

"That makes sense." It was also terrifying. Most of the

invaders attacking our world from their own reality were mindless, but a few had human intelligence—maybe better than human intelligence—and correspondingly greater power. "Except it doesn't explain why now."

"Unless it does. We don't know how many of them made it through the node in Montana before it was shut down. The invaders might now have the strongest presence they've ever had in our world. And that might mean they have the power —" He stopped speaking, then went on, "All of this is speculation. Lucia will learn more, and she will pass on what information she thinks we need. But I suggest you talk to the other custodians. If the Fountain was targeted because it was a named Neutrality, you may all be in danger."

"That's what I was thinking."

"Don't be afraid. We will protect Abernathy's, and you, with our lives."

"I hope it doesn't come to that." I still hadn't forgotten how Malcolm had looked when he was nearly killed by the Mercy. Sometimes it featured in my nightmares, when I wasn't dreaming about…the other thing. "I'll see if the others are available. Samudra might be asleep, though I don't know how anyone could sleep after this. And I'd like you—Campbell Security, I mean—to do something about the alarm on the front door, so it's obvious it's been turned on."

"Of course. I love you. We will solve this problem, I promise."

I smiled. "I love you, too."

Judy had waited patiently during that conversation, and after I hung up, she said, "I think you need to talk to someone."

My jaw clenched. "I'm fine."

"You're not fine. You've been through a lot of trauma and

it's a miracle you don't have PTSD or something. Or maybe you do, and you're just good at hiding it."

"All right," I said irritably, "let's say I need therapy. Who do you suggest I talk to? Any psychologist I go to will think I'm insane if I start talking about monsters and magical bookstores."

Judy rolled her eyes. "There are therapists at the Gunther Node," she said. "Why are you so resistant to the idea? Plenty of people see therapists these days. It's no different from going to a doctor because you have back pain, or whatever."

"I don't think there's anything wrong with therapy. I just don't think I need it. I talk to you and Viv about my troubles, and I tell Malcolm everything."

"That's not the same as having it out with someone who knows how to help you overcome your problems." Judy hopped off the stool and stretched. "Keep it in mind, okay? It can't be healthy for you to be wound so tight all the time."

So she'd noticed something, despite all my care. "I'll think about it," I promised. "Now, let's have lunch."

But before we could enter the break room, Madeleine emerged from the basement. She looked as tidy and clean as before, annoying me. "The wards are secure," she said. "I have increased their power as much as can be without making the store physically impregnable."

"Thanks," I said. "I guess we still need to be able to get into Abernathy's."

"Exactly." She regarded me with that same neutral expression I hated. I knew it concealed a different emotion, and it bugged me that I didn't know which one.

"Well…thanks," I said again, and stood aside to let her pass.

She didn't move. "You knew the custodian of the Fountain of Youth?"

"I did. She was a good friend."

"Then I am sorry for your loss."

She didn't exactly look sorry, but I decided to take her at her word. "Thanks. It hasn't really sunk in yet."

"That is how it feels to lose someone," Madeleine said, and just for a second, her composure cracked. "There is the… disbelief, saying 'What?' and going on saying it for many days."

Since I'd lost another friend just four months before, I almost replied with something sarcastic. But this was the most vulnerable Madeleine had ever been with me, and it was unexpectedly touching. "That's how it feels, yes," I said. "Like… why haven't I heard from her today?"

"Yes. That." Madeleine's expression softened. "It is a tragedy on many levels. Two named Neutralities gone."

"Yes, I—what did you say?"

Madeleine's eyes narrowed at my sharp tone. "I say it is tragic for more—"

"No, I mean—what about two Neutralities? Only one was lost."

"Only one today," Madeleine said. "The Well was lost long ago. You do not know this?"

I glanced at Judy, who seemed not at all surprised by this news. "I didn't. What's the Well?"

"The Wishing Well," Judy said. "It was destroyed before I was born. I didn't realize you hadn't heard that story."

"I thought a Neutrality couldn't be destroyed. Isn't that why everyone's so worried about losing the Fountain?"

"It was not the same," Madeleine said. "The Well was not

destroyed as the Fountain was. It was corrupted, put beyond use. But it is still there."

"I want to hear about this," I said.

Madeleine shrugged. She walked into the break room and took a seat. I hadn't actually meant for *her* to tell me about it, but I wasn't going to be rude. I sat opposite her at the folding table, and Judy leaned against the door frame.

"The Wishing Well is the oldest of the named Neutralities," Madeleine said. "It is in what is now Iraq. Baghdad. People would toss in a thing of value and make their wish, and the Well would grant it according to how valuable the thing was. The custodian gathered the offerings…it was as all the named Neutralities are, that they collect money and so forth. But the Well was different. Not all the offerings were retrieved, as if the Well kept some for itself. But that does not matter."

She leaned forward as if she wanted to put her elbows on the table but was too well-bred. "Some fifty years ago there was fighting in the Middle East. Not of the mundane type. Magical war. And not between factions, but Nicollien fighting Nicollien, family against family. One family decided to prevent the other from use of the Wishing Well. They killed the custodian and dumped his body into the Well."

I covered my mouth to hold back a gasp. "That's horrible!"

"They were not good people. The Nicollien Archmagus finally sent in others who destroyed both families utterly. They tried to retrieve the custodian's body, but it had vanished."

"I heard the water in the Well turned bloody after that day," Judy said.

"I do not know that," Madeleine said. "What is certain is that from that day forward, anyone daring to wish on the Well is cursed. Some die immediately, others suffer terrible misfortunes, but there are no exceptions. The Well is poisoned."

"So it might as well be destroyed," I mused. Two gone, four remain. But why had the oracle referred to the named Neutralities as guardians? I'd had one question answered, but that left a slew of them I didn't understand.

"Yes," Madeleine said. "I think the Arabian nodes have not given up trying to reclaim the Well, but they keep to themselves these days. Few foreign magi are allowed in the Middle East."

"I'd heard that. It's weird to think the whole area was shut down for reasons not relating to the Long War."

"Ours are not the only problems in the world, just the most serious." Madeleine stood and straightened her pantsuit. "You will call me if you see any problems with the wards, yes?"

"I…sure, I guess so." She'd sounded perfectly professional, and I'd responded without thinking. Well, if Madeleine could change even a little bit, I could be big enough to accept it.

We walked with her to the front door, where she nodded farewell and walked to Abernathy's magically reserved parking space and the sporty red coupe parked in it. I watched her drive away and said, "Was that surreal, or was it just me?"

"I didn't think she was capable of ordinary conversation," Judy replied.

"Maybe she's changing. She can't be happy, holding in all that anger and bitterness all the time."

"You're too optimistic to be real," Judy said.

"I'm not *that* optimistic. You didn't hear me invite her to dinner, did you?" I ran my fingers through my hair and yawned. "I wish I could go home and end this day already. I don't know if I can bear any more shocks."

My phone rang.

"You need to not hand the universe such amazing straight lines," Judy said.

I checked the display. Ariadne Duwelt, my liaison with the Board of Neutralities. "Hello?" I said.

"Helena. How are you?"

"Fine, just a bit rattled. Is everything all right?"

"We're concerned, naturally."

I almost laughed. Ariadne was as laid back as they came, and "concerned" was, for her, the equivalent of "freaking out." "The wards on Abernathy's were checked and they're as strong as they can be without preventing people from entering."

"It's possible it will come to that. We're still not sure how the invaders managed to destroy the Fountain, but we know they exploited a weakness in its wards."

The back of my neck tingled. That had come too glibly to be real. "I…think you're not telling me the whole truth."

Ariadne sighed. "We are trying to keep quiet the fact that it was a large number of intelligent invaders who were responsible for the destruction, all right? No sense stirring up fears."

"Sorry to contradict, but don't you think people have a right to know what danger they're facing? I don't know much about fighting invaders, but I do know it's important to base a fighting technique on the type of invader a Warden faces."

"We won't be able to conceal it for long, and you're right, people need to know. But we want to be able to give more concrete information. I'll call you when we know more. It's essential that we protect the rest of the named Neutralities."

Another warning tingle. "You make it sound like there's more to it than wanting to avoid more destruction."

"The named Neutralities are the biggest nodes in the world. Never mind losing their special advantages—we can't afford for the invaders to get their tentacles on that much raw power."

I glanced at Judy, listening to this call without disguising her interest. "The oracle said…it referred to the named Neutralities as 'guardians,'" I said. "Does that make sense to you?"

"It's not anything I've heard before, but I suppose you could call them that. Guardians of magery, certainly." She sighed again. "Keep doing your job, and prepare for word that Abernathy's will have to temporarily shut down. I'm not saying it will definitely come to that, but it might." She hung up.

"Guardians? Were you going to tell me this?" Judy demanded.

"Madeleine drove it out of my head," I lied. "Besides, it wasn't more than that. It just said two were gone, four were left, and it called the ones that remained guardians."

"That's weird. Guardians of what, I wonder?"

"I don't know," I said, "but I hope the invaders don't know more than we do."

3

I propped my chin on my hand and stifled a yawn. With the rest of the named Neutralities on the other side of the world, it made sense for us to schedule this call for midnight my time, but it didn't make me any less tired. I'd set up my laptop on the kitchen table, had a big mug of herbal tea at my elbow, and was just waiting for the call to come in.

The rest of the day had been uneventful, but I hadn't relaxed. I wasn't so much afraid for Abernathy's as I was for whoever the invaders might strike next. Granted, that could be Abernathy's, but deep down I felt the invaders, the intelligent ones, wouldn't be so obvious. I wished I knew their plan. No, I wished *Lucia* knew their plan, because I had faith in her ability to counter it, backed by the other Neutralities and the magi.

"Helena?"

I half-turned to look at Malcolm standing in the kitchen doorway. "I'm going to bed," he said, "unless you want me to wait up?"

I smiled. "No, but it's sweet of you to offer. I don't know

how long this will take. Probably not long, unless one of the others knows something I don't."

He came forward and kissed me. "Good night."

"Good night. I love you."

I watched him disappear through the doorway and sighed. That one little interaction left me feeling more relaxed than I had all day.

The laptop began chiming. I hit the button to connect to the video call. The camera light blinked on, and four smaller screens appeared. One of them showed me—did I really look that disheveled? I resisted the urge to comb through my hair with my fingers and sat up straighter.

Three men looked back at me from the other tiny rectangles. They all looked far fresher than I did—well, for them it was morning or midday. Though Claude Gauthier, custodian of the Athenaeum, always looked alert no matter what time of day or night I spoke to him. He claimed he hadn't slept in twenty-five years, which struck me as implausible, but who knew what weird effects a named Neutrality might have on its custodian? I, for example, hadn't had so much as a sniffle in the nearly three years I'd been Abernathy's' custodian.

Amarion Katsaros of the Labyrinth, on the other hand, had natural dark rings under his eyes that made him look older than his thirty years. I felt a pang, in looking at him, that he wasn't my friend Iakkhos, who'd passed away just ten months ago, but Iakkhos had been well over a hundred years old and had gone peacefully. I didn't know Amarion well yet, but he was as friendly and outgoing as Iakkhos had been, and it was easy to see why Iakkhos had chosen him as his successor.

And then there was Samudra Magar, his smooth dark skin and graying black hair giving him a distinguished elder statesman look. The custodian of the Sanctuary was always polite, but I had a feeling that he disapproved of me for being so young. From comments he'd made, I'd gathered I was the youngest custodian Abernathy's had ever had, and I'd come to realize Samudra didn't trust anyone younger than forty. Diane and Amarion came in for the same polite but chilly treatment, or I'd have felt more insulted. As it was, I returned him politeness for politeness and hoped his attitude might change over time.

Samudra spoke first. "Is everyone connected?" His English was heavily accented, but English was the only language we all had in common.

We all replied in the affirmative. "Thank you, Helena, for being willing to take this call at such a late hour," he continued.

"It's no problem, Samudra, thanks." I always had the impulse to call him "sir" that I'd so far successfully controlled.

"Well. It has been a terrible day for magery," Samudra said, "and a great personal loss for each of us."

"Mourning will have to wait," Amarion said. "Right now we should discuss the fates of our own Neutralities. The invaders will certainly come after us next." His English was perfect and unaccented despite Greek being his first language.

"The wards on the store are as strong as they can be and still allow us to use the oracle," I said.

"But is that enough?" Claude said. "I think, me, that Diane did not disregard her charge's safety. Granted that the Fountain's wards might not have been as strong as possible, but they would have been powerful regardless. We should be asking what the invaders have learned that allowed them to overpower wards of any strength."

Everyone was silent. "I was wondering," I finally said,

tentatively, "whether what happened to the Well might be important."

"What do you mean?" Samudra said.

"Well, I've only just learned the Well exists, so I don't know much about it. But it was corrupted by human action, right? What if the invaders did something like that to the Fountain, and it warped the wards, or something?"

Amarion's eyes narrowed like he was thinking hard. "I don't know," he said.

"It seems unlikely," Samudra said. "The Well is still there, and to my knowledge is still warded—powerfully so, to prevent any more tragedies."

"Perhaps not," Claude said. "It was not possible to ward it completely against physical intrusion, as that would draw mundane attention to it. But it is true those wards have a very strange shape, to my knowledge."

"Does the shape of a ward make a difference?" I asked.

"It can," Samudra admitted. "I have made it a point to stay informed about how the wards on the Sanctuary work, and the stone magi tell me the Sanctuary's node distorts its wards in peculiar ways. The example they gave was of a stone disc broken in half, not smoothly, but with jagged edges. Both must be aligned perfectly to make a whole. The wards are made jagged by the node, and the stone magi build matching wards that mesh into a single magical structure."

"I get it," I said. "So if the node behaved differently— warped the wards in a different way—would that weaken the wards? Because they no longer, um, mesh?"

Samudra's face had grown thoughtful as I spoke. "I cannot answer that, as I am not a stone magus," he said, "but it is a theory worth pursuing. I shall contact the Devarakonda Node when we are finished here and ask Mr. Chowdhury to send a stone magus. However, I cannot imagine a condition that would alter a node enough to change the way it affects the world."

"Nor can I," Claude said, "but nodes grow and shrink over time, so there is nothing inherently impossible about them changing in other ways."

"I agree that it is worth considering," Samudra said.

His approval warmed my heart, and I had to remind myself that I wasn't a lap dog, eager for praise from my master. Especially since Samudra wasn't my master. "Can I ask something about the Well?" I said. "You said it was still there, and I was told it could still grant wishes, but that they were cursed wishes. Why would anyone even make a wish, if they knew it was cursed?"

Amarion grimaced. "Some people are hard of learning," he said. "They believe their request is so pure it won't be tainted. Others think they've learned the secret way of asking that will grant them success. And some simply do not know the danger. Those are outsiders, usually, ordinary non-Wardens who toss a penny into the Well and make an idle wish. Because they pay little, the Well gives them little, and that's true for its curse as well."

"The Well has been corrupt for over fifty years," Claude said, "but the Wardens have not given up on reclaiming it. It would be a great boon to magery were they to succeed."

"I heard only the Middle Eastern magi are allowed to go there," I said.

Samudra nodded. "This is mostly true. The conflict in the Middle East makes it hazardous in places for foreign magi, particularly those of American and European descent. But there are those who go anyway, without official sanction, naturally." His pinched, disapproving expression told me those were likely hot-blooded young men with no common sense. I wondered if Malcolm had ever gone to the Middle East, either as a Navy SEAL or as a magus. He had plenty of common sense.

"So the invaders couldn't attack it without being noticed," I said.

Samudra began to speak, then subsided, his pinched expression becoming thoughtful.

"It would do them no good," Claude said, then fell silent as well. Amarion had an inward-turned expression, like he was thinking hard.

"What is it?" I said finally, feeling impatient.

Claude shrugged. "Possibly nothing. It is just…we assume the invaders have not attacked it because it is poison to them as well as to us, but that is a guess only. Perhaps we should not depend on guesses."

"I'll tell Khalil al-Hussein at the Najmeh Node of this possibility," Amarion said. "The Well is heavily warded, but I don't know how often they check the wards."

"But this leaves us with the other possibility," Claude said, "that the invaders struck at the Fountain in a non-magical way. I did not ask how Diane died, obviously, but if it was other than simply being drained of her magic…"

Silence fell over the four of us. I didn't want to think about Diane's death at all. Invaders usually killed by draining someone's magic, and it was an agonizing death, but there were a lot of ways to die that were equally awful, and if Diane… I shuddered and said, "I suppose we ought to tell someone about this possibility. I doubt anyone would think of telling us if Diane died a different way. Just…just killing her wouldn't do it, because Mr. Briggs was murdered and it didn't hurt the oracle—oh, I can't believe I just said that."

"Michelle Suzuhara at the Hampton Node spearheads this investigation," Samudra said. "I do not know her."

"Lucia does," I said. "And she should probably be told, too. I know the Board of Neutralities goes to her first when they need someone to, um, put pressure on the magi."

"Very well. Then you will discuss this with Ms. Pontarelli," Samudra said. "And each of us will discuss with our stone magi the possibility of the wards being distorted and therefore weakened."

"I—oh, Xerxes!" I exclaimed as a furry body leaped onto the table in front of the laptop. "Sorry, everyone." I grabbed my Persian cat around his fluffy midsection and unceremoniously dropped him on the floor. "He knows he's not allowed on the table, but he thinks if there's no dishes…anyway."

"Of course," Samudra said, and to my surprise he was smiling the smile of a fellow cat guardian. "He is large."

"Eighteen pounds of bird-chasing fur." Xerxes rubbed against my leg as if he knew I was talking about him. My pajama legs were always covered with white hairs.

"As I said, I'll warn Khalil," Amarion said as if Xerxes hadn't interrupted us. "And suggest he speak to Lucia as well. Her information may help them."

"Then I believe that is all," Samudra said. "I will text the rest of you if I learn anything." It always surprised me to get texts from Samudra, because I never thought of Nepal as particularly rich in technology—but that was probably my ignorance showing. All I knew about Nepal was high mountains and Sherpas.

We all added our agreement, and I reached to disconnect from the call when Claude said, "Helena. A moment."

I lowered my hand. "Yes?"

"What does the oracle say on this matter? Has it spoken to you?"

I felt like an idiot. I should have led with this. "I'm sorry, I should have said. It told me, before we learned of the destruction at Berryton, that two Neutralities were gone and only four remained. I didn't understand that, because at the time I didn't know about the Well. Then it called the four remaining ones 'guardians.' I asked Lucia, and she said that was an appropriate description of the named Neutralities, but she didn't say why."

The three men regarded me with a scrutiny that made me uncomfortable. If they'd been in the same room together, I was sure they'd have been exchanging sideways glances. "I have not heard of the named Neutralities being called guardians of anything, except, perhaps, their own secrets," Claude finally said. "But in a metaphorical sense…"

"The Wardens look to the named Neutralities as… mascots, maybe? Or totems?" Amarion said. "You must have seen that, Helena. We—the custodians—we're respected for our connection to our Neutralities, because the named Neutralities are special. Unique."

"Is that why, at the Conference of Neutralities, we were high in the unofficial ranking everyone assured me didn't exist?" I asked.

The others all laughed. "That is so," Samudra said. "So, as Claude says, metaphorically the named Neutralities are guardians of what magery means to the Wardens. Guardians of their morale, perhaps."

"I guess I have noticed that," I said. "Is there any chance the oracle might have been speaking more literally? It's really hard to understand it most of the time. It also talked about leaks, and there being one path, and sealing something. Any ideas?"

Amarion and Claude shook their heads. Samudra said, "None of that suggests anything to me yet. But we still know very little about the situation. More information may enlighten us."

His words made me feel uneasy. I hadn't told any of my fellow custodians what the oracle had said about its end because of Lucia's warning, but with the destruction of the Fountain...suppose the oracle was next, and that was what it had foreseen? "There's something else," I said. "I haven't told anyone but my husband and Lucia, but I think maybe you should know. About four months ago, the oracle told me it had seen its ending, and mine as well."

Samudra's eyes went wide. Amarion whistled in astonishment and said, "Helena, why didn't you mention this before?"

"Because Lucia was convinced it would only create panic if people thought the oracle was going to die. But now that a named Neutrality has actually been destroyed, I think...I need help." To my horror, my eyes grew wet, and I blinked away tears. I hadn't realized I was so fragile. Maybe I needed that therapist, after all.

"Lucia was right then," Samudra said, "and I do not blame you for keeping the secret. But *you* are right to tell us now. What, exactly, did the oracle say?"

I repeated the words that were seared into my memory. Such short sentences to spell my doom. "And it's repeated itself several times a week since then," I added. "Like I didn't get it the first time."

"Perhaps you did not," Claude said. "It did not say 'die.' It said 'end.' There are many ways in which something might end. When one marries, for example, it is the end of their life as a single person. Perhaps the oracle means only that dramatic change is coming."

Cool, wonderful relief flooded through me. "I never thought of that! That's possible, right?"

"It is possible," Samudra said. "But with the destruction of the Fountain, we should not ignore the possibility that the oracle spoke literally. I think we must prepare for the worst."

And just like that, the relief was gone. "You're right," I said. "I wish I knew how to do that."

"We will discuss with the stone magi, and give Ms. Pontarelli a chance to act," Samudra said.

"You should ask Lucia what she learned from Ms. Suzuhara, too," Amarion said. "We need to know how the Fountain was destroyed so we can keep it from happening to our charges. And—don't worry, Helena. We've all seen the oracle's predictions be thwarted."

"I know. Thanks, Amarion." I didn't say that I'd never known the oracle to be wrong in what it told me directly. If it was a prediction of the future, it could be averted. I hoped.

"Let us plan to speak again at this time in three days," Samudra said, "and text anything that cannot wait. Good night, Helena."

"Good night," I said, and disconnected. I stared at the blank screen for a few minutes before shutting my laptop and wearily trudging off to bed.

Xerxes followed me up the stairs until it became clear I was going to my bedroom, and then he trotted off in the direction of his cat bed in the spare room. His brother Cyrus, five pounds smaller than he and golden-furred, had early on colonized our bed as his territory, and while the brothers got along very well, Cyrus was an absolute tyrant when it came to his sleeping space. It amused me to watch them gradually make our house their home, how they had their own little quirks that translated into one or the other of them dominating certain parts of the house. I hoped their previous guardian, Jun, approved of our caretaking of her cats.

Malcolm was asleep with Cyrus puddled over his legs. The cat opened one eye and regarded me as I climbed into bed, but otherwise didn't move. He liked me well enough, but Malcolm was definitely his person, which I thought was funny because Malcolm hadn't been as enthusiastic as I was about adopting the boys. He'd pretended to be indifferent to them, but Cyrus had ignored Malcolm's apparent standoffishness and behaved exactly as if the cats joining our family had been Malcolm's idea. Malcolm's (well-concealed) delight at being the object of a Persian cat's affection had made me so happy.

I snuggled up next to Malcolm, who put his arm around me without opening his eyes. I loved cuddling with him; it made me feel secure and loved and successfully banished my demons for a few hours. Tiredness caught up to me, relaxing my body and making it impossible for me to keep my eyes open, but my mind wouldn't let me sleep. Recently my sleep-lessness was the result of fretting over the oracle's cryptic warnings. Tonight, I couldn't stop thinking about the oracle as mascot for all of magery. Did that extend to me, as Amarion had said? Should I behave more respectably? Not that I was disreputable now, but…these were questions with no answers, which meant they wouldn't go away.

Finally, I made myself think about tackling Lucia in the morning, imagined what I would say, and let the planning carry me off to sleep. With luck, I wouldn't dream.

4

"Lucia," I said to her voice mail, "I've talked to the other custodians and we have some questions. And I have things to tell you. Call me back." I disconnected and tucked my phone into my pocket, one not as deep as yesterday's. Stupid girl pockets.

"Did you call Madeleine yet?" Judy asked. She forked up ravioli and ate with blissful gusto.

"It's been a busy morning," I said, feeling defensive. "And I might be putting it off because I don't want to talk to her."

"I know, but she'd understand better than we do about the possibility that the wards could be warped."

I sighed and took a bite of my own ravioli. It was store-bought, not homemade, but one experiment along those lines had convinced me I would not add ravioli to my cooking repertoire. I compromised by buying the highest-quality fresh pasta I could find. "I *know*. I'll call her after I eat. I don't want to ruin my digestion."

Distantly, the bells over the door jingled. I groaned and

took another huge bite. Rare were the days when I got five minutes to eat my lunch in peace.

But the newcomer was a pleasant surprise. "Victor!" I exclaimed, hurrying forward to hug him. "It's been a while."

"I've been busy with training," Victor said. That much was clear. Victor was a big young man who easily passed for much older than his eighteen years, but when we'd first met, he'd been on the heavy side, not quite fat, but not muscular. Now he'd slimmed down a little, replacing fat with muscle, and looked like Denzel Washington's younger, fitter, and even more attractive brother.

"You want lunch? There's lots of ravioli."

"I'm good, thanks. Ate before I came."

"Well, come on back anyway. Or—is this business?" Victor, a genetic sport like me, was a precognitive, and sometimes his talent guided him in my direction.

"I'm not sure. I got cleaned up after my workout, ate lunch, and then, instead of going back to work, I saw myself here." He laughed. "It still feels weird that everyone at Campbell Security knows what I can do, and all I have to do is say I gotta go, and I'm gone."

"That's because they know you won't abuse the privilege." I took my seat at the break room table as Victor greeted Judy. "So—you saw yourself here? No idea why?"

"None. Hey, I heard about what happened in Georgia. Was the lady a friend of yours? I'm real sorry."

"Thanks. She was." A pang of sorrow shot through me, and once again I considered the possibility of talking to a therapist. But I was well-adjusted, so did I really need to? "Tell me what's up with your team. Malcolm said you've been moving around a lot, getting used to different fighting styles."

Victor beamed. "They think I'm about ready to head my

own team. Has to be with some experienced fighters, because I'm not great with knives yet, but…it's an honor."

"I'm so excited for you!"

"That's fast," Judy said. "You must be making better progress than you think."

"It's a little weird, not being a magus," Victor said. "Some people expect things of me because I'm naturally immune to being drained, and they forget I can't use magic. But it's all good. Everyone's been cool about it."

My phone rang. "It's Lucia," I said. "Hang around for a bit, will you? I want to hear more about what you've been doing." I excused myself and crossed the hall to the office before answering.

"What questions do you have?" Lucia said in her usual abrupt way.

"We want to know what Ms. Suzuhara discovered about the destruction of Berryton," I said. "We had some ideas—"

"What ideas?"

I hesitated, considered the unlikelihood of Lucia letting me control the conversation, and said, "We thought it was possible the invaders had destroyed the Fountain indirectly, not by trying to overcome its wards. Like how the Well was corrupted by the body of its custodian. Maybe that would warp the wards enough to break their protection."

Lucia let out a short sigh. "You're all very smart," she said. "That's more or less what happened. They used the Mercy's aegis-suppression field to render all the magi vulnerable. Then Lakin was killed in a way—I won't give you the details—"

"Thanks."

"But her death was used to corrupt the Fountain, which warped its protections and allowed the intelligent invaders to drain the node. Then, once the magic was gone, they broke the Fountain so it wouldn't be able to regenerate its magic."

I shuddered, picturing the intelligent invaders I'd met smashing the Fountain's basin, which I'd never seen. In my imagination, it was a scallop-edged fountain with water shooting out of a fish's mouth, and that was probably totally wrong. "So how do we defend against it?"

"I don't know." Lucia sounded more grim than usual. "We're working on it. Until then, I'm posting bodyguards for you and suggesting the other named Neutralities do the same for their custodians."

I hated the idea, but it made sense. "We don't have to shut down, do we?"

"That's the final resort. The stronger the wards, the harder it is to warp them, and an impenetrable ward is unbreakable by any force we know, including intelligent invaders. But if we have to shut down the named Neutralities, that's the same as if the invaders destroy them, at least so far as us getting any use out of them goes. Hang on." Her voice became muffled, as if she'd covered the receiver and was talking to someone else. When she came back, she said, "Any other questions?"

"I...don't think so. No, wait. Do you know how many intelligent invaders came through in Montana? Because I was wondering if they hadn't tried this before because there weren't enough of them."

There was a pause. "Don't go spreading this around," Lucia said, her voice almost too low to hear. "We don't know how many of the intelligent ones made it through before the Wardens shut down the node in Montana, but it wasn't a high number. They didn't do this through brute force. Suzuhara says the pattern of the attack is anomalous. She's still looking into it, but her preliminary assessment is that the invaders used new tactics—a strategy of attack unlike any we've seen before."

I felt a chill pass through me, even though I didn't understand the import of her words. "Why would they do that? Other than that it let them destroy a named Neutrality."

"We have no idea. But whatever came through in Montana, it has a different plan in mind. And that can't be good for the Wardens."

"No. Is that why you want to keep it secret? You don't want to spread panic?" Between Lucia and the Board, I felt crammed to the gills with secrets I couldn't share.

"Got it in one, Davies. But it's not a secret that will last. Suzuhara's investigation will be finished in a day or so, and that's when we'll release our information, along with an assessment of how much danger we're all in. Gives people something to focus on that isn't hiding inside a warded fortress."

"I can't not tell—"

"I'm used to your insane need to share everything with Campbell. Makes me glad I'm not married." Lucia chuckled to let me know it was a joke. "He's more tight-lipped than I am, so no worries on that front. And…let the other custodians know. They're almost certainly in the most danger, and they need to know what to watch out for. Like I said, another day, maybe two, and we'll have a plan of attack."

"All right." I didn't feel nearly so certain as Lucia sounded, but then her Neutrality wasn't in danger, so far as we knew. "I was going to ask Madeleine about the wards on the store, whether there was anything we could do to protect them against being warped."

"Just so you don't tell her why you have that theory, you're fine," Lucia said. "I'll call you if anything changes." She hung up.

I put away my phone and returned to the break room, where Victor and Judy were chatting. "Well?" Judy said.

"She says it's possible, and to have Madeleine check the wards. And some other stuff. The investigation is going well." I was having trouble remembering who I'd told what to, and who was allowed to know what. "A couple more days until it's over."

"I heard it was intelligent invaders like the ones we fought in Montana," Victor said. "Lots of them, and that's how they overpowered the node."

"Lucia didn't say," I lied. "I guess that's possible, though. But I want to know what else you've been doing! Still gambling?"

"Not in this state. It's no fun," Victor said with a laugh. "Besides, I got better things to turn my talent to now. Like—"

His eyes went distant, and a funny, confused look crossed his face. Then he focused on me and Judy. "You need to call Malcolm," he told me. "Right now."

"Um…okay," I said, pulling out my phone. "What do I tell him?"

"A car is going to plow into the front of the store in fifteen minutes. It will destroy the front door and wreck that thing that protects it from invaders in human suits. That's how they'll get in. If he gets a couple of teams moving *now*, it might not be too late."

I gaped at him, then, with shaking fingers, called Malcolm. The phone rang far too many times before he answered. "Malcolm, Victor's here and he's had a vision," I said, cutting off Malcolm's warm greeting. "I need some teams at the store immediately. He says the invaders are trying an attack."

"On my way," Malcolm said, and the phone went dead.

"You two need to get out of here," Victor said.

"I can't leave," I countered. "What if the car is a distraction, and the point is to get me out of the warded store? I have to stay here."

Victor's mouth set in a determined line. "Then I'll stay with you."

"Thanks." I didn't care if he was inexperienced. His presence comforted me.

"So what do we do?" Judy said. "Wait around for doom to fall on us? How in the hell is a car able to drive through the front door? The street's not wide enough for it to get up any speed!"

"Sideswipe, maybe?" I realized my hands were clenched so hard the nails bit into the flesh of my palms and made myself relax. "I'm not going to hide in the back. If the teams don't get here in time, and the invaders make it through the door, I want to know where they are. I'm going out front. Judy, you need to leave."

"The hell I will! I'm staying here."

"If they succeed in triggering the wards and it doesn't destroy the oracle, there'll need to be a custodian. There's no third person—it's just you and me. They can't be allowed to kill both of us."

Judy's face was red and furious. "If you think I'm going to run away—"

"It's not running away. It's sensible. *Please*, Judy." I stared her down, willing her to be sensible.

Judy looked away and swore viciously. "Fine," she said, gathering her purse. "But if they kill you, I'll never forgive you." She strode to the back door and slammed through it.

"Don't think you can get rid of me that way," Victor said. "Malcolm would kill me if I left you."

"Is it bad that I didn't even think about it? I don't want to be alone." I didn't bother with inane questions like *Are you sure?* or *Did you see me die?* Victor's visions always came true, but he tended to see events rather than people. My fate was still a mystery—unless the oracle was right, and this was what it had foretold. I unclenched my hands again and walked at a calm, measured pace to the front of the store.

I wasn't totally foolhardy; I stopped as far from the front door as I could get and still see it. The sunlight was dim, suggesting an overcast sky, though the forecast hadn't been for rain. It still made the street look warm and welcoming. Men and women dressed in shorts and lightweight dresses passed in both directions, laughing and smiling like the world was theirs for the taking. It made me feel sick, and I turned away so I wouldn't have to see them.

"Helena, you're shaking," Victor said. "It's going to be okay."

"Is it?" I laughed, a weak, anemic sound. "I wish I could be sure." Victor didn't know about the oracle's prophecy. I checked my phone's display. Eleven more minutes. My hands really were shaking. I closed them tightly on my phone and willed myself to be still.

"I'm glad you came by," I said. "Imagine if…"

"I'm glad I didn't ignore that vision," Victor said. "Used to be I'd tell myself it was my imagination when I saw something that didn't make sense. Like me being at Abernathy's mid-day when I ought to be at work. Now I go with it."

The door jangled open, and I let out a shriek I instantly muffled with my hands. The Nicollien who entered gave me a strange look. "You have to leave," I said, overriding what-ever he was going to say. "There's going to be an invader attack here in…nine minutes…and it won't be safe. Please, come back later, or tomorrow, or…" I felt a mad giggle building in my chest and pressed a hand against my throat to seal it in.

"A what?" The man looked confused, as well he should. "Shouldn't we call someone?"

"We did. They're on the way. But you need to leave."

"Then why are *you* still here?" His confusion deepened.

The giggle escaped halfway, sounding like a strangled duck. "This is my Neutrality and I'm not going to be driven away from it," I said.

"I can't just leave you!"

"Then…you can wait on the corner for the teams to arrive. Stay away from the front door—away from the store front entirely." Why wouldn't this idiot just go? His presence, and his annoying questions, had me wound tighter than a violin string about to snap.

The Nicollien looked like he wanted to argue further, but backed away out the door, letting it swing shut behind him. The bells jingled again, a merry sound that made me want to scream.

Victor grabbed the folding chair from beside the door, dragged it across the room, and made me sit. The chair was freezing cold even now, in the heart of summer, and it made me shake harder. Victor put his arm around me. "They'll get here," he said.

I nodded. I'd clenched my jaw tight against the shaking and couldn't have spoken even if I'd had something to say. All my attention was fixed on the door and the plate glass windows to either side of it. Cars drifted past, not going more than the speed limit, as was typical of this neighborhood. It was picturesque, and people tended to slow down to look at the stores and the trendy people. Judy was right; the two-lane road paralleling the store front wasn't wide enough for a car to swerve into the front door at any speed. There was no way the invaders could break through the door. What a stupid plan.

I checked my phone once more. Six minutes. Where the hell were the Wardens? My husband? Anyone who might be able to stop this horrible thing from happening? I wanted to cry angry tears at how weak and helpless I felt, but I didn't want to embarrass Victor, who was doing his best but was clearly afraid I'd burst into hysterics he couldn't deal with.

I couldn't help myself. "What else did you see?"

Victor shook his head. "Just the car, slammed into the doorway. And no, I don't know how they manage it. The car, and the door broken into pieces on the floor, and the frame twisted so you can see bits of metal and glass embedded in it."

I nodded. I'd seen the door trap installed, and that's what it had looked like. It seemed so fragile now.

I didn't want to look at my phone again, but I could feel the minutes slipping away. I remembered being in a car accident with Malcolm, how time had slowed so I saw every second of us sliding across the freeway. This was the opposite of that, this feeling that the seconds had shrunk to nothing, and at any moment I'd hear the squeal of wheels on pavement, speeding out of control...

Dark shapes hurried past the windows. Someone flung open the door. I sprang to my feet as a dozen men and women in fatigues poured through the doorway, spreading out to both sides. None of them carried drawn weapons, but they held themselves like experienced fighters, and it made my leaden heart feel feather-light.

Then Malcolm came through the door, dressed in the suit and tie he'd worn when he left the house that morning, and I sank back into my chair, all my joints suddenly too weak to support me. Malcolm came straight to my side and knelt, taking me in his arms. I clung to him and blinked away tears. I didn't want to cry in front of the Wardens. "About time," I sniffled.

"If I could have ward-stepped here, I would have," Malcolm said. "We'll take care of this. Go into the office."

I shook my head. "I need to see this, or I'll...it will stay in my nightmares for a long time."

Malcolm hugged me once more, then stood. "Are you armed?" he asked Victor.

Victor patted his right thigh. "No knives. Just the gun."

"That will be enough. Take a position on the left." Malcolm put a hand on my shoulder. "I'll stay with you, love. Don't worry."

I nodded and clung to his hand. I felt weak and sick and embarrassed and angry all at once. Those *bastards*, thinking they had a right to our world and its magic. How many people had died, over the centuries, because of them? Not just the ones the invaders actually killed, but the ones whose deaths had been indirect, or at the hands of the Mercy? I felt a sudden hot rage flash over me, and with it, a desire to be someone capable of damaging them directly. Instead, all I could do was sit and tremble like some fainting maiden in one of the stupider fantasy stories.

A distant humming grew louder and deeper until it was obviously a car's engine, one running hard and fast. I clutched Malcolm's hand and saw he'd drawn his gun with his other hand. The noise grew and grew until it filled the air. Two people had stopped outside the window and were pointing up the street to the left. "Make them move!" I shouted, but they were already running, and I heard screams that were barely audible over the roar of the engine.

Then everything happened at once—the squeal of tires,

the stink of exhaust and burning rubber, a blue flash of motion as a car sped past, impossibly spun, and accelerated into the front door. I screamed. The door blew inward, narrowly missing a couple of Wardens, and splintered chunks of it skidded across the pale cream linoleum toward me.

The hissing of a broken radiator filled the silence the impact had left. The car was an old Cadillac convertible, like something out of a '50s movie, probably made of solid steel and weighing more than a ton. Two women sat in the front seat, easily visible through the door thanks to no airbags and the roof being down. Neither of them looked even bruised.

They climbed out of the car without opening the doors and headed straight for the store, expressionless like Robert Patrick in *Terminator 2*. Without a word, the Wardens opened fire. The tremendous noise echoed through my skull, and I let go of Malcolm's hand to cover my ears. I hoped some of those Wardens were paper magi, able to create powerful illusions to fool hearing as well as sight. If not, we would have a hard time covering it up—armed vigilantes shooting two innocent women? No, Malcolm would have made sure to bring paper magi.

The women jerked and thrashed as bullets found their mark dozens of times. One of them fell backward onto the hood of the car, while the other sank to her knees on the pavement. The shooting stopped, and four Wardens clambered through the empty doorway, drawing long steel knives. I gasped as one of the fallen women opened her mouth wider than should be humanly possible, and a sickly green thing began to emerge. Two of the Wardens bore down on her, stabbing the invader before it could leave its human suit fully. The others stood guard over the second woman, but she just sagged limply in death.

The screams had started again. Malcolm patted my shoulder and said, "I'll be right back." He walked toward the door and beckoned to the Wardens. I could barely see, past them, the four knife-wielding Wardens lifting the bodies and carrying them to the car. I breathed out in relief. The Wardens would make it look like the "women" had died in the crash, and everything would be all right.

Malcolm returned to my side and helped me stand. "It looks like people are calling 9-1-1," he said, "and the police will be here shortly. I'm sending most of these Wardens away, to make it easier on the paper magi, but there will be guards for as long as they're needed. Where is Judy?"

"I sent her away," I said, "just in case…"

Malcolm put two fingers beneath my chin and raised my head so I had to meet his eyes. "Helena, you're in shock," he said. "Go upstairs and lie down. Judy won't mind."

"But I have to be in the store."

"I will call the Board and inform them that Abernathy's will have to close for a few days while we repair the damage. You can't be expected to work under those conditions." Malcolm put his arm around me and steered me through the office and upstairs to Judy's bedroom that had once been mine. "I'll talk to the police on your behalf. We'll tell them no one was in the store when the accident occurred."

"Thanks."

Malcolm kissed me, so sweetly, and said, "Try to rest. I'll take you home as soon as things are settled here."

I lay on the bed in the darkened bedroom after he was gone and stared at the ceiling. I'd stopped shaking, but it felt as if the shakes were hanging out just around the corner and might come back any second. That had been close. If Victor had ignored his vision, I would likely be dead now.

In all my preoccupation with wards and Diane's horrible death and the fate of the Well's custodian, I'd forgotten what that invader had told me one Christmas Eve day: all it would take to destroy Abernathy's was one invader in a human suit walking through the door and abandoning its disguise. We'd need some other way of warding the store. I should warn the other custodians of the possibility. I didn't know if that sort of destruction was enough for what the invaders wanted, but did that really matter?

What the invaders wanted. I didn't know that either. No one did, unless Ms. Suzuhara had had a breakthrough. It did seem an unusually direct attack, though. Maybe that mattered. They hadn't wanted me dead before—both the intelligent invaders I'd spoken to had been clear on not wanting me dead. How many times had I come close to death in the nearly three years since becoming Abernathy's' custodian? Ross Dunlop had held me at gunpoint…the giant invader had nearly killed me before I became the oracle, which also could have killed me…I'd been kidnapped and left to die in an abandoned warehouse… I realized I was shaking again, and tears leaked down my face. That had been in the space of only six months, and there had been more—so much more—

The door opened. "Helena?" Judy said. "Malcolm said you weren't doing well. I told him that was an understatement. Can I get you anything?"

I shook my head, then nodded. "Judy," I said in a shaking voice, "I think I need help."

5

I sat propped up on pillows in my own wonderful bed and turned another page. I'd been trying to study my augury, but *Old Tin Sorrows* had turned out to be a fascinating story, and after a few chapters I'd decided to read the book through and leave analyzing it for later. Cyrus snuggled up beside me—apparently I would do if Malcolm wasn't available—and I ran my fingers through his golden fur while he purred. His purr was so loud it sounded motorized.

The absent thought reminded me of the day's events, of the sound of that car drawing ever closer to the store, and I set my book down gently on its face and drew in a deep, shuddering breath. I'd thought I was doing better. Malcolm had taken me home and drawn me a hot bath, and I'd soaked in a pleasantly mindless stupor until the water was cold and my hands were pruny. I'd had a bowl of soup, comforting even on this sweltering July day. And then I'd gone to bed early with my augury. It should have been perfect and relaxing, but my mind kept veering back to memories I never wanted to recall.

Like the sight of those two "women" shot full of holes. I knew they were really invaders, but it had looked so real…

I picked up my book again and made myself read a few paragraphs before setting it aside. I should try to sleep. Things would look better in the morning. Maybe.

Malcolm came through the door and sat next to me. "Feeling better, love?"

"Yes. No. I hate feeling so fragile. It's not like I was even injured. I should be stronger than this."

"You *are* strong, Helena. But you've been under a lot of stress recently, and even the strongest person can snap if the pressure goes on long enough." He took my hand. "I think you need to talk to someone."

I sighed. "I know. I just don't know how to go about it. It feels so strange, thinking about seeing a mental health professional."

"I felt the same way the first time I saw a psychologist."

My eyes widened. "When was this? What do you mean, the *first* time?"

He smiled and kissed the back of my hand. "You remember the woman I killed accidentally in sparring? I'd been a SEAL for years before that, had killed…I didn't keep track, but more than a few of the enemy…but Roberta's death shook me. It was right after my father's death, when I'd come home to take up the family business and join a hunting team, and I started making mistakes in the field. Nobody died as a result, but that was pure luck. After that had gone on for three or four weeks, Tinsley pulled me aside and told me if I didn't get my head straight, the team was sidelining me. I fought him on it—thought it was a stupid, weak thing to do, and I should be able to work my problems out myself—but in the end, I humbled myself and went to the Gunther Node."

"And it worked?"

"Therapy isn't a magic pill, but at least in my case, talking to someone helped me work out the guilt I felt over Roberta dying. And a professional might see something you haven't considered."

I nodded. "All right. Should I ask Lucia?"

"Call Pringle in the morning. She will forward your call to someone who can see you—possibly right away."

"That seems fast."

Malcolm chuckled. "There are things the Gunther Node will do for the custodian of Abernathy's that they won't for the average Warden."

"I won't let it go to my head."

Malcolm hugged me. "I spoke with Ms. Duwelt and explained that it will take three days to repair the front door. She agreed that there was no point opening the store, though she suggested you might still go in for the mail-in auguries. Something about them piling up otherwise. I said I'd pass that along. And now I have, and I urge you to ignore them for a while."

I laughed. "I think a few days' rest might be good. It's so hard to have the oracle keep hammering home the point that we're both going to end."

"Which is why you need professional help." His hands strayed beneath my pajama top. "And other kinds of…help."

I raised my eyebrows. "Oh? And you think you can provide this…help?" I gasped as his hands moved north. "Ah…maybe you're right."

Malcolm kissed me, his lips lingering on mine. "But only if it's what you want."

I drew him down to lie beside me. "I can't think of

anything that would make me feel better than your hands on my—oh!"

"Then I think," Malcolm said, "we should explore the possibilities."

───────────

I WOKE BRIEFLY the next morning when Malcolm's alarm went off at 6:30, rolled over, and sank back into blissful sleep. When I woke more fully an hour later, I felt clear-headed and more rested than I had in months. Knowing I didn't have to face the oracle that day relieved my mind, leaving me with a familiar guilt over resenting the job I loved. I hadn't realized until then how tightly wound I'd become thanks to the oracle's constant reminders of our ending.

Malcolm was eating when I went downstairs, but got up when I entered the kitchen. "It's all right, I just want cereal," I said, taking a brightly colored box out of the pantry.

"All right, but you know I'm happy to fix you something." Malcolm went back to his meal. "You should use this day to relax. Read, have a bath, watch a movie. I'll make dinner."

"You are so sweet." I kissed his cheek. "I'll call the Gunther Node once I'm showered and dressed."

"Let me know how that goes. I think it will be good for you."

"Me too." I took a bite of crunchy sweet morsels in a variety of colors not occurring in nature. Though I remembered seeing pictures of morpho butterflies, an intense sapphire blue that burned the retina, and wondered if I was right about what Nature thought was appropriate.

Malcolm's phone buzzed with an incoming text. He

glanced at it, did a double take, and pushed his chair back. "Lucia says to turn on channel 2," he told me.

I got up and followed him into the living room. He turned on the television and flicked through the display to select channel 2. A very intense-looking male newscaster I didn't recognize—I never watched the morning news—was saying, "—more information as we receive it. Local sources say we're looking at a fast-spreading disease and have begun evacuation of nearby towns. The similarities to the Berryton disaster cannot be disregarded. To repeat: at 3:15 Central European Time this morning, reports of a disaster in a village near Barga, Italy began appearing in Italian news channels and were soon confirmed by the Italian government. What we know is that the entire population of the village, nearly five thousand people, was killed by an unknown agent sometime between the hours of ten o'clock p.m. and midnight CET. Official reports suggest a fast-spreading disease rather than violence, but an unknown biological agent cannot be ruled out. No correlation between the disaster at Berryton and the events at Barga has been officially made, but—"

Malcolm muted the TV and turned to look at me. "The Cracchiolo Node is near Barga."

"I know. Benedetto D'onofrio was just made its custodian at the Conference of Neutralities. Oh, Malcolm."

"So they're not just striking at named Neutralities." Malcolm tossed the remote at the couch, where it bounced and slid under a pillow. "This is bad."

"It's like they're tired of waiting for us to capitulate," I said. "They're going for total destruction."

"Interesting observation." Malcolm strode back to the kitchen and swept up his phone and his dishes. "Can I leave these for you?"

"I'm not an invalid, Malcolm, I can wash a few dishes."

I followed him through the house and up the stairs to the bedroom and watched him dress. "Does this mean nowhere is safe?" I asked.

"I have no idea what it means. I've never been to the Crac-chiolo Node and I don't know what its defenses are—were—like. The invaders may still be choosing vulnerable targets. But if we were wrong about the invaders going after only the biggest nodes like the named Neutralities, we suddenly have an entire world of nodes to protect. *And* we don't yet know what purpose the invaders have in total destruction. It might be a new threat to force the Wardens to capitulate."

"It certainly puts my problems in perspective."

Malcolm paused in knotting his tie. "I hope you don't mean that you think your troubles don't matter."

"No, just that I can appreciate having survived yesterday's attack. So much worse could have happened."

Malcolm came to my side and kissed me. "I can't imagine anything worse than losing you. Call the node. I'll be back around six."

I put my arms around him and snuggled into his embrace. "I miss you already. I love you."

After I'd waved goodbye to him as he drove away, I went back into the kitchen and cleared my bowl and juice glass. I'd only eaten half my cereal, and it was soggy now, the milk pale pink. I dumped it out and loaded the dishes into the dishwasher. Then I went back into the living room and found the remote. There was a stock photo showing on the screen of a beautiful medieval village on a hill, surrounded by green trees. When I turned the volume back on, the same male newscaster was saying, "—breaking news from Barga, Italy, where local authorities have quarantined nearby towns for fear of the outbreak spreading. No one has confirmed or denied the existence of a super virus, but officials are choosing to take precautions. More on this story as it develops."

I turned off the television and put the remote away, then stood hugging myself as I looked out at my grassy back yard, where the sun had burned off the morning dew. Five *thousand* people. It was too big a number to comprehend. How could the invaders have killed so many, so quickly? New tactics were definitely involved. I thought about calling Lucia, but decided it was none of my business, not the way the named Neutralities were.

I went upstairs and dressed in shorts and a T-shirt, feeling another vague flash of guilt at being dressed down on a work day. Then I found my phone and called the Gunther Node, not Lucia and not her assistant Dave Henry, but the number for the node's switchboard. Though likely it was more complex than that. I pictured it as an old-fashioned board with holes and wires and half a dozen young women making physical connections when people called in, but that was unlikely.

The phone rang twice, and then a cheerful woman's voice said, "How may I direct your call?"

"This is Helena Campbell," I said. "I don't know who I want to speak to, but I…I need to set up an appointment with a therapist."

"Oh, hi, Helena," the cheerful voice went on. "This is Marci Pringle. Let me put you through to the infirmary—just tell them what you told me and they'll set something up."

"Thanks," I said, but Marci Pringle had already hung up. I heard the hum of a live connection but no Muzak while I was on hold. I waited. It took only a few seconds before someone said, "Infirmary."

"Hi, this is Helena Campbell. I need…I want to make an

appointment with a therapist." I felt so stupid saying it, like I'd confessed to some embarrassing personal secret.

"Sure thing," the man said. "Does today work for you, or do you need something a little further out?"

I swallowed. "Um, today is fine, maybe this afternoon?"

"How does 3:30 sound?"

"I can do that." The abruptness left me feeling both dizzy and relieved.

"Come to Green 1 then and someone will direct you from there. Is there anything else I can help you with?"

"Thanks, that's all."

After I hung up, I lay back on the unmade bed and stared at the ceiling. Maybe I should have asked more questions. I didn't even know if the therapist would be a man or a woman. I wasn't sure I was comfortable talking to a man about my private business, but then I wasn't all that comfortable with talking to anyone, so it probably didn't matter. Would they want me to tell them about other things? Hypnotize me? I had so many questions…and in a few hours, they'd be answered. So there was no point in worrying.

I made the bed and tidied the room, which didn't need much tidying, and then went downstairs and contemplated the TV. I wasn't sure I could stand listening to more news about Barga, particularly news that had no idea what was really going on.

The doorbell rang, and I found Judy and Viv on my doorstep. "We thought you could use company," Viv said. "Did you hear about Italy?"

"Yeah. It's awful."

"*I* think it means the invaders are scared," Viv went on. "They've never destroyed anything on this scale before, and I bet it's because they know the Wardens can take them out. So they're making it look like they're more powerful than they are and hoping to bluff."

"Except that they *are* powerful if they can do that," Judy said, rolling her eyes.

"Unless it's like when the Mercy attacked all the steel magi. That used up most of their resources, and they weren't able to follow up the attack with another one."

"Which the invaders just did. It's only been two days since Berryton."

"You're making my head hurt. Do you want water, or something?" I asked.

Both shook their heads. "The Wardens made the wards on the store impenetrable while the construction's going on," Judy said. "I'm staying with Mike for a few days. I love him, but he has some appalling habits."

"Still not interested in living together?" Viv teased.

"Nope. Maybe someday, but I like my privacy." Judy dropped onto one of the couches in the living room and sprawled, heedless of her dress's lightweight fabric. "And I think he feels the same. At least, the way he drops his underwear on the floor six inches from the basket tells me he does."

Viv made a face. "I'm okay with a relaxed attitude toward laundry, but that's just laziness."

"Let's do something," I said. "The mall will open in about an hour. We can walk around and get smoothies. And then I have an appointment with a therapist this afternoon."

Viv sat next to Judy. "Good for you. It will help."

"I hope so. I don't know what to expect."

"Just be open and honest, and everything will be great." Viv poked Judy in the side. "Don't you agree?"

"Openness and honesty are a good idea in most cases, not just in therapy," Judy said. She sat up and smoothed her skirt, then cursed. "I forgot about your stupid cats. There's long hairs everywhere."

"They shed more in the summer. You can use the lint roller. Didn't you have dogs growing up? Those shed, too."

Judy accepted the lint roller with a scowl. "They were familiars that looked like dogs. The illusion doesn't extend to making them seem to shed."

"Well, a little cat hair never hurt anyone."

"Unless they're allergic," Viv pointed out.

"All right, except for then." A thought occurred to me. "I have to email the other custodians about what Lucia told me, and about what happened yesterday in the store."

Judy and Viv followed me into the kitchen, where I set up my laptop on the table and opened my email program. "I hope they're all all right," I said. "I should have done this last night, but I was overwhelmed."

"It's fine," Viv said. "If anything had happened, we'd have heard about it."

"I don't know. The Sanctuary is mostly off the grid." I typed my message about what Lucia had said as succinctly as possible. Then I hesitated. Where to start? Just thinking about yesterday's events made me tremble again. I told myself to stop being stupid and described the attack on the store, from Victor's warning to the deaths of the invaders. *I don't know if your Neutralities are vulnerable to that kind of attack,* I concluded, *but as long as you're consulting stone magi about the wards, you should find out the details. Though after what happened near Barga, maybe the threat isn't what we thought it was.*

I signed the email and hit Send. "That's all I can do for now," I said.

"Don't you wonder what the authorities in Italy are going

through?" Viv said. "I wish there were a way to reassure them they're not dealing with a bioweapon."

"They wouldn't believe anyone who told them the truth," Judy said. She brushed futilely at her skirt one last time and said, "Let's go. Shopping, and smoothies, and lunch."

I nodded agreement, but as I gathered my purse and put on my sandals, I couldn't help glancing back at the TV. Even though it was off, I imagined I could see the pictures of the unnamed village they hadn't shown—bodies fallen in the street, crashed cars, doors hanging open like someone had just stepped out—and wondered how long it would be before the invaders struck again.

6

Viv and Judy volunteered to drive with me to the node that afternoon, but I declined. I had no idea how long a therapy session lasted, and I didn't want to make them sit around if it was a long time. Not to mention it made me feel like a little kid taking her mommy along to the doctor. I was a grown woman, and needing therapy didn't make me weak.

I parked in the gravel yard next to the airplane hangar that was the entrance to the Gunther Node and crunched my way up to the smooth concrete. The thorny circle on the floor had recently been repainted and looked more pale pink than white now. I wondered whether magic went into the painting, or whether the circle was just a mundane way of marking the space where the teleportation happened.

I spoke my name into the telephone handset on the back wall, took my place within the circle, and two seconds later the world blinked, and I was elsewhere. The cavernous, three-story-tall central hub of the Gunther Node bustled with Wardens, some of them carrying folders or tablets, others

pushing mine carts full of glowing purple ore that was unprocessed raw magic. Nobody paid any attention to me, which
was comforting. I already felt like I was wearing a sign saying
Mentally Unstable.

The rainbow-colored spaghetti tangle of lines painted on
the polished concrete floor was no help to me, since I rarely
came here, but I didn't need it because I'd been to Green 1
before. I set off toward the big opening rimmed in green paint
where the infirmary was. The last time I'd been here, the hall
had been full of injured Wardens and the stink of sulfur and
burnt rubber. Now it smelled only of gardenias, a strange
contrast to the industrial hardness of cold concrete walls.
People still filled the hall, but they walked at a normal pace,
not the breakneck speed of a life or death situation. Again, no
one showed any interest in me beyond some polite nods and
smiles. I relaxed. This would be all right.

The wooden doors lining the hall had large glass windows
filled with wire mesh that reminded me of my middle school,
though that had smelled of paint and boiled cabbage rather
than gardenias. Almost all the rooms were unoccupied, something I knew because there were curtains on the inside and
most of them were drawn back to reveal empty beds and
dormant medical monitors. There were a lot of rooms, and I
knew there were other halls in the infirmary with even more of
them. It was frightening to remember a time only a few
months back when all these rooms had been needed. The
attack on the Gunther Node by invaders who'd breached its
wards had devastated the Wardens. We'd won, but at a
tremendous cost.

After a minute or so of walking, I neared a big open space,
this one brightly lit with white lights. It had a lower ceiling
than most of the halls in the node, and the walls were painted

a warm cream, giving it a comforting look most hospitals lacked. The operating tables filling it dispelled that comforting feeling, especially when I remembered the screaming that had echoed through this room the last time I'd been here. None of the tables were occupied now. It was quieter than the hall, as if people respected it as a place of healing even when no healing was going on.

I made for a circular desk in the center of the room that reminded me of a nursing station in a hospital, though I'd never seen one in the middle of a room before. Two Wardens in hospital scrubs, one maroon, one teal, stood behind the desk. The maroon Warden was typing rapidly and swearing under her breath at whatever showed on the computer screen. The teal Warden looked up from his tablet as I approached. "Ms. Campbell, right?" he said, coming around the desk to shake my hand. "Owen Jefferson. It's good to meet you."

"Um, you too," I said. "I don't know…what do I do now? Is there paperwork?"

"We have a couple of pages of questions for you, yes. Sorry about that. We try to make it as easy as possible, but this provides background for your therapist so she has something to start from."

So it was a woman. "What's her name?"

"Sydney Fallon. She has a lot of experience working with the kinds of trauma Wardens usually suffer." Owen rooted around behind the desk and pulled out a clipboard with some papers clipped to it and a ballpoint pen. "Be as complete as you can. There aren't any right or wrong answers."

I glanced at the top sheet. There was a place for my name and then a long list of questions with bubbles next to them like on a standardized test, only these were for responses ranging from "Never" to "Almost Always." I found a chair next to the wall and began filling out the form. Despite what Owen had said, I couldn't help thinking of how this Sydney person would interpret my answers. If I said, in answer to question five, that I felt something was wrong with my mind, did that mean I was crazy? It was tempting to guess what would make me look normal. I closed my eyes briefly and berated myself. I was here for help, and if I lied about how I felt or thought, that wouldn't happen.

There were four pages in all. I filled in bubbles, taking my time about answering and giving each question some consideration except the one about wanting to end my life, where I colored in "Never" so hard it nearly tore the paper. Then I returned the clipboard to Owen, who said, "Thanks. Wait here, and Sydney will be out in a couple of minutes."

I returned to my seat and watched Owen disappear through a door marked PRIVATE. I twined the strap of my purse around my fingers and let it roll from one side of my hand to the other and back again. Answering the questions had actually relaxed me, as if I'd already talked to someone about my problems. Not that I was going to leave—I knew this was just the beginning. But it surprised me how much looking at my fears and bad memories in a clinical sense had eased them.

The woman in maroon left the desk, giving me an absent smile as she passed, and I was alone in the room. I leaned back and closed my eyes. There was a hum in the air that sounded like distant machinery, or an air conditioner running on low. The room was comfortably cool, just like the entire Gunther Node, and I wasn't sure air conditioning was necessary, but the hum was soothing.

"Helena Campbell?"

I opened my eyes. A plump older woman stood in front of

me, smiling like meeting me was the best pleasure she'd had all day. Her silvering blond hair was pulled up in a twist at the back of her head, and she wore a flowing long-sleeved robe of some thin burgundy fabric embroidered abstractly in pale gold around the neck and cuffs. "Sydney Fallon," she said, extending a hand. "Please call me Sydney."

"Helena," I said. I stood and shook her hand. A flash of memory, Jun Li shaking Lucia's hand and Lucia falling unconscious, struck me just at that moment, and I suppressed a shudder. I didn't suppress it well enough, because Sydney's eyes narrowed briefly as if she'd noticed something off about me. But she said nothing, just indicated that I should follow her.

We went to a door, not the one marked PRIVATE, that led to a short hall so different from the main room it felt like stepping through a portal to an upscale office building. The floor was carpeted, just with a plain gray Berber, but it was the first carpet I'd ever seen in the node, even in Lucia's office, so it looked exotic and out of place. Wooden molding stained dark brown divided the walls in half; the upper walls were a light tan color, and the lower walls were a rich plum. The doors were a brown that matched the molding, with brass handles rather than knobs. Each door bore a nameplate, but Sydney walked too fast for me to read them. She stopped at a door labeled SYDNEY FALLON, LCSW and opened it for me.

The room beyond matched the hall for comfortable upscale furnishings. A wooden desk with more drawers than I'd ever seen in anything that wasn't a rolltop took up one corner, with a rolling black office chair pulled up in front of it and a computer monitor atop it. Two padded armchairs upholstered in mahogany colored leather, or maybe just a really good imitation, faced the desk, angled so they also faced each other. A colorful Persian rug lay atop the gray Berber, brightening the room, and a series of photo enlargements showing Middle Eastern market stalls hung on one wall. It was enough to make me forget we were probably deep underground.

Sydney gestured to me to have a seat in one of the armchairs, then took the other. "So how are you feeling?" she said. "I heard about the attack on Abernathy's."

"I'm fine—I mean, I wasn't hurt, and the fear has mostly passed," I said. "Is…this what we do? Talk?"

Sydney smiled again. I wondered if the smile was something she practiced, not to be deceptive but to make it the most pleasant, non-threatening expression she could produce. "Talk, yes," she said. "It sounds from your initial paperwork that you're dealing with post traumatic stress disorder, and we'll see if we can help you with that."

"PTSD. That sounds so serious. I don't feel—I mean, I always thought that was something soldiers got from battles. I haven't done anything nearly so dramatic."

"I wonder," Sydney said. "You were kidnapped last January, weren't you? By the Mercy?"

"Yes. But they didn't hurt me."

"And before that, I remember the Mercy tried to burn down Abernathy's with you inside."

"That's right. I fought back. And the oracle helped me put out the fire. So nothing really bad happened."

Sydney propped her elbow on the arm of the chair and rested her chin on her hand. "I wonder," she said again. "Why do you want to deny the pain and horror of your experiences?"

I blinked. "I don't," I began, and then fell silent. I *had* just dismissed what had happened to me as no big deal, but if those things had happened to, say, Viv, I'd have been horrified and frightened for her. "I don't know," I finally said. "Does that mean something?"

Sydney shrugged. "Why don't you tell me? From what you've said, it sounds like you think pain is only pain when it does actual physical harm. Have you ever been injured when you were in danger?"

"Yes. The magus serial killer—my husband shot me to stop him killing me. It made more sense if you were there." I hadn't thought of that night in years, and to my surprise, tears welled up in my eyes. Malcolm's face, so hard and furious without a trace of love for me, the agony of my shoulder being torn open by his impromptu weapon, the terror of having a gun pressed to my head—I'd cried over it afterward and thought that made everything okay. Clearly, I was wrong.

Sydney took a box of tissues off the desk and handed it to me without a word. I took one and blotted my eyes. "Sorry. I thought I was over that."

"Don't apologize for having feelings," Sydney said. "When things happen to us, we have emotional reactions—happiness, fear, loneliness, pleasure. Love and hate. That's a normal part of being human. Why do you think you started to cry just now?"

"I guess because the memories are powerful. It felt almost as if it were happening again."

"That's not uncommon, particularly when you haven't fully processed what you felt." Sydney sat back in her chair and clasped her hands in her lap. "Why don't you tell me about the attack yesterday? I know invaders tried to destroy the oracle, but not how."

I clasped my hands, mimicking her, and realized they were trembling. "Do you know who Victor Crowson is? The genetic sport who can see the future? He's a good friend of mine. He came to the store yesterday because he saw himself there—it's something that happens to him—and while he was there, he had a vision that the store would be attacked. I called for some teams to defend the store, sent Judy away, and Victor and I waited. He can see about fifteen minutes into the future, so we knew exactly when the attack would happen, and we had to sit there and *wait* because we didn't know if the attack was a feint to get me out of the store."

I drew in a deep breath and released it slowly. "The Wardens arrived just about a minute before the invaders came. They—the invaders—they were in human form, and they drove a Cadillac convertible into the front of the store, wrecking the door. And the car. Then the Wardens…they… they shot the invaders, killed them before they could enter Abernathy's, and did a bunch of illusions to cover everything up."

Sydney watched me closely, but said nothing. Her silence was the kind that made me want to fill it up with words, so I added, "It was awful. I couldn't stop shaking. That's what made me decide to see a therapist. It felt like the final straw."

"That's an interesting way to put it," Sydney said. "You hadn't thought you needed it before then?"

"No. I thought I was coping well with everything I've endured. I guess not."

Sydney again looked at me, long and considering. Her eyes were dark blue with stubby blonde lashes; she wore no mascara, no makeup of any kind, but her skin was translucent the way some blondes' are, and it gave her an almost luminous look. "Have you been sleeping well?" she asked.

"Mostly."

"Only mostly?"

I looked down at my clenched hands. "Sometimes I have

bad dreams. And sometimes I have trouble falling asleep, so even if I don't dream, I don't wake rested."

"What kind of dreams?"

I really wished she hadn't asked that question. "Dreams of my husband dying. He was almost killed during the attack on the Montana node, and in my dreams I see him battered the way he was when I found him, only I can't reach him in time, and he…" I wiped my eyes again. "That's probably normal, right?"

"I've found that 'normal' isn't a good guideline. It generally just means 'most common,' and we don't always aspire to be common." Sydney's eyes narrowed. "That's not the only thing you dream about."

She was too damned perceptive. This was something I really didn't want to talk about. Which probably meant I should. I looked directly at her and said, "I shot a man. To death. I dream about it sometimes."

Sydney didn't look shocked, or concerned, or judgmental. She said, "What happened?"

I swallowed, seeing once more Santiago's stunned, uncomprehending expression as the first bullet hit him. "I was in the Montana node with Malcolm. He couldn't move—they'd paralyzed him. We were waiting for someone to pick us up. Mr. Santiago, the Mercy leader…I think he came to make sure all the captured Wardens were dead." I closed my hands more tightly to still their shaking. "They were gassed. I couldn't save them because the gas nearly killed me and Malcolm, too. I wanted to save them." I heard the pleading note in my voice and shut my mouth.

Sydney just said, "And this Mr. Santiago—what did he do when he arrived?"

"We talked. Then he threw—threw Malcolm off the platform." Tears choked me, and I took another tissue. "I attacked him, but it didn't…he was so much stronger than me. He was going to kill me the way he'd killed Malcolm—I mean, I only thought Malcolm was dead—anyway. So I shot him."

"And killed him."

I nodded. "Seventeen times," I added. My fingers felt numb. "I didn't count. That's just how many bullets my gun holds. Actually, it was sixteen times, because I shot at him once before that and only injured him. But that's a lot, don't you think? I didn't need to shoot him so many times. Just once was enough."

"Do you think you were wrong to shoot him that many times? Or wrong to shoot him at all?"

"It's not wrong to fight for your life, is it? When the Mercy attacked the store, some of their people died, and I was indirectly responsible. But this—" My voice sounded ragged, and I cleared my throat. It didn't help. "I killed him. *I* killed him. I never thought—"

A sob racked my body, and I cried as I hadn't ever before, not in all the times I'd suffered terror and pain as a result of being Abernathy's custodian. It hurt, a dull throbbing ache centered on my chest that spread throughout my body with every gasp and every tear. I covered my face and waited for Sydney to put her arms around me, and hoped she wouldn't.

She didn't. She sat quietly until I cried myself out into a shuddering mess. Then she said, "I think you never let yourself grieve that loss until now."

I blew my nose. "What loss?"

"Loss of innocence. For all you've been at the center of a lot of turmoil as Abernathy's custodian, you've probably never done anything to counter your image of yourself as a gentle person who would never hurt anyone. And now you've taken a life. It doesn't matter whether you were justified or not, or even whether 'justified' is the right word. What matters is that you're not the same person you used to be, and that other person was ripped away from you in the most horrific way possible. You have a right to grieve for her, just as you would any death."

Her words struck me to the heart. I had never considered, in all the suppressing I'd done over shooting Santiago, that I'd hurt myself as well as him in pulling that trigger. I'd tried so hard to convince myself that I'd done the right thing, and that meant I wasn't entitled to feel pain, that I'd hurt myself all over again. "I never thought of it like that."

"I know." Sydney shifted her position slightly, making the folds of her dress ripple. "It sounds to me like you've been telling yourself that because you survived the things that have happened to you, they haven't affected you at all. But that's not true. We're all marked, every one of us, by our experiences good or bad. Imagine your wedding day. It was happy, wasn't it?"

I remembered all the near-disasters that had threatened to ruin it, and how I'd sailed through them without a single worry. "It was."

"You wouldn't dream of telling yourself you shouldn't hold that memory dear, or that you should forget about it now that it's past, would you?"

"Of course not!"

"The same thing is true of our painful experiences. I'm not saying you should cling to your pain, because that's harmful in a different way. But it's important to accept that they happened and that they changed you. And to accept, also, that you're not going to stay the same woman you were at twenty. Let yourself be changed."

I nodded. "That makes sense. I...I didn't want to remember killing Mr. Santiago, because I was angry and I thought Malcolm was dead and I wanted Mr. Santiago to suffer like I had. So I felt like...maybe like I'd shot him for revenge or out of anger instead of to save my own life. And that mattered, because I could still think of myself as a good person if I killed him out of desperation. But I killed him because I wanted him to die painfully, and I never knew I was the kind of person who could feel that way."

"And now you have to learn who you are after that moment," Sydney said. "It's something we can work on in the weeks to come."

"Weeks?" I flushed with embarrassment at how shocked I'd sounded, like the possibility of weeks of therapy was abhorrent. "I mean—I don't know how long this is supposed to take."

"It depends on how willing you are to work," Sydney said. "I'd like to meet with you weekly, if you can manage it. We'll talk, and I'll teach you some techniques for managing your thoughts and behaviors that will, over time, help you to heal." She stood, and I rose quickly after her. "For next time, though," she added, "I'd like you to make a list of all the bad things that have happened to you since you became Abernathy's custodian, and bring it with you. I think it will be revelatory."

We agreed on a time for our next appointment, and Sydney walked with me back down the hall to Green 1. "Call if anything happens you feel can't wait for next time," she said.

I said goodbye and hurried past the circular desk, not wanting to be drawn into conversation, though the Wardens manning the desk (not the same Wardens as before) didn't look inclined to start one. I felt emptied out, as if my crying had tapped some inner reservoir of pain and drained it. I hoped my face didn't look too ruined. Good thing I hadn't worn makeup.

I found a tech to return me to the node's entrance and walked to my car, which the sun had warmed to a painful degree. I started the engine and rolled down the windows to let out the heated air. Unlike the stifling air, the seat, radiating warmth, actually felt good against my body, as if I'd been sitting in a refrigerator for an hour instead of the comfortable temperature-controlled Gunther Node. After a minute, I put the car in gear and backed down the low incline to the road. I had so much to talk to Malcolm about tonight.

I'd left the node just in time to hit rush hour traffic, which delayed me enough that Malcolm was home when I pulled into the garage. The smell of hot oil and crisp vegetables met my nose as I entered the house. I found Malcolm in the kitchen preparing sweet and sour pork stir fry. "Oh, delicious," I said. Xerxes padded past me, twining around my legs, and I recognized the ploy of a cat who'd already tried to cadge meat from one Campbell and was trying his luck with another.

Malcolm put down his knife and hugged me tightly. "How did it go?"

"Well, I think. It was uncomfortable, but in a good way." I popped a pea pod into my mouth and closed my eyes in pleasure at how the fresh, green flavor exploded on my tongue.

"I understand," Malcolm said. "But you should probably sit down."

He sounded so serious my peaceful mood evaporated. I drew up one of the kitchen stools and sat opposite him at the center island. "Is something wrong? More attacks?"

"No, not that." He picked up the knife again, but didn't

resume chopping. "I'm afraid I have to leave in about two hours."

I'd been reaching for another pea pod, but his too-casual tone of voice stopped me mid-motion. "You're going on the hunt?" I felt irrationally abandoned, despite all my earlier talk about not being fragile. Surely there was no reason Malcolm had to hunt tonight, when I needed him?

Malcolm shook his head. "I'm ward-stepping to Australia," he said. "Ms. Suzuhara released her report on Berryton earlier today. The Wardens have worked out where the invaders will strike next, and we're going to stop them."

7

I sucked in an astonished breath. "But—that's good, isn't it? You don't sound like you think it's good."

"It is extremely dangerous," Malcolm said. He went back to chopping vegetables in a slow, measured way like he was using them as a focus for his emotions. "We have no idea how they're managing to drain entire towns, or even if they intend to do the same with their next target. Kalgoorlie is much larger than Berryton or that village near Barga. It seems impossible that the invaders have grown strong enough to destroy over thirty thousand people. So we have to expect the unexpected, which is virtually impossible."

"How do they know this city—what's it called?"

"Kalgoorlie. In Western Australia."

"How do they know that's where the invaders will attack?"

Malcolm turned away briefly to dump vegetables into the wok with a hiss and a puff of steam. "Do you remember the Pattern? At the Gunther Node?"

"I remember." I'd seen it back when the Mercy was intent

on conquering South America—a tunnel like a duct in a military base, with its walls covered with two-inch glass tiles in a mosaic of color that constantly shifted and changed as magi moved the tiles around. I'd been awestruck despite the fear that had consumed me at the time. "Shouldn't that have predicted all the other attacks? I thought it was magic to analyze the invaders' presence and identify where they are about to break through."

"That's true," Malcolm said, "but these new attacks have been different enough that the Pattern didn't identify them as part of the, well, pattern it identifies. Once Ms. Suzuhara's investigation turned up enough information, it was clear the Pattern was needed. Magi around the world have worked ceaselessly since the Berryton disaster to alter the Pattern to take account of these new tactics. And about three hours ago, their work paid off."

"And you're going to Kalgoorlie."

"I have to, love. They need the best fighters because they don't know what to expect."

"I'm sorry. That was whiny. I know you have to go. But I don't have to like it, right?"

Malcolm cast a glance over his shoulder as he stirred vegetables briskly. "No. One of the things I love about you is your determination to do what's right, even when it's something you hate."

"I wonder if that didn't get me into trouble, though. Sydney—the therapist—she says it sounds like I've been telling myself that because I've gotten through all these bad things and done what's right, I shouldn't let them affect me. Like I've been suppressing my pain and fear all this time." I laughed. "She wants me to write a list of everything awful that's happened since I became Abernathy's custodian. I was thinking about it on the drive home and it's already stunning to realize how much I've gone through."

"I remember telling you once you seem to attract trouble. Maybe it wasn't as much a joke as I thought." Malcolm added thin strips of marinated pork to the wok and continued to stir. The most heavenly aroma filled the air, and I breathed it in contentedly.

"Well, I only rarely go out of my way to encounter trouble. Mitch Hallstrom, for one, and I sort of walked into the Mercy's trap in their second oracle." I hopped down and opened cabinets to remove plates and glasses. "I assume you have time to eat, or you wouldn't be cooking."

"Believe it or not, Mother is coming here in a couple of hours to ward-step me directly to Kalgoorlie."

I paused in the act of setting plates on the table. "She is not. Seriously?"

"Lucia asked her to come out of retirement for this. I wasn't kidding when I said we didn't know what to expect. Mother's a powerful telekinetic, and who knows if that won't turn the tide in our favor?" Malcolm carried the wok to the table and set it down on the trivet with a flourish. "Let's eat, and worry about the future later. I want to hear more about your session today."

We ate, and talked, and I was almost able to push my fears for Malcolm to one side. But time passed far too quickly, and when the doorbell rang, it sent a shock of fear through me. Malcolm was upstairs getting changed, so I answered the door and got another shock: Madeleine was wearing white fatigues, and her normally elaborately styled black hair was braided and pinned tightly at the back of her head. "Come in," I invited. "You look so different."

"This is a time for being serious about the fight,"

Madeleine said. She surveyed my small formal front room with a curious air, and I remembered this had been her house once. The thought made me uncomfortable, like I had some duty to live up to her memories. But she said nothing, not even a comment on the décor, and I realized further that she'd never been here since we moved in. I felt a pang of shame over having excluded Madeleine from our lives so thoroughly. Then I reminded myself of all the things she'd done to harass me, including offering me one and a half million dollars to break up with her son, and the shame disappeared.

"You're early," I said. "Malcolm's still upstairs. Would you like to come into the living room?"

Madeleine nodded. If she took my words as criticism, she didn't show it. We sat in the living room in silence. I stared at the fireplace, dark and cold in the middle of summer, and thought again how weird it must feel for Madeleine to be back here. It occurred to me that maybe her never coming over was partly her decision. Maybe it was painful, seeing this place and remembering that when she'd lived here, her husband had been alive.

"This is a lovely room," Madeleine said, startling me out of my reverie. "You have made this place your own."

"Thanks." I couldn't resist. "Is it weird, being back here?"

"Yes. Though it has been remodeled enough that the similarities are less." Madeleine looked out the back wall of floor to ceiling glass windows to where the setting sun cast long, golden rays over the lawn. "But the yard is the same. I remember Malcolm and Ewan chasing one another, around and around until they fell down dizzy. And Alastair, running after them."

I had never heard her say her husband's name before. She hadn't sounded sad, or regretful, but her voice hadn't sounded dead either. Wistful, maybe? "I really regret never meeting him," I said quietly, letting my words reach out to her like an offering to a wounded animal that might turn and bite.

"He was the best of men," Madeleine said. "Malcolm, he looks so like his father. I hated him for years for that."

That stunned me into silence. Not that she would admit to hating her own son, but that for a moment, I saw the world through Madeleine's eyes. How must it have been, to lose the man you loved above all others, and to be reminded of him every day by someone who could never take his place? I couldn't think of anything to say that wouldn't sound fatuous. So I said nothing, and waited for Madeleine to speak again. Finally, she said, "You think I am evil, I know."

"I don't think that." *Much.*

Madeleine chuckled. "*Mais oui,* you will not say because you are not hard. You do not speak the hard truths. It is not a bad thing, but it is not the way I am. I admit I do not like you because I wish better things for Malcolm."

And just like that, any sympathy I had for her evaporated. "Okay, now I'm thinking it," I said angrily.

To my surprise, Madeleine laughed. "I speak wrong. I mean to say, I did not like you when you came into Malcolm's life. I thought Malcolm rejected Andria and chose you simply to spite me. But it is not true. I see that he loves you, and that you love him. And I cannot make him live his life to suit me. That is how I lose him, and in losing him, I lose his father all over again."

She'd stunned me again. As I groped for words, Malcolm came into the living room, dressed in his fatigues and fully armed. "Mother," he said. "What did you two find to talk about?"

"Things," Madeleine said before I could respond. "This

room, which is lovely. Are you ready? The wardstone is where I remember it?"

"In the shed in the backyard," Malcolm said. He drew me into his arms and kissed me. "I love you," he murmured. "I'll be back soon."

"I love you," I said, laying my head briefly on his shoulder. This never got any easier. "Take care."

"I always do." He released me and nodded to his mother.

"We will return," Madeleine said. "*Bonne nuit*, Helena."

I followed them to the sliding door that let out on the patio, then watched from the living room as they crossed to the little shed that looked like it ought to hold a lawnmower, but actually contained a stone warded weakly enough to be used for ward-stepping. As the shed door closed, I slid the patio door shut and walked like a sleepwalker through the house until I reached my bedroom. I sat on my bed, buried my face in my hands, and prayed silently for their safety, for the safety of all the Wardens. Maybe I should talk to a priest, or a minister, someone who could explain how to pray properly, but I didn't feel drawn toward any of the religious faiths I knew about and didn't know if I wanted my formless beliefs shaped in any particular way. So I prayed the way that felt right to me and hoped God didn't mind.

When I finished, I looked around the room and thought about what I could do to keep from going crazy with waiting. I didn't think I could focus on studying my augury, and I felt too restless to read. My eye fell on my phone, and I flicked through the contacts. I could call Viv and Judy, but the last time we'd all waited here together for news of a battle, it had ended with four people on my doorstep telling me my husband was dead. I was just superstitious enough not to want that to happen again.

My finger hesitated over a name, then pressed Call. After a few rings, Harry Keller picked up. "Helena? Did Malcolm go to Kalgoorlie?"

"He did, just a few minutes ago. I don't suppose Harriet is in contact with the fighters there?"

"She's not. She went to the Gunther Node to help analyze the Pattern. I'm sorry."

"That's okay. I'm just looking for something to do."

"I hear Abernathy's will be closed for a few days. That leaves you at loose ends, eh?"

"It was relaxing today. I'm sure I'll get bored before long."

Harry laughed. "You have the strongest work ethic of anyone I know, and I include Lucia in that category. Read a book. You handle them all day long, you ought to dip into one now and again."

I thought of *Old Tin Sorrows* and how much I was enjoying that. Maybe, if I could focus on that, it would calm me down. "You're right. I'll talk to you later. Thanks."

I read a chapter or two, then set the book aside and stretched. Maybe a movie would keep my attention better. I hadn't seen *Twelve Angry Men* in a while. I trotted down the stairs and turned on the television.

"—assures us there's no need to fear, but I ask you, what kind of virus kills a single town and then stops?" a strident female voice said. I looked up from the DVD cabinet at the TV to see a woman I vaguely recognized as some kind of news commentator addressing an unseen person to her right.

Just then, the camera switched to that person, a blond man in suit and tie who looked like a Ken doll, down to the shellacked hair. "There have been no more 'attacks,' as you irresponsibly call them, since the Barga incident," he said, as hotly as she had spoken. "The government acted quickly and decisively to contain the outbreaks. And if they *were* attacks, there's no pattern to them! A town in Georgia and a town in Tuscany that have nothing in common—"

"Both were about the same size. Both were relatively isolated. Exactly what you'd expect for a trial run of a new bioweapon. And several terrorist organizations have claimed responsibility. Let's be honest, Bruce, this is the face of terrorism in the 21st century."

"If it is, you're doing their job for them, Marie. People are already afraid, and your fearmongering in the absence of evidence is just going to cause more panic!"

I shook myself out of my stupor and found the remote, changing the input from the satellite box to the DVD player. That had been stupid. If Bruce was so worried about causing panic, why was he giving airtime to Marie? Or maybe I was wrong, and he was the guest on Marie's show. I didn't watch the news often.

I'd been so caught up in my own troubles, I had no idea what the world thought of the destruction at Berryton and Barga. It seemed so obviously an attack I couldn't understand why the Bruces of the world didn't see it that way. *Was* there widespread panic? I almost turned the TV back to the news, but realized in time that there was nothing I could do if there were, and I had enough fears without burdening myself with make-believe ones.

I put in the *Twelve Angry Men* DVD and went to make myself a bowl of popcorn. My school had done *Twelve Angry Women* my junior year, our drama department being disproportionately female, and I'd been on stage crew as usual, but I'd also understudied Juror #4, so I felt a kinship with E.G. Marshall, who'd played the role in the film. I loved the way the plot shifted over the course of the story, with each juror having his (or her, I guess) attitude and beliefs tested.

I settled in with my popcorn and Diet Coke, determined not to sleep until Malcolm returned, or called, or texted—anything to confirm that he was well and the counterattack had been successful. I lay back with my feet propped on a pillow and felt all my muscles relax. I couldn't imagine life without great films.

The buzz of a text startled me awake. I shot upright, spilling the remainder of the popcorn, and blinked at the TV screen. Only two jurors hadn't changed their votes. I snatched up my phone, and my heart thumped painfully when I saw Malcolm's name. He couldn't text if he was injured. ALL WELL. INVADERS TURNED BACK NO PROBLEM. HOME SOON.

I checked the display for the time. Just after ten. That had been fast. FAST WORK, I texted back.

WILL TELL YOU EVERYTHING WHEN I RETURN. I LOVE YOU.

His assurance warmed my heart. He was alive. He was coming home. LOVE YOU TOO.

I gathered up the spilled popcorn while the movie played out to its satisfying conclusion. Though now that I was older, I kind of wanted the movie to end with Henry Fonda being secretly paid off by the defense for having successfully convinced the jury to find the murderer not guilty. As it was, the final scene on the street outside the courthouse felt weak. But I was too cheerful to care.

When the movie was over, I put the DVD away and went upstairs to change into pajamas. I was just considering reading more of my augury when I heard the back door open and close. I flew down the stairs and into Malcolm's arms, burying my face in his shoulder and breathing him in. He smelled of sweat and gunpowder, but his fatigues were surprisingly cool.

"It's the middle of winter in Australia," he told me when I mentioned it. "Mid-sixties and very comfortable. I think I need a shower." There was dirt in his hair and on his face, and altogether he looked filthy.

I followed him into the bathroom and sat on the edge of the tub while he undressed. "It was a perfect operation, and I've seen very few of those," he told me. "So many things can go wrong—bad timing, or the enemy knows you're coming, or weapons malfunction—but everything went just as planned."

"So what did the attack look like? How are the invaders draining whole towns?"

"Our guess was right that the attacks are led by the intelligent invaders. They go in first, in disguise—all of them are skilled at illusions—and open thousands of rifts, cracks the smaller ones can get in through. That part, we don't understand, or at any rate don't understand how that's possible. But it was irrelevant. We used the Pattern to predict where the intelligent invaders would appear and destroyed them before they could let many of their stupider, smaller cousins into the city."

I shuddered. "How many were there? Of the intelligent ones, I mean."

"That's the frightening part. Only three." He turned on the water and stepped into the shower stall. "Three intelligent ones to wreak so much destruction. Lucia hasn't said how many came through in Montana. She might not know yet."

"I guess it's positive news. All the Wardens have to do is destroy all the intelligent ones, and their threat is ended."

"If we can find them. Until a year and a half ago, everyone believed the intelligent invaders were mythical, or at least long gone. The one you met in Abernathy's was the first one anyone had encountered in centuries. Assuming they've been here all along without us knowing, they've had all those centuries to learn how to stay hidden. We can kill the ones we find, but we've no guarantee that we've found all of them."

"I like my take on it better."

Malcolm laughed. "You do have a delightfully positive outlook on life."

I picked up his filthy clothes, which smelled worse when they were bundled up. "I'll put these in the wash, and then I'll be right back."

When I returned, Malcolm was toweling dry his hair and the bathroom smelled of the fresh scent of his soap. "I never appreciate being clean so much as when I'm just back from a mission," he said.

"Mmm. I appreciate you being clean all the time," I said, running a hand over his back, which was damp from condensation.

He laughed. "Let's go to bed. I still have to go to work in the morning."

I turned down the covers while he got into boxers and a T-shirt, then snuggled up in his arms and closed my eyes in pure contentment. "You know, I think Madeleine is mellowing toward me?" I said. "She was almost polite tonight. Well, polite for her, which means she said a couple of nasty things under cover of being straightforward and speaking truth."

"You don't have to put up with that, love."

"I know. This was…different. I wonder if it wasn't being in her old house that did it. She said something about watching you and Ewan play with your father on the lawn, and she sounded almost human."

"I wish she could be like she was when my father was alive.

She was still a hard person to get close to, but he made her into her best self." Malcolm sighed. "What makes you think she's mellowing?"

"She admitted she thought you'd chosen me purely to spite her. And that she could see we love each other. Maybe it's wishful thinking on my part, but it felt like maybe she's finally coming to terms with the idea of us."

Malcolm's arms tightened on me. "I suppose it's possible. I'm not holding my breath."

"Me neither." But it surprised me to realize, deep inside, I hoped it was true.

8

T he next day was Friday. I spent the morning chatting with Ingrid, our occasional household help, and the afternoon cleaning the pantry. I liked reorganizing things; it was soothing and the end result cheered me up. I'd probably get tired of housework if it was all I did, but now and again it was a welcome break from my job.

That evening, Malcolm and I went to the Kellers' for dinner. Their home was in a west side neighborhood in the hills, overgrown with trees and filled with '50s era homes that had once been ultramodern and were still attractive in an old-fashioned way. Squarish and blocky and vertical, the Kellers' home wasn't the sort of place I could see myself living, but it suited them and their unique personalities.

We followed the curving driveway that circled the house, giving visitors a tour of Harry Keller's magnificent rosebushes. In the heart of summer, they were radiant with color, deep reds and pale peaches, blush pink like the cheeks of a girl in love and dark purple-red close enough to black as to make no difference. Those last were the pride of Harry's heart. He'd spent years cross-breeding roses to get that extraordinary color, and if I hadn't known him so well, I might have suspected magic was involved.

The garden gnome by the Kellers' front porch winked at us saucily as we mounted the steps. It was a lone piece of tackiness in the otherwise elegant landscaping, but when I'd asked Harriet about it, she'd just laughed and said it was a private joke between her and Harry and wouldn't elaborate. I guessed it was something more than just where they hid their spare key —well, that was true, the spare key was on top of the door frame. But it always made me wonder.

Harry let us in. "Glad to see you," he said. "Dinner's almost ready. Come sit with me. Harriet says I'm just in the way in the kitchen."

"Because you are, dear," Harriet called out. "I hope everyone likes fried chicken."

I *loved* Harriet's fried chicken, served with baked potatoes drenched in butter and sour cream and baked beans whose recipe I had yet to master. The smells emanating from the kitchen made my stomach growl.

Harry chuckled. "We love having guests who appreciate Harriet's cooking so much," he said. "And I'm glad that thing at Kalgoorlie went off without a hitch. Hate to think of you still there, Malcolm."

"If I were still there, it would be a disaster the likes of which the Wardens have never seen," Malcolm said, the smile falling away from his lips. "I can't imagine even our glass magi being able to maintain illusions for so long. And there would certainly be civilian casualties."

"The custodian at the Morgan Node, Rafe Wheelwright, is

an old friend of ours," Harry said. "He said the fighting never came close."

"It was almost anticlimactic," Malcolm agreed. "We knew almost exactly where the intelligent invaders would come through, thanks to the Pattern, and took them out before they could fully implement their plan. So we never did have to fight waves of the small ones."

"Now, both of you know there's no talking shop over dinner," Harriet said. She'd removed her apron and held it balled up in front of her. "Let's eat, and talk of pleasanter things. I haven't seen Judy in weeks, Helena, is she doing well?"

I stuffed myself full of good food to the point that I almost didn't have room for Harriet's rich cheesecake topped with raspberry compote. Almost. I was full, not stupid. Then I rolled myself into the living room, accepted a cup of coffee in the tiny cups Harriet had brought back from Belgium in her fighting days, and settled into a corner of the sofa next to Malcolm.

"But the invaders will change their tactics now they know what we can do," Harry said, exactly as if the conversation hadn't been interrupted by food. "We can't count on it being that easy again."

"No, but that's typical of warfare," Malcolm said. "In an ordinary war, we would go on the attack, but since we have no way of reaching the invaders' reality, we can only try to guess their next strategy and thwart it before they can enact it."

"Why can't we reach them?" I asked. "Is it just that humans can't survive there?"

"That, and we're in the same position the intelligent invaders are when it comes to finding a place big enough to slip through," Harriet said. "They can use nodes, but that would be deadly to us. And no one's ever discovered what we *can* use. If that ever happened, I'm sure some clever Warden would come up with a way to protect a human in the invaders' reality."

"But even if we could get through and survive, what could we do that would be useful?" Harry said. "It's tempting to think of planting a bomb, or a flamethrower, but we don't know enough about their reality to know what would do us the most good."

"It would serve them right if we could send through a thermonuclear device," I muttered.

Malcolm laughed. "That *is* tempting."

"Well, with the Pattern recalibrated, we should have no trouble tracking the incursion again," Harriet said. "The report on Berryton confirms what we saw in Barga and Kalgoorlie. The Pattern just wasn't set up to account for the intelligent invaders."

"It should have been," Harry said. "It's not like there weren't intelligent ones in the world before this."

"Well-hidden," Harriet said, "and not taking an active role in attacks. Though I'm sure they directed their mindless cousins often enough."

I remembered the creature that had dragged itself out of my friend Kevin's lifeless body, remembered it wrapping its tentacles around me and biting my shoulder, and I closed my eyes tightly against those memories. When I opened them, the others were looking at me in concern.

Malcolm took my free hand in his. "Are you all right?"

"Just remembering. They're utterly terrifying. Not because they're strong and aggressive, but because they don't think we're worth any consideration. We're just like bugs to them, something to stomp or crush and sweep out of their way."

"We are bugs who have stopped them advancing for over seven hundred years," Malcolm said. "That attitude of theirs is pure bluff. The invader you faced in the Gunther Node wanted you to feel despair."

"It sort of worked. I only survived because they didn't feel like killing me." And because Jun had sacrificed her life to spare mine. More memories that tore at my heart.

"We destroyed three of them at Kalgoorlie," Malcolm said, squeezing my hand gently. "They are as vulnerable as any invader."

I was sure the fighting had been more difficult than he was letting on, but I didn't want to challenge him in front of our hosts. So instead, I said, "I stabbed one of them in the eye. It knows we're not helpless."

"No, but we are dependent on wards," Harry said, "and it sounds like, from Michelle Suzuhara's report on Berryton, that's become a weakness. If we can't figure out how they're warping the wards, any warded location is vulnerable."

Nobody had a response to that. I didn't know what Ms. Suzuhara's report said, because I'd been busy and Lucia hadn't called me, but it was that lack of a phone call that told me it must contain more or less what the custodians and I had guessed: warping the wards enough to take advantage of the gap, or whatever it was, and then killing the node's custodian horribly and thereby destroying the node.

"What's special about the node in Kalgoorlie?" I asked.

Everyone shifted as if coming out of a private reverie. "The Morgan Node is the biggest in Australia," Malcolm said. "In fact, it's one of only two Neutralities in all of Australia. The other nodes are all small and under Nicollien or Ambrosite control."

"Only two that we know about," Harry pointed out.

"Much of Australia is hostile to human life. It's like the Himalayas and the Alps—could be nodes the size of Neutralities all over the place, but nobody's in a position to discover or use them."

"I hope there aren't any secret Neutralities in Australia," Harriet said. "The invaders would certainly make use of them. Desert conditions don't bother them."

"You're wondering why that node was attacked," Malcolm said. "Lucia sent out an update this morning addressing that question. It seems there's nothing all three nodes—four nodes, if you count the failed attack on Abernathy's—had in common. Berryton, Morgan, and Abernathy's are large, but the Cracchiolo Node is relatively small as Neutralities go. Berryton and Cracchiolo were isolated, small communities. Cracchiolo and Kalgoorlie were inland. The Fountain of Youth in Berryton and Abernathy's are named Neutralities, and so forth. So there's no common factor that would help us in identifying the next target."

It irritated me that Lucia hadn't told me this. I reminded myself that she was busy and said, "Unless there's some similarity we just haven't seen yet."

"I'm certain some Warden or other is busy digging deeper into the mystery," Harriet said. "There has to be some reason those targets were chosen. The ones that aren't named Neutralities, I mean. It's obvious the invaders would want to deny those to the Wardens."

I recalled what the oracle had said about 'guardians' and wondered, not for the first time, if that had a literal meaning in addition to the metaphorical one. "Have either of you ever heard the named Neutralities referred to as guardians?" I asked.

Harriet's brow furrowed. "What makes you say that?"

"It was something the oracle said. The other custodians said it was because the named Neutralities are like mascots for all of magery, but I wondered if it might mean something more. I guess it's because the oracle is cryptic, but it never says anything unimportant."

Harry rubbed his nose with one long, bony finger. "Interesting," he said. "There are lots of theories about why the named Neutralities are even a thing—you've never heard those?"

I shook my head. "I've never thought about it."

"Well, there's really no reason for the named Neutralities to exist. There's a whole chapter in *A History of Magic* about them, but it's all nonsense as far as I'm concerned. Not all nonsense, I suppose—the book does point out that as far as any glass magic is concerned, they're all just really big nodes. No magic has ever revealed how they work or why they even exist. And they resist being investigated."

He chuckled. "When Harriet and I were kids, there was some Warden or other who attempted to discover what made the Labyrinth work. She and Iakkhos got into a huge fight about it, and Iakkhos finally said if she was so hot on the subject, she could take her chances with the Neutrality. She went into the Labyrinth and came out five months later, after everyone believed she was dead. She claimed it had only been three days and that's all she would say on the matter."

"I know Abernathy's can't be inventoried, or it would destroy the oracle," I said. "But I don't know if it's ever taken direct action to stop that happening. There's always been a custodian to prevent it. Even when Silas had to move the store—"

I stopped, struck by a thought. "Abernathy's didn't take its node with it, right? It moved from one node to another.

Rebecca Greenough is custodian of that Neutrality in London."

Harriet nodded. "You look like you've had a revelation, dear."

"I don't know. Maybe. It's more a thought. If the oracle is independent of its node—oh, I don't know what I'm saying. I just had an image of the oracle as a lightbulb that could be screwed into any socket. And if that's true for the oracle, it might be true for the other named Neutralities. So the attack on Abernathy's and on Berryton wasn't on the node, it was on the Neutrality."

Harry and Harriet had politely confused looks on their faces, but Malcolm said, "You mean there must be something about Barga and Kalgoorlie that has nothing to do with their nodes."

"Maybe it was who the custodian was, or what the Neutrality produces, or—"

"Lucia probably knows this already," Malcolm said, "but you should call her anyway."

"That sounds like you're ready to go," Harriet said with a laugh. "Let me get you some cheesecake to take with you. There's always far more than Harry and I can eat."

"Far more than you'll let me eat, you mean," Harry grumbled.

Cheesecake box in hand, we got in Malcolm's Mustang, and I called Lucia as Malcolm navigated the driveway in reverse and headed for home. I left her a message I hoped was intelligible without being too wordy and hung up. "Now that I've said it twice, it doesn't seem like much of a breakthrough," I said.

"Possibly. I mentioned they've already eliminated the obvious qualities, like geography and population, but I don't know that anyone's examined the purely practical output of the node. Or the possibility that it might be the custodians the invaders intended to eliminate."

"That hits a little too close to home, Malcolm."

"Sorry." He rested his hand briefly on mine. "You're speaking with the other custodians tonight?"

"At midnight again. It's going to be another late night. You're sure the work on Abernathy's won't be finished tomorrow?"

"The store is scheduled to reopen Monday morning. We can both sleep in tomorrow to our heart's content."

I smiled. "That sounds lovely. Then we could have a picnic and go to an afternoon movie, just like ordinary people who never have to work Saturdays from ten until six."

"I like the sound of that. Though—" He laughed. "I admit ten years ago I would have hated the idea. Of course, ten years ago I was in the Navy and a thrill-seeker. A picnic was something we guys did to impress girls we wanted to sleep with."

"That still works, you know. I never realized how sexy it is to watch a man doing dishes of his own free will."

Malcolm roared with laughter. "Did you just tell me that so I'll do the dishes all the time?"

"No. Maybe. Did it work?"

"You'll find out tomorrow." He winked, making me laugh.

When we got home, Malcolm disappeared into the office to do finances, something he enjoyed more than I did, and I got into my pajamas and curled up with *Old Tin Sorrows* for a few chapters. More than that was too much to take; the story had grown more intense, and I couldn't guess who the villain was. Maybe that was what the oracle was trying to tell me— that the true villains were hiding in plain sight, and I lacked the understanding to identify them. The idea that more humans might be behind the attacks filled me with horror. The Wardens had eliminated the Mercy as a serious threat, but they'd never eradicated every single member, and while it was unlikely that any of those who remained were leaders, maybe that just meant some people had gotten major promotions.

I went downstairs and made hot chocolate, maybe a little weird on a warm night like this, and took a mug to Malcolm. He accepted it with a smile, and I sat near him and enjoyed my own drink in companionable silence. "I'm almost done," he said. "We could watch a movie until midnight."

"That would be nice. Something funny. Something without death in it."

We settled on *My Favorite Wife* and cuddled together on the couch while Cary Grant made a fool of himself trying to avoid telling Gail Patrick his long-missing first wife had come back. Back in the days when we'd done this in the apartment over the store, movies had usually ended with the two of us taking each other's clothes off and occasionally making it as far as the bedroom. Now, I felt so content, lying there in my husband's arms, I didn't need sex to bring us close together.

"Remember what I said about the man I was ten years ago?" Malcolm murmured. "He had no idea what waited in his future. And he wouldn't have appreciated it if he knew."

"I won't tell you what I was doing ten years ago, because I was seriously underage," I said.

He laughed and stroked my hair. "I like to think," he said, "that it took me just long enough to grow up that I could fall in love with you when you were the perfect age."

"Mmm. I like the sound of that."

His arms tightened on me. "Ah, love, what would I do without you?"

"I believe the consensus is that you would be miserable and lonely."

"Very true." He kissed me, and for a few minutes I forgot about the movie. Then Cyrus leaped up to investigate what Malcolm was doing that wasn't petting him, and we settled back in to watch.

It was about twenty 'til midnight when the final credits rolled—or didn't roll; those old movies just had static screens listing the cast. We disentangled ourselves, and I kissed Malcolm goodnight and got my laptop set up on the kitchen table. I felt more at peace than I had in weeks.

A flash of memory struck me, of my first sight of Malcolm, standing by the cash register in Abernathy's with a look of surprise at seeing me, a stranger, instead of Mr. Briggs. I'd thought he was gorgeous, of course, but had no idea what the future held for us. Married. How far we'd come.

I settled in at the computer and gestured to Xerxes to sit on my lap. He ignored me, as was his habit. He liked to pretend lap-sitting was all his own idea. I propped my elbows on the table and waited. I wasn't sure what news I had for my fellow custodians, given that they'd all probably heard the report on Berryton and what had come of the attack on Kalgoorlie, but the idea of sharing information with people whose concerns were mostly like mine made me feel even more at peace.

The computer chimed, and I hit the button. "Good day— and good evening," Samudra said. "I trust everyone is well? Helena, you are unharmed? We all heard about the attempt to destroy Abernathy's."

"I'm fine, thanks. It was incredible good luck, though."

"I'm surprised the oracle didn't warn you itself," Amarion said.

"I—yeah, it doesn't seem to see threats the way we do. Probably it knew Victor would be there, and that was all the warning it took."

"Or warned Victor itself," Claude said. "We do not know the mechanism by which his magical talent operates. The Mercy's oracle tapped into the same mystical space as Abernathy's, so perhaps the other precognitives do the same."

"I never thought of that." It was an intriguing idea, though one I didn't know how to investigate. A thought for another time.

"So our theory about the wards proved true," Samudra said. "Though no one yet knows *how* they are doing it."

"And the situation at Abernathy's tells us how they were getting past the wards," Amarion said. "That was daring, trying to smash through like that."

"I wanted to ask whether all of you have similar alarms set up on your Neutralities," I said. "Now that we know they're willing to take such drastic action, those alarms aren't enough."

"We do not have the alarm on the Sanctuary itself, but on the walls surrounding it and the gates leading to the…you might call it an enclosure," Samudra said. "A stretch of empty land between those gates and the Sanctuary's buildings. Though the invaders would find it difficult to drive a car into the walls, shattering them. The Sanctuary lies atop a sheer cliff, accessible only by foot. But we will not be foolhardy. My people are even now assessing the possibilities and preparing for an assault, possibly by air."

I immediately pictured invaders in parachutes dropping into the Sanctuary complex. "I hadn't thought of that."

Samudra smiled. "It would be extremely hazardous. The

wind blows constantly around the precipice. But even that slim chance should not be overlooked."

"The Wardens have been doing construction around the Labyrinth all day," Amarion said. "They tell me they'll have an improved alarm system in by tomorrow morning. I'm looking forward to having them out of here, honestly. Not that I don't appreciate their efforts, but the noise makes it hard for people to concentrate on their journey."

"The Athenaeum's heart is impregnable," Claude said. "Because access to it is distributed around the world, it is those places that must be accessible, not the node itself. We weaken the wards once a year for me to enter and maintain my charge, but at all other times the wards are as strong as possible. And that time is another four months off. The invaders may try some other approach, but I believe even killing me will not gain them what they want."

It made me uncomfortable, how he spoke so casually of being killed, so to cover my discomfort I said, "I haven't been back to the store since the attack. I feel bad that I'm not more worried about it. It gets wearying, hearing over and over that we're both going to die, or end, or whatever."

"It makes sense," Claude said. "Is there anything we can do?"

That cheered me. "I don't know," I said. "It's so nice of you to offer. If I think of anything, I'll let you know."

"I would urge you to tell us anything the oracle says," Samudra said. "Perhaps we will see something you have not."

"Right. And there's always the possibility that whatever's going to happen to the oracle might affect us as well," Amarion said. "We've already seen it's possible for named Neutralities to be destroyed. It's not such a stretch to imagine them ending for some other reason."

His words triggered a memory from earlier that evening. "I was thinking," I said, "about how Abernathy's was moved from one node to another, and how maybe that means the named Neutralities are independent of their nodes."

"This is true," Claude said. "The Athenaeum was moved from Germany to Switzerland during the First World War. It was not such a production as moving Abernathy's," he said to my surprised gasp, "and I understand it was a matter of one woman packing its core into a suitcase and taking it by train. But the principle was the same."

"So maybe the other two Neutralities the invaders went after were attacked for qualities other than their nodes."

Amarion was nodding. "That makes sense. More sense than trying to figure out what the nodes had in common, which is nothing."

I was about to say something about what Ariadne had said about the size of the named Neutralities' nodes when Samudra said, "Unless it means something entirely different."

"What do you mean?" Claude asked.

"I am not certain," Samudra said, "but I feel, deep within me, as if this puzzle is far from being solved."

I nodded, and the other two did the same. Then my computer let out a low moan, like an animal in pain, and I jumped in surprise. "Did you hear that?"

"I did," Claude said. He leaned forward and appeared to fiddle with something on his monitor, maybe the volume control. The sound came again, deeper and more painful. "It is not I."

"Wait a moment," Amarion said. He pushed back his chair and disappeared from view. I messed with my own volume control, but the sound didn't happen again. No one spoke. I realized Xerxes had been on my lap for a while now, and I'd been petting him without being aware.

Then Amarion's face came into view, his hands clutching both sides of his monitor. His eyes were wide and he was breathing heavily. "Get to safety," he panted. "Get out—go now!"

As quickly as he'd appeared, he vanished again, this time jerked away by some unseen force. I sucked in a startled breath. Then Amarion screamed, a hoarse, horrible sound filled with such desperate agony I cried out myself. The screaming went on, incoherent and wordless, for what felt like forever—until it cut off as abruptly as if his tormentor had pressed a button.

There was a dull scraping sound, stone over wet stone. Something filled Amarion's little rectangle. It was nothing human, with its pointed jaw filled with serrated shark's teeth, its pebbly skin, and its flat black eyes the size of saucers placed close to its nose slits. It was bright blood red—and in a moment of horrible clarity, I realized it was actually covered in blood. Human blood.

It took hold of Amarion's monitor and tilted it until it was looking at me at a weird, inhuman angle. Its bloody lips twisted in a smile that showed bits of flesh clinging to the horrible teeth. In a voice that pushed every one of my primal panic buttons, it said, "*You're next.*"

9

I screamed and slammed my laptop shut, sending Xerxes flying as I scrambled backward until my chair fell over and hit the floor. I kept going, clawing my way back until I came up against the center island. I couldn't stop seeing the invader's hideous face, bloody with what was left of Amarion. I closed my eyes and flung my arms over my face, panting in mindless terror. *You're next.* Any moment now, I'd feel its teeth on me, tearing out my throat.

"Helena!"

I heard Malcolm run into the kitchen, his bare feet slapping the tile unnaturally loudly. He crouched beside me, putting one arm around my shoulders and supporting me to a sitting position. I clung to him, my chest aching from how hard my heart was pounding, my throat raspy from screaming.

"Helena, what happened? Are you hurt?"

I shook my head. "The Labyrinth," I said. "Amarion is... they're under attack, Malcolm, you have to stop them." Tears spilled down my cheeks. "He's dead. It's too late. He's dead."

"The Labyrinth is under attack?"

I nodded. "It killed Amarion. I've never heard anything so terrible." I opened my eyes. Malcolm had his gun in his other hand, and his eyes scanned the room for hidden threats. "It said I was next," I whispered, and burst out crying.

Malcolm shoved his gun into the back waistband of his boxers and helped me stand. My knees wobbled too much to support me. Deep inside, I screamed at myself to toughen up, to stop sobbing like a baby, but the memory of Amarion's final screams rang in my ears. My friend, who'd died horribly at the teeth and claws of an invader while I listened helplessly. Nothing in the world could make me strong enough to bear that.

Malcolm lifted me in his arms and carried me to the living room, where he deposited me on the couch and knelt beside me. "I have to call Lucia and the node in Athens," he said. "I'll be back."

I nodded and clutched a throw pillow like a shield against memories, and gradually my tears subsided into shuddering breaths. No. I wasn't going to let this throw me. I could only help Amarion by doing what I'd done, telling someone who could maybe get Wardens to the Labyrinth in time to prevent it being destroyed. And by refusing to let my fear keep me from doing my job. Maybe that meant I was suppressing my pain, but at the moment, I didn't see any alternative that wouldn't leave me a sobbing wreck.

I wiped my eyes and lay on the couch, hugging my pillow and staring at the blank television screen, until footsteps heralded Malcolm's return. I sat up, and Malcolm sank onto the cushion beside me and took me in his arms. "There are teams going to Knossos right now," he said.

"But it's probably too late."

"If we don't go, it certainly will be. Can you tell me what happened? I'm afraid my instructions to Desmona Papadopoulos were along the lines of 'go now, don't argue.'"

"Did she? Argue?"

"Des is an old friend of mine. She hung up before I could finish talking. I have absolute faith in her ability to handle anything that might have happened at the Labyrinth."

I drew in a deep, shuddering breath and discovered I'd stopped shaking. "We were in the middle of our call," I said. "There was a noise—Amarion went to see what it was. Then he came back and shouted at us to get to safety, and something grabbed him, like…like snatching him out of his seat. Then he screamed. It was—" I swallowed, controlling myself. "I'd never heard anything so awful. It cut off, and that's when the invader looked into the camera and said I was next. Or we were next. I don't know who it was talking to."

Malcolm kissed the top of my head. "I'm so sorry, love," he said. "This is exactly the sort of thing I wish you wouldn't have to witness."

"Yes, but isn't it part of my job? I mean—not that being a custodian means I have to see terrible things, but if the invaders are striking against named Neutralities, that puts me front and center, unless I want to abdicate." I hugged him more tightly. "You said it yourself—I'm strong, and I can deal with this. I just need a better way of dealing than suppressing my fears and my awful memories."

"You're right. You are the strongest woman I know." Malcolm loosened his grip enough that he could look into my face. "Desmona will call when it's all over, if only for more of an explanation. She'll tell us what happened. But you ought to go to bed."

"I can't sleep after that. Not until I know the worst."

Malcolm nodded. "I understand. Do you want to wait here, or in the bedroom?"

"Here. If you'll wait with me."

He chuckled. "You couldn't pry my away from your side."

We sat together and waited. Neither of us wanted to watch a movie, and I didn't suggest turning on the television to see if the news would report a mysterious disaster near Knossos. Like the Fountain of Youth, I didn't know exactly where the Labyrinth was, but Iakkhos had told me it wasn't in a town. So it wasn't likely to show up on the mundane news the way Berryton had.

I wondered what would happen if the Labyrinth were exposed to the world, like how some archaeological sites were revealed when new digging happened. It had been built in the 1400s, far too recently for the typical Greek archaeological dig, but not new construction either. It might mean disaster for the Wardens if they couldn't cover it up. I didn't think even the most powerful magnifica illusion could conceal something that size.

Despite what I'd told Malcolm, I was drifting off when Malcolm's phone rang. I sat upright and stared at it. Malcolm answered, saying, "Des?"

There was a long silence. I couldn't hear Desmona Papadopoulos's voice even as a murmur. Malcolm nodded. "I didn't know that would happen, but it makes sense," he said. Another long pause. "If Lucia—" he said, then stopped as if Desmona had cut him off. "No, yes, I understand. Small blessings." This time, the pause was long enough I got antsy, wishing he'd put her on speaker. "All right," Malcolm said finally. "Thanks. That's as good a result as we could hope for. Yes, I'll tell her. Goodbye."

He set the phone down on the coffee table and stared at it. "Well?" I said.

Without looking at me, Malcolm said, "The Labyrinth is destroyed. Des's teams arrived in time to save perhaps a quarter of its population. Fortunately, the Labyrinth's concealed location means the disaster won't appear on the evening news. But—" He rubbed his face with both hands, a gesture of such exhaustion it made me want to yawn. "Des said, with the Labyrinth's node destroyed, the Labyrinth immediately began to decay. It already looks—you've never seen it, but it used to look as new as when it was first built. Now it looks a hundred very hard-lived years old. She estimates it will disappear entirely in a matter of hours. Protection for the Wardens, so no mundane entity can discover it and draw the right conclusions, but it means there will be no reclaiming it."

"I'm so sad. I understand the need, but it still feels like a loss." I leaned against his shoulder. "Did she say…were they able to recover Amarion's body?"

Malcolm stiffened. "I'm not sure you want to know."

"Now I'll imagine the worst. Please, just tell me."

He put his arm around me. "Amarion was devoured," he said. "Des didn't know how that allowed the node to be destroyed. Her people are looking into it."

I shuddered. "Poor Amarion. It's so awful. He said they weren't done fixing the invader alarms—that's how they got in. I hope Claude and Samudra will take—oh, damn, I need to call them. Or text them."

I ran upstairs for my phone and decided a group text was faster than a phone call to each man separately. I quickly sent off the message—Amarion dead, the node destroyed—and then sent a second message begging them to be careful. When

I finished, I looked up at Malcolm. "Is the house safe? I can't sleep if there's a chance one of those invaders could get in."

"The house is as safe as Campbell Security can make it," Malcolm said, "but...I hesitate to point this out, but if the pattern holds true, the invaders will only attack you if you're on the premises of Abernathy's."

It was a horrible, pragmatic thing to say, and it made me feel instantly better. "I think I can sleep now," I said. "If you hold me."

"You never have to ask," Malcolm said.

We cuddled in the darkness of our bedroom, listening to the night noises outside our window. The chirruping hum of a million insects made a nice background to the night birds that lived in the fir that rubbed against the corner window. I'd never learned what birds they were, but they let out low coos like unusually deep-voiced pigeons. Malcolm's breathing was a steady counterpoint to the other sounds. "Is it weak to say I'm afraid to return to the store?" I whispered. "Especially since I now have a good idea what kind of end the oracle saw?"

"Not weak to feel fear," Malcolm said. "Weak to let it control your actions, possibly."

"I'll go back. I have to. It's like Lucia told me—if we shut down the named Neutralities, we might as well have lost them to the invaders. And if we're going to defeat them, we'll need the help only the oracle can provide."

"I'm afraid I'm not as strong as you. I'm tempted to lock you safely in the house until we've worked out the invaders' plan."

I laughed quietly. "I love that you want to protect me, even though you know what I have to do."

"It's true. I can't bear the thought of losing you."

I snuggled closer. "It won't happen. I'm not going to let them get to me."

"I'll hold you to that," Malcolm said.

WHEN I WOKE the following morning, Malcolm was gone, and his side of the bed was cold. A half-sheet of lined paper on his pillow read *Had to go to node to consult with Lucia. Might be a while. Sorry. Love you.*

I suppressed feelings of disappointment and squinted at the alarm clock. 9:43. I hadn't slept that late in months. I rolled out of bed and stretched. We might still be able to salvage our peaceful afternoon.

My phone rang while I was in the middle of breakfast. It wasn't Malcolm; it was Viv. "Hey," I said. "I haven't seen you in a while."

"I've been busy at the Gunther Node. What do you know about what happened at the Labyrinth? Have you heard anything?"

Memories of Amarion's screaming filled my mind. "Yes. But I'd rather not talk about it. It was awful."

"You say that like you were there. Hel, don't hold out on me."

"I was in a video call with the other named Neutrality custodians when the invaders attacked. I heard Amarion die. It was awful, Viv."

Viv whistled. "Are you all right?"

"It's not like I was attacked or injured, so—" I remembered what Sydney had said, and went on, "I mean, I can't stop remembering how it felt. I was so scared."

"Well, yeah, of course you were! Look, I don't want to

bring up painful memories. There's just a lot of rumor running around and I was wondering if you knew the truth. Did the Labyrinth really disappear?"

I'd finished most of my cereal, but my appetite had disappeared. I rose to clear my bowl. "Malcolm said it did. Or was in the process of disappearing. I guess by now it's entirely gone. He said it was to prevent mundane authorities from seeing it and getting excited. So that's three named Neutralities left."

"You're not going back to work, are you?"

"On Monday? Of course I am. If we're going to defeat the invaders, we need all the resources we can muster, and that includes the oracle." I watched the colorful bits of cereal circle the drain and disappear. I sounded like someone who had no fears. Too bad actually getting rid of my fears wasn't as easy as making bold statements.

Viv clearly wasn't fooled by my boldness. "Helena, that's so dangerous! Nobody knows how the invaders keep getting past the wards. They need to seal up Abernathy's until all the intelligent invaders are destroyed."

I stopped with my bowl held under a stream of water to rinse it. "Is that what people are saying?"

"I guess, but mostly it's my opinion. Better to lose the benefits of the oracle for a few weeks or months than to have it destroyed entirely." Viv sounded less emphatic now, but I could tell when she felt strongly about something.

"They're altering the wards so the invaders can't warp them at Abernathy's. Everything will be fine. And suppose it takes much longer than weeks or months to hunt all of them down? This is the best course of action." I still didn't feel as certain as I sounded, not with Amarion's screams still ringing in my memory. But I had faith in Malcolm's assertion that the wards would be secure and that the invaders couldn't try that stunt with the door again, and that was enough to carry me through my insecurities.

Viv sighed. "All right, but I'm scared for you."

"I'm scared for me, too, but I know what I have to do."

"That's what bravery is. Hel, do you think this war will ever be over?"

I didn't point out that the invaders destroying our world would end the war just as much as the Wardens triumphing would. "I don't know. Doesn't it feel like we've entered the endgame, what with the invaders changing tactics? Maybe we'll see the end sooner than we think."

"I thought the invaders wanted humans to capitulate. This is more like they're going for total destruction."

"I think so, too. But that means they could make mistakes, if they're changing the way they do things. And we've already destroyed some of their leaders. I choose to be optimistic."

Viv laughed. "That's one of the things I love about you, your endless optimism. That, and how you keep a tight leash on your curiosity. You haven't even asked why I've been busy at the Gunther Node."

That comment had slipped right past me. "Okay, why have you been busy at the Gunther Node?"

"It's my new job. I'm working for Mr. Wallach as a lab assistant."

I gasped. "Viv! What about the diner?"

"That was getting old. I'd already worked there about a year and a half longer than I'd promised myself I would, because the tips were good and the hours were flexible. But I've always been intrigued by Mr. Wallach's inventions, and a few weeks ago I asked to be a tester for the portable ansible, which was so unbelievably cool I can't even tell you. And when the test run was over, he said I'd been a big help and did I want a full-time job?"

I could easily picture Viv in a lab coat and goggles, though knowing Viv, the lab coat would be tie-dyed. "That's amazing! And probably scary. Some of his inventions aren't exactly safe."

"Safe is boring. Besides, he's a very careful experimenter. Doesn't do human trials until he knows exactly what the results will be. A real job, Hel. Doesn't that just blow your mind? Me, with a real job." Viv sounded more pleased than astonished.

"I think it's great. And you'll get to see so many amazing inventions up close. Did you know he worked on time travel once? Though he said it was impossible."

"I didn't think Mr. Wallach thought *anything* was impossible." Viv yawned, audible even over the phone. "You want to hang out today? Jeremiah's out of town until Monday night."

"Malcolm and I were going to do a picnic and a movie this afternoon. But he went to the node this morning, and he wasn't sure when he was coming back."

"If it turns out you need company, let me know. I have to get in the shower. I overslept this morning and now I'm playing catch-up."

"I'll call you later. Congratulations again!"

After hanging up, I finished washing the rest of the dishes. Then I assessed my house. I found cleaning therapeutic, and I needed something to boost my spirits after the previous night. But between me and Ingrid, the house looked good enough that there weren't any massive cleaning projects to tackle. So I went back upstairs to the bedroom and sat on the edge of the bed, staring at my bedside table. There was something I could do—something that, after last night, I could add to—but thinking about my traumatic history since becoming Abernathy's' custodian led me to reliving those terrible events, and then all I wanted to do was curl up and forget again.

I sighed and opened the drawer. My notebook, a spiral-bound student's notebook from the nearest dollar store, looked back at me. I withdrew it and clicked the pen clipped to its cover a few times, then opened it to where I'd left off and began writing. I'd gotten as far as my second Christmas as custodian, which meant the Conference of Neutralities. Where I'd been attacked and bitten by invaders…and seen someone killed horribly by them…and gone deep into the bowels of the hotel surrounded by those monsters to fight them… I sighed again and made a few more notes. It was a miracle I was even sane.

When Malcolm came home, he found me lying on the bed staring at the ceiling, clutching the notebook to my chest like a breastplate. "Sorry that took so long," he said. He sat beside me and took my hand. "Have you been resting? You look like you need it."

I handed him the notebook, which was folded open. "Read that."

He raised his eyebrows, but flipped the notebook over and read aloud:

Held at gunpoint four times
Threatened with knife once
Beaten nearly to death
Shot at several times, injured once

"That was me," he said. "Helena—"

"I forgave you. Just keep reading."

He cleared his throat and went on:

Kidnapped twice
Attacked by invaders multiple times, bitten three times
Witnessed seven murders

Nearly died from becoming the oracle twice
Nearly died from being trapped in a burning building
Serious car accident
Saw two invaders disguised as women shot and killed
Killed Rafael Santiago

When he got to the end of the list and handed the notebook back to me, I said, "I didn't include the oracle telling me we were going to die, because that's still a secret. And I didn't include all the little things, like…oh, knowing that Nyla committed suicide rather than face justice, and Kevin dying so the intelligent invader could get close to me. But that's still a lot."

"I have always said you're the strongest woman I know," Malcolm said. "I didn't realize until now how true that was." He took my hand and helped me sit up so he could hold me. "Love, you have every right to be changed by these experiences. And I've seen that change. Do you want to know how I think it's affected you?"

"Made me a dripping wreck who can't forget the sound of screaming?"

He held me closer. "It's made you someone who can't bear to sit by and watch evil destroy others. Almost every one of those things happened to you because you couldn't not take action. And yes, that means you have some terrible memories. But there are people who are alive now who wouldn't be if you'd kept yourself safe. You chose this path, and I believe it was the right one. And in time, you'll come to terms with your history. Until that happens, and long afterward, I will be by your side, feeling unspeakable awe that someone like you chose to link her life to mine."

I gaped at him. "That's…amazing. How do you always know what to say?"

Malcolm smiled. "I learned it from you, love." He kissed me, a light touch that gradually deepened until I was breathless. I put my arms around him and reveled in his kiss. He was right, I could endure this, because the alternative—hiding from the monsters—would turn me into someone I'd hate.

"Do you want—" Malcolm murmured.

"I'll always want," I said, and tossed the notebook across the room.

I woke Monday morning to a sense of nameless dread. It took me several seconds to remember I was going back to work today and that was the source of my dread. I dragged myself out of bed and into the shower, trying to think positive thoughts. The store was protected against invaders, even the intelligent ones. I had an important role to play in the Long War. And maybe the oracle would give up on reminding me of its, and my, upcoming end. I'd never realized how much I'd come to look forward to communicating with my strange friend until those communications had gone sour.

Malcolm had made breakfast: chocolate chip pancakes and sausages, both of which I drenched in maple syrup. "I will never understand some of your eating choices," he said, watching me fork up a dripping bite of sausage.

"This is delicious. It's salty and meaty and sweet all at the same time."

He shook his head in mock despair and ate his own sausage, totally free of syrup. "I can drive you to work today, if you want," he said. "I have to give the final approval to the new alarm system."

"That would be nice." I took another gooey, delicious bite. "Did I tell you Viv is working for Mr. Wallach now?"

"No, you didn't. That sounds…actually, it sounds like a recipe for disaster. They have the kind of personalities that would reinforce each other's most adventurous qualities."

"I'm sure it will be fine. Viv's not stupid, and Mr. Wallach only looks like he's reckless."

Malcolm nodded. "And for all we know, this partnership will result in amazing discoveries."

I scraped up the last of my syrup and sucked it off my fork. "That's a very positive attitude. I'm collecting those today. It's way too easy to fall into despair, what with everything that's happened, so I'm choosing to look on the bright side."

Malcolm stood and held out his hand for my empty plate. "I'm glad to hear it."

Judy was in the office opening the mail when we came in. "I want to know what the front door really looks like," she told me.

"Um…didn't you look at it already?"

"Yes, but the letter with the instructions says they put an illusion on it to make it look normal. You can see through illusions, and I'm curious as to what was so extreme they had to cover it up."

Malcolm had already left the office, heading toward the store front. Curious myself, I followed him. The store felt bright and new today, as if the oracle had needed a break, too. Even the deeply shadowed aisles between the bookcases seemed less dark, and the air had the fresh linen scent of line-dried laundry. My resolve to be optimistic increased.

I came through the last bookcases and stopped, stunned.

Malcolm stood next to the door, feeling along its surface with his face nearly pressed against it. "What do you see?" he asked.

Where the old wooden door with a glass center had been stood a magnificent piece of what looked like leaded crystal, beveled and faceted to collect sunlight and turn it into fractured rainbows. It was impossible to see clearly through it; the world beyond appeared as colored angular lines, with the moving ones from cars and people passing looking like ripples in a pond. It looked more like a magic mirror than a door. If it had come to life and told me I was the fairest of them all, I wouldn't have been surprised.

"It's amazing," I said. I walked forward in a daze, blinking away the brightness. "It looks like solid crystal."

"That's how it feels, too," Malcolm said, stepping away from the door. "And sounds, if you knock on it. I'll get someone over here to adjust the illusion. It ought to cover all five senses, but although it smells like wood, it feels slick like crystal."

He put his hands on his hips and surveyed it. "The rest of the magic is active. It will now kill an invader outright if it touches the door, and it still operates as before to prevent an invader in a human body from entering. But it's also proof against anything short of a nuclear warhead impact, and the magic that reinforces its physical resistance extends to the entire building. It occurred to me that there was nothing stopping someone from blowing a hole in the wall from either side, or the roof, so we took care of that possibility."

"So how is this different from regular wards?"

Malcolm leaned against the counter, graceful as a cat. "Stone wards are a function of magic reinforcing stone's natural tendencies to protect and guard. A stone ward...I suppose you could say it anchors itself within the stone, and the more magic a stone magus pours into it, the stronger it gets, until it creates an impenetrable ward."

"Which would do us no good, because we have to keep Abernathy's open."

"Right. This magic is more like a web, but an irregular one. Lines of magic extend from the focus—the door, in this case—and interweave in a random pattern until they're threaded through every inch of the walls and roof. The randomness increases its effectiveness because it's a highly redundant system. If one line breaks, there are fifty others doing the same job. But that's metaphorical, because the lines can't break."

I touched the crystal of the door, then jerked my hand away, afraid of smearing the perfect surface. My fingers hadn't left a mark. "That sounds better than a stone ward. Why don't we use these instead, all the time?"

Malcolm shook his head. "It requires too much magic to operate. With a stone ward, it requires a lot of magic to set, but the magic just sits there within the ward, powering it passively. This system needs magic poured into it constantly, and that's expensive so far as *sanguinis sapiens* goes. But don't worry," he added, forestalling me as I opened my mouth to protest, "it's only an impractical solution, not an impossible one. We have plenty of *sanguinis sapiens* to maintain it indefinitely."

"That's good, I guess." I crossed the room to hug him. "I already miss you. I've loved the last few days of having nothing to do but spend time together. I'm sure we'd eventually get tired of each other, but not for a long while."

"I agree," Malcolm said.

We walked back through the store and kissed goodbye at the back door. When I returned to the office, Judy had a stack of bills at her elbow and was frowning at the computer screen. "Anything wrong?" I asked.

"Just the usual finances details. And Mike wants me to move in with him."

I sat on the corner of the desk and picked up the fat stack of augury requests. "Wow. I thought you said he wasn't interested."

"He's not. He's worried about me living here when there's a chance invaders might destroy it." Judy sighed and pushed back from the desk. "I don't know. He may have a point. I'm just not sure we should move in together for that reason. I could tell he was…oh, he wasn't begrudging or anything, but he was clearly more interested in my safety than in building a life together."

"That doesn't sound good."

"I'm probably saying it all wrong. I guess I mean if he could find another way to keep me safe, he'd be as hot on that as he is right now about me moving in. Does that make sense?"

"Yeah. But the store is totally safe now. You should see it— the door is a giant crystal. On a bright day, I'm going to need sunglasses."

"I'll tell him that. Actually, I'll tell him to ask Malcolm about the details of the protections." Judy sighed. "Sometimes I think about our future—me and Mike, I mean—and I just don't know what I want."

"But you love him, right?"

"Love isn't always enough. What if we're too independent to really fit together? Long-term relationships need compromise to work." Judy twined the keyboard cable around her fingers. "But then I think about how far we've come, and I wonder, haven't we already learned to compromise? To over-come our differences? So…I don't know."

"I think you should be more concerned about whether it's what you want. Because if it's not something you want to do, it's a bad idea."

"I know." She moved her hand restlessly and appeared surprised to find it tangled with the cord. "Some days, I can picture us together for the rest of our lives. And other days, that feels like a huge burden."

I tapped the sheaf of envelopes on my palm. "That sounds like you're not ready to make the decision."

"True." She looked up at me. "Right now I'd settle for Mike and my father getting along. They're superficially polite, but I can practically hear them thinking 'filthy Ambrosite' and 'degenerate Nicollien' whenever conversation stalls."

I swore under my breath. "Why can't they all see how stupid they're being? We need unity if we're going to win this war. Especially now that the invaders are stepping up their game."

"I wish I knew. Sometimes it feels like the Nicolliens and the Ambrosites actually enjoy having someone to hate. It's like having a favorite sports team, only a million times more intense." Judy stood. "You probably ought to get to those. They didn't stack up nearly as much as I expected while we were closed, but there's still a lot."

I didn't tell her I'd sort of been using our conversation as a delaying excuse. "Yeah. Let's see how many I can get done before the Nicolliens show up."

Back at the front counter, I set the stack of envelopes down and withdrew the first letter. Without opening it, I walked into the oracle—and into an ambient red glow like the light of a dying star. "Wow," I said involuntarily. I'd intended not to speak to the oracle unless it spoke to me first. "I—it's hard not to feel this is a bad omen for the rest of the day."

I returned to the counter and scrawled NO AUGURY on the outside of the folded paper. Judy would print out a copy of the nice little note I'd taken to mailing people whose requests were refused. It felt like the polite thing to do.

The second augury, though, was normal, and so were the next three, which was all I could manage before ten o'clock. The oracle never spoke, though I could feel its presence nearby, its attention fixed on something else. I sometimes wondered what it did all day long. I didn't think it needed much attention to give auguries, and I always had the sense that it *was* doing something, just nothing I could comprehend.

At ten o'clock, I let in the three people who waited outside. "Quiet morning," I commented as I accepted the first augury slip. "I thought we'd be swamped."

"I think most people expected Abernathy's to be closed longer," the woman said. "How are you holding up? That attack must have been terrifying."

"I'm all right, thanks. And everything worked out okay, so…" Feeling myself on the verge of once again suppressing my feelings, I made my escape into the oracle.

The rest of the morning was so peaceful it was hard to remember how awful things had been last week. I filled augury requests, then had lunch with Judy, then filled more augury requests. As two o'clock drew near, and no Ambrosites lined up outside the door, I felt superstitiously as if the end of the world had come and no one needed auguries because they were all off fighting the last battle of the war.

I was about to remove the second to last augury request from its envelope when the bells over the door jangled. It had relieved my mind that the magi replacing the door had either left the bells in place or installed new ones. It made me feel less like my whole world was in upheaval. "Welcome to—oh, Ariadne!" I exclaimed. "How can I help you?"

Ariadne Duwelt pushed her short red hair back from her face as if the wind had disordered it. "Hi, Helena," she said. "I'm here on behalf of the Board of Neutralities. It looks as if Abernathy's wasn't even touched in the attack."

"I know. The repairs are better than perfect. I wish you could see what the new door actually looks like." I liked Ariadne, who was far nicer than my previous Board liaison, Timothy Ragsdale, but her permanent semi-smile always made me feel as if she were secretly laughing at a joke I'd missed.

She smiled that secretive smile again now and said, "We're all grateful you weren't hurt. Have you caught up on the mail-in auguries?"

That irritated me a little. I supposed, in a sense, she had the right to check up on my job performance, but the question made me feel like a child being nagged about her homework. I waved the envelope in my hand at her. "They've gone so fast today. I'm glad having to shut down for a few days wasn't more disruptive."

Ariadne nodded. "I have a few requests from the Board, but they can wait until you've finished that one."

"No, it's all right. The Accords say I have to take walk-in requests before mail-ins, and I think that's sensible."

Ariadne's smile grew into a real one. "I bow to your knowledge of the Accords."

I laughed. My knowledge of the Accords had gotten me into trouble with the Board and then out of trouble again. "I'll have to take those one at a time, so it may be a while."

"I'm free all afternoon." Ariadne looked at the folding

chair beside the door as if she were considering the possibility it might dump her on her butt, came to the conclusion that the odds were not in her favor, and leaned against the counter with the air of someone prepared to wait all day.

Inside the oracle, I unfolded the paper she'd given me. *How many intelligent invaders are presently in our world?* An interesting, direct question, and not one anyone else had ever asked. I set off looking for the blue-lit augury. Knowing how many of the enemy there were might help when it came to knowing if the Wardens had eliminated all of them, though that assumed no more intelligent invaders would enter our world. Probably the Board would make use of the information in ways I hadn't thought of.

I pulled the book *Blake's Complete Writings* off the shelf, feeling the electric tingle of a live augury, and flipped through the pages before remembering it was against the rules to read someone else's augury. Tucking it under one arm, I returned to Ariadne's side and handed her the book. "I think we can do all of these and add up the total at the end," I said.

Ariadne nodded. She was already engrossed in studying the book. I took the next request—*How can we best defend the named Neutralities?*—and left her to her reading.

There were five augury requests in all, most of them related to protecting the remaining named Neutralities. It felt a little weird reading the questions, like listening to a conversation between two people discussing my personal habits. I reminded myself this wasn't about me, at least not directly, and set the last book on Ariadne's stack. "Looks like $10,725," I said.

"I've got a check," Ariadne said.

"That's fine. I'm not worried about the Board stiffing Abernathy's," I said with a smile.

I wrote the receipt out, only then wondering where Judy was, and found Ariadne a box to carry her books in. "I hope those are helpful," I said.

"So do I," Ariadne said. "Just between us, the Board is looking for a new approach to counter the new tactics of the invaders. Please let us know if the oracle gives you any hints."

"I will."

The door swung open, making us both turn. "Hi," Viv said. "Can you believe I'm here on business?" She didn't look like a businesswoman compared to Ariadne, who wore a light-weight sky-blue suit and open-toed pumps; Viv had on striped green and white shorts, a cropped lemon-yellow T-shirt that matched her hair, and gray suspenders decorated with colorful buttons bearing cute sayings.

I tore my gaze from one that read I CAN KILL YOU WITH MY BRAIN—all right, that one wasn't so cute—and looked past her at the other person coming through the door. "Mr. Wallach, hi," I said.

"I was afraid we'd have to fight the crowds," Wallach said. For a change, he wasn't wearing scrubs, of which he seemed to have an endless supply. Instead, he wore an old-fashioned black suit with wide lapels and white pinstripes, black and white saddle shoes, and a tie wider than his lapels. It should have looked ridiculous, but on him it had a weird, sprightly dignity, if those three words could be used together.

"No, it's been quiet," I said. "Good luck, Ariadne."

Wallach held the door for her and let it swing carefully back into place, though it no longer slammed shut if you let go of it at the wrong time. "I hope you're doing well, Mrs. Camp-bell," he said.

"I'm fine. I'm happier now that the new alarm system is in

place. Though I guess it's more a defense system than a simple alarm."

"Here's my request," Wallach said, extending a torn piece of paper toward me. I took it, glancing at Viv, who was bouncing on her toes with excitement. Her lemon-yellow bob swayed with her movement.

"Um…is there something I should know about?" I asked. "You seem more chipper than usual."

"Go ahead and get the augury, and we'll tell you," Viv said with a wide smile.

I raised my eyebrows. "That doesn't fill me with dread at all."

"It's nothing to worry about," Wallach said.

I took the piece of paper into the oracle. Immediately I felt its presence surround me, pressing down on me with the lightest touch that I knew would become unbearable over time. "So you're interested in this augury," I said. Despite myself, I felt heartened by its awareness. So long as it didn't start talking about endings, I enjoyed having it near.

I unfolded the paper and read, *Where is the navel?* "Huh," I said. "Navel of what?"

The oracle's attention never wavered. In the distance, blue light flared. I headed in that direction. "I know he said not to worry," I continued, "but Mr. Wallach has done a lot of crazy things in the past, and I can't help thinking he doesn't have the same definition of 'safe' as most people. You'll steer him right, won't you?"

The book was a pretty hardcover titled *One Was a Soldier*. I examined it without opening it for a few seconds before heading for the exit. The oracle followed me the whole way, giving me the impression that it was looking over my shoulder.

I handed the book to Wallach with a flourish. "$4500," I

said. "And you'd better let Viv tell me what has her so excited, or she might pop."

Wallach rooted around in his suit for his wallet. "Go ahead," he said.

Viv grabbed me by the shoulders. Her radiant smile prompted a smile from me, though I didn't know what we were happy about. "We know how to end the Long War," she said.

I stared at Viv, dumbfounded. "You *what?*"

"Isn't it amazing?" Viv said. She let go of me and went back to bouncing on her toes. "Nobody ever thought to look for a solution like this, but it's really obvious once you know. Obvious even to me, and I'm no scientist."

I turned to Wallach just as Judy emerged from the stacks, looking disgruntled. "What do you mean, end the Long War?" I said.

"What?" Judy exclaimed. She sounded as incredulous as I had.

"I don't know the mechanics of the solution yet," Wallach said, "but the principle is, as Ms. Haley says, obvious. If we can misalign our reality with the invaders', they won't be able to enter anymore. Problem solved."

Judy and I exchanged glances. "That sounds...really simple," I said. "It seems someone ought to have thought of it before."

"You'd think so, yes?" Wallach said. He finally dug his

wallet out of the depths of his amazing suit coat and started counting out bills. Judy stepped forward to accept the money, but her wide eyes told me she was still stunned. "But it's only been in the last five or so years that we've understood much about the non-Euclidean geometries defining the space invaders come from, or how that intersects with the Euclidean geometry of our world's effective reality."

"And now it's not simple at all," I said. I'd understood the individual words he'd used, but taken all together, they left my brain feeling mushy.

"Well, the details, as I said, I don't know yet. But I'm certain it's possible." Wallach finished counting bills and put his wallet away. "I'll probably have a number of augury requests in the coming days. I'm not so proud as to think I can do this entirely myself." He patted the cover of his augury like a baby.

"Have you told Lucia?" Judy asked.

"I left her a memo. If she wants more information, she can come to my lab for an explanation." Wallach's smile went smug. I couldn't blame him. Getting Lucia's attention sometimes meant resorting to cryptic measures.

"You should keep this quiet until you have a practical plan," Judy said. "Otherwise you might raise people's hopes only to dash them. What if it turns out the mechanics are impossible?"

"Oh, I don't think that's the case," Wallach said, "but I agree with you about keeping it secret. I prefer not to have people nagging me with questions in the early stages of development."

"And I get to help!" Viv exclaimed. "I'm experienced at interpreting auguries now that I've helped Jeremiah with so many. I think I have a gift for it."

I couldn't think why this whole situation made me uneasy. "I agree," I said, wishing my words didn't feel false. I was sincere; if Viv hadn't taken the job with Wallach, I'd have suggested she train as a professional interpreter. So why did I feel like a mom patting her child on the back for learning to dress herself?

"Thanks for this," Wallach said. "Like I said, I'll probably be back often."

"We'll be ready for you," I said, and waved goodbye before shutting the door.

"That was unreal," Judy said. "And it does feel like someone should have thought of it before, but he's right that it wouldn't have occurred to anyone until recently."

"I have no idea what he was talking about. Misalign our reality?"

Judy leaned against the counter. "Well, you know how our reality is orthogonal to the invaders'?"

"And 'orthogonal' means 'at right angles.' That's about all I know."

"Mr. Wallach is talking about shifting our reality so it no longer matches up to theirs. Like scooting it over half an inch so the cracks are covered, only this shift would make it impossible for new cracks to form."

"Wow. Is that possible?" Her mention of cracks reminded me of something I'd heard recently, but I couldn't put my finger on it.

"For Crazy Wallach? Almost certainly. At the very least, he'll come up with three new magical technologies out of the research." Judy ran her fingers through her short black hair. "No more Long War. I can barely imagine it."

"I don't want to imagine it." At Judy's look of surprise, I added, "I mean, obviously I want the war to be over, but daydreaming about it will make it harder for me to handle the reality that it's not over yet."

"That makes sense." Judy looked beyond me at the plate glass window. "Looks like we have a customer. I'm glad no one was here when Crazy Wallach dropped that little bombshell. He's going to have enough trouble keeping the secret when people start asking what he's researching now."

I smiled pleasantly at the Ambrosite who entered and accepted her augury request. When I entered the oracle, its attention was elsewhere again. "I'm sorry I don't understand you better," I said. "You were clearly interested in Mr. Wallach's augury, but I have no idea why. I hope it wasn't a message to me that I missed."

The rest of the day passed uneventfully, with only a few people coming in before closing. One of them confirmed that they'd expected Abernathy's to be closed until tomorrow, which suggested tomorrow might be as busy as today had not been. When I finally locked the front door at six o'clock, it was with an unexpected sense of relief that nothing awful had happened. The only really exciting thing had been Wallach's announcement, but since that hadn't been accompanied by gunfire and explosions, I couldn't call it excitement.

"You'll be all right?" I said to Judy anyway. "Alone here?"

"I'm fine. The store is secure, and the neighborhood is safe." Judy set the computer to hibernate and pushed in the office chair. "I'm looking forward to a quiet night alone."

"Let me know if anything happens."

I waited outside in the rear parking lot for Malcolm. The heat of the day lingered, though the parking lot was in shade most of the afternoon. It smelled of hot asphalt and buttered popcorn from the theater next door and the tang of heated metal radiating off the beater car nobody claimed ownership of. I'd never felt frightened of living in the apartment over the store in the whole time I'd lived there, and the only time I'd been in danger had been from my ex-boyfriend, Chet, when he was under the influence of an illusion. Now, though, I wasn't sure I could be as carefree as Judy—but then, she hadn't been present for the attack on the store, and didn't have troubling memories to disturb her calm. And I had faith in Campbell Security as vouched for by Malcolm. She would be fine.

My mind wandered back to Wallach's announcement. Judy's example had made sense to me: shift our reality out of sync with the invaders. How that could happen, I couldn't begin to imagine. As I understood it, our "reality" wasn't the same as the physical world, so I didn't think Wallach had moving the universe in mind, but what else was there?

Come to think on it, what else *was* there, out there in the place where the invaders' reality met ours? The invaders, I'd been told, had attacked many realities, draining them of their magic and moving on. If we shifted ourselves out of their reach, would that prevent them latching on to some other world, or would they simply move to the next? Unease rose in me again. I wasn't sure we had a right to condemn some other reality to the invaders' attack. On the other hand, we had the right to defend ourselves…oh, it was all too confusing, and I didn't know enough to take a position either way.

Malcolm's car pulled into the parking lot, and I waved. I'd tell him about Wallach's plan, and maybe he could help me understand the ramifications. And then maybe my uneasy feeling would go away.

MIDMORNING OF THE NEXT DAY, I was searching for an augury when the oracle's attention suddenly pressed down on me, painfully this time like being caught in a vise. "What?" I said, more sharply than I'd intended because of the unexpected pain.

They strike, I thought. **They fall. No more cracks.**

"I don't understand," I began.

Then I did.

I dropped the augury request and darted for the exit, though I didn't know who I could tell. If I was fast enough, maybe the Wardens would be able to save the invaders' next target.

"Write your request again. Sorry," I told the waiting Nicollien. "The invaders are attacking," I said to Judy. "I need to warn someone."

"Call Lucia—no, call Dave," Judy said. "Where are they attacking?"

"I don't know. The oracle said it was happening. Maybe it showed up in the Pattern, but—I have to warn someone!"

I called Dave Henry and got his voicemail. Cursing, I tried Malcolm. "The invaders are attacking again," I said when he answered. "I don't know what to do."

"Take a breath," Malcolm advised me. "Where are they attacking?"

"The oracle didn't say. Why would it tell me and not mention the important part?"

"Abernathy's might be in danger again. There's no reason the invaders might not make a feint elsewhere and focus their real attack on the store. Did you call Lucia?"

"I tried Dave. He's not answering."

"Leave it to me. Don't let any of your customers leave for now. You're perfectly safe, but if invaders swarm the store, anyone outside might not be." Malcolm abruptly disconnected. I put my phone away and turned to my mystified customers.

"I've just learned the invaders are trying another attack," I said. Gasps and muttered profanities swept through the small crowd. "We're not sure where, but if they attack here, we're all safe."

"You think they might attack here?" an elderly woman said.

"I have no idea. I think not, or the oracle's warning would have been different. But everyone should stay inside for a while, until we find out what happened."

Movement outside the plate glass window caught my eye, and I pushed past Wardens until I stood next to it. Three familiars were leashed securely to a lamppost just outside. I was used to that, since familiars weren't allowed inside Abernathy's, but their presence still made me uncomfortable. Normally they sat, or climbed over each other, behaving like the dogs they were disguised as. Now, however, they strained at their leashes in eerie silence, all of them apparently desperate to get free. They reminded me of dogs in a movie who've just heard a dog whistle.

Someone beside me said, "That's strange." He was looking at the familiars, too, his brow furrowed in concern. Outside, a couple of young men holding hands walked past, turning to watch the straining familiars. Then one of the creatures, a bright orange-furred beast with six multijointed legs, let out an unearthly howl that shivered down my spine. The young men recoiled and hurried on, faster than before.

"I'm going to see what's wrong with Pestilence," the man beside me said.

"No, don't!" I cried out as he moved toward the door. "It might be a trap!"

"Familiars can't harm people," the man said. He opened the crystal door.

The orange familiar lunged for him. I cried out, but the man didn't react. He went down on one knee and took the creature's elongated muzzle in one hand. A ripple went through the familiar, a full-body shudder that shook the man's hand. Then the familiar collapsed.

Now the man cried out. He rolled the familiar onto its back and pressed a hand against its bony chest. Another, more violent shudder ran through the thing, but other than that, it didn't move.

Someone beside me shouted and pushed forward to the door. The other two familiars had fallen and now lay motionless on the sidewalk. One of them had fallen halfway into the gutter. Two women hurried to their side. One of the women was crying.

All around me, people took out their phones. Some scrolled through the displays, while others texted or made phone calls. A few took pictures of the dead familiars and were scolded by their neighbors. Judy and I looked at each other. "I'm calling my father," Judy said. "What are the odds that three familiars mysteriously died just here and nowhere else?"

"And died just as the invaders are attacking?" I said.

My phone rang. "It was Sheffield," Malcolm said. "In northern England. The oracle wasn't the only one that knew about it, because the Wardens were there almost as soon as the attack began. They kept it from becoming a total disaster, but more than two thousand people were killed."

I closed my eyes and tried to remain calm. "And it looks like the others? A fast-acting illness?"

"No," Malcolm said. "It looks like biological warfare. And that's how it's being reported."

"Terrorism," I said. "If the invaders wanted panic, they've got it." I couldn't imagine anything more terrifying to the average person than the possibility of a biological attack that could strike anywhere, at any time.

"We have to stop them permanently soon," Malcolm said in a low voice as if there were people nearby he didn't want overhearing this conversation. "The world's governments can't not take notice of this, and they're going to react. Badly, from our perspective."

"Malcolm, something else happened." I quickly described what had happened to the familiars.

"That can't be a coincidence," Malcolm said.

"Judy's calling her father—actually, hang on," I said. Judy was waving at me frantically.

"It's happening everywhere," she said. "There are reports coming in from all over. Familiars just dropping dead. Father is communicating with other Nicollien leaders around the country and they report the same thing."

"But is it an attack?"

"Father thinks so. There's nothing else that could kill all the familiars, all at the same time—not even Ambrosites could work that kind of magic. He believes it was meant to be a distraction from the latest attack on the node in Sheffield—you know it was Sheffield?"

"Yes. Hang on." I told Malcolm what Judy had said, and added, "If it was meant to weaken the Nicolliens in Sheffield, it wouldn't work. There aren't any familiars left in Great Britain."

"It's possible it was intended as a more global distraction," Malcolm said. "If we hadn't had the Pattern and the oracle's warning, we would have been dealing with the familiars' deaths when the attack in Sheffield happened, and the invaders would have destroyed the city and the Bridgerton Node."

"But now it seems there might be no more familiars. What will the Nicolliens do?"

"Adapt. I know, it sounds harsh, but there is no alternative. Building up another cadre of familiars would take years, and we don't have years. And maybe this is what we've needed all along—to remove the primary source of friction between the factions. Removal of the familiars by a third party, instead of the Ambrosites demanding it or the Nicolliens doing it grudgingly, might be the best option."

"You don't really think this will make the factions get along, do you?"

Malcolm sighed. "No. But your optimism is infectious."

I laughed, and quieted myself before I could draw more than a few irritated stares. "I guess we'll have to wait and see. Do you know if there are any similarities between the Bridgerton Node and the others?"

"No. Lucia will investigate, and if there's anything, she'll announce it. I have to go, love. I'll see you tonight."

I hung up and put my phone away. More Wardens were on the street, just standing around doing nothing—but as I thought that, I realized the familiars' bodies had sagged like deflated basketballs, and patches of bright blue goo showed on their skin. Some of those Wardens were no doubt paper magi, skilled at illusions and more than capable of concealing what had happened there on the sidewalk. And the others would dispose of the bodies. Not that that took much doing, since the bodies of dead invaders, which is what the familiars really were, broke down quickly once they were destroyed.

"All right, form a line again," I said, drawing the attention of the dozen or so people staring at their phones. "Your auguries might be even more important now, and you can't help the familiars or the people in Sheffield by standing around doing nothing." *Taking up space in my store* was what I wanted to say, but the Nicolliens looked devastated enough I didn't want to be harsh with them.

Half of them left without auguries. I thought, from observing them, they were ones who'd left their familiars at home and either wanted to check on them or had gotten word that they, too, were destroyed. We finished the rest of the auguries in glum silence, me speaking only to tell someone how much their augury would cost. By noon, the store was empty, and so was the street outside. Just a couple of blue blotches showed where the familiars' bodies had lain, and I assumed those were hidden by illusion.

"This is awful," Judy said. "Everyone's reporting their familiars dead. One hundred percent fatality. The Nicolliens won't recover from this."

"And it won't even prompt the Ambrosites to make common cause with them, want to bet?" I stood in front of the crystal door and admired the rainbows. They calmed me.

"I wouldn't take that bet." Judy headed for the break room. "Let's eat before some other disaster strikes."

But nothing happened. I refrained from looking at any news feeds, afraid to learn the extent of the disaster at Sheffield or what the news thought was the cause of all that death. Bioterrorism, Malcolm had said, and I could see how that would be a compelling explanation. The press would go nuts trying to find similarities between the three incidents they knew about. Probably about as nuts as the Wardens were going as they tried to work out why the invaders had chosen those targets. The named Neutralities were obvious, but why the other two nodes? I had no ideas, other than my feeling that the oracle knew more than it was saying.

Inspired, I slipped into the oracle's space about ten minutes until two, when a few Ambrosites had lined up outside. The oracle paid me no attention. "I have a question," I said, "and I don't know if you'll answer it, but…do *you* know why the invaders chose the targets they did? I mean, it seems obvious that they wanted to destroy the Fountain and the Labyrinth, and us, of course, but why the other three? Or were they just a distraction? Because if they were—if they were meant to conceal the invaders' interest in the named Neutralities—it didn't work."

I waited. After a few seconds, I thought, **Gaps. Leaks. Seal the cracks.**

That was where I'd heard that phrasing before. "You've said that before," I said aloud. "I don't understand what it means."

The oracle's attention became oppressive, and I had to force myself to stand upright against the pressure. **Force increases. Seal the cracks. Many holes, few holes, one hole. They fall. The guardians remain.**

"Force increases…many holes…" It still didn't make any sense, unless… "What comes through the cracks?"

Power. The oracle's voice thundered through my body, blurring my vision. **Seal the cracks**. Then it was gone.

I clung to the nearest bookcase until my vision cleared and my knees stopped wobbling. "Thanks," I said, though I hadn't gotten anything to be thankful for except, possibly, not being crushed.

I left the oracle and went to let the Ambrosites in. "Great

day, huh?" the woman at the head of the line said. "Those Nicolliens finally got what they deserved."

My head still ached from the oracle thinking through me, and I remembered the devastated face of a woman kneeling beside her fallen familiar. "Excuse me?" I said icily.

The Ambrosite didn't react to my sharp tone. "They should have destroyed their familiars a long time ago. This just proves how wrong they were. They ought to be grateful the creatures just died and didn't turn on them the way they did two years ago."

I snatched the augury slip out of her hand. "That's right," I said. "Because they're all idiots who don't actually care about winning the Long War. Not the way you sainted Ambrosites do."

"What?" The woman sounded puzzled. It made me angrier.

"Look," I said, pitching my voice so the whole store could hear me, "I hate familiars. If it turns out they really are all destroyed, I won't be sad. But at least I'm not so full of self-righteousness that I take pleasure in other people's pain. And unlike the lot of you, I'm not so obsessed with defeating other humans that I can't see who the real enemy is!"

The woman had gone totally still. Everyone had their eyes on me. "You people have serious problems, you and the Nicolliens alike," I said. "At what point did you all decide it mattered more to put one over on *your fellow humans* than to work together? It's disgusting. And I'm sick of it." I waved the augury slip in the woman's face. "I swore to be impartial. So I'm impartially declaring Abernathy's a faction-free zone. You do whatever the hell you want when you're out there, but in here, I'd better not hear anything against either faction. And yes, I'll tell the Nicolliens the same thing. Now, get your augury slips ready, and I'll be back." I turned on my heel and stomped away into the oracle.

As if it had been waiting for me, the oracle's attention bore down on me instantly. "I'm in a bad mood, so whatever you have in mind had better not be cryptic," I snarled.

Guardians fall. Guardians remain. Seal the cracks.

"See, that's exactly what I didn't want to hear. Who is sealing what cracks, and how?"

There was a pause. **There is an ending. I will end. Helena will end.**

I bit back a furious shriek and closed my eyes, practicing my calming breathing. "All right," I said when I finally felt capable of speaking in a normal tone. "You and I are going to end. I don't understand why you keep telling me this when you won't say anything else. I don't know if it's something we can prevent, or if it's inevitable, and either way I don't know how to prepare for it. Can't you *please* give me something else? Some hint?"

Nothing happened, but the oracle's attention was still present. Finally, I thought, **Lose the battle. Win the war,** and the oracle retreated.

I did some more calming breathing as I thought about this. Losing battles did not seem the way to win a war, and even if it was, I still had no context for the cryptic remark. We'd already lost battles—was that the key? Losing the right battles?

I rubbed the bridge of my nose against the headache forming behind my eyes and looked around for the woman's augury. I hoped it was a book called *Stop Being Stupid*. Probably there wasn't any such book, but I could hope.

It was actually a book titled *Driven to Distraction*, which was almost as good. I certainly felt the factional nonsense had driven *me* to distraction. I handed her the book with a narrow-eyed stare. "$650. Judy will take payment."

The woman had the decency to look embarrassed. I accepted the next augury slip and walked away.

When I returned, there were more Ambrosites, and all of them were whispering as if they were in church. The whispering increased when I appeared. With luck, that meant all of the ones who'd been present for my angry speech were telling the others about it.

After the fourth augury, I came back to find Viv and Wallach waiting near the counter. "Hi!" I said, feeling much more cheerful. "I'm afraid you'll have to wait your turn."

"We're in no hurry," Wallach said. He looked awfully relaxed, as did Viv. She wasn't bouncing the way she had yesterday, though she still looked as chipper as always.

She still looked chipper when I finally reached their augury, despite how bored she must be at waiting. I unfolded the paper. *Where can we find the right joints?* "Interesting," I said.

"It's starting to come together," Wallach said. "Faster than I expected, actually."

I nodded and went into the oracle. The bright blue light of an augury glowed very nearby, bright enough that it made the rest of the room look dim. I edged through the narrow aisles until I came to the shelf where the augury lay.

Except it was two auguries. A year ago, that would have sent me into a panic. Now I knew it was just the oracle being helpful. I took the first, a fat, oversized hardcover titled…I blushed. *The Complete Illustrated Kama Sutra.* I hoped Wallach was as hard to embarrass as Viv. I opened the cover to see *Darius Wallach, $2250* written inside in silver ink. I closed the book and tucked it securely under my arm. There wasn't anything salacious on the cover, but I still felt its contents would be visible to everyone in the store.

Then I reached for the second augury, which was on a higher shelf and required me to stretch. Most likely, this meant Lucia was on her way. The oracle seemed to anticipate her requests more than most people.

The book was a slim paperback with a colorful cover depicting a transforming teen. Animorphs. The title was *The Warning*. "I guess you never know," I said, flipping the book open.

Inside, the silver ink spelled out the words *Helena Davies, No Charge.*

I riffled through the pages as if more information might leap out at me. "A warning," I said. "Why do I need a warning? I'm already prepared for the worst."

The oracle didn't respond. "And maybe it's not that. Maybe it means something else." It reminded me that I had yet to interpret the *Old Tin Sorrows* augury, though I'd finished reading the book last night. It had been intense, and disturbing, and I hadn't been able to stop thinking about it. Now I had two auguries to deal with, and no guarantee that they were related. "All right. Thanks."

I handed the big book to Wallach, whose eyebrows went up. Viv giggled. "I don't see what this has to do with our question," she said.

"I do," Wallach said, but he didn't elaborate. He paid for the book, and he and Viv left without any more conversation. I felt a little forlorn. Usually Viv chatted with me when she came into the store…but now she had a job, and chatting probably wasn't allowed.

It took until almost five o'clock for the last Ambrosites to clear out, by which time I felt frazzled and headachy and a little embarrassed at my outburst. But when I mentioned that last to Judy, she said, "They deserved it, and you know it. I wish I'd recorded it so I could play it for everyone who comes to the store. And put it on permanent loop for my father. You'd think he would see the importance of not building tension, but no. Maybe this thing with the familiars will change his mind."

"Maybe." I picked up my Animorphs book and flipped through it. "Did you ever read these?"

"Nope. Why? I thought they looked dumb, honestly."

"They're not dumb. I read a few when I was young and liked them okay. I just don't remember any details that might help interpret this augury. Except the kids are fighting alien invaders that can take over human hosts, so there's that similarity."

"Well, it's short," Judy said. "It shouldn't take you long to go through it."

"I hope not." I set it aside and stretched, making my spine crackle with a series of tiny pops. "I have another therapy session tonight."

"What's your therapist like?"

I yawned and covered it with my hand. "She's very matter-of-fact. Doesn't try to comfort me when something upsets me, which is nice. I like her in a distant way—like, we're never going to be buddies, and that's okay."

"Interesting." Judy headed past me toward the break room. "I'm going to sweep, and then if you don't mind I want to leave early. I need a shower before tonight. Party at Father's house, and they'll almost certainly be talking about the familiars crisis."

"Sounds fun. I'm glad I'm not you."

"Yeah, you just have to face your personal demons," Judy said.

THE CORRIDOR to Green 1 felt shorter this time, possibly because I knew what to expect at the end of it. Also, at that time of evening, the node was at its busiest, and a lot of people nodded or waved to me as I passed. It was all so friendly I almost forgot why I was there. My grip on my notebook, though, kept me from becoming complacent. I was nervous about showing my list to Sydney. She'd said it would be revelatory, and that was true, but what if she'd meant revelatory to her? I couldn't imagine what a trained psychologist, or whatever a LCSW was, might make of my recitation of traumas. It felt like she'd asked me to strip naked so she could criticize my posture.

The Wardens at the central desk were, again, unfamiliar to me. It made me wonder how many bone magi Lucia employed that I knew so few of them. "Ms. Campbell," the woman hailed me. She was tiny and looked younger than me, but her smile was confident. "You can wait right over there, and Sydney will be with you shortly."

"Thanks." I took a seat in the indicated direction and positioned my notebook on my lap.

Almost immediately, the nearest door opened, and Sydney emerged. She was wearing another shapeless, flowing dress, this one turquoise blue. My favorite color. "Hi, Helena. Come this way, please."

The hall and the office hadn't changed except for there being a dark blotch on the wall farther down the hallway where a bulb had burned out. Sydney saw me looking at it and said, "It takes Maintenance time to get to all the little things. Personally, I think they should give us a box of lightbulbs so we can handle it ourselves, but that would make too much sense."

I sat in the chair I'd used last time and again set my notebook on my lap. Sydney seated herself opposite me and said, "Well. How have you been?"

"Okay, I guess. You heard about the familiars? And the Bridgerton Node?"

"I did. I admit I'm more frightened by the deaths of the familiars than by the attack. If the invaders can reach that far, who knows what else they might be capable of?"

I shook my head. "I bet they took advantage of some link they have to all invaders, even the bound familiars. If they could do that to humans, they would have already."

"I hope you're right." Sydney held out a hand. "Is that your list?"

I opened the notebook to the right page and handed it over. Sydney took it and read down the page, slowly enough that I became nervous again. If she thought I was unhinged… or if I *wasn't* unhinged, but should be…

"This is thorough," Sydney finally said. "I admit I'm surprised at how much you've been through. How did you feel, writing all this out?"

I considered that. "At times, I felt relieved, like I'd lost a burden I'd carried for so long it felt like part of me. Other times, though, it felt like living through it again. Like—" I swallowed. "When the Mercy were actually in the store, and Mr. Santiago held a knife to my throat to get me to do what he wanted…I don't think I'll ever forget how that felt."

"Understandable." Sydney interlaced her fingers and rested them on her knee. "Does that memory bother you often?"

"Sometimes. It's always unexpected, though. I'll be doing something completely unrelated—I won't even be in the store—and that memory springs up and I have to stop what I'm doing and calm myself."

"I see. It's that realistic a memory?"

"Very." I realized my breathing was ragged and took a deep breath to slow it down.

Sydney looked at me as if she knew what I was doing, though I was sure I hadn't been obvious. "Sometimes, when our memories of something traumatic are powerful," she said, "it's because our minds are trying to make those events turn out differently. As if dealing with them differently now will alter the original event."

I thought about this. It was certainly true that all my most terrible memories, the ones I had trouble shaking, were of things I wished had happened differently. "That makes sense," I said. "But I know I can't change the past, so why does it happen?"

"Your head knows you can't change the past, but your heart doesn't." Sydney leaned forward as if to give her words greater emphasis. "And you'll go on doing it until you've accepted those events as part of who you are now. Particularly the ones that have changed you in ways you don't like."

The eye of memory immediately threw up an image of Santiago the way he'd looked just after I shot him, that horrible look of pain and bewilderment, and I closed my eyes against it. "How do I do that?" I said.

"We'll start by working on those distressing thoughts," Sydney said. "Do you know what mindfulness is?"

"I've heard people talk about it, but I don't know more than that."

"Mindfulness is about living in the moment. Being fully

present and aware of where we are and what we're doing, and not being overwhelmed by what's going on around us or our distracting thoughts. Everything you've endured is in the past, but you've been reliving it as if it were the present. You know that's not true. Practicing mindfulness will help anchor you in the actual present, and allow you to eventually leave those memories where they belong—in your past."

"That sounds difficult." Actually, it sounded kind of New-Agey, not something I could ever see myself doing, but I'd committed to this, and I could give it a try.

"It takes practice. I'll teach you some meditation techniques, but the rest is up to you." Sydney sat back in her chair. "The other thing I'd like you to do is more difficult. I want you to choose three events from this list you feel are most disturbing. Maybe the ones you remember most often, or the ones that hurt the most—you decide how you want to go about it. Then for each of those events, I want you to write a detailed description of what happened and how you felt at the time. You should be as open as you can—I won't read these."

I once more remembered Santiago and said, "I don't know if I can do that."

"Why not?"

"Isn't it the opposite of what I want? I'm trying not to remember so vividly."

Sydney smiled. "The point of this exercise is for you to confront and embrace your memories in a safe way. Writing about, for example, being held at gunpoint might bring up painful memories, but you're not actually in danger. There's no one there with a gun to your head. And writing about the feelings you had at the time helps you acknowledge that it's okay to feel fear or other emotions when something bad happens."

"Other emotions? Like what?"

Sydney's smile broadened. "I'd rather not put ideas into your head. Do the exercise, and you'll discover what emotions you had."

I glanced at the colorful photos on the wall. "All right."

Sydney stood and opened a drawer in the desk. She withdrew a sheet of paper and handed it to me. "This is for you to read when you get home. It's an overview of the mindfulness techniques we'll discuss today. Remember, this takes practice, and part of meditation is not being critical of yourself when your thoughts wander. Now, close your eyes and feel the air on your skin…"

An hour later, I was on my way home with a lot of new things to think about. Despite my resolve, I'd felt really stupid meditating. My mind wandered frequently, caught up in thoughts of the auguries I had to interpret and what tomorrow might bring at work and a dozen other pressing problems. I hadn't done any physical labor, but I felt exhausted from jerking my mind back to the present so often. And I dreaded the other part of the assignment: recording the events that had hurt me most. I didn't want to think about them, and I didn't see how writing about them would help.

"It just seems so…I don't know. Pointless?" I told Malcolm as we got ready for bed.

"I'm sure it's not pointless," Malcolm said. "Your therapist wouldn't waste either of your time on something pointless."

"Okay, wrong word. I guess it's that I don't know what the point is. I can't look at any of what Sydney wants me to do and identify how specifically it will help me. So I feel like I'm flailing around and looking like a fool."

Malcolm went into the bathroom and picked up his toothbrush. "Maybe you should ask her that question."

"Maybe I should." I got my own toothbrush and went to work. Knowing how all these things helped would make a difference in how I approached them. I'd be more enthusiastic, for one.

I spat, rinsed, and put my toothbrush away, then walked to my side of the bed. The notebook lay on my bedside table, taunting me. I sighed and put it away in the drawer. I'd face my demons some other time.

I climbed into bed and snuggled up to Malcolm, who put his arms around me. "This is the kind of therapy I prefer," I said. "When I'm with you, my memories don't trouble me."

"It's an impractical kind of therapy, unfortunately," Malcolm murmured. "Given that I can't follow you around all day."

"I know. This is enough." I smiled into the darkness as another memory, a good one, emerged from the back of my mind. "I was thinking the other day of how we met. I would never have guessed, from that day, that we would someday end up here."

Malcolm chuckled. "I remember. I thought you were cute, but hopelessly out of your depth. Honestly, I didn't think you'd last a week, let alone three years."

"I almost didn't. And I was out of my depth. But I survived."

"You did." He held me closer. "And the better I knew you, the more I was attracted to you. Your courage, your perseverance, your sense of humor…and then there was a day when I realized I couldn't imagine my life without you."

"I felt the same. Oh, Malcolm, I love you."

"And I love you." He kissed me, though it was a kiss that only fell partly on my mouth in the darkness. I shifted and kissed him back, enjoying the feel of his lips against mine. Then I snuggled in closer and let myself drift off into sleep.

"JUDY," I said the next morning, "do you think it's possible to receive an augury for another person?"

"Sure. That's what *aug. fam.* is."

I shook my head. "I don't mean ask for an augury on another person's behalf. I mean get an augury for yourself that's really meant for someone else."

Judy paused in her typing. "I'm not sure I follow."

I tapped the Animorphs book on the desk's edge. "I studied this all morning before I came to work, and I really feel like the warning isn't directed at me. More like I'm supposed to warn someone else."

"A specific someone else?"

"Yes. I think it's meant for Mr. Wallach."

Judy held out her hand for the augury and flipped through the pages as if she could read its meaning as easily as skimming it. "Warning against what?"

"Well, there's really only one thing he's working on, right? Shifting our reality." I accepted the book back from her and dropped it into my capacious purse. "But I don't get it. It's such a good idea, why would the oracle warn him against pursuing it?"

"It could be the way he's pursuing it is wrong. Or he's on the wrong track."

"But he's received auguries about it. If the oracle thought he was on the wrong track or something, it wouldn't give him responses. Not depend on someone else to deliver a warning."

Judy went back to typing. "Well, if he comes in today, you can ask him."

I shrugged and left the office.

There weren't many mail-in auguries that day, but all of them had to do with the current disaster. Most of them asked for predictions about where the invaders would strike next. All of those resulted in the NO AUGURY response. That worried me because it could mean so many things, none of them good. I particularly worried about the possibility that the oracle wouldn't give an answer because it couldn't—that the invaders' tactics were so different it couldn't predict their movements. I reminded myself that the oracle had told me about the attack on the Bridgerton Node and then remembered it had only done so at the moment of the attack. That was no comfort.

I stood surrounded by red-tinged light, clutching the latest failed augury. "I hope I'm wrong," I said. "Maybe it's just that these have to be mailed to their recipients, and the invaders strike so quickly, they'll have attacked before these people ever get their responses. So it would be a waste of their time and money. It doesn't have to be that you don't know."

The oracle's attention never shifted. I closed my eyes and drew in a calming breath. Why not? Now was as good a time as any to practice Sydney's meditation techniques. And I could certainly use inner peace.

I drew in another deep breath, focusing on how it filled my lungs, how it streamed out of my nostrils. I pictured it colored like the light, red air being changed to blue inside me so it made a long indigo streamer that swirled away into the distance. It was a fun image…and I was getting distracted already. I drew in another breath and focused on the air brushing my forearms and my face. There were no fans in the store, and the air was generally still, but within the oracle, breezes occasionally moved. The air was warm and strawberry-scented, and if I relaxed enough, I could feel it stirring the fine hairs on my arms.

I let myself feel that for a while, then shifted my attention to my sense of the oracle. It still wasn't paying me any attention—no, that was wrong, I could feel its notice like a tingling tickle across my skin that wasn't dispelled by the warm breaths of air. I embraced the feeling and focused on it until that sensation filled my whole world. It was like sinking into a beanbag, if beanbags were filled with shaving cream instead of pellets. The deeper I sank into meditation, the more aware I became of the oracle's presence and the more I distanced myself from my awareness of my own body.

The oracle drew nearer, observing me like a cat approaches a new ball of string. I felt an unexpected warmth creep over me, not so hot as to be painful, but comfortable like the sun on a clear spring day. My excitement rose as the oracle focused all its attention on me. I felt closer to it than ever before, close enough to understand its thoughts—

My concentration snapped. Suddenly the warmth was gone, and the oracle had withdrawn to somewhere nearby, its attention once more elsewhere. I scowled and opened my eyes. That had nearly been something interesting.

I went back to the counter and scrawled NO AUGURY on the paper. If only the oracle would explain—but it never did. I hoped its lack of response meant something positive, like that there was nothing to worry about. Or that whatever happened, it believed I was strong enough to deal with it without its direct guidance.

13

V iv and Wallach showed up around 4:30, just as the Ambrosite rush had trickled to nothing. Viv greeted me cheerily, but I knew her well enough to recognize when she was feeling a little down. "Anything wrong?" I said.

"No, of course not," Viv replied. She smiled broadly and said, "This is the most interesting job I've ever had, and I include those two weeks I was a pearl diver."

Wallach, on the other hand, didn't conceal his scowl. "Let's hope this augury is more successful," he said, handing me a torn piece of paper.

"Wasn't the last one? I thought you said you could see how it related to your work." The augury request read *How should the anchors be connected?*

Wallach scowled more deeply. "Never mind," he said. "Let's move this along. I still have work to do."

Stung and a little confused by his irritability, I made my escape into the oracle. I was used to Wallach's occasional grumpiness, but that had always been directed at a recalcitrant problem, not at a person, and now he seemed upset with me as well as with the oracle. The light was blue-tinged, not red, so at least I'd be able to present him with something to focus his irritation on.

I rounded a corner and found the augury, another slim paperback—no, another Animorphs book. *The Threat.* "Weird," I said. When I opened the cover, I got another surprise: this one was for me again. "This is really strange," I said. "What do you have in mind, I wonder?"

Instantly, the oracle's presence bore down on me, painfully sharp instead of the usual slow pressure. I cried out and tried to wrench away from it, but the pain followed me. "Stop!" I shouted. "What do you want? Why can't you just speak?"

The pain lessened from a spike jabbing my shoulder to a pinprick. **Warn,** I thought. **Danger.**

"You could have just said that. Warn Mr. Wallach? What danger?"

Warn. Danger. The anchor vanishes. The oracle's presence disappeared.

I rubbed my shoulder and rotated it to ease the lingering pain. That had been slightly less cryptic, but if it could tell me what warning to give, why had it also given me an augury? Unless the augury wasn't like the previous one, and was actually for me. I'd have to study it and find out.

I headed for the exit and then remembered I hadn't received an augury for Wallach. There must be one, or the light wouldn't have been blue. Sighing, I set off in search of another tiny blue star.

When I found it, it wasn't so tiny. It was another fat hardcover book you could bring down a pigeon with. The title was in huge red letters across the cover: *Extraordinary Popular Delusions and the Madness of Crowds*. I set the Animorphs book on top of it and returned to the store's front.

"Here you are," I said to Wallach, handing him the big book. "$3500. I hope you don't have to read the whole thing. That's a long one."

"Ms. Haley interprets the auguries," Wallach said. He handed the book to Viv, who pretended to groan under its weight and then offered Judy several tubes of *sanguinis sapiens*.

"There's one other thing, Mr. Wallach," I said. "I received an augury yesterday about your work. It was a warning."

Wallach's eyes widened. "A warning? About what?"

"I'm not sure. I think it's about your new project. Something about how it's too good to be true? And the oracle spoke to me now and repeated the warning. It said, 'the anchor vanishes.' Does that mean anything to you?"

The old scientist's face cleared. "I already know about that. I don't see why the oracle wants to give me a warning about dangers I'm already aware of."

"I don't know, either," I said, feeling a little defensive of the oracle, as if he'd called its competence into question. "But I don't think you should dismiss the warning."

"Of course not," Wallach said with a smile too paternalistic to be anything but insulting.

I suppressed an angry retort and said, "Good luck with your augury."

Viv looked like she wanted to say something, but just hefted the enormous book and followed Wallach out the door.

"Did that seem weird to you?" I asked Judy, who'd silently taken payment from Viv and now lined up the tubes of raw magic on the counter.

"No weirder than anything Mr. Wallach does," Judy said.

"I mean that he was so dismissive of the oracle's warning. Most people, if they hear the oracle's spoken to me, get all flustered."

"He's not most people." Judy swept up the vials in both hands and headed for the basement. I flipped through the Animorphs book and wished I remembered the series better. Fighting alien invaders in secret, using magical powers—all right, technology, but it might as well have been magic. The back cover copy mentioned a new Animorph who started out as a help, but became dangerous when he began breaking rules. If it applied to Wallach's new project, this combined with the first book suggested strongly that whatever Wallach was inventing to shift our reality would have unexpected, negative effects.

I sighed and carried the book to the office, deposited it in my purse, and rubbed my eyes with the heels of my hands. It seemed the oracle, rather than warning Wallach directly, had decided to put the burden on my shoulders. Since Wallach was experimenting with something world-changing, if I failed to get him to take me seriously, those negative effects could include widespread destruction and maybe death. Like I needed that kind of responsibility. I could barely manage myself and my personal demons.

I heard footsteps on the basement stairs, running ones, and emerged from the office to see Judy slam the basement door shut and run toward me. "Another attack," she panted. "Someplace in Louisiana I can't pronounce." She displayed her phone, whose screen was filled with a long text from her father.

I squinted. "Natchitoches," I read. "I'm probably saying it wrong, too. What happened?"

"Father says the Wardens were there in time to save most of the population. Only a couple hundred deaths. But that's a problem."

"Yeah, any number of deaths is a problem."

Judy shook her head. "The problem," she said, "is every time the Wardens stop the invaders after they've begun their attack—whenever the city is identified publicly as a victim of the 'biowarfare'—we run the risk of having someone wonder what, or who, is keeping the disaster from becoming greater. Right now—" Her phone chimed with an incoming text, and she held up a finger for me to wait while she read. "The news outlets are reporting it as an attack gone wrong, like the terrorists failed to properly deploy their weapon. Their words. But if this continues, somebody's going to start asking inconvenient questions."

"How could they possibly figure out the truth? Failed 'attacks' might be suspicious, but there's not enough evidence to reveal what's really going on."

"I don't know," Judy said grimly. "But Father's concerned, and he's the most cautious thinker I know. If he thinks there's a problem, we should be worried."

I leaned against the door frame. "I'm worried that the oracle didn't warn me like it did for the Bridgerton Node attack. It was too busy warning me about Mr. Wallach's augury. The oracle's priorities aren't the same as ours, but if it's more concerned about what Mr. Wallach might do than about a city being destroyed—"

"Crazy Wallach might be in over his head, you mean?" Judy sighed. "I don't see what we can do about either of those things, except keep doing our jobs."

"I just wish it didn't feel so much like this is the end of days," I said.

I SAT in my bed with the notebook on my knees, laid down my pen, and flipped back through my pages of notes. The *Old Tin Sorrows* augury had me stumped. Three crimes, many suspects, a powerful motive…there was an obvious interpretation, but it was so obvious I was reluctant to go there.

I turned back to the end, where I'd stopped halfway down the page. *Not a bull in a china shop*, I wrote. The main character admitted his method for solving crime was to go stomping around until the bad guys got nervous and made mistakes, but I was certain the bad guys in my own situation were invaders, and they weren't likely to respond to that method. And this augury had been in response to the first attack and the destruction of the Fountain, and I knew who'd done that. It was why that was eluding me. And how, to a lesser extent.

I sighed. I'd eliminated every possibility I could think of but the first, most obvious one. I turned to a fresh sheet and, at the top, wrote: *Invaders are eliminating Neutralities one by one until only one is left.*

It was at the heart of the book. The old man had written a will that divided his fortune among his surviving family and staff, and one of them had been killing off potential heirs—though that person's motive had turned out to be not what I'd expected. It fit really well. The invaders destroyed powerful Neutralities, winnowing them, but why? Again, the invaders had a motive I couldn't fathom. And why the ones they'd chosen?

Not all are equally powerful, I wrote. The Cracchiolo Node in particular was an average-size node, smaller than the Gunther Node and out in the middle of nowhere. If there was a pattern to their attacks, I couldn't see it. *Need to ask Lucia about the pattern.*

What about cracks? The oracle had said sealing cracks was important, and I had a feeling that was related to the business with the Neutralities being destroyed. If it wasn't about Wallach's project, maybe cracks referred to the damage to the wards, warping them, and if we sealed the cracks, we could protect the Neutralities? Something else to suggest to Lucia, since I didn't have the power to do anything like that.

So the Neutralities were being destroyed. It reminded me of something else the oracle had said, something about holes being plugged until there was only one. That made me wonder if the Wardens should be doing anything about the destroyed Neutralities. Those might be considered "holes." *Holes,* I wrote, then chewed the end of my pen. What else might this augury mean? Drawing each letter with deliberate slowness, I wrote *The villain is the least obvious suspect.* I didn't know what that meant, because we knew who the villains were, but it felt right.

I turned that page over and hesitated at the top of the next blank page. I'd been studying the augury so I wouldn't have to face this, and that had been a good excuse for a while, but now I was just being cowardly. I squeezed my eyes tight shut for a minute, then blinked at the page and clicked the pen open and shut a few times. *Mitch Hallstrom belonged to the Mercy, though we didn't learn that until later,* I wrote. *Judy and I believed he was the killer who'd been draining magi of their magic...*

I wrote until my hand was sore. Details I'd forgotten, like the smell of arborvitae and the greasy feel of concrete under my face, swarmed down my pen onto the paper. I remembered how it had felt when Hallstrom splayed his palm against the bare skin of my stomach and had to set my pen down and swallow hard to keep from throwing up. Then I wrote *Malcolm shot me* and stopped, reading those three words over and over again. *It was the only way*, I wrote, and stopped again. I swore loudly and crossed out those words so violently my pen tore the paper. *He shot me*, I wrote, ignoring the splotches where my tears struck the paper. *I loved him, and I thought he loved me, and he looked at me as if I was a bug and sent that twisted piece of metal through my shoulder. And it doesn't matter that I understand why he did it, it doesn't make me forget that look on his face. But because it hurt him—*I crossed that sentence fragment out too. *I can't let it affect me because it would hurt him so much, all over again, because it wasn't true, he* did *love me, and—*

I tossed the pen aside and wiped my eyes. I'd told him I'd forgiven him, and I'd meant it, but I'd been strong for all the wrong reasons.

I went in search of Malcolm and found him in the office, answering email. "Are you busy?"

He shook his head, but his eyes were still on the monitor. "I'm…not now," he finally said, clicking Send. "Is everything all right?"

"I was writing about Mitch Hallstrom," I said, "and how you shot me."

His face went very still. He said nothing.

"I didn't want to make you feel bad, because I knew you felt so guilty at hurting me," I went on, "but that means—I didn't—" Tears streamed down my face. "You looked as if you didn't care about me at all. Like I was just another obstruction. I could understand everything else, but not that. And believing you didn't care for me…that hurt so much more than being shot."

Malcolm stood and gathered me into his arms, holding me

as I cried. "I was so afraid for you," he murmured. "I thought if Hallstrom knew you meant more to me than just an innocent bystander, he'd never let you go. Or that he'd hurt you to make me suffer. If I hadn't looked indifferent…Helena, he held your life in his hands. I am so, so sorry you suffered, and if I could have any moment to live over again, make different choices, it would be that one."

I sniffled. "I don't see how you could change it. I'd still have been in his power."

"I got lost on the way to his house. If I'd gotten there five minutes earlier, I would have arrived before you were captured, and you wouldn't have been involved." He stroked my hair. "I don't usually play the game of 'what-if', because trying to second-guess yourself is a fool's errand. But in this case, it's hard not to imagine."

"I didn't know." I wiped my eyes and looked up at him. "You know I really, truly don't blame you."

"It doesn't sound like that's what this was about." Malcolm cradled my face in his hand, stroking my cheekbone with one thumb. "That night, you looked at me—I don't know what you were thinking, but you looked at me with such hope it broke my heart, because I knew the only ending to that standoff would leave you bloody on the ground and hating me forever. I know I can't change your memories, but I want you to know—no matter how I looked that night, I loved you, and I hope you believe I always will."

I leaned into his touch. "I shouldn't need that reassurance, but I do."

"I don't think 'should' matters," Malcolm said, and leaned in to kiss me. His lips on mine were so tender, so much the way they'd felt the first time we'd kissed, that more memories rose up, all of them wonderful. I put my arms around his neck and kissed him back, feeling peace unfold like a flower in my heart.

"I don't know if that's what Sydney had in mind with that assignment, but it worked," I said a few minutes later.

"I'm in favor of anything that makes you kiss me like it's the first time," Malcolm murmured.

"That's how it was for me, too. Except the first time, I thought you were saying goodbye, so my heart was broken."

"I told myself it was goodbye, but I couldn't stop thinking about it." Malcolm brushed my hair back from my face. "And now we're here."

"Now we're here," I agreed. "Come to bed. I want to hold you and let that memory fade."

"You have excellent ideas," Malcolm said, and we went upstairs together.

I HANDED WALLACH THE PAPERBACK. Its eerie cover featured a bearded man in a top hat with his hands outstretched as if welcoming something. Lightning forked in the background, and two smaller figures in the center raced toward an old-fashioned carnival. Wallach read the title aloud. "*Something Wicked This Way Comes.* Is this a joke, Mrs. Campbell?"

I'd slept poorly last night despite Malcolm holding me, and I wasn't in a mood to be polite. "The oracle chooses the auguries, Mr. Wallach, not me. I'm sorry if it's not what you expected, but I have work to do."

Wallach didn't budge. "You've been unrelenting in your negative comments and your claims that the oracle has spoken to you. Is there some reason you want this project to fail?"

"Fail? Why would I want that? You said this would stop the

invaders permanently. I have a husband who puts his life on the line on a regular basis to fight invaders. Why wouldn't I want you to succeed?"

"And yet you claim to receive auguries about my work, as if you were qualified to pass judgment?" He jabbed a finger at the other book I'd brought out of the oracle, the one with my name on the title page in silver ink. This one wasn't an Animorphs book; it was titled *Cassandra: Princess of Troy*. Even I could understand the symbolism there: Cassandra had been cursed to prophesy the truth and never be believed.

His animosity was winding my nerves to the breaking point. I said, "Look. I don't just take books off the shelf and pretend they're from the oracle. I think it's enlisted me because you're not paying attention to the auguries it gives you."

"The oracle doesn't know any more about this project than you do." He cast a glance at *Something Wicked This Way Comes*. "If it's not going to be helpful, it can stop providing answers. I don't need its assistance to understand the principles behind my theory."

His attitude made me feel defensive of the oracle. "Is that what your auguries are telling you? Are they warning you, too?"

Viv opened her mouth to reply, but Wallach overrode her. "It's none of your business what my auguries say."

"Well, it's not just auguries. What about when it spoke to me directly about anchors vanishing?"

Wallach's jaw tightened again. "It's something I've accounted for already. Everything's proceeding the way I expect. Unless the oracle can tell me something concrete, I can't use its nebulous 'warnings.'" His voice put sarcastic air quotes around the last word.

Viv looked worried, her attention darting back and forth

between Wallach and me like she was watching Mom and Dad fight. "Maybe we should listen to what Helena says," she said. "If the oracle spoke to her, isn't that important?"

"This project will change the future of every human being on this planet," Wallach said. "You know it's dangerous, Ms. Haley, I've explained that to you. The results are worth the danger."

"But—" Viv hesitated, then shut her mouth.

"Look, Mr. Wallach," I said, "I've relayed the oracle's warning. You've had your own auguries. It's up to you what you do with them. But I've never known anything good to come of ignoring what the oracle prophesies."

"And you and I both know the oracle's auguries can be invalidated under the right conditions," Wallach said. "I know what I'm doing and I don't need any more warnings, particularly ones about dangers I'm already aware of." He slapped his augury down on the counter. "Ms. Haley, let's go."

"But what about—" Viv said, gesturing to *Something Wicked This Way Comes.*

"We don't need it." He slammed through the crystal door, sending rainbows scattering over its surface. Viv followed him with one last backward glance at me.

I closed my eyes and bit back several profanities. Then I looked at my next customer. "Okay, Brandon, let's keep moving, okay?"

Brandon gave me a skeptical look. "Did you say the oracle spoke to you?"

"It does sometimes. It would be more exciting if I understood half of what it said." I took his augury slip and stepped into the oracle.

The oracle's attention pressed down on me as if it had been waiting for me to come back. **Warning,** it said.

"I'm not the one you need to tell that to," I replied. "Though it doesn't look like he's listening to either of us. If you could give me something more specific, maybe that would help."

Warning. Something comes. Dreams come true.

"That doesn't seem like something bad. Though if you mean literal dreams, I've had some real nightmares I wouldn't ever want to come true." I'd never thought of the saying in those terms before.

Dreams come true. Pay the price. Warning.

I thought about that one. "You pay the price for a dream to come true. Maybe a dream in the good sense, something you really want. You get your dream, but at a price…so what if the price is too high? Or—like that story I read in English class, where the husband and wife buy each other the perfect gifts by sacrificing their treasured possessions, and then they can't use the gifts because of the sacrifices?"

Price. Warning. Something comes. I will end. Helena will end.

I let out a hiss of frustration. "Why don't you—wait." Either it had switched warnings mid-stream, or… "Is Mr. Wallach's plan related to our ending? Will it cause us to end?"

The oracle said nothing, but its presence still bore down on me. **I will end,** it finally said. **Helena will end.** It left me as swiftly as it had appeared.

I leaned my forehead against the nearest bookcase and drew in a calming breath, though I was too agitated for meditation. The oracle didn't have emotions, at least none I could perceive, so the frustration I felt was all mine. But I couldn't help wondering whether it was as impatient with my lack of understanding as I was with its cryptic, incomprehensible warnings.

I straightened and set off in search of Brandon's augury. That, at least, was simple and straightforward. Either there was an augury or there wasn't, and Brandon's question, *How should I invest my gambling winnings?* was not one the oracle was likely to want me to weigh in on.

14

L aserPinz wasn't the best bowling alley in the Portland area, but it did have one feature Judy, Viv, and I loved, and that was Lanes After Dark. Thursdays after eight o'clock, they turned the overhead lights way down and turned on black lights and the neon light strips outlining each lane, revealing that the rather bland bowling balls and pins glowed in the dark. So did the stripes on the rented shoes, the wall decorations of colorful zigzags, and the cream toppings on their famous chocolate pudding cups. Viv liked to say it was all very Eighties, but I thought no one decade could possibly have produced anything this simultaneously tasteless and awesome.

I lined up between the glowing green lines of our lane, hefted my neon pink bowling ball, and took a few quick steps to send it spinning toward the pins. A perfect strike. I pumped my fist in the air and trotted back to our table. "That's another one for me."

"I'm only letting you gloat because we're playing laser tag after this," Viv said, "and you suck at that."

"Bowling is the only sport I'm any good at," I admitted, admiring my score.

Judy licked a dollop of radiantly white cream off her spoon. "I can't believe you talked me into coming here."

"You say that every time, and then you change your tune when the laser gun is in your hand," Viv said. She hopped up and retrieved her ball, which glowed blue like it was radioactive. "I'm not sure it's healthy for you to enjoy shooting people that much."

"It's therapeutic. It keeps me from lashing out at idiots." Judy took another bite of pudding. "I don't know what they put in this stuff, but it's addictive."

I ate some of my own pudding cup. "How do they make the topping glow, I wonder?"

"Tonic water glows under a black light," Viv said over her shoulder. She let go her ball and watched it drift into the gutter. "I don't know why I bother."

"You're getting better," I protested.

"Not so anyone can tell." Viv hovered over the ball return. "We need to join a softball league so I can be successfully athletic."

"No way," Judy and I said in unison.

"I played Pee Wee softball for one season when I was seven," Judy said. "I got hit by the ball ten times. Two times, I wasn't even on the field. I swore off softball forever."

"That's quitter talk," Viv said. She released the ball and leaned hard to the left as if that would keep the ball on track. Three pins fell. "Are you sure we can't play with those bumper pads blocking the gutters?"

"You'll never learn not to throw gutter balls if the pads are in the way," I said. "My dad never let us use them, even when we were little."

"Your dad is a monster," Viv grumped. She returned to her seat and took a long swig of Diet Coke as Judy got up to take her turn. "But you seem to be in a better mood. I was starting to worry about you."

"I'm trying to avoid thinking of all the horrifying things in my life. Bowling has a very soothing, focusing effect on me." I scraped pudding off the sides of the clear plastic cup and licked it off my spoon. "And it helps that there were no new attacks today anywhere in the world."

"There's nothing we can do about them if there were," Judy said, lifting her ball to chin height before taking a couple of swift steps and releasing it. "Except what we're already doing."

"Yes, how is Mr. Wallach's project coming along?" I asked.

Viv shrugged. "It's at a stage where I don't understand most of what he's doing. The initial work was all about finding a shape for the magic that will shift our reality. It's like a frame-work…we bought about a hundred Tinker Toy sets off eBay to model it."

"So it has a physical shape."

"Sort of. The model does, but that's just to show the magic what it needs to look like. The actual solution is only partly physical, like an aegis." Viv took another drink. "But that's bone magus territory, and a lot of what Mr. Wallach does, I can't even see."

Judy dropped into a chair next to us. "You don't sound enthusiastic."

Viv tossed her cup at the nearest trash can. It bounced off, and she stood and, grumbling, retrieved it and threw it away. "I'm worried," she confessed. "None of the auguries gave any positive advice—positive in the sense of helping us move forward. They were all a lot of warnings about things. Which is good, because they helped us avoid some major missteps, but…wouldn't you think the oracle would want to see this happen?"

"The oracle doesn't see things the way we do," I said. "I can never guess what it will do. What worries *me* is that it saw fit to give me auguries to back up the ones it gave Mr. Wallach. I think something is wrong with his plan."

"Me too. But I have no idea what." Viv sighed. "It all looks perfect. The modeling came together just right, all Mr. Wallach's theories are proving correct—it's almost too good to be true."

"Which is one of the things the oracle warned me about," I said. "Getting a dream at a price that's too high."

"But if Crazy Wallach's plan was detrimental to the Long War, the oracle wouldn't give any auguries about it," Judy said. "Which suggests there's some other problem."

"I don't suppose you still have that last augury?" Viv said. "The scary one?"

"I do," I said, "but I can't sell it to you because it's in Mr. Wallach's name. I held onto it in case he changed his mind. You'll have to convince him."

"That's unlikely. I think he's mad that the oracle hasn't been more helpful. Helpful according to his wishes, I mean."

Judy glanced at the monitor. "Helena wins. As usual. Do we want another game?"

"I'm tired of losing. I want to shoot things," Viv said.

I pushed back my chair. "Sounds good to me."

We returned our balls and shoes and headed for the laser tag arena. In the dimness, the people around us were shadows blotched with glowing white, mostly T-shirts and tennis shoes. My own shoes, which I'd worn instead of sandals because I knew Viv would insist on laser tag, had white stripes on both sides that made me look like I was wearing those wooden Japanese sandals with blocky soles.

I threw away my empty drink cup outside the door to laser tag and followed Viv through into an even darker space. It was warm and close in the antechamber, like being wrapped in a heavy, slightly damp blanket, and I found it comfortable even though bowling had warmed me up. The room smelled of sweat and ozone and, very faintly, someone's cologne, a musky odor that wasn't entirely pleasant. To me, it was the smell of imminent defeat. I was as bad at laser tag as I was good at bowling.

I accepted my sensor harness and laser pistol, listened to the safety lecture reeled off by a bored youth, and waited for the signal that we could enter the arena. Beside me, Viv examined her gun like it was a real weapon, and Judy stood balanced on the balls of her feet, looking like a coiled snake ready to strike.

The bell rang, and Judy darted forward and disappeared around a corner. Viv and I followed with less alacrity. Almost immediately, my vest buzzed with someone's successful hit. I groaned and flung up my arms. "I didn't even have a chance to hide!"

"You're not supposed to hide, you're supposed to shoot the enemy," Viv said. She turned and ran, shooting into the darkness, and I heard another buzz, presumably from her victim. I groaned again, this time silently, and set off to locate the enemy.

After about five minutes, it was Enemy 4, Helena 0, and I was trying to remember why I'd agreed to this. Despite what Viv had said, I found a quiet corner and crouched while my breathing and heart rate slowed. The lights in the arena were dim, and the black light radiance combined with the lights on the harnesses made everything surreal, like we were in a dream landscape where things glowed that shouldn't, or somewhere deep underwater. I set my gun down and rubbed my hand. I'd been holding it so tightly my palm ached.

Helena, I thought. **Danger.**

My heart lurched. I grabbed the gun and pointed it into the darkness. I'd never spoken to the oracle outside its space before, and that frightened me more than its warning did. "What danger?" I whispered.

Danger. They fall. The guardians remain.

"Oh, *hell*," I said, and ran for the exit, and my phone.

Except I'd gotten turned around in the darkness, and everywhere I turned led to a dead end. I wanted to scream with frustration. This room wasn't much bigger than Abernathy's, and I couldn't get lost there!

I rounded yet another dead-end corner and lowered my gun. The walls here were black and soft, covered in something velvety, with symbols painted on them in white that glowed purply-bright under the black lights. I needed to calm down and think sensibly.

I turned—and came face to face with Santiago.

I screamed and brought my gun to bear on his chest, where the lights of the harness gave me something to aim at. I squeezed the trigger again and again, backing away as I did because he didn't fall with the first shot or the second. He just kept coming.

My heart pounded so hard it hurt, and I could barely breathe, could do nothing except keep shooting until the gun ran out of bullets. "Stop!" I screamed.

"What the hell?" Santiago said. Only it wasn't Santiago. The voice was that of a teenager. "You shot me already, lady, you don't got to keep firing. What's wrong with you?"

I blinked, lowering my gun. The young man was tall and heavyset, bulky rather than fat, and his hair was cut military short. He scowled at me like my shots had actually hurt him. "I…I'm sorry," I managed. "I thought you were…"

"Hey," the young man said. He came forward, and I took an involuntary step back. "You're really scared. Game too much for you?"

I wasn't about to tell him the truth, that I'd freaked out and mistaken him for the man I'd killed. "I need to get out of here," I said.

"Exit's this way," the young man said. He waved a hand back the way I'd come. "You need help?"

I wanted to say no, that I was fine, but I was shaking so hard I didn't think I could hold the gun much longer. "I got lost," I said, trying a laugh so he wouldn't think I was crazy. Crazier than he already thought, anyway.

"Yeah, it's confusing," the young man said.

He led me around two corners, and there was the exit, down a short hall I could swear I'd been down three times already. "Thanks," I said, and hurried along to the antechamber, where I dropped the gun and bent over with my hands on my knees, breathing the musky air deeply. Then I found the locker where I'd put my things and pulled my phone out of my purse. Conscious of the bored attendant, who was watching me with idle curiosity, I tapped out a text to Malcolm: ATTACK HAPPENING ON NAMED NEUTRALITY DON'T KNOW WHICH ONE HELP

"You get scared in there?" The attendant didn't bother to conceal his disdain.

I remembered seeing Santiago's face, how he wouldn't stop advancing on me, and the shakes started again. I turned my back on the attendant without responding and stared at my phone, willing Malcolm to reply. Except he wouldn't, would he, because he'd be texting Lucia or someone who could find out what had happened. So a lack of response was a good thing. It didn't stop me wishing for reassurance.

People started emerging from the arena, stripping off their harnesses and handing them to the attendant along with their guns. "Looks like Helena turned tail early," Viv said with a grin that showed brilliantly under the black lights. The grin disappeared. "What happened?" she asked, putting an arm around my shoulders.

"I can't talk here," I whispered, then repeated myself more loudly so she and Judy could hear me over the noise of the rest of the players.

We left the bowling alley and walked to Judy's car. Night had fallen, but even though it wasn't any darker outside than it had been in the building, it was a natural darkness, broken by the white streetlights and the glowing LASERPINZ sign over the door. The fresh air made the shakes retreat, but I didn't feel completely comfortable until I was safely inside Judy's car. It was still warm from the heat of the day and I again felt like I was wrapped in a soft blanket, though this one smelled of sweet mint from the air freshener.

"What happened?" Judy asked.

I took a deep breath. "The oracle spoke to me. It said there was danger and that the guardians were falling...no, that they remain...I can't remember. I texted Malcolm."

"That's not what scared you, though," Viv said. "You looked like you'd seen a ghost."

A semi-hysterical giggle escaped my lips. "I guess I did," I said. I giggled again, and then I was laughing like a madwoman, completely incapable of controlling myself. Tears ran down my cheeks, and in my hysteria I couldn't tell if they were tears of laughter or fear or sadness. I hugged myself and mentally screamed at myself to pull it together as Viv and Judy exclaimed over me.

Distantly I was aware of a calm, collected central Me, and I reached out to her and felt I'd found something more real than my fears. I held onto that central self until calmness radiated out from it, stilling my laughter and shaking and tears. I wiped my eyes and said, "Sorry."

"Don't be sorry," Viv said. "Hel, you're scaring us. What happened?"

I took another calming breath. "I think I had a flashback or something. I mistook one of the players for Mr. Santiago, and I freaked out."

"I didn't even think about that possibility," Judy said. "I'm sorry we came here."

"No, it's okay." The shakes were almost completely gone. "I think I was on edge because of the oracle's warning, and the guy was the same size as…anyway, I'm not going to avoid everything that might remind me of past traumas, because I'd never go anywhere."

"I don't know much about PTSD, but I know you have to be careful about the things that trigger those memories," Viv said. "I think putting a gun in your hand was a mistake."

"It sure scared the guy I shot," I said with a chuckle that didn't sound at all manic. "Maybe you're right. It's not like I'm losing much if I never play laser tag again, right?"

"I don't want to downplay your emotional reaction," Judy said, "because it worries me, but shouldn't we also worry about something happening to the named Neutralities? What if Abernathy's is under attack?"

"I don't know what to do," I said, gratefully seizing on this as a way to stop thinking about Santiago. "If it is the store, we shouldn't go there, and it's not like we can reach the other two Neutralities."

"Back to your house," Viv said. "Malcolm will have learned what's going on."

As Judy navigated the freeway at higher speeds than I was comfortable with, my phone rang. "Malcolm," I said, my heart in my throat. "What happened?"

"Invaders attacked the Sanctuary," Malcolm said. "They made an assault by air."

My mental image of invaders in tiny parachutes resurfaced. "Is Samudra okay?"

"The Sanctuary's protections are more robust than even I knew. Not one invader reached the premises. I'm told they were vaporized mid-air."

Now my mental image expanded to include falling invaders burning up like meteors in the atmosphere. "That's such a relief."

"How did you know it had happened?"

"The oracle spoke to me." Now that I was well away from the scene of my nightmare, I could reflect on that impossibility. "It's never done that to me before. Not when I wasn't in Abernathy's."

"Except when it was touching your dreams—but that's not quite the same."

"No." I shifted into a more comfortable position and glanced at the speedometer, then wished I hadn't. "I don't know what it means."

"Are you coming home?"

My phone buzzed with an incoming text. I glanced at the display in time to see Samudra's name. "Yes. Samudra just texted me. We'll be home in a few minutes."

"Lucia sent enforcers to the store, in case the invaders tried a simultaneous attack," Malcolm said. "Take care. Just because they've never attacked a custodian outside their Neutrality doesn't mean it won't ever happen."

"I will. I'm pretty sure Judy could outrun them." Judy snorted amusement. "I…I'll be home soon." I felt awkward about repeating my experience for him in front of Judy and Viv, even though they'd seen my emotional outburst and wouldn't judge me if I had another.

"I love you," Malcolm said. "Stay safe."

I ended the call and checked my texts. "Malcolm said invaders attacked the Sanctuary and were driven off before they even touched the ground," I said, "and…Samudra says everything is fine and wants to set up another video call with me and Claude."

"That's good," Viv said, too casually.

I glanced back at her. "Okay, what are you not saying?"

Viv met Judy's eyes in the rearview mirror. "We know you've been through a lot, Hel," Viv said, "but you've been acting strange ever since Montana, and we wish you'd say what's bothering you."

"Which is a polite way of saying 'talk, or else,'" Judy said. "Which is what I've wanted to say for the last four months, only Viv convinced me it was better to let you decide to come clean on your own. But it's clear we've gone past that point."

I turned my head to look out the window at the freeway speeding past. Lucia had said—but Lucia's primary concern was the welfare of all magery, and she was paranoid when it came to her responsibilities. I'd obeyed her wishes, but now I wished I hadn't, because *my* primary concern was my Neutrality, and I knew better than Lucia what mattered most to myself and Abernathy's.

"Lucia made me promise I wouldn't tell," I said, not

looking away from the window, "and I thought she was right, which is why I didn't say anything. But now I think maybe that was the wrong decision." I took a deep breath. "Four months ago, the oracle told me it had seen its end, and mine too."

Viv sucked in a startled breath. Judy said sharply, "You mean death? Or some other kind of ending?"

"See, that's why I should have told you. I assumed it meant death, but Claude, and now you, pointed out that that's not the only interpretation. It's been telling me it and I are going to end for the last four months, and it's wearing on me. Between that, and the attacks on the store, and everything else that's happened to me since I became custodian—"

"I'm amazed you're even sane," Viv said. "Helena, you know you don't have to worry about us spreading the news. That's why Lucia told you to keep quiet about it, right?"

"Yeah. And I'm sorry. I guess, in part, I also didn't want people treating me like I'm fragile. Except it turns out I am, so I'm not sure what the point of that was."

"You're not fragile," Judy said. She took the next exit and turned right, heading toward my neighborhood. "You've faced tremendous challenges and survived. So you've got a little emotional scar tissue. Nobody would blame you for backing down, but you never have. I was more worried about you when you were pretending you didn't have a problem."

"Me too, really." I finally turned to look at Judy, whose eyes were on the road, and then at Viv, who was watching me. "I guess that's what threw me about tonight. I thought I was getting past the thing about killing Mr. Santiago. I haven't dreamed about him for over two weeks."

"It takes time, sweetie," Viv said, putting a hand on my shoulder. "But no more laser tag."

"No more laser tag," I agreed.

15

When we got home, Malcolm was in the living room, watching TV with the sound off. He stood and came around the couch to hold me when I entered the room. I clung to him, wishing it wasn't so obvious that was what I was doing. "Are you all right?" he asked. "You're trembling."

I hadn't realized the shaking had started again and reached inside myself for that place of calm. "Later," I said. "I need to talk to Samudra. He said half an hour. Fifteen minutes, now."

"This is insane," Judy said. She was staring at the television, which I now realized was silent despite the images playing out on the screen. "Barcelona. Why Barcelona?"

I focused on the TV and felt sick. A banner across the bottom of the screen said that this was prerecorded footage from Barcelona, but in the darkness, it could have been any city—any city in flames. The camera showed a street scene that teemed with agitated movement. The fires were burning cars whose flames reflected off the jagged edges of broken windows. Men carrying sticks or lengths of pipe ran past, ducking into alleyways or flinging lumps that might have been stones or bricks into the few remaining unbroken windows. They ignored the camera. It looked so much like a scene from a movie I almost asked Malcolm who was starring in it.

"A terrorist group threatened to unleash their bioweapon on Barcelona about five hours ago," Malcolm said. He still had his arms around me, but his attention was on the grisly scene playing out in front of us. "City officials declared it was a hoax, but then people began complaining of illness, and panic set in. This——"

The scene shrank to a little square in one corner of the screen, and a newscaster came on. Malcolm found the remote and turned on the sound. "——as it develops," the newscaster said. She looked as calm as if she were reporting on the weather. "So far, there have been no reports of widespread death as has occurred in other cities around the world. City officials remain silent in the face of widespread looting and destruction."

The camera view shifted, and the newscaster turned to face the new camera. "In other news, the final death count in Natchitoches has reached two hundred and seventy-one. The CDC intends to release preliminary findings about the disease-causing agent at noon tomorrow, along with recommendations for how people can protect themselves against another attack. Presidential spokespersons urge citizens to remain calm. We will continue to update these stories as more information becomes available."

The station's logo filled the screen, and Malcolm turned the TV off. "It's been like that all evening," he said. "There was no invader attack on Barcelona. Fear and misinformation did all the work."

"It's going to get worse, isn't it," Viv said. "As long as the invaders keep attacking, panic will rise."

"And what happens when it's New York or London or Shanghai?" Judy said. "Barcelona is huge, but it's not the biggest city in the world."

"Not all of it is burning, but enough to be a disaster." Malcolm looked at Viv. "We need Darius Wallach's solution soon."

"I wish I could tell you how much longer it will take," Viv said. "We're working as fast as we can."

"That wasn't a criticism."

"I know, but we feel the pressure, I promise." Viv sank onto the couch and buried her face in her hands.

"But it will be a permanent solution," Judy said. "No more Long War."

My phone buzzed with an incoming text. "Samudra. I forgot. Sorry, I have to make a call."

"We're leaving, anyway," Judy said. She hugged me, such a rare gesture of affection from her I was startled. "See you tomorrow."

Viv hugged me too. "I'll see if I can convince Mr. Wallach to pick up that augury," she murmured. "Hang in there, okay?"

When they were gone, I set up my laptop on the kitchen table. Malcolm turned the TV back on and turned the volume down low. "Let me know if I'm disturbing you," he said.

"I was going to say the same to you," I replied. The video call light was blinking, and I clicked the button and saw Samudra and Claude appear in their little rectangles. "Sorry about the delay," I told them.

"We do not need to rush," Samudra said. His color was up, and he looked more alive than I'd ever seen him. "The attack was deflected perfectly, and if they did not attack the Athenaeum or Abernathy's at the same time, I think it unlikely they will attack again soon."

"It was unexpected, yes?" Claude said. "I did not think they would be so bold."

"Me neither," I said. "It's scary."

"And yet we continue to fight them off," Samudra said. "With the Pattern adjusted to predict their incursions, no new cities have been destroyed. And our Neutralities' defenses are more secure than ever."

"I just don't want to become complacent," I said. "They changed tactics once, and they might do it again."

"But Samudra's point is sound. We should not fall into despair." Claude scratched his large nose. "What do you know of this plan of Darius Wallach's?"

I sat up, startled. "I didn't think anyone knew about that. He said he wanted to keep it a secret until it was further developed."

Claude laughed. "It is a great secret, so naturally everyone knows. In seriousness, the rumor is simply that he has a new weapon in development. Do you know more? I assume he has asked for an augury."

"Several." I fought a brief battle with myself and made a decision. "I don't think I should say anything. He said it's easier if he's not dealing with a lot of questions in the early stages of a project. And if it turns out not to work, I think it's better not to have raised people's hopes. But I can confirm it will change the course of the war."

"Disappointing, but I understand," Claude said.

"So we will continue as we have been, fulfilling our responsibilities and staying alert to new dangers," Samudra said. "I cannot speak much longer. The Sanctuary is busier than ever in these desperate times. The records show that never have there been more petitions brought to our doors than in the past week."

"People come for a single prophecy, right?"

"We call it a revelation," Samudra said. "We guide Wardens through a process of meditation and study, and those who successfully complete their journey are granted a vision of their future, clear and unambiguous. Not everyone is successful, and only one revelation is given to an individual in his or her lifetime, so in the normal course of things we receive very few aspirants. Now we are busy night and day."

"I've seen an increase in mail-in auguries," I said, "but a lot of them, the oracle won't answer. Like, anything asking where the invaders will strike next. Either the oracle doesn't want to waste people's time on auguries that have to come the slow way through the mail, or it wants us to rely on our other resources."

"The Athenaeum, too, has never been busier," Claude said. "It is that people search for answers in every place they might be. It has drawn magery together."

"Except it hasn't, because of the stupid Nicollien and Ambrosite fight," I said. "I wish they'd get over themselves already and see how they're hurting themselves."

"The Board's decision to limit the times each faction can use a Neutrality has made our job difficult," Samudra said. "I have already petitioned for an exemption. There is simply no practical way to divide access to the Sanctuary by the time of day."

I felt more cheerful hearing this. "Maybe it will force the factions to get along. If they're trying to achieve inner peace, I mean."

"Possibly," Samudra said, but he didn't sound confident. "I

fear the answer will simply be to partition the Sanctuary and confine each faction to a different area."

My cheerfulness evaporated. "You're probably right."

Samudra nodded. "Let us stay in touch. If there are any more attacks on our Neutralities, we should notify one another."

We set a time for another video call three days from now, and I disconnected. I leaned back in my chair and ran my fingers through my hair. For once, I wasn't worried about invaders or my personal demons, but about the factions. There had to be some way to make them see sense.

I walked to where Malcolm sat watching the news. He wore a distant expression that told me he wasn't seeing what was on the screen, which happened to be more footage of Barcelona. I sat and leaned against him, startling him out of his reverie. "Anything new?" I asked.

He shook his head. "More of the same. Frightened people using violence to hide the fact that they are frightened. But it seems the rioting is confined to only a few sections of the city, and police are already acting to contain it."

"That's good."

Malcolm turned off the television and stood, bringing me to my feet. "I'm unexpectedly tired," he said, "and I have a feeling tomorrow will be a busy day."

"Really? Why's that?"

He shook his head again. "I don't know. It's just a feeling I have."

"Then let's cuddle." I took his hand. "And I need to tell you what happened tonight."

DESPITE MALCOLM'S PREMONITION, Friday was a quieter day than we'd seen all week. After lunch, I sat in the office at work and stared at my phone, which displayed my contacts list. Sydney had said to call if there was anything that couldn't wait until the regular therapy visit. Having that flashback might count, but I'd talked about it with Malcolm, I wasn't suppressing it, and maybe I was overreacting.

I set my phone down and closed my eyes, focusing on my breathing, how the cool, citrus-scented air filled my lungs and then left my body. I let myself feel the pressure of the air on the skin of my arms and my face. I became gradually aware of how the cloth of my shirt rubbed gently against my collarbone, how my sandals pressed against my soles. The hum of the computer came to my attention, a low vibration I'd never noticed before. Once again I had the sensation of sinking gently into a pool of foam, all my senses alert to the world around me.

A pressure on the back of my neck told me the oracle was paying attention. The pressure spread across my body, not painful, more like a deep, caressing touch. I leaned into it, and the pressure increased. Everything surrounding me felt heightened, the smell of citrus richer, the hum of the computer louder. *Are you doing this?* I thought to the oracle, afraid to break my concentration by speaking. *Are we in your space?*

The oracle said nothing. Its attention filled me, made my bones hum. My breathing came more rapidly, and as I focused on slowing it down, I realized I was seeing things behind closed eyes. Not exactly the specks or waves of light I was used to; these were more like bright webs that uncurled and spread and curled again. They reminded me of jellyfish undulating through water, though without tentacles. I watched the moving webs, forgetting about controlling my breathing. They changed color as they moved, from red to purple to blue to green and then back again. The light show was so beautiful I again asked the oracle silently *Are you doing this?*

Again, there was silence from the oracle. I watched in rapt fascination, following a web until it slid out of sight, then watching another. I wasn't sure how long I'd been doing this when the oracle said, **Helena. Something comes.**

For once, the oracle's cryptic utterance didn't annoy me. It was hard to feel annoyance, or any negative emotion, in my current state. *When?* I thought. Not my usual response, but at the moment, nothing bothered me.

The oracle didn't respond at first. After a few seconds, it said, **Not when. How. Seal the cracks.**

I think that's what Mr. Wallach has in mind. Sealing the cracks that let the invaders enter our world.

Three fall. Three remain. The anchor vanishes. Something comes.

The pressure of the oracle's attention made me feel like a drum skin, stretched tight over my bones. The colored webs grew brighter and began flashing. I felt the oracle drift away and reached for it, desperate to maintain that overwhelming, beautiful connection. *What anchor? Can I stop it vanishing?*

They change. Adapt. I will end. Helena will end.

The webs of light whirled around my head, dizzying me. Then they vanished. I floated in blackness for a while, my mind numb, until my eyes fluttered open and I realized I'd fainted. My cheek was pressed against the smooth hardness of the melamine desk, and a trickle of drool leaked from the corner of my mouth. I sat up and the world spun around me. Gripping the edge of the desk, I closed my eyes and drew in a deep breath. My lungs ached as if I'd forgotten how.

I wiped my cheek and concentrated on breathing until my

head didn't feel so swollen. When I opened my eyes again, the room had settled down. Even so, I sat for a few minutes longer, just in case I was wobbly.

I was positive I hadn't been within the oracle's space. It had reached out to me from wherever it existed. And it was reasonable to assume it could do so because I'd managed to put myself in a receptive state by meditating. Whether I'd fainted because its presence had overwhelmed me, or I'd just forgotten to breathe, I didn't know. But its communication hadn't been any clearer than usual, which frustrated me now that that blissful moment was past. Maybe the oracle was too alien to ever express itself in a way I could understand.

My phone display had turned off while I was communing with the oracle. I turned it on again and hesitated with my finger over the number for the Gunther Node. I might still be overreacting, but if that laser shooter had been a real gun, an innocent person would be dead today. I stabbed the screen with unnecessary force and waited for the call to go through.

I'd anticipated having to wait a while, but they connected me with Sydney almost immediately. "Helena, are you all right?" she said.

"I don't know. I had a sort of flashback last night. I thought I saw Mr. Santiago, and I shot him. Not really. It was laser tag. But I thought it was real."

"I see. And how do you feel today?"

"Uncomfortable. Afraid of myself. It was so unexpected, I can't help wondering when it will happen again."

"Describe the setting. Where were you? You said, laser tag?"

I explained what the laser tag arena looked like, and how I'd mistaken the young man for Santiago. Sydney said, "It sounds like that environment enhanced your mind's confusion over then and now. Would you have tried to shoot that young man if you'd met him on the street at noon?"

"I...don't think so. He didn't actually look anything like Mr. Santiago when I saw him clearly."

"Your reaction is typical for someone who's experienced a traumatic experience. You may have heard stories of soldiers with PTSD having flashbacks in response to a perfectly ordinary stimulus. A car backfiring, or a string of firecrackers going off. You were in a strange place with a gun in your hand and you saw your enemy, as you thought. You probably don't have to worry about the same thing happening, as I said, on the street at noon."

I breathed out in relief. "So I just have to pay attention to my surroundings?"

"More to the point, don't play any games with pretend guns again." Sydney chuckled. "I'm sorry I didn't warn you this might happen. My mistake."

"It's okay. It was frightening, but honestly, I feel more confident now. Like this is something I can control. Not like worrying I might hear a car backfire."

"That's true. Next time we meet, we'll talk about possible triggers and what you can do to manage them. Is there anything else you need to talk about?"

"Not anything serious. I'm practicing meditation." I didn't mention the experience with the oracle. That was outside her area of expertise.

"Excellent. I'll see you next week."

I hung up and put my phone away. I did feel more confident. For the first time since killing Santiago, I felt at least some of my emotional reactions were under my control. No more laser tag.

I propped my elbows on the desk, rested my chin on my

hands, and tried to recall what the oracle had told me before I fainted. It had said something about changing and adapting—no, it had said "they" change and adapt. If this was a warning, the oracle might have meant the invaders. That frightened me. The Wardens had found a way to counter their tactics, but that only made it more likely that the invaders would figure out some new way to attack.

I called Lucia and left a message: "The oracle says the invaders are going to adapt to our tactics. It didn't say how, but I thought you should know." Then I put my phone away again and stood. There was nothing more I could do except fill augury requests and hope Viv convinced Wallach to be sensible.

Viv showed up alone around 3:30, when the last of the Ambrosites had left. She wasn't smiling. "I'm here for that scary augury," she said. "I know I'm not allowed to study it unless Mr. Wallach gives me permission, but I'm hoping if he sees it lying around, he'll give it to me just to get it out of his hair."

"That's perfectly acceptable," I said. "It's only $500. I think the oracle is tired of being ignored." I handed her *Something Wicked This Way Comes* and accepted a handful of bills while Judy wrote out the receipt.

"He's getting close to a practical solution." Viv flipped through the pages, which I could see were clearly printed and not runny, which happened when an augury was illicitly gained. "At least, close to a test run. But Lucia is constantly in the lab, and I think he's feeling pressured."

"Lucia must be worried if she's hovering," Judy said.

"I told her today the oracle says the invaders are going to change their tactics," I said. "At least, that's how I understood it."

"When did the oracle speak to you?" Judy asked, her eyes narrowing.

I described my encounter with the oracle. When I finished, Judy said, "And you passed out? That sounds dangerous."

"I think I just forgot to breathe."

"Um, yeah, that's the dangerous part," Viv said. "Especially since the oracle either didn't notice or didn't care."

"It doesn't really understand people." I didn't like Viv criticizing the oracle, not when I could remember how wonderful it had felt to commune with it. "It didn't hurt me. That was all my fault."

"Whatever," Judy said. "You should be careful. The oracle may not want to hurt you, but if it sees you as its only way to communicate, it may put you in danger by accident."

"I *am* careful," I said irritably. "And I think the possibility of the invaders attacking successfully again is more important than my problems."

"But there's nothing we can do about that," Viv said, "except hope Mr. Wallach has a solution soon."

"I hate feeling helpless," Judy said. She slapped the receipt book down on the counter.

"So do I," I said, "which is why I don't feel scared about speaking to the oracle. What if its warning is all we get the next time the invaders attack?"

Viv shuddered. "Don't let's think that way. I'm going to take this back to the node and hope Mr. Wallach sees sense."

When she was gone, Judy said, "All the mail-in auguries have been processed. I'm going to run to the post office. Are there any other errands?"

"I don't think so." I sat on the metal stool behind the counter and put away the receipt book. "I hope someone comes in soon."

"If you don't want to be alone——"

"It's not that. I can't bear not being able to do *something* to help. I shouldn't feel trapped by the store, but I do."

"Promise me you won't try that thing with the oracle unless there's someone else here." Judy looked as serious as I'd ever seen her, and it frightened me.

"I won't. Promise."

I watched her leave, then looked out the plate glass window at the warmly-lit street and the people passing by. Some of them wore paper face masks. Nobody seemed at all surprised by this. I realized I hadn't heard what the CDC had reported at noon. I couldn't imagine anyone believing those flimsy masks could protect anyone from a biological weapon.

It did make me wonder, though, what the mundane world thought was going on. Being drained of magic by an invader left signs of more ordinary illness, like heart attack or stroke. I didn't know anything about medicine, so I couldn't guess what bioweapon could cause those effects. Something traumatic, definitely.

I hopped down and headed for the basement. When I had nothing else to do, I cleaned. It always made me feel better. It would take a hell of a lot of cleaning to fix the mood I was in.

16

I woke early the following morning and took a long, relaxing bath rather than try to fall back asleep. Malcolm was still dead to the world when I finally toweled off and dressed. His premonition had come true; he'd come home three hours later than usual and looked bone-weary when he did. "People are overreacting," he'd said, "seeing invaders where there are none. Everyone at Campbell Security spent the day ward-stepping all over the world to investigate false alarms."

Now I watched him for a minute, sprawled on his back with his mouth open in a peculiarly vulnerable position, considered snuggling up with him again, and decided he needed rest. Tomorrow would be soon enough for cuddling and maybe more.

Mike Conti was in the office with Judy when I arrived, startling me. It wasn't like their relationship was a secret, but they were both so discreet I'd never seen him on the premises except in the front room, waiting for an augury. "I didn't expect to see you," I said. "Malcolm said everyone at Campbell Security had a rough day yesterday."

"I'm actually headed in to work again," Mike said. "Following up on a couple of calls from yesterday." He turned back to face Judy, who was scowling as she scanned the computer screen. "I still say you're not safe here."

"I'm done having this discussion," Judy said. "Helena, I left the mail-in auguries on the front counter. Mike, shouldn't you be at work?"

Mike's lips thinned in disapproval. "Fine. You want to be that way, I won't argue with you. See you later, Helena." He strode to the back door and slammed it shut behind him.

"I...sorry I barged in on that," I said.

Judy blew out her breath and shoved away from the desk. "He won't *listen*," she said. "I'm getting sick of his overprotectiveness."

"I understand, but you know that's how he is. Not overprotective—I mean that he cares about what happens to you, and he shows that care by trying to protect you."

"I know, but he's taking it too far. He knows this place is safe, and he ought to honor my wishes." Judy ran her hands through her short black hair, disordering it. "I just—"

"Just what?" I asked when she didn't finish her sentence immediately.

"I just wish he actually wanted me to move in. Not so he can protect me, but because it's what he wants." She sighed. "It's irrational, I know, because I haven't told him how I feel, and it's not fair to him to expect him to read my mind. But if I tell him I want to move in with him, he'll go for it even if it's not what he wants—does that make sense? Because I think I'm babbling."

"It makes sense. You decided you want to live with him?"

"Yeah. I get so cranky on the nights he doesn't come over because I really miss him. I want him around so I can be cranky over his disgusting habits instead." Judy laughed. "He's not at all who I thought I'd end up with."

"Really?" I perched on the desk. "Who did you think you'd end up with?"

"Oh…someone tall and lanky. Someone into fine dining and art. Probably a Nicollien, given how they're always in and out of Father's house. Not a short, stocky Ambrosite whose idea of a fun evening is a sports bar or an MST3K movie." She laughed again. "I never knew I'd end up liking those things too."

I didn't know what MST3K was and didn't feel like derailing the conversation to ask. "But you went to that art show three weeks ago."

"Yeah, well, it turns out he likes art, too, and didn't know it. We've both changed."

"So tell him that, and see what he says. Maybe there's something else going on behind his desire to protect you."

Judy shrugged. "Could be. We have to get past this latest fight first. I'll call him later when we've both cooled down."

"Fair enough," I said, and headed for the front room.

When the Nicolliens filed in at ten, I'd already done most of the mail-in auguries and was feeling cheerful. One look at my customers dispelled that cheer. I'd never seen a more despondent group. "What's wrong?" I asked the first woman in line. "Not more attacks I haven't heard about?"

"It's trying to fight without our familiars," the woman said. "You won't understand because you're not a front line fighter. No offense," she added quickly, and sounded sincere. "It's just not something I can explain to anyone who's never been bonded to a familiar. You feel like you lose senses you didn't know you had."

"I get it." I accepted her augury slip. "I'm sorry."

The woman smiled mirthlessly. "You hated them, I know. I doubt you're all that sorry."

"Not that they're gone, no. But I know how close you all were to your familiars, and I'm sorry for that loss. I didn't rejoice over their deaths."

"Not the way the Ambrosites did," came a bitter voice from the middle of the line. "They gloated."

"Not in here, they didn't," I said. "And no more bad-mouthing Ambrosites unless you want me to kick you out."

The man went silent.

"I'll be right back," I said, and made my escape.

The oracle hadn't paid me any attention all morning, but now the pressure of its regard followed me through the stacks to the woman's augury. "Is this one important?" I asked. "Or is something else going on?"

The oracle said nothing, just continued to watch me. I'd come to realize that this meant something important was about to happen, something that interested the oracle. "All right, but you have to speak if you want me to understand," I said. "Though your speaking isn't a guarantee of me under-standing, I guess." I gathered up the woman's augury and navigated the little passageways to the store's front.

"Here—" I began, then was startled into silence. Someone else had entered while I was in the oracle, someone I was never happy to see. William Rasmussen, Nicollien leader for the Pacific Northwest, stood in an empty space near the door as if he were a magnet with an opposing pole pushing all the other people away. He looked like a professor of some obscure academic discipline with his plain dark suit and glasses, but his cold blue eyes revealed that he was a man with power who wasn't afraid to use it.

"Mr. Rasmussen," I said. "Welcome to Abernathy's."

"I have an augury request," he said. He nodded at Judy as if she were a colleague instead of his only child and extended a folded piece of paper to me. I bit back a protest that he should wait his turn—I knew from experience the Nicolliens always deferred to him—and without responding went back into the oracle.

This time, the oracle's attention was almost painful. "What is it?" I demanded. "If there's something you want me to know—"

They come. Union and division. Last chance.

"I don't understand." I unfolded Rasmussen's augury request. *How do we make up for the loss of the familiars?* Despite my dislike for Rasmussen, I felt a twinge of sympathy for him. When Malcolm had lost his magic, he and his team had struggled so hard to accommodate his changed abilities. Learning to fight without familiars had to be similar.

He chooses. Tip the balance. The oracle's attention vanished.

That had been even less comprehensible than usual. Did it mean the choice, whatever it was, would tip the balance, or was it an instruction to me to do so? Since I had no idea what the choice was or what balance had to be tipped, I had to muddle through and hope things would become clear.

I emerged from the oracle into chaos. The waiting Nicolliens had broken out into loud arguments, some of them shouting at each other. Most of them brandished phones. Rasmussen, still in his circle of solitude, had his head down over his phone's display and his brow furrowed. Judy stood next to him, reading over his arm because she was too short to see over his shoulder. As I approached him, he raised his head, and for just a moment a look of terrible indecision crossed his face. Then it was gone, and he was steely William Rasmussen again.

"That's enough," he said in a voice pitched to cut across all the arguments. "We will have to go immediately. Collect your teams and assemble at my home for ward-stepping."

"That's lunacy," someone called out. I heard a couple of muted gasps. "Without familiars, there's no way we can fight."

"Magi fought the Long War for centuries without familiars," Rasmussen said without turning around. "We have an obligation that transcends our temporary concerns. We will fight. And we will succeed."

"What's going on?" I whispered to Judy.

She had her attention fixed on her father. "Another attack," she whispered. "Not one the Pattern predicted. In Palembang in Indonesia. They're going even though they're at half strength, and they're going to get killed."

Rasmussen put his phone away and held out his hand. "My augury, Ms. Campbell," he said. "I shouldn't have to ask you to make it quick, as I'm sure you see the urgency."

"Of course." I gave him *My Enemy, My Ally* and saw him do a double-take. Probably he'd never seen a Star Trek novel before and certainly never expected one as an augury. He glared at me as if the book were my fault. I shrugged and tried not to look annoyed. "$25."

"Excuse me?"

"It surprised me, too. I guess the oracle wants—"

The door swung open, setting the bells jingling. Another familiar figure filled the doorway, this one tall and dark-skinned with muscles stretching his T-shirt taut across his shoulders and chest. The light gleamed off his bald head.

"Blessings be upon this place," Ryan Parish said. The Ambrosite leader looked like a bodybuilder—that made sense, that's what he was—but was as formal in his manners as Rasmussen.

"Mr. Parish," I said, forestalling more arguments, "this is Nicollien time. I'll have to ask you to leave."

Parish ignored me. "Will," he said, approaching Rasmussen. "You heard?"

"We're leaving immediately," Rasmussen said.

"You're under strength after the familiars—"

"Don't you dare rub that in my face again, Ryan," Rasmussen spat. "Ambrosites may be juvenile, but Nicolliens aren't. We will fight regardless."

"That's not what I meant," Parish said. He drew himself up to his full height like a soldier standing at attention. "I said some ill-judged things four days ago about Nicolliens and their lost familiars. I was wrong. I let my pride and hatred blind me to who the true enemy was, and I regret how long it took me to realize the truth." He held out his hand. "The Ambrosites are going to Palembang, and we need the Nicolliens to join us. To fight together as we should have done all along."

Rasmussen looked at Parish's enormous hand, then at the augury. I held my breath. Despite my confusion over the oracle's words, I was sure intervening at this point would be a colossal mistake. Judy's hand closed on my arm painfully tight.

Slowly, Rasmussen reached out and clasped Parish's hand. "You're right," he said. "This fight has gone on far too long. Anyone who's willing to work with Ambrosites, follow me. If you can't control your animosity, we don't want you. Choose." He shook Parish's hand, then shifted the augury from one hand to the other and looked at the cover more closely. "I'm not sure I needed more than this title," he said.

"Keep it," I suggested. "It's going to take more than one battle to bring the factions together."

He glanced over his shoulder at me. "You're right. Thank you, Ms. Campbell." He left the store after Parish. Almost everyone followed him. When the store was nearly empty, I said to the lone remaining Nicollien, "Why not you, Brittany?"

Brittany Spinelli, Malcolm's long-time enemy and an uneasy friend to me, shrugged. "I hate Ambrosites," she said. "They caused the deaths of too many Nicolliens to change that. I'm never going to be friends with them no matter what Will Rasmussen tells me to do. I'll go to Palembang on my own terms." She shifted her weight in a way I was familiar with, one that said she was adjusting the set of her concealed guns. "I don't need that augury, after all. Be seeing you, Helena."

When she was gone, I sagged into the counter and let out a deep breath. "Did that just happen?"

"I didn't think Parish had it in him to be so humble," Judy said.

"Do you think it will last? The truce?" I gathered up the receipt book and put it away behind the counter.

"I don't know." Judy's face paled. "Another attack. One the Pattern didn't see coming."

"They're already changing their tactics," I said.

We stared at each other in silence for a moment. Finally, I said, "I'll call Malcolm. He may not know about it yet."

Malcolm didn't answer his phone. I texted him and got no reply. Anxiety built in my chest until I couldn't bear to eat the tuna salad sandwich I'd brought for my lunch. We tried calling Lucia and got no response from her, either. Two o'clock rolled around with no sign of any Ambrosites. The silence nearly drove me mad.

Finally, with a bitter curse, Judy went online looking for news, something neither of us had wanted to do. The mundane world knew so little about what was actually happening, their reporting couldn't be accurate. I didn't want to watch them panicking when I knew they didn't have the truth. But with so many hours passing with no news from Warden sources, we couldn't bear the silence any longer.

The stories appeared almost immediately: terrorist attacks on Palembang, city in crisis. The news said the terrorists had made a number of small attacks, disappearing when the military showed up only to appear somewhere else. The death toll was estimated at upwards of ten thousand. "That's wrong," Judy said. "They always guess too high." Three terrorist organizations had claimed credit, and two of them had threatened follow-up attacks unless their demands were met.

"I wish we know how much of this fighting was the Wardens stopping the invaders before they could do more damage," I said. "It looks disastrous."

"I picture our people chasing invaders all over the city," Judy said. "Damn it, I hate that Mike and I fought just before he left. It makes me worry more that he won't come back."

"Don't be superstitious. It doesn't change anything."

"I know." Judy leaned her chin on her hand and sighed. "How are they doing it? The invaders, I mean? They're good at illusion, but I didn't think they were so good they could make themselves completely unseen."

"I don't know." I remembered running through a hotel pursued by hostile familiars and closed my eyes to dispel the image. "If they were even disguised as wild dogs, someone would have said something."

My phone rang. I opened my eyes and snatched it up. Malcolm. "Are you all right?" I said.

"I'm uninjured. The attack is nearly over." He sounded out of breath. "Too many deaths, unfortunately, but we prevented the invaders from destroying the Maladewi Node."

Judy's phone rang. "Mike?" Judy said. She stood and walked away from the desk toward the back door, speaking in a low voice.

Distracted, I hadn't heard all of Malcolm's next words. "I'm sorry, what was that?"

"I said the Pacific Northwest contingent worked as a unified team, Nicolliens and Ambrosites together," Malcolm repeated. "It was unbelievable."

"Ryan Parish came into Abernathy's and apologized to Mr. Rasmussen," I said. "*That* was unbelievable."

"I wondered what had happened to bring them together." Malcolm's breathing was slowing. "But it may be too little, too late, because that unity hasn't penetrated to all levels of Warden society. Too many lives were lost because Nicolliens and Ambrosites from other places around the world wouldn't work together. The invaders led us a merry chase all over Palembang, making a thousand small strikes across the city. If this is their new strategy, it's one we'll have trouble countering."

"I'm sure Lucia will want an augury on how to do that. Malcolm, how are they doing it? How have they avoided being seen?"

"By leaving no survivors," Malcolm said grimly. "And in their undisguised forms, they now have a limited invisibility that makes them appear to be shadows if you don't look too closely. We believe their intelligent masters conferred it on them. But at some point, now that those intelligent ones can direct their stupider cousins, I fear they will stop caring about not being seen, and then the real disaster will strike."

"What will happen then?"

"They attack from hiding now because that inspires greater fear and makes their attacks more effective. If they stop hiding, it will be because their numbers are great enough that they no longer need that advantage. Then the Wardens will fight not only the invaders, but the world's military forces as they scramble to face a foe they have no experience fighting."

"But the Wardens would go public then, right? Show the world how to fight the invaders?"

Malcolm sighed. "I don't know. The US military, at least, does things a particular way and isn't likely to take orders from civilians, as they'd see us. I choose to hope we'll find another solution."

"Or that Mr. Wallach will."

"Or that. Love, I have to go now, but I'll be home in a few hours. Possibly just as you're getting off work."

"Stay safe. I love you."

I hung up and looked at Judy, who was still talking quietly to Mike. I sat in the office chair and stared blankly at the monitor, my mind filled with images of thousands of slavering invaders overflowing the streets of Portland. Looking at pictures of Palembang, some of them showing bodies in the street, it was hard to remember it hadn't happened here. I'd never felt so helpless.

"He said they're coming back soon," Judy said, waking me from my reverie. "It was a victory. Just not a bloodless one. Our estimates say maybe twenty-five hundred dead."

"That's so many."

"Not as many as ten thousand. I'm clinging to that because it keeps me from falling into despair. That, and the Wardens themselves didn't lose many."

"I guess that's a relief." I pushed back from the computer. "Let's get cleaned up. I'd say we should close up early, but I don't want to go home to an empty house. It will just make me worry, even though I know Malcolm's fine."

Judy's phone buzzed with an incoming text. She glanced at the display. "That was Father," she said, "telling me he's well and asking me to invite Mike to dinner. He says the three of us have things to talk about. I hope that means he's going to apologize for being a jerk. Which means I should get Mike alone first and suggest strongly that he do the same. I want this civil war over."

"So do I," I said, and went downstairs for the bottle of glass cleaner.

I was busy spritzing the countertop when the door opened and Viv came in. She held the slab of crystal open for Wallach, who carried a cardboard box big enough he couldn't see over it. Its bottom sagged as if it contained something heavy, but Wallach, not a young man, hefted it onto the counter with ease. He was in black scrubs printed with multicolored palm trees and wisps of his white hair were coming free from the pouf. "Sorry, were you cleaning that?" he said.

"I was, but it's okay…can I help you with something?"

"Just give me a corner to set up in," Wallach said. He opened the box and removed a stack of folded white cloths, which he set on the counter, then a Tinker Toy contraption that looked like it went through five dimensions. That, he carried to the farthest corner from the door. It was about two feet high and bristling with rods like a wooden porcupine that had been flattened by a truck and stretched over an armature of a different shape.

"Um…" I couldn't think which of all the questions

brewing inside me I should ask first. Finally, I went with, "What is that?"

"It's an anchor," Wallach said. He messed with the connector wheels for a bit, achieving no difference that I could see. "Part of the realignment magic. Ms. Haley, can you bring me a sheet?"

Viv took a cloth from the stack and shook it out. It was, in fact, a white bedsheet. She handed it to Wallach, who flicked it a couple of times before letting it float down to cover the anchor. With the bedsheet over it, the Tinker Toys looked even more like an animal, one standing perfectly still as if avoiding a predator. Wallach regarded it for a moment, his hands on his hips. "That's one," he said. "Mrs. Campbell, do you have a stepladder?"

"In the basement," I said. "Why—"

"The second anchor has to go somewhere high," Wallach said.

"I was going to ask, why are the anchors here?" I said.

"Oh," Wallach said. "Because we're going to use Abernathy's node as the power source for the realignment magic."

17

"The *hell* you are!" I burst out. "Make Abernathy's the center of your experiment? I don't think so!"

Wallach looked surprised at my outburst. "It's perfectly safe. The oracle doesn't use a tenth of the power generated by its node—"

"How do you know that? The oracle isn't like anything else. What happens if you're wrong, and you suck all the power out so it dies?"

"I've studied this node on and off for twenty years, Mrs. Campbell." He sounded placating rather than angry, and it made me even more upset, like he thought I was a child to be soothed. "The oracle sits atop the node rather than being integrated into it—"

"I know that." I hadn't known that, not really, but it fit with what I'd suspected after hearing Claude talk about the Athenaeum moving, and with the transport of the store from England to Portland.

"—And it generates its own power," Wallach continued as

if I hadn't interrupted him. "The node is simply a backup, if that."

That, I really hadn't known. "That doesn't make sense," I said. "Ariadne Duwelt told me the named Neutralities are the largest nodes in the world. If the oracle isn't using the node, why would it need to be so large?"

"It's not about need," Wallach said. He returned to the box and hoisted out another contraption, this one bigger than the first and resembling a scared cat. "The oracle's proximity to the node encourages its growth—you know nodes grow and shrink naturally over time? All the named Neutralities have the same effect on their nodes, though some, like the Sanctuary and the Labyrinth, are more integrated than others. The oracle will be in no danger."

I still resented his high-handed assumption that he had the right to use my Neutrality any way he chose. "You're planning an untested experiment on Abernathy's' premises. Even if it doesn't drain the oracle's power, how do I know there won't be other side effects? I heard about the houseflies!"

Wallach scowled. "The interbreeding worked," he muttered. "Create a couple of self-propelling organic cameras the size of ponies and nobody ever lets you forget about it."

"It's going to be fine, Helena," Viv said, a note of pleading in her voice. "We've done all sorts of testing and planning, and it's perfectly safe."

"And this will end the Long War, Mrs. Campbell, I can promise you that," Wallach said.

"Meaning that even if you screw up, it won't matter, because there won't be any more invaders to fight?" I said sarcastically.

Wallach closed his eyes and tilted his head heavenward as if praying for patience. "Mrs. Campbell," he said, finally looking at me, "you have done nothing but try to obstruct this project from the beginning. You—no, let me finish. You are worried about irrelevancies and issues I've already corrected for. I'm not sure where your hostility comes from, but I promise you this: *I know this plan will work*. I've poured a lifetime's worth of scientific study into it, I have performed small-scale tests successfully, and I have absolutely no doubt that this magic will permanently prevent the invaders from accessing our world. Now, if you insist on standing in my way, I'll call the Board of Neutralities and get an injunction. I would prefer you cooperate willingly."

I gaped, stunned by his attack. "I have *not* tried to obstruct you," I managed. "The oracle gave you all those auguries, not me. It cares enough about this project that it even gave me auguries to warn you when you didn't listen to your own. Mr. Wallach, I want your plan to work. But if the oracle thinks something is wrong, don't you think you should listen?"

"I did." Wallach set the Tinker Toy cat on the counter. "I identified the flaws the auguries suggested and corrected for them. Why isn't that enough for you?"

It was a good question. I had only my instincts to tell me Wallach wasn't listening to the oracle's warnings. That, and Viv's concerns. "Viv, what do you think?"

Viv bit her lip and looked from me to Wallach. "I...think we've covered everything," she said. "All the plans and all the tests have gone perfectly. Helena, everything's going to be fine."

"I don't like the idea of Abernathy's being involved," I said. "Why not the Gunther Node?"

"That really could be disastrous," Wallach said. "Not because this could endanger the node, because it can't, but there are so many people at the Gunther Node it complicates the magic. The store isn't nearly so crowded."

I opened my mouth to protest again. Wallach held up a hand to forestall me. "Why don't we let the oracle decide?" he said. "I'll ask for an augury predicting our success. Will that satisfy you?"

I thought about it. "All right. But if it says to stop, you stop. No more grousing about how the oracle isn't being cooperative."

I handed Wallach a sheet of paper torn from the back of the ledger—we were running out of pages from having done that so often—and watched him write his question in big, looping cursive even I could read. *Should I go ahead with this project on Abernathy's' premises?*

I folded the paper in half and put it into my pocket. "I'll be right back."

As I expected, the oracle's presence was tangible the second I stepped inside. **Danger, Helena,** it said. **Warning**.

"I know that. You need to give me an augury that's obvious so there's no quibbling." I sidled through one of the narrower corridors, looking for the blue glow.

Seal the cracks. Resonance. Ending. I will end.

I stopped. "You don't mean this could be what kills you, do you?"

No. Seal the cracks. Many, some, one, none. Power strikes.

"I *really* don't understand."

Ahead, blue light flared. **Here, or nowhere,** the oracle said, and slipped away.

That had felt fairly unequivocal. What Mr. Wallach proposed to do was seal the cracks allowing invaders into our world. And it sounded like the oracle wanted the plan to happen here. But I didn't like the sound of "danger."

I followed the blue light to a bookcase near the back of the room. The augury was on an upper shelf, and I had to stretch to reach it. The title on the bright red and orange cover read *Feel the Fear…and Beyond*. I read it a few times, waiting for the oracle to give me more guidance, but it never returned. Finally, I made my way back to the front of the store, where I half expected to see the Tinker Toy cat mounted on the wall. But Wallach and Viv, as well as Judy, who held a broom, stood around the counter, waiting.

I handed Wallach the augury. "It's no charge," I said. "I don't know how easy that is to interpret, but the oracle spoke to me, and I think it says you should go ahead."

Wallach flipped the book open and jabbed a gnarled finger at the page. He read silently, his fingertip following the lines of text. He closed the book and did it again, and a third time. When he closed the book for the final time, he said, "I'm satisfied if you are, Mrs. Campbell."

"This is important enough I want it to succeed," I said. "What do you need?"

"Just that stepladder. Oh, and some water."

"For cleaning?"

Wallach smiled. "For a drink. I'm thirsty."

I went down to the basement for the stepladder while Judy got Wallach and Viv bottles of water. The basement was cool and quiet year-round and smelled of damp concrete and cleaning solution. Wooden filing cabinets lined two of the walls, with metal safe deposit boxes taking up most of a third. In the back corner was the stained porcelain sink, the broom closet, and, propped against the wall beneath the stairs, a three-step folding ladder. I hauled it out and lugged it upstairs, leaving the basement light on. It was superstitious, I knew, but even after nearly three years, I still felt haunted by the ghost of Mr. Briggs, who had been custodian before me and was murdered when he wouldn't falsify an augury.

I set up the ladder in the front room and watched Wallach drag it to the corner opposite the other Tinker Toy sculpture. He took a hammer and some nails out of the box and tapped the nails into the wood, making me protest. "This is the only damage I'll do," he promised. He held the Tinker Toy cat against the wall and, with zip ties Viv handed him, fastened it to the wall between the nails. I kept expecting it to come apart in his hands, but it held together as if it was glued. Maybe it was.

Viv handed Wallach another sheet, which Wallach again flicked open and allowed to settle over the contraption. It, too, looked more like an animal once it was covered, only this one, because it was attached to the wall, looked like the ghost of a cat with its sheet trailing down to puddle on the floor beneath it. The colored rods and wheels were faintly visible beneath the white cloth.

Wallach stepped back with his hands on his hips and his head tilted to one side, examining it. "I think that's it," he said. "Now, I need access to the exact center of this room."

"Um…that's somewhere among the bookcases," I said. "I don't know how to figure that out."

"I have an app for that," Wallach said. He pulled out his battered smartphone with the cracked screen and shook it a few times, then tapped the screen so it lit up bright green. The glow played across his dark skin, giving his face an odd purplish sheen. He tapped it a few more times. The green glow turned blue, a color almost identical to that of a live augury. Wallach held the phone flat high above his head so the light shone on his white hair, tinting it pale blue.

Beams of red light like the lasers you see in movies shot out from the four sides of the phone, extending all the way to the walls except in the direction of the oracle, where the beam struck a bookcase. Where they touched the walls, the lights turned pink and shot out sparks like a Fourth of July sparkler. The one touching the bookcase, however, just ended.

"Huh," Wallach said. He walked in the direction of the oracle, taking slow, long strides. Soon he was lost to sight. I followed him, feeling nervous about letting him loose inside the oracle even if it wasn't active.

Wallach continued to hold the phone high, tilting his head back to see the display. Despite this, he didn't run into anything or trip over the stacks of books on the floor I totally intended to pick up someday. He seemed to be following the red beam of light, which flicked from bookcase to bookcase, sometimes intersecting on a book and making it glow like an evil augury, red instead of blue.

After about a minute of this, Wallach stopped and looked around. "Do you mind if I climb one of these shelves?"

I hesitated. Despite being very hale, Wallach was in his seventies and not exactly spry. "Are you sure that's safe?"

"Of course. Don't worry, I won't sue if I break my leg," Wallach said with a smile. I shrugged and made a "go ahead" gesture.

Wallach tucked the phone into the breast pocket of his scrubs and hauled himself up, shoving a few books aside with his feet. I watched, biting my lip nervously, as he settled himself and then pulled out the phone again. The red beams of light shot out of it again, but this time I couldn't see where any of them ended. Wallach tilted the phone one way and then the other, glaring at the display, which to me still seemed like a blank blue light. Then he set the phone atop the bookcase and climbed back down, feeling his way with his feet. I held my breath until he was solidly on the ground again.

"That's the center of the room," he said, gesturing to where the phone lay. "The last piece goes there."

It surprised me that the center of the room wasn't the same as the center of the oracle, those four monolithic bookcases that stood facing each other in a square where I'd so often spoken with the oracle, or been spoken to. "What's the last piece?"

"It's how the magic connects to the node." Wallach headed for the exit, and I followed him. "It will take some time to make that connection, but we should be able to do this in about two hours."

"Two hours from now?"

"You sound surprised. What were you expecting?"

I shook my head. "I don't know. Something big and flashy. I mean—you're planning to move our reality, right? That ought to be huge!"

Wallach laughed. "I suppose that makes sense. No, it's a simple piece of sympathetic magic. I've placed anchors at the joints of the city, and then the fulcrum connects to the node and fuels their movement."

We emerged from the stacks to find Viv and Judy talking quietly behind the counter. "And when one set of joints moves, the rest of them do," Wallach continued. "It causes a ripple effect across our reality, shifting us out of alignment. When it's complete, the only invaders left will be the ones trapped here, and it should be easy work for the Wardens to eliminate them."

Despite my reservations, I had to admit it seemed perfect. "What's the fulcrum?"

"This," Wallach said. He reached into the box and pulled out the biggest gemstone I had ever seen outside cheesy '80s fantasy movies. It was an oval easily three feet across, black as night and faceted like a giant insect eye. Wallach held it like it weighed a ton, but waved off my offer to help carry it. So I followed him back into the stacks to where he'd left the phone, where he did give it to me so he could climb the bookcase again. I handed it up to him—it must have weighed twenty pounds or more—and watched him settle it atop the bookcase. It wobbled slightly when he climbed down, but didn't fall.

Wallach turned off the phone's display and put it back into his pocket. "Two and a half hours," he said. "I have a few other things to do, but I'll be back then."

"Okay," I said, glancing once more at the black gem before following him out of the stacks once more. I thought about asking him what else he had to do, but that carried with it the risk that they were complicated things he might try to explain to me, and decided against it.

Once we were back at the counter, Wallach said, "A few other people will be present for the event. Lucia, obviously, and some of my colleagues who worked on the prototype. Will the store be open?"

I checked my watch. "Actually, it should happen just before closing."

"Good. You're welcome to observe, of course." Wallach picked up the now-empty cardboard box and said, "Is there somewhere I can leave this? That fulcrum is going to be incredibly valuable when this is all over, and I'll want to retrieve it."

"Sure." I gestured at a spot behind the counter.

Wallach deposited the box and nodded to us. "I'll see you soon." He headed for the door. Viv hurried after him.

When the door swung shut, Judy said, "Viv didn't look happy."

"This is a big deal. I know it sounds simple, but it can't be…I don't know. Trivial?" I looked through the window at where Viv and Wallach were getting into one of the Gunther Node's signature white vans. "I know Mr. Wallach feels confident, but I won't rejoice until it's done."

"I can't believe you agreed to it. Do you honestly think it will work?"

"I don't know. I hope so. At least, I got the feeling the oracle was satisfied." Though as I said that, I wondered if it were true. "Satisfied" wasn't exactly the vibe I'd gotten. More like "resigned." "But he was right about one thing. This is so important to the fate of the world, the Board of Neutralities would almost certainly have overridden me if I'd continued to make a stink. So it's better if we cooperate, don't you think?"

Judy shrugged. "I guess so. But maybe you should see what the oracle thinks of having that big-ass black diamond smack in the middle of it."

"It's not in the middle of it, that's what's weird." I shook my head. "I was thinking something along those lines. I'll go take a look."

Being able to enter the oracle's space without an augury request was a relatively new thing for me. It had only been about a year since I discovered my ability, but until recently I had done it often, enjoying the moment of contact with my strange friend. Since it had started warning me of our ending, the experience had soured. This was the first time in over four months I'd gone in voluntarily. It was a strange feeling, like I imagined going back to church for the first time after a long absence would feel.

The oracle's presence, to my surprise, was elsewhere. "Are you all right?" I asked. "That gem isn't bothering you?"

The oracle shifted. Its attention brushed me, then darted away.

"It's not at your center, so I thought maybe that meant it wasn't a problem," I went on. I walked through the aisles until I came to where the gem lay atop the bookcase. It didn't look like it was doing anything. "I really hope I didn't misunderstand you. I know Mr. Wallach was ignoring your auguries, or at least I thought he was, but it seemed like everything was fine."

Its attention shifted again. **Danger. Here or nowhere. Seal the cracks.**

"That's what he plans to do. Seal the cracks. But even if there's danger, even if there are side effects, isn't that worth sealing off our reality from the invaders'?"

Ending. I will end.

I sucked in a startled breath. "But you said…I thought you said this wouldn't hurt you. Mr. Wallach says it won't even touch your power source."

No. I am alone. Not the node. Seal the cracks.

I shook my head, feeling stupid and helpless. "I'm really sorry I don't understand you. I have to trust that if you were in danger…except that might not matter, right? If your ending, our ending, is inevitable. But it really does sound like this isn't what kills you."

I will end. Helena will end.

I grimaced. "Why do I have the feeling you don't understand time?"

Instantly, the pressure bore down on me so hard I cried out. **I will end. Helena will end. It happens.**

"Am I right? You mean you don't know when it will happen?"

I and not-I happens. Burning happens. Ending happens.

"I'm…going to take that as a yes." I and not-I—that had to mean the second oracle the Mercy had created, the one Abernathy's had destroyed. And the Mercy had tried to burn down the store before that. If the oracle didn't understand time, if all those things happened, for it, simultaneously or something, then maybe it couldn't tell me when it would end because it didn't know. What use this information was, I had no idea, but anything that would help me interpret the oracle's cryptic pronouncements, I'd take.

"All right, so you don't know when your ending will come," I said.

Immediately, the pressure lessened. **Seal the cracks,** the oracle said, and it was gone.

I rubbed the back of my neck, which was as sore as if something physical had borne down on it. The black gem still didn't look any different. I hadn't really learned anything new, but I had to hope this would all work out.

I returned to the store front to discover Judy was gone. I retrieved my bottle of glass cleaner and polished up the countertop. I'd never needed the calmness that came from cleaning more. Just a little over two hours, and we'd see the end of the Long War forever.

Lucia showed up at just after five with her assistant Dave Henry in tow. "Wallach wanted to do this by himself," she said. "Like flipping a switch. I told him if reality was going to move, I was going to be there for it."

"That's how I feel," I said. "Something this momentous ought to be bigger than just...I don't even know what the magic looks like."

"Me neither." Lucia leaned against the counter and crossed her arms over her chest. It might be a momentous occasion, but she was still wearing her usual plain T-shirt and yoga pants. Dave took up a parade rest position next to her, his eyes scanning the store like he was looking for hidden threats.

"Have you heard anything from Indonesia?" I asked.

Lucia snorted. "Have I heard anything from Indonesia. I've heard practically nothing else. All of it reports from my Wardens that the end of times is here because our Nicolliens and Ambrosites worked together to fight the latest invasion. I wouldn't believe it if the reports hadn't come from some of the least imaginative men and women I've ever known."

"Ryan Parish apologized to Mr. Rasmussen publicly. In the store."

Lucia's eyes widened. "It *is* the end of times. You sure it wasn't his evil twin?"

"Pretty sure. Besides, it was a good thing, so doesn't that technically make Mr. Parish the evil one?"

Lucia laughed. "I'll take it. If it lasts."

"It had better last," Judy said. "I'm sick of my father and my boyfriend being unable to share a meal without it turning into Waterloo. With both of them starring as Napoleon."

"I can imagine." Lucia glanced past me at the window. "Looks like Wallach's team is arriving."

I followed her gaze to where a van, not one of the Gunther Node's white ones, was pulling up in front of the store. At this time of day, when the stores were closing down, there were usually curbside parking spaces, but this van was oversized and I wasn't sure it would fit. And then it did. I blinked, thinking maybe I was wrong about the length of the blue van, but it hadn't gotten any shorter and it still fit into the narrow space. It wasn't an illusion, because I'd be able to see through that, but pure alteration magic. I had no idea what kind of magus could pull that off.

The van's doors opened, and three people got out. One of them drew my attention immediately, because she was the tallest woman I'd ever seen, taller even than most men. Her ginger curls spiraled around her face, and her pants, ordinary teal scrubs, were just a little too short for her, which was sort of miraculous that it was only a little. She towered over the two men, one of them middle-aged and balding with fat-rimmed glasses that gave him a Clark Kent look despite his age and lack of hair, the other an Asian man who might have been younger than me. Despite a serious case of bed head, he looked alert and cheerful.

The middle-aged man pushed open the door and held it for the other two. "—last thing I want to do," the woman was saying in a heavy English accent. "Hi. Darius told us to meet him here. I've never been in Abernathy's." She looked around, turning slowly like she wanted to take it all in. "It's a little rustic, isn't it?"

"Camouflage," I said, feeling nettled even though I knew it didn't matter what people thought of my store's appearance. "I'm Helena Campbell, custodian of Abernathy's."

"Sarah Osenbaugh," the woman said, extending her hand. "Darius strong-armed you into this, didn't he? He can be a tad obsessive."

"Which is why he gets results," the middle-aged man said. "Jon Pirolli. Nice to meet you."

"How do you ever find anything in here?" the Asian man asked. He, too, was surveying the stacks, but where Osenbaugh had looked dismissive and maybe a little amused, he seemed genuinely amazed.

"We don't," I said. "That's how the oracle works. We don't know what's in here—"

"So anything could be in here," he said, concluding my sentence. "Amazing. I bet I could get this place to cough up the lost works of Shakespeare if I had three weeks and a couple of interferometers."

"Um…"

He turned to look at me and grinned. "Scary thought, huh? Don't worry, I don't experiment on living creatures— that's what Abernathy's is, right?"

"Um…yes. As far as I can tell."

He stuck out his hand. "Rick Jeong," he said. "It's actually Jeong Hak-Kun, but I got sick of people pronouncing my name to rhyme with 'raccoon.' And I'm a huge fan of Feynman."

That made almost no sense, but I smiled and nodded anyway. "Mr. Wallach said you all would be coming to see this. Were you part of the experiment?"

"Darius based the experiment off my work in sympathetic magic," Osenbaugh said. "I told him it was insane, but that only made it more appealing to him."

"Rick and I did some of the hands-on work," Pirolli said. "We built most of the anchors."

"Not without a lot of arguing," Jeong said. "What's wrong with basic 3D modeling, I'd like to know?"

"3D modeling of a 5D system is—"

Jeong waved Pirolli off. "Yeah, yeah, insufficient parameters, I know, but—"

"Would you all like some water?" I said, sensing an imminent descent into irrelevancy.

They all accepted bottles of water, and silence fell. I had no idea what to say to three people who seemed every bit as eccentrically brilliant as Wallach. Judy drummed her fingers on the counter. I messed with the receipt book, flipping through the pages before putting it back beneath the counter.

Jeong idly capped his water bottle. "So, Ms. Campbell—"

"Please, call me Helena," I said.

"Okay. Helena, what's it like, working so closely with the kind of entity Abernathy's is?"

"I—well, it's…unusual. I guess that's the obvious answer, right? But sometimes it feels like coming up against something unspeakably alien, and sometimes it's like chatting with a friend. It doesn't communicate easily, and half the time I don't understand it, but there's a closeness I can't describe."

"Nathaniel Briggs never saw it that way," Pirolli said. "It was always just another job to him."

"Did you know him?"

"As a casual acquaintance. We weren't close friends."

I remembered reading Mr. Briggs' diary, how he'd written of the oracle as something he could control, and nodded. "I don't think Mr. Briggs ever realized the oracle's true nature."

"So why you?" Osenbaugh asked, her eyes narrowed in thought.

"I don't know. Maybe because I'm a genetic sport, or maybe because I was willing to do things no other custodian had." I wasn't going to tell them that the oracle had predicted my existence and chosen me for its next custodian. They seemed nice, but that was a private thing I shared with very few people.

"Interesting," Osenbaugh said.

The bells jangled, and Wallach and Viv entered. Wallach held an oversized tablet in a translucent violet case, and Viv carried an ordinary red steel toolbox, hefting it with both hands like it was heavy. "Ah, you're here," Wallach said. "Ready to watch history be made?"

The other three laughed like he'd made a joke. I waited for Wallach to get upset at being mocked, but he didn't react. Maybe it really was a joke, one I wasn't privy to.

"One minute," Wallach said. He set the tablet on the counter and headed off into the stacks without even a nod to me. After a startled moment, I followed him. I caught up to him when he'd reached the room's center. Wallach stared up at the black gem. "Magnificent, isn't it?"

I looked up. The black gem seemed no different than

before, except—no. If I looked closely at its edges, I could see the faintest wavering in the air, like heat haze. It blurred the thing's outline so it looked less like an insect's glittering eye and more like a lump of glass. "I don't know what it's supposed to look like," I said.

"It's supposed to look like that. The fulcrum is now connected to the node and drawing energy nicely. All according to plan." Wallach climbed up and awkwardly shifted the gem until it tilted precariously on the edge of the shelf. I hurried to stand beneath it, though if it fell and I tried to catch it, it might break my arm. Wallach, though, gave it a shove that made it rock, its swaying gradually increasing until it slipped and plummeted to the ground. I cried out as it struck the linoleum floor with a sharp crack.

"Sorry about the noise," Wallach said. He crouched and wormed his arms beneath the stone, which appeared undamaged. "It's lab-created black diamond," he said when he saw my astonishment. "It would take more than a seven foot fall to damage it, particularly now it's connected to the node."

"Oh. It looks fragile. Like glass."

Wallach hefted the stone and walked away. I hurried after him. I was starting to feel like a puppy chasing after a constantly moving red ball.

The others hadn't moved in our absence, though Lucia was talking quietly on her phone. Wallach set the gem on the counter and stepped away. "Ladies and gentlemen," he said, "in a few minutes, we will make history."

Lucia ended her call and turned to face him. "Let's hope that's true."

Wallach picked up the tablet and turned it on so the screen glowed blue. "The principle is simple," he said. I recognized the tone of voice: I'd gone to college for a few semesters, and this was exactly how most of my professors had sounded when they were about to deliver a lecture. "Thanks to Sarah's work with sympathetic resonance, we were able to establish a connection between these physical models and the magic shaped by them." He pointed at the sheeted Tinker Toy cat hanging on the wall like a cut-rate Halloween decoration. "The oracle identified the places within the city where reality hinges—places that are susceptible to being moved. The 5D models now located at each of these places, fueled by the magic of this node, will shift our reality around the fulcrum, cutting us off from the invaders' reality."

I raised my hand. It had been years since college, but that ingrained reaction hadn't vanished. "Can it really shift our whole reality?"

Wallach smiled. "Think of a tablecloth spread over your dining room table," he said. "Suppose you need to adjust it so it hangs down evenly on both sides. You tug on one side, shifting it, but wrinkles form, so you tug elsewhere until it lies smooth again. What I'll do is similar to that, except those secondary 'wrinkles' smooth themselves out. Over the minutes after I initiate the process, the effect will spread throughout our reality. So it's not instantaneous, but it is extremely fast."

"Four minutes and forty-three seconds, to be precise," Pirolli said. He tapped his wristwatch. "I'll time it."

Wallach flicked the gem with his fingernail. A high, clear tone rang out through the room, like a note sung by a child soprano. He nodded. "We're ready. Feel free to talk—it won't disturb the magic."

Nobody spoke. Maybe it wouldn't disturb the magic, but it would make me, at least, feel weird. Wallach turned his attention to his tablet and tapped the screen. The light went from blue to clear white. Wallach continued to tap and swipe. I sidled up to Lucia and whispered, "How will we know it worked?"

"No idea," Lucia murmured. "I hope it's not explosive."

So did I. I stole a glance at the gem. It still didn't look any different, aside from the slight heat haze.

Movement caught my eye, and I looked up from the gem at the hanging cat. Its sheet rippled in a breeze I couldn't feel, making it look even more like a ghost in a frat party haunted house. Instead of the traditional oooOOOooo sound, I heard rainfall pattering on the roof, as loud as if the second-story apartment wasn't there. I looked out the window, but afternoon light filled the street, bright and strong without even the dimness of a slight overcast.

The sheet covering the other anchor started rippling too, but its movement looked more like a puddle of spilled milk flowing endlessly off the edge of a table. It was the weirdest mix of mundane and eerie I'd ever seen.

Wallach took a few steps in that direction and held out his hand, the fingers splayed wide, to the anchor. The flapping sheet went wild, twisting in an intangible wind. I looked closely. Though the sheet still defined a shape, there was nothing visible beneath it. The colored rods and wheels no longer showed through the cloth of either anchor.

Wallach turned and pointed his hand at the second anchor, whose sheet also went into flapping convulsions. He tapped and swiped some more. The white light dimmed and took on a greenish tint. "Ms. Haley," he said.

Viv opened the toolbox and pulled out a tuning fork that looked like it was made of bronze. She tapped it against the black diamond. Another clear tone rang out, higher pitched than the first. The air rippled around the gem, the heat haze made stronger and more visible. A strong, unidentifiable scent filled the air. After a few breaths, my brain insisted it was peanut butter, but those moments of uncertainty told me whatever it was was truly alien, and I'd translated it into something I understood.

Viv struck the diamond again, sending out a lower sound that set my teeth on edge. I clenched them together. "Once more," Wallach said, and the next tap produced a note midway between the others. The pleasant sound echoed through the store, and I saw Osenbaugh and Pirolli exchange smiling glances. Jeong had his phone out and was tapping furiously, occasionally looking at Wallach.

Wallach took a few leisurely steps toward the bookcases and came up short, his shoulders tensing. "That's one gone," he murmured, I thought to himself. He turned around and walked back to the anchor on the wall.

As he passed me, I got a look at his tablet. It showed a map of Portland's roads as far south as Beaverton and as far north as the Columbia River. Tiny green lights, and one red one, glowed in a random pattern strewn across the screen. The red one was far to the west. Just before he was too far away for me to see the screen, one of the green dots turned red. "What does that mean?" I said, curiosity overriding my fear of disrupting the magic.

"Two anchors have been destroyed," Wallach said.

Lucia swore under her breath.

"It's all right, there are redundancies built into the system," Wallach said. He used his fingers to shrink the display and then turn it. "Everything is fine."

Jeong was still tapping rapidly. I wondered if he was texting someone or taking notes. Osenbaugh said, "It should have reached activation by now."

"It's fine," Wallach snapped. "Ms. Haley. Again."

Viv, looking nervous, tapped the diamond again. The sound that emerged was the same pitch as the last one, but instead of harmonizing with the lingering echoes of the other note, it sounded discordant.

Wallach thrust the tablet at Osenbaugh and strode to Viv's side, snatching the tuning fork out of her hand. "Sarah, count them off," he said. He stood poised to strike the diamond again.

Osenbaugh fixed her gaze on the tablet. "Three," she said. "Four."

"There's not enough energy going into the system," Pirolli said.

"There will be," Wallach said. He struck the diamond, not the gentle taps Viv had used, but a hard blow like a hammer. The note rang out again, producing yet another discordant ripple of sound that made my skin vibrate. I backed away from the diamond and ran into Judy, who'd done the same thing.

"Five," Osenbaugh said. Pirolli hovered at her side, looking like he wanted to snatch the tablet from her.

Light blossomed where the two anchors were, a pinkish-yellow light that made me think of a spring morning. Pirolli and Osenbaugh relaxed. "That's it," Pirolli said. "They're drawing it in."

"Six—no seven," Osenbaugh said.

"It's fine," Wallach repeated. He lowered his hand holding the tuning fork and tension visibly flowed out of him. "It just has to outpace—"

The anchors' light brightened. Osenbaugh's hands tightened on the tablet. "Eight. Nine. Ten. It's accelerating!"

Wallach swore and dropped the tuning fork. He ran to Osenbaugh's side and snatched the tablet. "No, no, no," he muttered, swiping at the tablet. "No. It's not fast enough!"

"Shut it down," Jeong said, lowering his phone. "Shut it down before it collapses."

"No! We're so close," Wallach shouted. He shoved the tablet at Pirolli. The anchors' light increased again until it was too bright to look at. Wallach held one arm over his eyes and walked toward the anchor on the wall. His steps were slow and halting, as if he were fighting a wind only he could feel.

Painful pressure seized me. **Danger,** the oracle said. **Ending.**

"Stop!" I shouted. "Don't do it!" I headed for Wallach and immediately was caught in the same wind that pressed him back from the anchor. I heard the other scientists shouting things I couldn't understand, and Lucia calling my name, but I couldn't have stopped walking if I'd wanted to.

"It just needs an adjustment," Wallach shouted over the noise of the discordant melody that had grown in volume along with the increased brightness of the anchors.

I took another step. Wallach had almost reached the anchor. He looked like a black blotch against the painfully bright light. I reached for him—

The sound cut off so completely I felt deafened. Glass shattered nearby, and I screamed silently as something grabbed my outstretched hand and twisted it painfully to the left. I jerked my hand away and fell to my knees, breathing heavily. All I could see was a pulsing yellow-pink light and black afterimages that might have been people. They were located where the others had been, at least, but they were motionless. I squeezed my eyes shut and hoped I hadn't been blinded.

Gradually, sounds emerged from the silence as if someone were turning up a volume knob. I heard muttered conversation, and someone put an arm around my shoulders and supported me into a sitting position. I hadn't realized I'd collapsed. "Helena," the person said faintly. I recognized Judy's voice. "Helena, show me your hand."

I still couldn't see anything. I held out my left hand and screamed when Judy touched it. It felt raw and burning at the same time. "It will be all right," Judy said, which seemed preposterous. I held it away from my body and keened at how the air brushing over it felt like acid poured over my skin.

More sounds, still unintelligible, reached my ears. I heard Lucia talking steadily the way she did when disaster struck and she was giving orders. I blinked, and found the brightness had faded from yellow-pink to pulsing red. The black afterimages looked more like people, though I still couldn't make out details, and they had moved to converge on a spot nearby. "What happened?" I said.

"The anchors exploded," Judy said. "Mr. Wallach—I don't know what happened to him. And Viv…"

Cold dread washed over me. "What happened to Viv?" I focused on Judy. I could see her now, but as if she were behind smoked glass. She looked as if the explosion had stunned her.

"She broke the diamond," Judy said. "I don't know why. It exploded in her face." Her arm closed more tightly on my shoulders. "She's not moving."

19

I pushed myself one-handed to my knees and stood, wobbling until Judy steadied me. The pain in my hand had lessened so it now only felt like a rasp stripping the skin from my bones. With Judy's help, I walked to where Pirolli and Osenbaugh knelt beside Viv, each holding one of her hands. Her eyes were open and sightless. I didn't think she was breathing. "What—" I said, then realized I didn't know what I'd meant to say.

"Give them space, Davies," Lucia said. She stood in the corner beneath where the anchor had been, looking down at Jeong, who knelt beside another fallen form. I approached them cautiously, feeling as if the floor was rippling underfoot and might knock me down if I stepped wrong.

The only thing I recognized about the figure beside Jeong was the black scrubs printed with colorful palm trees. Wallach looked like a wax sculpture melted over a fire and twisted out of recognition. My numb brain insisted on trying to make what was left of him look human and failed. I felt cold and sweaty at the same time, bright sparks filled my vision, and I fell to my knees and lowered my head to keep from passing out. I heard people talking around me, but they sounded as if they were underwater. I breathed deeply with my eyes closed and waited for the dizziness to pass.

"Helena. Helena." It was Jeong. "Are you all right now?"

I nodded and opened my eyes, then wished I hadn't, because I was again looking directly at what was left of Wallach.

"I need to look at your hand," Jeong said.

I held it out—and screamed. My left hand was nothing but a club, with the same waxy, twisted look Wallach's body had.

Judy grabbed my head and made me look at her. "He'll fix it," she said. "Do you understand me? You just touched the edge of the effect. It can be fixed. Helena. Breathe."

I nodded and sucked in air, holding my breath for a few heartbeats and letting it out again. My hand didn't feel like a club. When I wasn't looking at it, it felt like my fist was clenched, and if not for the fact that I couldn't open it, it would have been a perfectly normal feeling.

Jeong took hold of my hand, and I clenched my teeth on another scream, because my skin still felt raw. But almost immediately, the pain vanished. "Have you had a major healing before?" Jeong asked.

"Yes."

"I've deadened the nerves so you can't feel anything, but... Helena, this is a major reconstruction. It looks like all your bones are still there, but fused." Jeong's calm manner was so at odds with his words I wanted to laugh. Fused? The idea was terrible and ludicrous and couldn't have anything to do with me. "We're going to take you to the Gunther Node and put you under before trying to fix it."

He sounded way too calm. "There's something you're not telling me," I said.

"I don't want you to worry. We can fix this."

"But...?"

Jeong sighed. "Darius was the expert on this kind of reconstruction. I don't know of anyone who comes close to his level of expertise."

"And he's dead." I felt as if my fear had been numbed along with my nerves. "I can't believe he's dead. What are we going to do?"

"We'll figure it out." He looked past me. "I'm more worried about Viv."

And just like that, fear pulsed through me. "Is she..."

"She's not dead. But she took the full backlash from breaking the fulcrum. I have no idea what that did to her."

I turned around. Osenbaugh and Pirolli still knelt beside Viv. Now that my vision was fully clear, I could see she was her normal color and her eyes were closed now. She no longer looked dead; she looked asleep. "Why did she do that?" I asked. "What happened? I don't understand any of this."

Jeong and Judy helped me stand and assisted me to the metal folding chair beside the door. It wobbled as I sat down, but I was used to its peculiarities and held myself steady. "I can't explain the details of the magic," Jeong said, "but basically, we knew the anchors would vanish as the magic spread through the system. It was something Darius planned for. But they vanished faster than we expected. I don't know why yet. The point is, countering that meant pouring more magic into the system. Tapping into the node more...you can picture it like poking a straw into a drink. We swapped out the first straw for a wider one."

I nodded. "So the magic killed Mr. Wallach?"

"Not the magic itself. He tried to adjust the anchor manually before it activated, to keep it from vanishing. But he wasn't fast enough. The anchor started to shift our reality, and he got caught in its field." Jeong pointed at my hand, which I refused to look at. "So did you."

"That doesn't explain why Viv broke the diamond," Judy said. "I didn't think that was possible."

"I don't know what she was thinking," Jeong said. "Breaking the fulcrum stopped the magic pouring into the system, like unplugging a lamp, but she was there for the creation of the diamond. She knew it was unbreakable. At least, we all thought it was." He stood from where he'd been crouching next to me and looked in Viv's direction. "She probably saved us all. With the anchor disrupted by Darius, that distortion field would have spread to engulf this whole room."

I nodded. I couldn't stop looking at Viv and the bone magi trying to save her. It reminded me so strongly of how Jun had died four months ago, of the bone magi huddled around her and how it had ultimately been futile, that I closed my eyes and prayed more fervently than I ever had before.

Footsteps sounded on the linoleum, and I looked up at Lucia. "Can you walk?" she asked me.

I nodded.

"You and Rasmussen are going with Henry. Jeong, do you need any help getting Haley into your van?"

"I think we can manage it," Jeong said. He glanced over his shoulder. "What about Darius?"

"I've called for assistance. I'll stay with him until they get here." Lucia looked at my hand and quickly looked away. "I've called Campbell and Washburn and they'll meet you at the node. Jeong, I want a full report on this debacle as soon as you and your colleagues have had time to analyze the situation."

"Understood." Jeong put a hand on my shoulder. "Don't worry, Helena. Everything will be fine."

I wished I knew him well enough to judge whether he was offering me empty assurances. Instead, I said, "Thanks."

I was recovered enough to walk under my own power to the little white van, where I sat in the back seat while Judy rode shotgun. The last thing I saw before Dave pulled away from the curb was the three scientists carrying Viv's unconscious body to the blue van. That made me cry when nothing else had.

We rode to the Gunther Node in silence. I tried once to open my left fist and felt only as if someone had closed their much bigger hand around mine. The rest of me felt as numb as my hand, but with an emotional deadness rather than a physical one. Now that the immediate terror had worn off, my mind circled around and around might-have-beens. If I had refused Wallach access to the store's node. If I'd pushed him to listen to the oracle's warnings. If I'd made Viv stop working for him. If I'd—the possibilities were endless, and all of them felt like my fault. I'd known there was danger, and I hadn't acted decisively.

The gardenia scent of the Gunther Node should have been calming, but today it made me feel ill. I followed Dave down the passage to Green 1 and waited, still feeling numb, while he spoke to the bone magi at the desk. I caught them staring at me and almost turned my back on them. I didn't need to feel like a freak on top of everything else. Judy eyed me, but said nothing.

Finally, Dave and one of the bone magi came to my side.

"This is Veronica," he said, indicating the woman in maroon scrubs. She looked familiar. "She's going to show you to your room, and in a few minutes they'll do an initial analysis. It's going to be fine."

I nodded and let Veronica lead me back down the hall to one of the little rooms with the curtained windows. Judy sat in a chair opposite the bed while I kicked off my shoes and lay back. Veronica looked like she wanted to shoo Judy away, but was afraid to. "You don't need to undress or anything," Veronica said. "Someone will be in shortly." She pulled the curtain across the window and left.

"I can go if you want me to," Judy said. "But I don't think you ought to be alone."

"I'm worried about Viv. Maybe you should find her."

"Those scientists told me she would be in isolation while they treat her." Judy clasped her hands on her knee. "I'm worried about her too."

The door opened. A young, dark-skinned woman with her black hair pulled back from her face in a soft pouf entered, followed by Jeong. I recognized her; she was Wallach's assistant, or something, and they resembled each other strongly. "Ruby Wallach," she said, offering me her hand. "You tried to save my grandfather."

"I'm sorry," I said. "It's a terrible loss."

Ruby nodded. "Let's take a look at your hand."

I hesitated. "Are you sure…I mean, you must be grieving…"

"I am," Ruby said, "but he would want me to honor his memory by carrying on his work. And you were injured trying to save his life."

I extended my left hand, still not looking at it. I couldn't feel her touching me, but I did feel the rotation of my wrist as she turned it one way and the other.

"You're right, Rick," she said. "All the bones are there. I think we can reconstruct the hand." She released me, and I lowered my hand out of my line of sight. "Helena," she said, "I don't want to lie to you. This is an extremely complicated magical procedure, and my grandfather was the expert. But with a combination of surgery and magic, I think we stand a good chance of success."

I shuddered. Surgery. "I want you to try. But what happens if you fail? I mean, could you make it worse?"

Ruby considered the question. "That would depend on what you thought of as 'worse.' You might end up with a partially functional hand, or only three fingers. To me, even partially functional is better than what you have now. But you may disagree."

"No, I'd rather have some fingers than none." I took in a deep breath. "How soon can you do it?"

"They're prepping an operating room right now. You will need to change into a hospital gown because it's a surgical procedure." Ruby opened a cabinet and pulled out a pile of cloth. "Take everything off and put this on so the ties are on the side. Then we'll come back for you."

"I'll go," Judy said. "Is there a waiting room?"

"I'll show you," Jeong said. "Good luck, Helena."

Judy hugged me. "I'll tell Malcolm everything when he gets here."

I'd almost forgotten Lucia had called Malcolm, and the thought that I probably wouldn't see him before the procedure made my chest ache. "Thanks."

When everyone was gone, I undressed awkwardly, one-handed, and put on the gown. It was already tied, for which I was grateful because I couldn't have done that myself, but it was loose enough to slip over my head regardless. I'd never had an operation before and was surprised at how comfortable the hospital gown was. All those movies with people walking around with their butts hanging out…either they'd been playing for laughs, or hospitals had gotten fed up with being made fun of and had changed their styles. I sat on the edge of the bed and wished I had slippers. My feet were cold despite the room being the same comfortable temperature all of the Gunther Node was.

In a few minutes, someone knocked on the door and entered without waiting for me to respond. The man was pushing a wheelchair and had a pleasant smile. "Ms. Campbell, I'm your ride," he said. "I know, you're not an invalid, but the floors are cold and hard and we don't want you uncomfortable."

I felt plenty uncomfortable anyway, but decided a wheelchair was better than truly being an invalid and having to go on one of those wheeled beds. The nurse—I assumed that's what he was—tucked a soft blanket over my lap and legs and wheeled me out of the room. I hid my malformed hand under a fold of the blanket and pretended no one was staring at me.

He pushed me down the corridor to Green 1 and then beyond it to a wide door that swung open without being touched as we approached. Beyond lay another corridor, more brightly lit than the main one and with a lower ceiling. It looked like any of the hospitals I'd ever been in and smelled faintly of antiseptic and gardenias. The nurse pushed my chair halfway down the hall and through a door on the left which also swung open without him touching it. If he was doing it with magic, that was quite the useful skill.

The new room, larger than the one where I'd changed,

was just as brightly lit as the hall, but curtains hanging from a rail in the ceiling made it look dimmer even though the curtains were currently drawn back. When they were pulled out, they would surround the operating table at the center of the room, shrouding its occupant and her surgeons. I realized I was shaking and without thinking clasped my hands together —or, rather, put my good hand over the injured one. I wished I hadn't. It felt so wrong, lumpy and too-smooth and more like a leather sack of marbles than a clenched fist. I snatched my hand away and closed it on the armrest, which was cold and angular but at least felt normal.

"Hey, are you cold?" The nurse tucked the blanket more closely around me, then checked my eyes. "You're in shock. Somebody should have noticed that before. Let's get you up here so you can lie down, that will help."

I nodded and let him help me sit on the table, which to my surprise was warm despite being very hard and smooth. "The illusion makes it more comfortable," the nurse said. "Lie back." He spread the blanket over me, and the shakes subsided.

I didn't tell him illusions didn't affect me. At least the warmth was real. The lights were too bright, and I closed my eyes and wished desperately that Malcolm was there. Probably they wouldn't let him be there for the surgery, but I needed his arms around me, if only for a few minutes.

The door opened. "Ready to get started?" Ruby said. "Why is she lying down, Paul?"

"She was in shock," Paul said.

"Not a surprise." Someone put a warm hand on my forehead, and I opened my eyes to see Ruby standing next to me. Rick Jeong was there too, standing beside the door, along with an older man I didn't recognize. All of them were suited for surgery, though none of them wore masks. Since I didn't really know what the point of a surgical mask was, I couldn't tell if this was normal or not.

I drew in a shaky breath. "How long will this take?" I asked.

"We're not sure," Ruby said. "From your perspective, no time at all, because you'll be asleep. Do you want to know the details, or will that make you more worried?"

"I...think I'd like to know."

"All right. Right now, your hand is...you could think of it as a seed pod containing all the bones and flesh of your undamaged hand. We're going to cut into that pod and free what's inside, then rebuild any structures that were destroyed by your encounter with the anchor's field. It's a complex procedure only because hands are complex." Ruby smiled, a reassuring expression that almost made me forget that she'd just used the words "cut" and "rebuild" in relation to my hand.

"I warned you that my grandfather was the one who understood this procedure best," Ruby went on, "but the three of us have enough experience combined that I'm confident this will be successful. You already know Dr. Jeong—" Jeong waved at me. "And this is Dr. Morris. Do you have any other questions?"

"You're all bone magi?"

"Dr. Morris is a facial reconstruction surgeon, not a magus. He's here for the actual surgery and to supervise the reconstruction of your hand. He'll also help with your rehabilitation, if that becomes necessary."

Rehabilitation. I clenched my good hand against a return of the shakes. "I think I want you to start now," I said, "before I think about this too much and freak out."

The three of them chuckled. "See you soon, Helena," Ruby said, and the lights went out.

I blinked. The light was all wrong for early morning and felt artificial, not like sunlight, and my bed was unnaturally hard and tilted up at the head. I scratched my head and felt cloth brush my face. What—?

"Helena," Malcolm said. I blinked again—he wasn't in bed beside me. The bed was too small for that. In fact, it wasn't my bed. Malcolm sat beside me, holding my other hand in both of his. He was unshaven and there were dark rings under his eyes like he hadn't slept in days.

Memory returned. I looked at my left hand, with which I'd scratched my head without thinking. It was heavily bandaged and looked three times its normal size. I sucked in a horrified breath and closed my eyes.

"Calm down, Helena, it's fine," Malcolm said, moving closer and putting his arms around me. "The reconstruction was successful—it's just going to take time to heal completely."

"It looks swollen. It looks like a grapefruit. Malcolm—"

He turned my face toward him and brushed his fingers across my cheek. "There's a plastic ball under the wrappings. It's to hold your fingers in place while the tendons heal so they don't heal crookedly. It's *all right*, love. I wouldn't lie to you." He pressed something small into my right hand. "Don't let this upset you, but your wedding ring was embedded in your flesh. It doesn't look at all damaged."

I examined my ring, a simple gold band that shone brightly under the fluorescent light attached to the wall, and started shaking. I slid my right arm around Malcolm and held him, pressing my face against his bristly cheek. "I'm sorry," I said tearfully. "I believe you, it's just—it's all too much."

"I know." He kissed my damp cheek. "It's perfectly reasonable for you to be upset. In a few days, they'll finish the healing, and the doctors say your hand will be completely restored."

I nodded. "How long did it take?"

"You were in surgery for thirteen hours. I've been here for the last three, waiting for you to wake up—they wanted you to wake naturally so you wouldn't lose any memories."

"I could lose memories?"

"It happens sometimes when you're roused from an induced unconsciousness abruptly. They weren't in any hurry. What do you remember?"

I thought back over the afternoon—yesterday afternoon, according to Malcolm. Wallach's fulcrum and the anchors. The magic, and the anchors vanishing. Wallach diving for the anchor and me trying to stop him. Viv—

"*Viv*," I said, clutching Malcolm's shirt. "What happened? Is she all right?"

Malcolm's face went still. "She's still unconscious," he said. "At least, she was three hours ago when they brought me here. Physically, she's unharmed, but…nobody's ever been struck by that amount of raw magic and survived. So they have no idea what to expect."

I sat up. "I want to see her."

"Not yet. Let me get Dr. Wallach. She'll want to make sure there aren't any lingering effects. Then you can get dressed and we'll go to Viv's room."

I waited impatiently for far too long before Malcolm returned with Ruby. The doctor smiled when she saw me. "You're alert. That's good. Give me your hand—no, your good hand." Her hand was warm and firm and closed over mine reassuringly. "Vitals are all strong, you're breathing naturally, no infections…as soon as we finish the healing of your hand, you'll be as good as new. It's a relief."

"Really?"

"There was a chance the anchor's field might have had lingering effects that could have spread throughout your body. A small chance, so I didn't bring it up, but it would have extended your recovery time by weeks. But everything's fine." She released me and opened a cupboard by the bed. "I want you to relieve yourself before I let you go, just in case there are other problems we weren't aware of. But here are your clothes, and as soon as you've done that, you can go. You'll be hungry in about an hour. Don't gorge yourself or you'll vomit. Malcolm, you'll need to monitor that. Talk to Rick before you leave to set up a time to return for the final healing."

I used the tiny bathroom and felt better. I hadn't realized how much I'd needed to go until I'd peed about a gallon of liquid. Ruby checked my physical condition again, smiled, and said, "I'm glad everything worked out. I'll see you in a few days."

"Why are you a doctor, but Mr. Wallach wasn't?" I blurted out. It was irrelevant, but I'd been wondering it ever since meeting Ruby.

A shadow passed over Ruby's features, and I felt like kicking myself for bringing up her dead grandfather. "Grandpa was too impatient for school," Ruby said. "He left high school at sixteen and then…well, it was the Fifties, and he was a smart black man—even if he hadn't been impatient, it would have been hard for him to get a degree. So he was self-taught for the most part, studied with the Wardens when he could, collected knowledge from all over the place."

She chuckled. "He faced bigotry and racism his whole life and never cared. It was all about the knowledge. I asked him once how it felt being a black man in a white man's world, and he looked at me like that was the dumbest question of all time. Said black and white meant nothing when our world was under siege by monsters that didn't give a damn what color we were. I wish I had that kind of confidence."

"I'm really sorry for your loss," I said.

Ruby nodded. "Thanks. I also wish he'd been less of a stubborn ass, because maybe he'd still be alive. He was convinced this magic would be his legacy. Like he didn't already have a hundred legacies to his name."

I didn't like to say I thought the oracle had been right all along, and Wallach had ignored its advice and that had gotten him killed. It would have been cruel, and it would also have raised the question of why the oracle had apparently given in at the end, if giving in had meant Wallach's death. "I wish it had worked," I said instead.

"Me too." Ruby smiled sadly. "You may have trouble falling asleep tonight. Hot bath, herbal tea or cocoa, and don't force it. See you soon."

Malcolm helped me dress, and we left the room. It was on the opposite side of the corridor to Green 1 from the one I'd been taken to first. I didn't feel wobbly or tired, I wasn't hungry; if not for the continuing numbness of my left hand, I would have felt in perfect condition.

Jeong was at the central desk in Green 1, chatting with one of the nurses. He looked even younger under the lights of the enormous room than he had in Abernathy's. "How old *are* you, anyway?" I blurted out.

He laughed. "I'm twenty-seven," he said. "I have a condition where my body's self-repairing abilities work way too well. Keeps me from aging as fast as the average person. It's a rare side effect of the bone aegis. Feel more confident now?"

"Is it bad for me to say yes?"

"Not really." Jeong pushed off from the desk he was leaning against and picked up a tablet. "Let's see...it will take two days for the tendons to finish repairing themselves—"

"What do you mean?"

He glanced up at me before returning his attention to the screen. "We induced a regenerative field in your hand, very localized, to encourage your tendons to repair themselves. The alternative was keeping you in a medical coma for those two days, something we never like to do because there are potentially harmful side effects. The field will disappear in a few days, at which point we'll complete the healing process. Come back on Tuesday—it can be in the evening, if that's easiest—and...that will be it."

He spoke so casually of regeneration it made my head whirl. Malcolm said, "We'll be there. Thank you, doctor."

"Call me Rick," Jeong said. "I'm glad something in this mess worked out all right."

"I'm sorry about Mr. Wallach," I said.

"Me too. It's a huge loss." Rick looked suddenly even younger, his eyes shadowed with pain and his lips pinched tight. "I can't believe you tried to save him. Didn't you know how dangerous that was?"

"I didn't. I have a history of doing stupid things without realizing how dangerous they are."

Rick smiled. "I'm glad we didn't lose you. Two losses are bad enough."

A chill passed over me. "Two losses? You mean...Viv is dead?"

Malcolm put his arm around me, supporting me as my knees wobbled.

"Oh, no, she's alive," Rick reassured me. "I shouldn't have

said it that way. I don't have any idea of her condition, I'm afraid, but I do know she's not dead. And that means there's hope."

"We're going to see her now, if she's allowed visitors," Malcolm said.

Rick checked a different tablet. "She is. And she has the best bone magi helping her."

"Thanks," I said, but I noticed he hadn't said she would be fine, and that scared me.

20

Malcolm kept his arm around me as we walked back through the halls. I was grateful for his support. Now that my fears for myself were mostly eased, I could focus on my fears for Viv. I needed someone who could tell me what was wrong with her, and more importantly, tell me what it would take for her to recover.

The infirmary corridors all looked the same to me, but Malcolm walked with confidence to a room with the curtain drawn and opened the door. I took two steps inside and stopped, my heart in my throat. Viv lay unmoving in the hospital bed, her bright magenta hair the only spot of color in the room because she was paler than usual, her lips white and cracked, her eyelids sunken. An IV drip led to her left arm, and she was hooked up to a couple of monitors that beeped and hissed quietly. On a rolling bed beside her, Jeremiah stirred and sat up. "Helena," he said, his voice hoarse. "You're well."

I raised my bandaged hand. "Mostly. But Viv—"

"No change," Jeremiah said. He sat with his feet dangling above the floor and ran a hand through his hair, scratching his head. "The accident drained a lot of her magic, but they've restored that and she still won't wake up."

"Does she...what about her brain function?" Just saying the words made me feel ill.

"That's all normal, too," Jeremiah said. He hopped down and took Viv's hand in his. "She's not a vegetable. But they can't get her to wake up." He rubbed the back of her hand with his thumb. "She doesn't respond to anything."

I walked to the other side of the bed. Viv's breathing was shallow but steady, barely noticeable. "She saved us, Rick said. She broke the fulcrum and saved everyone in Abernathy's... maybe saved the oracle too."

"Forgive me for not being comforted by that," Jeremiah said.

"No, I didn't—that's not what I was thinking. I meant, how did she know it would work? The diamond fell off one of the tallest bookcases and didn't even crack when it hit the floor. Viv couldn't possibly do more damage than that. And she knew it was indestructible."

"I don't know," Jeremiah said. "I haven't talked to anyone about what happened. Viv didn't even tell me what she was involved with, working with Wallach—said she wanted it to be a surprise." He laughed bitterly. "That phone call from Lucia was some surprise, all right. The kind of surprise I could go my whole life without getting."

"So you don't know about the realignment magic?"

Jeremiah shook his head. "Are you all right? They said you were caught up in the explosion that killed Wallach and did this to Viv."

"I'm fine, I guess." I pulled a chair next to Viv's bed and

sat. "Mr. Wallach found a way to keep the invaders from getting into our world ever again. He wanted to shift our reality away from theirs, seal the cracks they use to get in. And it almost worked."

"That's insane. No wonder—" Jeremiah closed his mouth, pressing his lips tight against more words escaping.

"No, really, it was working. The anchors—the parts that connected the magic to our reality—they started to move. That's what killed Mr. Wallach. He got caught in the field and it—" I remembered that twisted wax figure and swallowed bile. "And I brushed up against it." I waved my bandaged hand at him again.

Jeremiah nodded. "Was anyone else hurt?"

"No. Just the three of us. It could have been so much worse."

"She's not dead. That means there's hope." Jeremiah didn't sound hopeful.

The door opened, and Lucia entered. She didn't look surprised to see us there. "I understand the surgery was successful," she told me. "Glad to hear it."

From Lucia, that counted as gushing happiness. "Thanks. They'll finish the healing in a few days."

"You're still the luckiest person I've ever met." She stood beside Jeremiah and regarded Viv. "No change?"

"None. Does anyone know what happened yet?" Jeremiah said, his voice tight with frustration.

Lucia didn't take her eyes off Viv. "Pirolli is still analyzing the fulcrum. He and Osenbaugh have recreated the event, as far as possible without repeating it, and he says there was a microcellular event that altered the fulcrum to make it vulnerable to, as he put it, a percussive intervention." She scowled. "He means it was weakened enough that hitting it could break it," she said to my obvious confusion. "God save me from academics."

"But Viv couldn't have known that," I said.

"I won't know what Haley did or did not know until she wakes up." Lucia's scowl deepened. "About all we do know is she bashed it with her toolbox and the fulcrum shattered, releasing all the energy it had absorbed from the node along with its direct connection to the node's energy."

"She should not have survived that," Malcolm said. "The power of a node is fatal to humans."

"I know that, Campbell. She's lucky all it did was drain most of her magic. Right now I have my best minds working on the problem. Haley ought to be dead, or at the very least brain-fried." Jeremiah's exhausted face went paler, but Lucia didn't notice. "I don't even know enough to speculate. It might have something to do with the node itself. Nobody really understands how the named Neutralities affect their nodes, and I only learned the oracle is separate from the node yesterday, so it's even weirder than I thought. Or something about the store's environment affected her. It's all just random guessing at this point."

My stomach chose that moment to rumble with hunger. Lucia's lips curved in a half-smile. "And life goes on," she said.

"Not for everyone," Jeremiah growled. "Don't you dare make light of this, Lucia."

The smile vanished. "I've lost the most brilliant magus this node has ever seen, Washburn. The oracle was nearly destroyed. I am sorry for your personal tragedy, but don't *you* think you're the only one who's suffering here. Haley's alive, and we'll figure out how to rouse her. Until then, I have work to do." She nodded at me. "Are you going back to work tomorrow?"

I'd lost track of what day it was. "I guess so. I feel fine, just hungry. My hand doesn't even hurt."

"I'll have a few auguries for you. Call Judy Rasmussen and let her know you survived. I made her go home around midnight. Right now I have to deal with the fallout from Palembang." She was gone before I could ask what had happened with Palembang. She'd made it sound like everything was well there when we'd spoken before the realignment's failure.

Jeremiah was staring blankly at the wall, his hand closed into a fist. I put my hand on his arm. "She's right. They'll figure it out."

He nodded, but didn't look at me. "Go get some food," he said.

"You should come with us."

He shook his head. "I'm not hungry. I'll have to leave eventually to go to work tomorrow. Until then…I don't want to leave if there's a chance she'll wake."

"I understand." I hugged him impulsively and left.

I thought Malcolm would take me to the central hub to be teleported out of the Gunther Node, but instead he led me along the magenta line to a big, low-ceilinged room that smelled of roast chicken and green beans. "The cafeteria," he said. "It's a little early for lunch, but they feed people twenty-four hours a day."

"I had no idea this was here." The cafeteria was unexpectedly cheery, its walls covered with posters done in a World War II art style, but with slogans altered to apply to fighting the Long War. I gazed at a picture of a Forties-era housewife in a cheerful polka-dot apron whose thought bubble read *What the invaders don't know WILL kill them!* and wondered if there was a Warden marketing department that came up with these things.

Malcolm helped me fill my tray with chicken and a pile of green beans—even the food felt like WWII-era dining—and then cut the chicken into small pieces I could manage. Despite what Ruby had said, I didn't feel much like eating, but my stomach ached with hunger, so I valiantly ate my meal and idly eavesdropped on the few other diners in the room. They weren't talking about anything interesting, but maybe they were just influenced by the poster that read *Be like Dad and Keep Mum!*

While I was eating, Malcolm pulled out his phone and texted someone. Moments later, another phone buzzed with an incoming text. Malcolm withdrew my phone from his back pocket and handed it to me. GLAD YOU'RE WELL. STOP SCARING ME, Judy's message read. I typed a reply one-handed and went back to eating. "I'm glad she went home," I said. "Was I really there for thirteen hours?"

"Sixteen, counting the time it took you to wake up," Malcolm said. He took a drink of coffee, which was all he'd helped himself to, and added, "I'm starting to feel the exhaustion of having fought at Palembang and then spent the night napping fitfully."

I pushed my tray away. "Let's go home, and you can sleep."

Malcolm didn't look as if he were exhausted, but I kept up a steady stream of conversation with him on the drive home anyway, to keep him awake. "Have there been any more attacks?" I asked.

"Not to my knowledge. But I've been preoccupied."

"Lucia would have said something." I stared out the window at the passing cars. I'd lost enough time that I was disoriented by the sun being high in the sky instead of on the horizon the way my body told me it should be. "Was it really that remarkable, the factions fighting as one?"

"It was. Ambrosite teams split up and took the roles the familiars used to play in the fight. It wasn't a perfect integration, but I could see how it will become so. I hope it set an example for the rest of the world."

"Wouldn't it be wonderful if the factions disappeared in our lifetime?" I leaned my head against the glass and breathed in the scent of warm leather and cinnamon air freshener. "Weird, too, but wonderful."

Malcolm rested his hand on my leg, squeezing gently. "I'll believe it when I see it. That's not the sort of animosity that gets set aside overnight. It took me years to overcome my knee-jerk reaction of assuming the worst of Nicolliens."

"But you overcame it. That means it's possible."

"I overcame it in large part because of you, love. Not everyone has that advantage." He pulled into our garage, turned the engine off, but didn't open the door. "Very few Wardens came to this world as adults, free of those prejudices."

"I know. But don't you think there have to be some who are tired of the fighting?"

"I hope so." Malcolm came around to open my door for me, something he did rarely enough that it warmed my heart when he did.

I made him shower and get into bed, something he clearly needed, then cuddled up beside him until he fell asleep. As Ruby had implied, I didn't feel tired myself—well, I'd slept for sixteen hours, so that made sense. I eased myself out of bed, though Malcolm was deeply enough asleep I wouldn't have woken him anyway, and went downstairs to the living room. I settled on the couch and turned on the television, flicking through the channels until I found one showing a dumb game show. I turned the volume low and let my mind wander.

My phone ringing startled me out of a dull reverie. It was Judy. "I'm tired of being patient," she said without preamble, "and I want to know you're all right. A badly-spelled text isn't enough."

"I'm all right. Almost. There's some healing still to finish in a few days."

"And is Viv awake?"

"Not yet." I felt this was an optimistic thing to say. "They still don't know what's wrong."

Judy sighed. "This was a disaster. Is it true it almost killed all of us?"

"I think so. At least, they told me if Viv hadn't done what she did, the field would have engulfed the store."

"And Mr. Wallach is dead. I'm so glad he didn't spread the news around about what he intended. Imagine the whole magical world demoralized today instead of just us."

I hadn't felt demoralized until just then, what with my personal tragedy and my worries about Viv, but now I felt sick and weary. "I hadn't thought of it like that."

"Really? I haven't been able to think of anything else. That was our best chance at stopping the invaders, and now it's back to fighting a defensive war." Her voice was almost plaintive.

I rolled onto my side and hugged a pillow to my chest. "Now I feel tons better, thanks."

"Sorry." Judy sighed again. "Father's been on the phone all morning, organizing training sessions. He and Parish have been working on new fighting strategies that incorporate Ambrosite and Nicollien tactics. He…Helena, it's weird to say this about my own father, but he seems happy for the first time in years. Like he secretly wanted this to happen, except I know that's not true."

"It has to be a burden lifted, don't you think? I mean, being angry all the time…that can't be healthy for anyone."

"That's what I think. He and Mike had a long talk late last night after I got back from the node. They might actually end up friends. Is that bizarre, or what?"

"I hope the rest of the world figures out how much better it is without the factionalism. We need that kind of boost."

"Right. Even if nobody knows how close we came to ending the Long War."

I examined my bandaged hand and wondered how I was going to get a shower. "Lucia sounded like everything hadn't gone well at Palembang. Do you know anything about that?"

Judy sighed. "It was what Mike and Father were talking about—how the invaders kept popping up and then disappearing. It's something the Nicolliens used to train familiars to do. So our teams were successful because every group had someone who could predict where the invaders would appear. But the Nicolliens from other parts of the world were useless without their familiars. *And* the Ambrosites, not ours, the other ones, mocked the Nicolliens like it was all a game, even though they were inefficient too. Mike and Father were both furious about it."

"I wonder if Lucia is going to rip into them. The others, I mean. Now that she has proof that Nicolliens and Ambrosites can work together and are more effective when they do."

"I hope she does. Are you coming in tomorrow?"

"Yeah. I feel fine, except for only having one hand for a few days."

"Good. I was going to visit Viv later today, see if I could talk Jeremiah into going home for some real sleep."

I felt slightly guilty that that hadn't occurred to me. "Good idea. Maybe I—"

"Stay home and rest, Helena. I'll call if anything changes." Judy hung up before I could argue with her.

I turned off the television and lay back on the couch. My mind still felt scrambled, as if everything that had happened in the last twenty-four hours was disconnected from everything else. It seemed impossible that this time yesterday I'd been worried about the fighters going to Palembang and been completely unaware of what waited in my future. But I didn't want to rest. I wanted to do something. Sure, Wallach's plan had failed, but that didn't mean it was time to give up. The problem was I didn't have any idea what I could do short of talking to the oracle, and I'd have to go to the store for that. I wasn't sure driving was a great idea.

On the other hand…I'd communicated with the oracle when I wasn't in its space, and there was no reason I couldn't try that. And even if I didn't succeed, I might manage to calm my fevered brain.

I sat up and rearranged the pillows, then lay back with my hands crossed over my stomach and closed my eyes. It had been an unusually hot day, and the air conditioning was running, a distant purring sound that became louder when I focused on it. I breathed in through my nose, out through my mouth, and listened to the purr. Aside from that, the house was quiet.

I became aware of the thrumming of blood in my ears, a lower sound than the air conditioning. My bare feet rubbed against the couch's suede upholstery, soft and relaxing. I breathed in again and smelled the woody scent of the diffuser on the mantel, faint because it needed to be changed—but thinking about it was a distraction. I focused instead on the feel of the air brushing my face, how my skin tingled with awareness.

Again I felt as if I were sinking into thick, welcoming foam that enveloped me in its warmth and softness. I let my mind wander, not thinking of anything in particular, just waiting for the oracle to speak through me if it wanted to.

My memory touched on a recent augury, nothing special, one of hundreds of auguries I'd performed over the past almost three years. The book had been missing its dust jacket, and its cover was bright cranberry red, the color of my favorite dress. I recalled thinking that at the time, commenting on it to the oracle, who had been paying attention for no reason I could remember.

Helena. Danger. Ending.

I know, I thought, not wanting to disrupt my meditation with speech. *Mr. Wallach is dead. Did you know it would happen?*

Warning. The anchor vanishes. It happens. He is not. He chooses.

But we could have saved him. We could have made him listen.

HE CHOOSES.

The thought reverberated through me, wiping away all other thoughts and making me temporarily numb. *I understand,* I thought. *I wish he'd chosen otherwise.*

The oracle was silent, but the pressure of its awareness bore down on me like a heavy blanket. I embraced the feeling, letting it press me down into the imaginary foam further. After an endless moment, the oracle said, **They fall. The guardians remain. Seal the cracks.**

I don't understand. I thought that was what Mr. Wallach had in mind, and that failed.

Many, few, one. Power strikes. I will end.

Impatience fractured my calm, and I concentrated on my

breathing for a while, hoping I hadn't lost my connection with the oracle. *Do you mean you will end when only one is left? One of what?*

The guardians fall. The guardians remain. I will end. Helena will end.

Do you mean death, or some other ending?

The oracle said nothing, but its attention increased. I had a feeling I'd confused it. *Do you know death? What happened to Mr. Wallach?*

I know ending. He ends. I end. Helena ends.

I drew in a sharp breath, and my connection to the oracle shattered. Breathing heavily, I lay on the couch with my eyes squeezed shut and wiped tears away before they could leak into my ears. That had been about as definitive as I could expect. The oracle had seen our death. Maybe it didn't understand time, maybe it couldn't tell me when it would happen, but I was convinced that waited in my near future.

I wiped away more tears and sat up. Crying wouldn't solve anything. Since the oracle couldn't tell me when it would happen, I could only keep on doing my job and hope that would help the Wardens find another solution to the invaders' attacks. What I was not going to do was give up.

21

I'd never realized how much I depended on having two hands in my job. Some of the auguries were large and heavy, too big for me to easily lift one-handed. I ended up balancing those on my hip like an angular, motionless baby. I took the latest one to the counter and awkwardly heaved it up to lie flat on the countertop. "This one is $1700," I said, flipping the cover open. "Did you have any more requests?"

"That's the last," Dave Henry said. He opened his familiar aluminum briefcase and extracted bundles of cash to hand to Judy. "Thanks. I hope we can get these interpreted before the next attack. It would be nice to go on the offensive for once."

"Is that even possible?"

Dave shrugged. "Maybe. Lucia has some ideas, but I'm not allowed to discuss them. You know how she is."

"I understand."

Dave put the books away in the briefcase and nodded to me and Judy. "Be seeing you."

I accepted the next person's augury slip. The Nicollien

woman was short and slim, built like Judy, but she had the hard look of a front line fighter, and I knew better than to make assumptions. Her question read *Can I trust my new teammates?* I wondered if by "new teammates" she meant Ambrosites, and was tempted to tell her she didn't need an augury for that. Instead, I smiled and walked into the silence of the oracle.

It hadn't paid attention to me all morning, but now I could feel its presence like someone hovering at my shoulder. "I don't know whether to be heartened by this question, or annoyed," I said as I paced the narrow aisles. "I mean, at least she's asking, but on the other hand, she shouldn't have to ask." I pulled the augury off the shelf—a skinny little paperback, fortunately— and headed back for the store front.

The woman was the last of the Nicolliens that morning, and accepted the augury (*Brian's Hunt*) with no change of expression. "Are you forming a new team?" I asked as Judy wrote up her receipt.

She nodded curtly. "I don't like working with new people," she said, "and Ambrosites...don't worry, I won't bad-mouth them, I'm just saying it takes some getting used to. On both sides."

"I understand. Good luck."

When she was gone, Judy said, "How many is that?"

"Fifteen people asked for auguries related to combining forces with Ambrosites. Most of them were positive ones, too. Not passive-aggressive or anything."

"I'm glad. The invaders could attack again at any moment, and we need to be at our strongest." Judy put the receipt book away. "I'll fix lunch."

I leaned against the counter and picked at the bandage on my hand, which still didn't hurt, though my skin itched constantly. Whatever regenerating field the doctors had created, it didn't feel like it was doing anything. It did make me wonder, though, if I would need rehabilitation to get my new tendons working properly. The thought didn't disturb me the way it had a day ago. I'd stopped being freaked out on my own behalf and had moved on to mourning Wallach and being afraid for Viv.

Viv still hadn't woken up. Rick Jeong had come in early this morning to remove what was left of the anchors and had told me there was no change in her condition. Whenever I had a free moment, like now, my thoughts went to her and to Jeremiah. There had to be something I could do—though even I knew that was a ridiculous thought. I hated being helpless.

I went back into the stacks and the oracle's space. "Do *you* know what happened to Viv?" I asked.

The oracle's attention was focused elsewhere. It gave me no answer. "Please," I said. "You were here when it happened. You must know *something*."

Still the oracle said nothing. I leaned against the nearest bookcase and breathed in air scented delicately with lilacs. It was so peaceful I wanted to cry at how little it reflected our world's current situation. Any time now, I expected to hear of a new attack, or of some disaster arising from the fear generated by the attacks.

I walked through the stacks to the break room, which smelled deliciously of pungent dressing and parmesan cheese. Judy was already eating her chicken Caesar salad and only glanced at me when I sat down to mine. "You're worrying again," she said between bites. "You need to stop. It doesn't do anyone any good."

"I know." I took a bite of salad. It tasted as good as it smelled, but I wasn't very hungry. "I can't stop trying to understand the oracle's warnings. It's still telling me we need to seal the cracks. When it bothers to speak to me."

"Lucia will figure it out. Keep her informed about the oracle, and let her deal with it."

I grimaced and laid my fork down. "The oracle is my responsibility. That feels like passing it off to someone else."

"It's more like using your resources. Lucia can do more with that information than we can." Judy swigged some Diet Dr. Pepper and set the bottle down with great deliberation.

"I think—" I stopped speaking as the room swayed around me. "What was that?"

"What was what?"

Another wave of dizziness struck me. **The guardians fall**, the oracle said. **Danger. He flees.**

I gripped the table with my good hand and squeezed my eyes shut in the hope that would control the dizziness. "Something's wrong with one of the other named Neutralities. It's under attack."

"Which one?" Judy demanded.

"I don't know. It could even be both." I fumbled my phone out of my pocket and dropped it when the dizziness struck again, making me feel like the room was spinning like a top. "I think we're under attack, too!"

Judy put a hand on my shoulder. I opened my eyes and had to squeeze them shut immediately because Judy looked like she was tilted almost horizontally. "What's wrong?" she said.

"Can't you feel it?" I thought I might throw up if the movement didn't stop.

"Feel what?"

He flees. The guardians fall. We stand. The oracle's

voice reverberated through me. I risked a peek and saw the room had stopped spinning.

"What was that?" I said.

"Helena, I told you, I didn't feel anything."

"I was talking to the oracle." I crouched to retrieve my phone. The room stayed still. Quickly, I called Lucia and got her voicemail. "One of the other named Neutralities is under attack," I said. "I don't know which." I shoved my phone into my pocket and ran, ignoring Judy's questions, through the stacks and into the oracle. I hurried through the narrow aisles, sidling past the bookcases, until I reached the oracle's heart, a spot where four tall bookcases stood facing each other in a square. The oracle pressed down on me like a giant thumb, and for once I didn't mind.

"What's going on?" I asked. "Something's happening."

They strike. The guardians fall. Stand strong.

"Are we under attack, too?"

We stand. He flees. Listen.

Dizziness hit me again, but faintly, like a memory. I rested my bandaged hand on one of the shelves and closed my eyes again, breathing slowly and letting my sense of the oracle wrap around me like a warm wool blanket, not quite soft enough to be truly comfortable. As I did so, the oracle bore down on me more heavily, making me feel like I was going to burst with its presence. But it stopped short of the point at which I would have to assume its body as I'd done twice before. I hugged it to me and waited.

Every inch of my exposed flesh tingled with goose pimples, and I felt as if I could see through my skin. I gradually became aware of the store surrounding me and remembered how it had felt to be the oracle, how all the books and shelves and walls had been a part of me, and in my imagination I felt that way again. I felt rooted to the floor, strong and immovable, and breathed in the scent of leather and old paper that I realized was the oracle's true scent.

Faintly, I heard cries of panic in a language too garbled to identify. They grew louder, as if a fight had broken out somewhere nearby and was drawing closer. The smell of old paper mingled with the smell of smoke—no, incense, a dark, rich odor that filled my lungs and spread through my body.

Then new sounds arose, terrible, skin-crawling, hissing squeals that came from nothing earthly. As the noise, too, drew closer, I cringed, wishing I could hide from the things that made it. Footsteps echoed through the oracle, the sound of someone running across marble, not linoleum. The person was coming my way. Without opening my eyes, I reached for the runner, found a handful of cloth, and dragged the person toward me.

Whoever it was stumbled and fell into me, knocking me into one of the bookcases. Immediately my sense of the store vanished, and with it the keening, hissing squeal. I opened my eyes. Claude Gauthier sprawled at my feet, breathing heavily, his hair and clothing disordered.

I gaped. "Claude! How—"

He flees. We stand. Here, and there, and here.

"Helena," Claude gasped. "Where are we? Is this Abernathy's?"

I ignored him for the moment. "You did this before, with the other oracle," I said. "But that was because the two of you shared the same oracular space. How did you reach across a continent and an ocean to bring Claude here?"

The oracle was silent, though I still felt its presence. Claude got to his feet and dusted himself off. His eyes were wild, and he was still breathing heavily. "Is it the oracle to whom you speak?" he said in a low voice, like he was afraid of interrupting me.

I nodded and held up a finger, asking him to wait. "Is that too hard a question?" I asked. "Um…can you tell me if we're in danger?"

The guardians fall. Four are gone, two remain. He flees. Here, and there, and here.

"The Athenaeum is gone," I said, and looked at Claude. He nodded. I didn't think he'd heard the oracle speak through my thoughts. "How did we save Claude?"

Again the oracle was silent. Then it said, **We are one. We are apart.**

"I…think this may be too complicated for you to explain to me. We made a connection with the Athenaeum? Could you always do that?"

We are apart. If we touch, we end.

"And the Athenaeum was already lost, so——" A horrible thought struck me. "Can the invaders use that connection to come here? That would bypass the wards, I'm sure."

We are apart.

"All right." I looked at Claude, who was watching me without betraying any of the confusion he might justifiably have felt, what with me talking to the air like that. "I don't know how it worked, but I'm glad. They would have killed you."

"They nearly did," Claude agreed. He looked around with interest. "I have not seen the store ever. It is extraordinary."

I let out a deep breath. "We need to call Lucia. She'll want to know what happened."

My phone rang the instant we left the oracle, as if it had been impatiently waiting for me to emerge into a place that had cell reception. "Which Neutrality?" Lucia demanded.

"The Athenaeum. It's lost. The oracle…I don't know how it happened, but it brought Claude Gauthier to Abernathy's before the invaders got him."

"That's not even the weirdest thing I've heard all week. We can discuss it later. How did they break through the wards?"

"Um…why don't you talk to Claude?" I handed Claude the phone.

As he spoke to Lucia, Judy came through the stacks. She looked pissed. "Why does no one ever tell me what the hell is going on?" she exclaimed. "And where did Claude come from?"

"Switzerland," I said. "I don't know what happened." I described the events of the last few minutes. Judy's expression went from angry to thoughtful. "I think the oracle was able to overlap with the Athenaeum, or something," I finished. "Which means it probably can't do it again, if the Athenaeum is destroyed."

"That sounds dangerous," Judy said. "But what a relief that he wasn't killed."

"Yeah."

Claude abruptly handed me back my phone. Lucia said, "From what Gauthier tells me, Abernathy's isn't in immediate danger. The protections on the store aren't stone wards, so they're not vulnerable to the attack the invaders just pulled on the Athenaeum. I'm sending enforcers to watch the neighborhood in case they try an attack on one of you directly."

"Okay. How likely do you think that is?"

"I no longer know what to expect from them. There were three other simultaneous attacks when they destroyed the Athenaeum. Not cities, but pinpoint attacks on Neutralities in Istanbul, Hong Kong, and outside Scranton. The invaders have changed their tactics again, and I wish I knew why."

"It's like they don't care anymore about preserving our world."

"It—what did you say?" Lucia's voice went sharp.

"Um…that they don't care about preserving our world?"

"Why would you think they ever cared about that?"

Stammering, I said, "It was something that invader told me, about wanting to basically farm us. It made it sound like they wanted cooperation. But this is more like total destruction."

"It is. Damn. I'll call you later." She hung up.

I lowered my phone slowly. "The attack hit more than the named Neutralities," I told Judy and Claude, and related what Lucia had said.

"There has to be some pattern to it," Judy said. "Something those Neutralities all have in common."

"I don't know if that's true," I said. "What if they're just trying to throw the Wardens off-balance? If the real targets are the named Neutralities, and the other attacks are to draw Warden resources away from protecting them—"

"That makes sense, I guess." Judy let out a deep breath. "Only two left. It's terrifying. Makes me wonder what happens if—" Her mouth snapped shut, and she looked away from us.

"That is true," Claude said. "If they are all destroyed, what does that mean? What if the named Neutralities are guardians in a literal sense?"

I nodded. "The Wardens need to stop them before we find that out."

———

It was late afternoon, and I was dusting shelves, before Lucia called again. "You were right," she said. "That's how their tactics have changed. The invaders have given up on the possibility of convincing humans to cooperate, and they're going for total destruction."

"I don't understand," I said. "I thought that was always the plan. That the cooperation thing was a lie they told the Mercy."

"The lie was that they would give power to some humans to make them co-equal with the intelligent invaders." Lucia spoke rapidly, like the words were spilling out of her. "It was always optimal for them to take our world without having to fight for it. Wasted resources and all that. That's been their strategy for over seven hundred years. But now, maybe because of the destruction of their human allies, maybe for some totally different reason, they've settled on breaking humanity. Starting with its defenders."

"So there *is* a pattern to their attacks. There must be. They choose their targets according to what will best defeat the Wardens."

"Smart girl. Yes. We've gone back to our original efforts to analyze the attacks with this new information in mind."

"But the named Neutralities are separate from that pattern."

"What makes you say that?"

"It's just what the oracle has been saying all along, that they're the guardians. I really do think it means that literally. There's something about the named Neutralities that makes them fundamentally important, not just as a distraction to the Wardens."

"You might be right. We'll keep that in mind. Until then, Henry's on his way over again. We need Abernathy's more than ever, now that the Athenaeum is gone. Damn Darius Wallach. I need him too, and—" Lucia's voice was hoarse.

She cleared her throat and said, "Stay safe, Davies," and hung up.

I put my phone away and went back to dusting. It still confused me, the difference between the invaders wanting our cooperation and the invaders wanting our destruction. They needed our magic, and I could understand them wanting it given, if not willingly, then at least without a huge fight. But if they destroyed us, didn't that make our magic inaccessible to them? I wished I understood better what it meant.

Claude was reading in the break room when I finished. It was an ordinary book, not an augury, he'd taken off the shelves. "You want to stay with me and Malcolm?" I asked. "Until we figure out what to do?"

"I do not wish to intrude."

"It's a big house, and I like having guests."

He shrugged. "Very well. I must make calls, and I think, me, that you and I and Samudra should talk. Samudra will need to know how the wards were thwarted, so that he may perhaps stop it happening at the Sanctuary."

"Do *you* know what happened to the wards?"

Claude closed the book over one large knobby finger and pursed his lips in thought. "I told you how the Athenaeum's heart is—was—protected by an impenetrable ward. It appeared to me that they used that impenetrability to their advantage. Their advance force bore similarly unbreakable wards that were...in harmony, perhaps? It is as if their wards confused those on the heart into thinking they were the same, and thus allowed them to pass through." He shook his head ruefully. "We should perhaps be grateful the intelligent invaders were in no position to direct their stupider cousins, all these years."

I thought about what Lucia had said about their intent,

what I had guessed, and said, "I think there were a lot of things we took for granted all those years."

DAVE HENRY CAME in just before closing and apologized for his lateness. "Traffic," he said, handing over an augury slip. I opened it and read *What is the pattern to the invaders' attacks?*

"I hope the oracle can help with this," I said. I folded it into my pocket and walked into the oracle's space—and into the reddish glow of a dying star. My heart sank.

"Are you sure?" I said. "This would make such a difference. I wish I could at least tell Lucia why you won't answer. Is it that there really is no pattern? Or is searching for a pattern the wrong approach?"

I felt the oracle's presence an instant before I thought, **The guardians fall. Four are gone, two remain.**

"Does that mean it's the named Neutralities that matter? Or—I don't know what you mean."

Seal the cracks.

An idea occurred to me. I hurried back to where Dave waited, grabbed the pen beside the ledger, and scribbled out Lucia's question. "Ask something else," I urged, thrusting the paper and pen at him. "Ask 'How do we seal the cracks?'"

"What about the other augury?"

"The oracle refuses to answer. Hurry, try that question. I can't ask for an augury for myself, so you'll have to do it." I was about fifty percent sure the oracle would reject the question on the grounds that I'd given it to Dave, but fifty percent was good enough for me to take the chance.

Dave wrote the question and handed the slip to me. "Thanks," I said, and hurried back into the oracle.

The light was clear and blue-tinted, and I breathed out in relief. "I don't know why this didn't occur to me before," I said as I paced the aisles looking for the augury. "You keep talking about cracks, and it's past time we figured out what it meant."

It didn't take long for me to locate the blue light. I dragged the book off the shelf; it was a weighty hardcover with a lurid cover titled *Plague of Frogs Vol. 1* and looked like a comic book compilation. I tucked it into the crook of my left arm and opened the cover. *Dave Henry, $500* was written there in silver ink. I closed the book and headed for the exit.

Dave raised his eyebrows when he saw the size of the augury. "$500?" he said, opening his briefcase. "Is that good, or bad?"

"I never know." I scrawled out a receipt. "Sometimes I think the cheap ones are because the oracle believes they're important. But then it gives out a cheap one to someone whose request is frivolous, and then I wonder if that's true, or if I'm wrong about what's frivolous."

"I choose to be grateful the oracle answered the question. And hope Lucia isn't so irritated that it wouldn't answer the original question that she doesn't take this one seriously." Dave closed the briefcase and nodded a farewell.

It was six o'clock, so I locked the door behind Dave and then stood for a moment looking through the crystal. Everything beyond was slightly blurry and warped out of true. It felt like a metaphor for my life lately. My relief that I'd withstood the invaders' attack was overwhelmed by my fear about how they'd somehow overcome the wards on the Athenaeum. There was no reason they might not try that here.

My phone rang. I looked at the display, and my heart lurched when I saw Jeremiah's name. "Jeremiah," I said. "Is she awake?"

"No," Jeremiah said. His voice sounded choked. "Helena, it's not good news."

I clutched my phone so hard it hurt. "She's not…"

"She's alive, but…" Jeremiah cleared his throat. "This morning her magic levels were low. They thought it was the normal ebb and flow—it's natural for magic to increase and decrease even over the course of a day. So they replenished them, and by noon they were low again. Her magic keeps draining away, and the mechanism that ought to replenish it naturally isn't working."

"I don't understand. Can't they repair it?"

"That's what I thought. But the bone magi said it's not reacting to anything they do. Like it doesn't respond to their magic and can't be repaired."

I leaned against the counter, afraid I might fall without its support. "That's…what does that mean?"

"It means Viv is dying," Jeremiah said.

22

The monitors hooked up to Viv made occasional hissing, humming noises that sounded overly loud in the quiet room. Viv herself was still and utterly silent, her breathing barely visible as the rise and fall of her chest. Her lips were still pale, but glimmered with the ointment they'd used to treat the dryness. Her skin, always fair even in the heart of summer, was almost white, as if the color had leached away along with her magic. I held her hand, which hung limp and unresponsive in mine. My eyes were painfully dry, and I once again felt numb. This couldn't be happening. Viv could not— My mind sheered away from completing that thought.

"After running a few more tests, I think I know what happened," Rick said, startling me out of my painful reverie. "Viv took the full brunt of the magical backlash, which contained not only the magic the fulcrum had absorbed, but the fulcrum's connection to the node itself. The human body is built to absorb magic—it's how we can be revived if something happens to drain our magic, that ability to take it in. Viv's body tried to protect itself by absorbing some of the magic, diverting it, and it did that to a degree that the backlash only knocked her unconscious."

"Is that why she won't wake up?" Jeremiah asked.

"I'm getting to that." Rick touched the second IV bag, turning it so he could examine its glittering contents. It looked like a sack full of pale blue diamonds. "The problem is the mechanism that regulates magic production was severely damaged by the overload to Viv's system. Not only is it not working, it's too damaged to repair itself, and because it's magical rather than physical, it's not something a bone magus can fix. Viv's using her magic at a normal rate, but it's not being replenished. She's unconscious because…you might think of it like shutting off an overheating computer to keep it from frying itself. When she's unconscious, she uses less of her magic."

"I thought people couldn't use their magic. Isn't that what an aegis is for?" I said.

"Can't use their magic consciously," Rick said. "We use magic passively all the time, sort of like how our blood oxygenates our bodies. This is like if Viv was bleeding from a wound that won't heal."

Jeremiah was as pale as Viv. "Isn't there anything you can do?"

"We can keep her alive indefinitely through transfusions," Rick said, flicking the IV bag with his fingernail. "And I haven't given up on finding an alternative. But I don't want to give you false hope. It doesn't look good."

Malcolm put his arm around my shoulders. I let go of Viv's hand and took Jeremiah's, squeezing it tightly. He didn't respond, and when I looked at his face, I saw his eyes were unfocused as if he were staring at something none of us could see. "Keep trying," he said. "There has to be something. A transplant?"

"Like I said, the mechanism isn't physical," Rick said, "so there's nothing to transplant. You're right, that would be an ideal solution, but it's not possible."

Jeremiah nodded, his eyes still distant.

"Try to get some rest," Rick said to Jeremiah. "She's not in any immediate danger, and we'll call you if there's any change. Or if we have a breakthrough."

Jeremiah looked at Viv. "I can't sleep at home," he said. "It's way too quiet."

"He can stay here, right?" I said. "There's even that bed. It won't disrupt anything."

Rick shrugged. "I don't see why not. I'll let the nurses know. Helena, come with me. I want to look at your hand, as long as you're here."

He ushered me and Malcolm into the next room over, empty even of medical monitors, and gestured to me to sit on the bed. I thought he'd unwrap the bandages, but he just took my good hand in his and closed his eyes. "The regenerative field is starting to fade," he said, "which means it's almost finished healing you. The bones are all strong, though that's no surprise because they were completely intact. Muscles are maybe a little on the underdeveloped side, but some hand exercises will soon fix that." He released me and opened his eyes. "You're going to be fine."

I let out a deep breath. "I'm so relieved."

"Lucia's right, you're incredibly lucky." Rick gripped my shoulder briefly, the gesture of a man much older than he appeared to be. "I'm sorry about your friend."

My smile fell away. "Did she really save us all by breaking the fulcrum?"

"It was fueling the anchors, and the anchors were out of control. Their field would have engulfed the store and everyone in it." Rick looked grim. "She saved us."

I wished that made me feel better.

Neither Malcolm nor I spoke much on the ride home. I was preoccupied with going over everything that had happened and trying to convince myself I couldn't have done any more than I had. My mind kept coming back to Wallach's auguries. The oracle had warned him repeatedly, he'd ignored the warnings, and that was all on his head, but it had warned me too, and I felt that was on *my* head.

"Blaming yourself?" Malcolm said.

I startled. "How did you know?"

"You hum when you're thinking of things you wish you'd done differently. A low note, just for a few seconds."

I'd never noticed that. "I'm sorry."

"You don't owe me an apology. Is there anything you want to talk about?"

"I just wish I'd pushed Mr. Wallach harder about the oracle's warnings. I'm sure he could have figured out a way to fix the problem with the anchors if he hadn't been so impatient."

"I agree. But it was his decision to make, Helena. All you could do was warn. You couldn't force him to be more patient."

"So I need to stop feeling like I failed?"

"That feeling doesn't change the past, does it?"

I sighed. "No. I guess it's part of how I hate feeling helpless.

Malcolm touched my hand lightly. "That's one of the

things I love about you. Though I could do without you almost getting killed."

"I know." I leaned my head against the window. "I wish this war were over. I wish I didn't feel so much like it might end in victory for the invaders."

"We haven't given up yet," Malcolm said.

Claude had already gone to bed when we arrived home. Well, he was still on Switzerland time. I trudged up the stairs and started to undress. I'd worn a pullover shirt and a skirt with an elastic waistband, things I could get into and out of without help, but I felt so unexpectedly weary I struggled anyway.

Malcolm helped me extricate myself from my shirt and unfastened my bra for me. "I wish I weren't so tired," I said, touching his cheek.

He put his arm around my waist and pulled me close. "Soon enough, love," he said, and kissed me lightly, a touch that gradually deepened into something more. It warmed me all over. I kissed him back and felt his hand move down my back to settle on my waist. Maybe I wasn't all that tired.

Malcolm's phone rang.

I cursed. Malcolm chuckled and released me. "Hold that thought," he said, picking up his phone. His face went still as he read the display. "Yes?" he said. The stillness gave way to an intent look. "When? All right. Tell her I'll be ready in ten minutes."

"What's wrong?" I asked when he hung up.

"That was Tinsley," Malcolm said. He stripped off his shirt and went to the dresser, where he took his fatigues out of a drawer. "The Pattern has predicted another attack. If we go now, we'll beat the invaders to it."

I saw my opportunity for an intimate interlude slip away. "Where?"

"The Danvers Node near Toronto. Juliet's ward-stepping here in ten minutes to take me to the Gunther Node." He fastened his pants and sat on the bed to put on his boots. "I'm really sorry about this."

"You know I understand." I found the T-shirt I was using for a nightshirt and pulled it over my head. "Tell the team I wish you all luck. And come back to me."

He smiled, a little ruefully. "I wish I could make that promise."

I went downstairs with him and into our backyard. Juliet Dawes emerged from the wardstone shed as we approached. Juliet was a stone magus and a good friend, but she didn't do more than give me a little wave. "You ready?" she asked Malcolm.

Malcolm nodded. He kissed me, said "I hope to return soon," and entered the shed with Juliet. I watched the shed door close on them, realized my fist was clenched tight, and turned to go back into the house.

The clock on the microwave read 7:46. We'd gone straight from Abernathy's to the Gunther Node to see Viv and hadn't eaten. Malcolm would be starving when he got back. I looked at my bandaged hand with a scowl. "You're not helping," I told it. Cooking one-handed was not an experiment I wanted to try.

I dug around in the fridge until I found a container of leftover cannelloni, one of my favorite foods to make. While it was heating, I ran upstairs and changed my skirt for my pajama pants and felt a little better. When I returned downstairs, I got out a tray and put the cannelloni and a can of Diet Coke on it. I added a hunk of

Italian garlic bread and a couple of snickerdoodles and, balancing the tray carefully, returned to my bedroom. Eating in bed was one of my favorite indulgences when Malcolm was on the hunt.

But it didn't relax me. I couldn't stop thinking about what Malcolm and his team could be facing in Toronto. The Pattern might have predicted this attack, but the Wardens were still fighting a defensive war so long as they couldn't take the fight to the invaders in their space. I popped the can open, using my left arm to hold it close against my chest, and took a long drink. I was not going to sleep until Malcolm was safely home.

I finished my meal and set the tray on Malcolm's side of the bed. Nibbling a cookie, I looked at the TV screen and fought a war with myself. Watching the news would only make me miserable because I was in no position to help. On the other hand, I didn't think I could bear not knowing. I finally gave up and found the remote. The attack might not have started yet. Maybe the world still rolled on in blissful ignorance of what was about to happen in Toronto.

I turned on the television and flicked through channels until I found one of the all-news networks. The newscaster, a slim African-American man, didn't have the manic edge to his voice that would indicate a terrorist attack. He was talking about some summit meeting between world leaders. I moved on. The next news channel showed a man and a woman, both blond and eerily similar to one another in face and build, talking about something the President had done that was either great for the economy or a financial disaster, I couldn't tell which. I was about to change the channel again when the female newscaster got the strangest look on her face, an expression of confusion blended with horror. "I've just been told another terrorist attack," she began, then went silent, listening to an unseen speaker.

"Emily?" her co-host said.

Emily blinked and shook her head slightly. "Toronto is under attack," she said, her voice clear and as calm as if she were reporting sports scores, though her eyes were wide and her pupils dilated. "The terrorist bioweapon has been deployed west of the city. Casualties are already being reported. It's spreading faster than in other cities." Now her voice shook. "There is still no evidence of how the weapon was deployed. No terrorist organization has yet claimed responsibility. The Canadian Armed Forces have mobilized—"

Again, she went silent. Her co-host looked like he wanted to shake the information out of her; he was leaning forward, and his hands gripped the edge of the desk. "That's all we know," she finally said. She turned to look at her co-host with the bleakest expression I'd ever seen anyone wear. "We will have live reporting from the scene when…when someone…"

"We'll be right back," the male newscaster said, and they cut to the station's background screen and theme song.

I drew my legs up to sit cross-legged in the middle of the bed and changed the channel back to the first news station. The newscaster was speaking rapidly in a low, intense voice. "—spreading throughout the greater Toronto area," he said. "The Canadian Armed Forces have set up a cordon to catch the terrorists responsible. Residents of Toronto and the surrounding areas, including Niagara Falls, are urged to stay indoors. More on this as it develops."

That station, too, went to commercial. I muted the TV and took a deep, calming breath. None of this was going the way it should. The Wardens had left in plenty of time to stop the attack, or at least minimize the damage. If this attack was worse—

My phone rang, and I let out a little shriek. I scrabbled it toward me and said, "Judy, did Mike—"

"He left. Are you watching the news? It's awful."

"I don't understand why it's so bad."

"Me neither." Judy blew out her breath; it made a whistling sound in my ear. "They wouldn't report it if the invaders made themselves known, would they?"

"Why would the invaders do that?"

"I don't know. It just seems like the next logical step for them, if they're going for full-on destruction."

I scratched my nose, which was a mistake because the bandaging made it itch more. "They still have to consume our magic. They wouldn't want to do anything that would interfere with that."

"Maybe. If they kill all the Wardens—"

"Hang on. The news is back on." I lowered the phone to my lap and turned up the volume.

"—live from Toronto. Isabella?"

"We've been told the event started in Mississauga, west of Toronto," Isabella said. She was a youthful Latina with her hair pulled back starkly from her face, and she looked as grim as the blonde newscaster had. "The Army has cordoned off the area and begun the evacuation of Toronto to the north and northeast. Prevailing winds are blowing south, and residents of cities on the lake are urged to remain indoors."

"Is this being classed as a terrorist attack similar to what happened in Natchitoches?

"Jackson, the authorities have not made an official statement, but the spread of the disease is what we saw in Natchitoches and in other cities around the world. According to my source, who asked to remain anonymous, the effects of the bioweapon are identical: muscle spasms, followed by heart attack or stroke or both. I think the same unknown terrorist group is responsible here."

"Thank you, Isabella. As yet, no organization has claimed responsibility—"

I shut the TV off. I didn't need to listen to their ignorant speculation. "Judy?"

"Still here."

"When did Mike leave? It seems impossible that they were too late to stop the attack."

"He's been gone almost an hour. Long before they started reporting. I'm worried."

"Me too." I took a bite from my second cookie. "But I don't want to call or text Malcolm and distract him."

Judy didn't reply.

"Judy? You still there?"

"Helena," Judy said in a faint voice. "What channel are you watching? Never mind. Turn to channel eight."

Mystified, I turned on the TV and changed the channel. It was the middle of prime time, but instead of a sitcom, the evening news anchor was speaking. "—live broadcast," he said. "What can you tell us?"

A hissing, bumping noise came over the speaker, the sound of someone fumbling a microphone, and beyond that, a rising and falling hum I couldn't identify. "I'm not sure yet," a male voice said. "We've passed the cordon and no one in authority has seen us yet. The streets are a mess of cars trying to move northeast and people fleeing on foot."

"Are you in danger?" the newscaster asked.

"I don't think so. The previous attacks were all limited in scope, and despite what the Army's said about evacuating, I don't think the bioweapon's range will reach this far. We're going to continue south—wait."

The channel went silent. Finally, the newscaster said, "What's wrong? Keith, what's wrong?"

Keith's heavy breathing came over the microphone. "I thought I saw something, but it's just the lighting here. We're moving on."

"For those of you just joining us, you're listening to Keith Scarren, reporting live from Mississauga, the site of the latest terrorist attack," the newscaster said. "In just a moment, we'll go to Rebecca Hayes for commentary on the tactics used by the terrorists and what we can expect to see as this attack progresses. Keith, any news?"

"We've moved out of the main streets so we can go more quickly, stay away from the evacuees," Keith said. "I don't think—what's that?"

"Keith?"

"I don't understand what I'm seeing," Keith said. "The shadows are moving away from the lights, and—*run, run!*"

The newscaster half-rose from his seat. "Keith? *Keith!*"

A horrible, anguished scream filled my bedroom. I'd heard that sort of scream before. Memories I'd suppressed, memories of seeing a woman writhe in agony as dozens of unbound familiars drained her of her magic, rose up in awful clarity before me. I clutched a pillow to my chest and closed my eyes, incapable of shutting off the sound.

After a few seconds, it cut off as sharply as if I'd found the remote. I opened my eyes. The newscaster looked as horrified as I felt. "We've...lost contact with our correspondent," he said faintly. "We'll try to...to reconnect with him, but now let's go to Rebecca Hayes."

The scene shifted to a plump, attractive woman whose

mouth hung open in astonishment. "I," she began, then fell silent, clearly at a loss for words.

When she didn't continue right away, I told Judy, "That reporter saw the invaders."

"Yes, and was killed by them," Judy said. "Where the hell are our fighters?"

"I wish I knew," I said. I'd never been so afraid for Malcolm in my life.

23

There wasn't anything else to say. Judy and I ended our call; neither of us said it was so we could be free for a call telling us that Malcolm and Mike were okay, but I knew that's what she was thinking. I watched the news channel's "expert" talk a lot of nonsense about the nonexistent terrorists and what their bioweapon was capable of. They never did regain contact with Keith, though I hadn't expected them to. Poor, stupid, dead Keith, who'd gone foolishly into danger and paid for it with his life.

Eventually I startled awake, realized I'd dozed off, and sat up in bed. I didn't want to sleep until I heard from Malcolm, but my body didn't feel the same. I thought about waking Claude to tell him about the attack—all right, I selfishly wanted company—but decided, since there was nothing he could do about it, it was better to let him sleep.

I rearranged the pillows, curled up, and fell asleep thinking of shadows detaching themselves from the bases of lampposts and swarming a crowd of people who screamed and fled.

My phone woke me out of a fitful sleep. I snatched it up, and my heart turned over in my chest when I saw Malcolm's name. SAFE AND WELL LONG STORY HOME SOON.

I clutched the phone to my chest and breathed out a prayer of thanks. After typing out a reply, I lay back on the pillows and closed my eyes. Malcolm's text and my long nap had cleared my head and left me wide awake. Malcolm would know what had happened in Toronto, why it had taken so long and why the invaders had been free to attack that reporter. I had no idea what the world would make of the man's final words, but it couldn't be anything good.

It seemed only minutes before I heard the back door open and close. I flew down the stairs and into Malcolm's arms, holding him tightly enough he let out a gasp. "It's fine," he told me. "We stopped the attack. Not soon enough, but it didn't wipe out Toronto."

"What happened? I was watching the news, and they kept reporting on how the bioweapon was spreading, and the Wardens didn't seem to even be there."

"Come upstairs. I need to get out of these clothes." He smelled terrible, like stale sweat and blood and the bitter tang of gunpowder residue. I followed him into our bathroom and leaned against the door frame as he undressed, too tense even to appreciate the sight.

"The initial attack in Mississauga was a feint," he said as he turned on the shower. "There were so many invaders, we didn't at first realize that the ones we were fighting hadn't attacked any humans. Everywhere we went, the invaders stopped their attack as soon as we showed up. It took us time to recognize where the real attacks were happening and shut them down. By then, the destruction had spread as far as Toronto's city limits, and the place was a disaster—enormous traffic jams, the Canadian Army all over the place, people fleeing on foot."

He was quiet then, lathering up and tilting his head back to rinse his hair. I said, "Did you hear about the reporter who was killed on live TV? How he saw the invaders?"

"I did," Malcolm said grimly. "I think the world has heard it by now. Thankfully, the speculation about his death is all entirely wrong. Though I don't know how anyone would figure out from that recording that he was killed by invaders from another reality."

"That's what I hoped. That they'd think…I don't know. Maybe that the bioweapon makes people delusional before they die."

"I heard someone suggest that very thing." Malcolm stepped out of the shower and toweled off. "But it might not matter. If the invaders continue to display such cunning tactics—"

"The Wardens aren't giving up, are they?"

"No. But I imagine Lucia is formulating a possible plan in which she approaches the mundane governments of the world to tell them the truth and enlist their help."

That struck me to the heart with fear. "That sounds desperate."

"Desperate times, Helena. And I can't say I disagree with the idea. Humans are dying, and if they don't know the truth, they can't defend themselves. As it's clear we Wardens are doing such a damn poor job of defending them."

I put my arms around him. "Don't say that. You're doing your best."

"I am. But the factionalism is still rotting us at the core. I saw more cooperation tonight, but not enough." He sighed and put his arms around me. "I'm exhausted. Let's sleep, and hope tomorrow looks brighter. It certainly can't be bleaker than tonight."

I wished he hadn't said that. It was the sort of statement that could inspire a heartless universe to prove it wrong.

I woke when Malcolm's alarm went off about four hours later and shot upright, propelled by a dream that dissolved around me. All I remembered was the fire alarm going off inside Abernathy's, something I was convinced was true for about twenty seconds until my rational brain told me it was just the alarm clock.

Malcolm slept undisturbed, and for a few minutes I thought about letting him sleep in. Surely there was nothing at Campbell Security so urgent that he had to be there right at nine o'clock? But then I remembered the disaster of the previous night and reluctantly shook him awake.

He woke abruptly, and I snatched my hand away, knowing from previous experience that he sometimes overreacted when he woke from a deep sleep. Blinking, he focused on me.

"The alarm went off," I told him, "and I wasn't sure if you were allowed to sleep in."

"I'm not," he said. "I have to meet with Lucia at eight." He rolled out of bed. "You don't have to get up."

"I'm awake now, and hungry. I'll make breakfast—" I remembered my injured hand and scowled. "Or not."

Claude was in the kitchen eating cereal when I went downstairs. "I hope you do not mind that I took advantage of your hospitality," he said with a smile.

"No, of course not. I'm glad you didn't wait for me. Did you hear what happened last night?"

Claude shook his head. "Was it an attack?"

"The invaders hit Toronto. It was a disaster." I quickly explained what had happened. I was just telling him about the reporter who'd been killed when Malcolm joined us. Claude's expression grew grimmer the longer I spoke.

"The invaders grow bolder," he said. "If we cannot find a way to attack them directly, they will overcome the world."

"I know there are Wardens investigating the possibility of entering the invaders' reality," Malcolm said. He took a couple of bowls out of the cupboard. "But I am afraid their efforts won't bear fruit soon enough."

I retrieved a box of cereal from the pantry and a container of milk and sat opposite Claude. "And there are only two named Neutralities left."

"There is a plan to regain the Well," Malcolm said. "A desperate plan, which seems fitting. But the Well's power might tip the scales in our favor."

"I thought it was too corrupted to be used," I said.

"Corrupted, yes, but too corrupted, no one knows," Claude said. "Repairing the Well requires someone to enter it, and previous attempts have ended in fatalities. But Khalil al-Hussein is a clever man, and I would not be surprised if he had discovered a different path."

The thought cheered me, though my rational brain knew how long a shot it was. "Could we—no, wishing the invaders out of existence is impossible, or they'd have done it before now."

"Correct," Claude said. "But wishing for a weapon that would interrupt their attack, or a device to allow us to pene-trate their reality—those things are not impossible."

I poured myself a bowl of cereal. "Or something that

would seal the cracks? Now that the oracle has told us they exist?"

"That, too," Claude said. "May I join you at Abernathy's today? I will need access to the internet to follow up on my duties."

"Sure. Does anyone know you survived?"

"I texted several people at the nearby nodes." Claude's expression went grim again. "Unfortunately, many died at the Athenaeum who were key to its operation. It means I have fewer people to notify, sadly."

"I'm so sorry."

Claude nodded. "It is a tragedy, but life goes on. We will attempt to regain connection with the tens of thousands of access points throughout the world, and we will see what may yet be done."

I thought he was way more optimistic than I would be in his situation, but I said nothing. I was teetering on the brink of despair and didn't feel like jumping in.

Malcolm dropped us both off at Abernathy's before rushing off to the Gunther Node, promising to return for me in the evening so I could have my hand checked. After he left, I remembered I also had a therapy visit scheduled for that evening. It was going to be a long night.

I got Claude settled at the computer and took my handful of mail-in auguries through the store. As I sorted through them, my phone rang. It was Jeremiah. My heart lurched painfully. "Any change?" I demanded.

"She's restless," Jeremiah said. "Like she's having bad dreams. I hope it means she's near waking up."

"What do the doctors say?"

"They won't commit to anything, but they said it was possible that she was nearing consciousness. But that's a bad thing, if it accelerates her loss of magic." Jeremiah sounded near the breaking point. I couldn't blame him. "It's already accelerating," he went on. "Not much, but they said it was definitely draining faster than yesterday."

"I wish I could be there."

"I took some time off. I don't want to leave her. I'd be useless at work, anyway." Jeremiah laughed bitterly. "I'm useless here."

"Don't think that way," I said. "When she wakes up, she'll need you."

"I'll keep you posted," Jeremiah said. "They say she's in no immediate danger, just—" His voice broke off.

"Thanks. If anything…changes, I'll be there."

I held the phone in both hands after Jeremiah ended the call and stared at the window with ABERNATHY'S painted on it in reverse. Invaders destroying the world, the named Neutralities ending, Viv…it was enough to put me in despair again. And yet, what could I do except my job? I set the phone down and picked up the stack of augury requests. They all seemed so pointless.

As if the universe knew I couldn't handle any more crises, the morning was peaceful. Very few people came into the store, all of them with auguries the oracle fulfilled without fighting me, and we heard nothing more about the attack in Toronto. Claude joined me and Judy for lunch and told us more about the attack on the Athenaeum. Strangely, it didn't discourage me, probably because Claude had survived and was even more optimistic than I usually was.

"I am making plans to resurrect the Athenaeum," he said. "There are records of how it came to be, and I think, me, that it is possible to repeat the experiment."

"So the Athenaeum didn't start out fully-formed?" Judy said.

"It was, in the beginning, merely a power source," Claude said. "Designed to allow us to store records in a time before digital existed. But as the records increased, so did the power source, and as it did so, it seems to have developed a rudimentary consciousness. I do not know how intelligent it was at the end, because I feel when I communicate with it that it holds back. But it was capable of learning and developing on its own. Its new interface, for example. We did not design it to replicate a physical electronic tablet. That was its own creation."

"That makes me even sadder that it's gone," I said. "Like the invaders killed a living thing."

"It angers me," Claude said. "And makes me more determined to see it reborn."

The afternoon was just as quiet as the morning. To my surprise, the few Ambrosites who came in could talk of nothing but working with the Nicolliens in Toronto. "They have techniques we'd never heard of," Allie Sanford told me. "I thought it would be difficult, coordinating with them, I mean, but it's like we fit right into their formations. I wish I could describe how satisfying it felt."

"Is the rest of the world falling in line?"

Allie shrugged. "I hope so. Toronto was a nightmare, and our teams were the only effective ones. I think some of the others have seen that and are willing to give it a try. This is not the time to hold onto old grudges." She laughed. "I'm one to talk. I hated Nicolliens as much as anyone. But now I feel stupid at having felt that way for so long."

Since Allie was a good friend, I refrained from telling her I thought she'd been stupid, too. "So long as it's happening now, I don't think there's any point in dwelling on the past," I said.

Allie saluted me with her augury. "That's very wise. See you later, Helena."

At ten 'til six, I gave the shelves a final dusting and trotted downstairs to put my cleaning supplies away. When I returned to the office, Mike was there, his hand on Judy's shoulder. She wore a furious scowl and had both her hands on her hips. "You don't want to live together," she said, "you just want me where you can keep an eye on me."

"That's a stupid thing to say," Mike said.

"Oh, so I'm stupid now?"

"Sorry," I said, and turned to go.

"It's okay, Helena, we're done talking," Judy said. She stepped away from Mike and sat at the computer.

I hesitated in the doorway. Mike let out a deep, frustrated breath and headed for the back door. I glanced at Judy, whose eyes were bright with tears, and said, "Mike. Wait."

Mike turned. "Yeah?"

It was none of my business, but I couldn't bear any more tragedy. "Judy wants to move in with you."

"Helena!" Judy exclaimed.

"She doesn't," Mike said flatly. "She's made that clear."

"Only because she doesn't want you to do it out of pity." I avoided looking at Judy, who I was sure was glaring at me. "She wants it to be what you want."

"Of course it's what I want!" Mike said, throwing up his arms.

"There's no room for me in your life," Judy said. "We might as well admit that."

Mike swore explosively. "You're so damned independent,"

he said. "You don't want to give that up. I've been trying to get you to come over for days now, and you keep putting me off."

"I don't see why you care," Judy shot back. "You're so protective of your personal space, there's no way I can fit in there."

Mike's jaw tightened. "That's not true."

Judy arched an eyebrow at him. "Isn't it?"

He shook his head. "I cleaned it up," he said.

"You what?" Judy said.

"I cleaned. I rearranged the living room. I bought another dresser so you'd have space for your things and cleaned out half the closet. There's even a laundry basket in the corner of the bedroom. It was *supposed* to be a surprise, but you're so damned stubborn you didn't take any of the hints I dropped."

"I hate surprises," Judy said, her voice faint. "Mike…you didn't have to do that."

"I want you to live with me," Mike said. "So yeah, I had to do that."

Judy stood. "I didn't know. I'm sorry."

She walked toward him. He met her halfway.

I backed out of the room and shut the door on the two of them kissing. My heart felt lighter than it had in days. Of course, now I couldn't leave the store, but I could give them a few minutes.

MALCOLM and I dropped Claude off at our house before stopping for cheeseburgers and heading for the Gunther Node. I ate happily and told Malcolm what had happened with Mike and Judy in between bites. "I'm glad I said something, because I couldn't stand the thought of them going on fighting," I said.

"They're both independent enough I'm surprised they make it work," Malcolm said. "I would have bet hard money that Mike would never settle down. I wonder if he just needed to find a woman he didn't feel depended on him for everything."

"Judy's definitely not that. Not that she doesn't depend on him, but she doesn't have her whole life wrapped up around him—is that what you mean?"

"Yes, exactly that. I hope they're happy together."

"And Mr. Rasmussen and Mike are getting along. You know, I feel like things might not be so terrible after all. Is that bad? Given that the world is in danger?"

Malcolm took the freeway exit to the Gunther Node and waited at the top of the ramp for the light to change. "I think humans can only take so much misery before something gives. Looking for moments of happiness when tragedy strikes is normal. It doesn't mean we don't take tragedy seriously, it just means we need a balance."

"I hope that's true. It's like what I'm doing in going to therapy—learning to accept the bad things that have happened without letting them overwhelm me."

"And remembering the good things that have happened, too."

I put my hand on his knee and squeezed gently. "So many good things."

Rick Jeong wasn't in Green 1 when we arrived, but he'd left a message that he'd be back in an hour or so. Just enough time for me to see Sydney. I left Malcolm waiting and found my own way to Sydney's office, knocked, and waited for her to let me in. Today she wore a flowing dress in emerald green with a colorful peacock embroidered on the skirt. "How are you today, Helena?" she asked.

I settled myself in my usual chair. "Better than I was this morning."

"Oh? Why is that?"

I explained about how despairing I'd felt over the attack in Toronto and the destruction of the Athenaeum, and how I was happy for Judy and Mike. "I don't know why something relatively small could offset something as large as the near-destruction of a city," I said, "unless it's because the small thing is personal. But I feel more positive, like the Wardens will figure this out."

"I think you're right about how we're affected more strongly by personal things." Sydney shifted her weight and propped her elbow on her chair's arm. "Speaking of being affected, did you write out the descriptions of the three events?"

"Yeah. It was…freeing, actually. I haven't been disturbed by those memories since. But it feels like that's too easy. If all it takes to overcome trauma is to write about it, nobody would ever need a therapist."

Sydney laughed. "You're right, it's not that easy. But sometimes, giving ourselves permission to relive events in a safe space opens the door to finally beginning to heal. Tell me, did you learn anything new about those events? A new perspective, or a detail you'd forgotten?"

I remembered my breakthrough in understanding why being shot by Malcolm had been so terrible. "Yeah. There were a few things I'd never realized."

"Seeing things from a different perspective helps break you out of the self-destructive pattern you've been trapped in, where you involuntarily recall painful memories. The more you can do that, the easier it will become."

I nodded. "That makes sense."

"Tell me about your mindfulness exercises," Sydney continued. "How are they going?"

"I'm not good at them yet," I confessed, "and that's probably because I don't practice often. But a strange thing happened with my meditation. It's brought me closer to the oracle, close enough that I've made contact with it while I wasn't in its space."

Sydney's eyes narrowed in thought. "What does that mean?"

I explained about the oracle's presence and how I'd spoken to it often in the last year, and added, "The point is that the oracle exists within the bookshelves of Abernathy's, but a few times, I've meditated and spoken to it while I wasn't in that space. I don't know what it means."

"I don't know anything about the oracle, so I can't help you," Sydney said, "but it sounds like when you meditate successfully, you make yourself receptive to the oracle's communication. I assume it exists all the time, and not just when the oracular space is active?"

"I think so. I have the feeling it has things it does when it's not talking to me, and I don't think it simply stops being just because I'm not there."

"And what has the oracle said to you during your meditation? Is its communication different from when you're in its space?"

I shook my head. "No, it's always the same sort of thing. Warnings, mostly."

"Then I'd encourage you to seek it out. Maybe it understands more than you think."

"That's almost certainly true," I said.

We talked a while longer about mindfulness and what had happened at laser tag, and when Sydney said, "I think we'll continue this next week," I was surprised at how fast the time had passed. She escorted me back to Green 1, where we said goodbye.

To my surprise, Malcolm was gone. I tried texting him, but as usual had no signal. Rick wasn't there, and the nurses at the central island were busy and paid me no attention. I decided to visit Viv as long as no one else was demanding my time. This was the Gunther Node's quiet time, when everyone was either going off-shift or eating dinner, and despite my returning anxiety over Viv, I felt at peace.

When I'd nearly reached Viv's door, it opened, and Malcolm emerged. He seemed surprised to see me. "Helena, come quickly," he said.

My peaceful feeling evaporated, and I ran the last few steps to his side. "What's wrong? Is she—"

"Viv's still unconscious," Malcolm said. He held the door open for me. "But there's been a change."

Viv looked exactly as she had the last time I'd seen her, white and still like a wax figure. Jeremiah stood beside her, his hands closed loosely into fists and his head lowered. Rick held one of Viv's hands and had his eyes closed. When I entered, he looked at me with those too-young eyes and said, "Viv's magic is draining more rapidly. There's going to be a point past which transfusions will be ineffective."

I felt like he'd punched me in the stomach. "When?" I managed faintly.

"I don't know for sure. A few days." Rick laid Viv's hand down and flicked the glittering diamond IV bag with his fingernail. "But we have a solution."

I sucked in a breath. "Why didn't you start with that?"

"Because it's impossible," Jeremiah said. "They'd have to give Viv an aegis."

M y mouth fell open. "An aegis?"

"In a magus, the aegis acts as a secondary control system," Rick said. "It regulates magic production and distribution, which is how it lets the magus tap into his or her own magic. If the aegis is damaged or destroyed, the person's own system picks up the slack. But that means the opposite must be true—if the natural mechanism regulating magic is damaged, an aegis should be able to take its place."

"Must be?" I said. "Should be? Those sound like it's never been tried before."

"It hasn't," Jeremiah said. "And it's impossible. She's unconscious, damn it, there's no way she can consent to the Damerel rites."

He sounded so angry I was taken aback. "But—it would be to save her life. Do they need consent under these circumstances?"

"Not that kind of consent," Malcolm said. "You remember when I received my new aegis I had to make the conscious decision to accept it. A person must be awake and clear-headed to undergo Damerel."

"And nobody knows if she's even a viable candidate," Jeremiah said. He glared at Rick, who was unmoved by his hostility. "It'd just be another kind of death sentence."

"With this, she has a chance," Rick said. "It's certain death if we do nothing."

I put my hand on Jeremiah's arm, which tensed. "He's right," I said. "You know Viv wouldn't hesitate to take the chance."

"Viv's reckless." Jeremiah closed his eyes. "But it doesn't matter. If they can't get her to wake up, she can't have the aegis implanted."

"I'm working on that," Rick said. "But we won't do anything unless you give us permission."

"I can't do that. I don't own her."

"You know her better than anyone. And giving permission is the wrong word. More like…confirming that it's what Viv would want." Rick glanced my way. "But you need to make the decision soon."

Jeremiah let out a deep breath. "All right," he said, looking at me. "If she were conscious, she wouldn't think twice about it." He smiled, a little half-twist of his lips. "She'd probably be excited."

"Then think about what aegis would suit her best," Rick said, "and I'll work on rousing her and putting a team together for the Damerel rites. Helena, why don't you come with me and we'll take care of your hand first."

I'd forgotten the other reason I'd come to the Gunther Node that evening. I squeezed Jeremiah's arm lightly and then followed Rick to another room down the hall, holding

Malcolm's hand. Rick had me sit on the unmade bed and took my bandaged hand gently in his.

"It may look a little strange," he warned me. When I stiffened, he laughed and said, "Not deformed. I mean the skin may be slightly discolored or mottled and your fingernails will be rather long. A side effect of the regeneration field." He unwrapped the bandaging to reveal a hard white plastic ball around which my fingers curled, just as if I were preparing to pitch a softball. When he removed it, the stiffness I'd felt the last few days disappeared, and my fingers felt light and untethered to my hand. I held still, afraid to move them.

Each finger had been individually bandaged, and once the outer wrappings and the ball were gone, I looked like a mummy, though one the years had been kind to. Rick carefully removed the rest of the bandages. He was right, my skin looked yellow and dry in the fluorescent lights of the hospital room, and my nails were at least half an inch long.

"Okay, Helena, I want you to close your hand," Rick said.

I tried, and my fingers quivered but didn't move. "It's all right," Rick said, seeing my distress, "you're just stiff from not moving that hand for a few days. Pretend you're closing your hand on a doorknob."

I closed my eyes and pretended I was reaching for the door. Slowly, my fingers contracted—not much, but enough that I could feel it. It didn't hurt, just felt tight like I was squeezing a rubber ball. I opened my eyes. I thought I'd closed it more than that.

"I'll give you some exercises to work on your mobility," Rick said. "Your skin color should return to normal eventually—I'm sorry I can't tell you how long. You can use ordinary lotion to treat the dryness. Keep it out of direct sunlight for a week, wear gloves if you can, and call me if you feel any pain or numbness. But it looks perfect."

I brought my hand close to my eyes. It looked exactly as it always did, except the scar in the web of my palm where I'd cut myself in tenth grade art class was gone. In fact, my skin, aside from being yellow, was free from the few dark brown beauty marks I'd always had and looked…perfect. I felt along the bones of my fingers and the center of my palm. "I can't believe it," I said. "It's completely restored."

"You can thank Dr. Morris for that," Rick said. "He's a craftsman. Ruby and I just healed the surgical incisions so you wouldn't scar and created the regenerative field."

"Even that's more than enough. Thank you, Rick."

"It was my pleasure. We're all putting it on our CVs. Makes us look impressive." Rick grinned, and I smiled back.

Malcolm put his arm around my shoulders and hugged me. "I'm so relieved," he said.

"Were you worried?" Rick said.

"Yes. Reconstruction on the level you described…I didn't say anything, because I didn't want to worry Helena, but I knew how difficult it would be."

"Thank you for not saying that," I said. "I would have freaked out."

"I have to go," Rick said. "I have a theory I want to test, a technique that will wake Viv long enough for us to perform the Damerel rites. I'll send Ruby to talk to you and Jeremiah about Viv's aegis."

"Me? Why me?"

"You're her closest friend. Once I wake her, we'll only have a short time before her magic drains permanently. There won't be time for her to make a decision on what aegis she feels drawn to. So you and Jeremiah will have to figure that out."

Rick ran a hand through his hair, messing it up further. "Ruby will supervise the creation of the aegis. All we have to do is get Viv conscious, and...really, I think this will work."

I didn't feel nearly so confident, but I nodded.

When Malcolm and I returned to Viv's room, Jeremiah was sitting in the room's lone chair with his head in his hands. "I can't do this," he said.

"Jeremiah, it will save her life," I said.

He looked up at me, his gaze as bleak and hopeless as I'd ever seen. "We're talking about a procedure that has a ten percent failure rate even in a healthy, prepared candidate. How prepared can she be, if she wakes up to a bunch of people gabbling at her about what happened and what they want her to do? There's no way this can work."

"The alternative is that she slips away from us," I said. "I can't bear that. And I'm sure Rick and the other bone magi will work out how to make it as safe as possible."

Jeremiah turned to look at Viv's still face. She moved just then, twitched as if she were aware of his regard. Her lips turned down in a frown, parting slightly, and her hands atop the blanket closed into loose fists. I gasped and took a few steps to stand by her side.

"It's an autonomic reaction," Jeremiah said. "They think she might actually be dreaming, based on her brain activity. So she's still herself in there. Helena, if she dies from the Damerel rites, I might as well have killed her."

"Don't think that way!" Anger flooded through me, and I almost slapped him for being so self-centered. Instead, I said, "You're not the only responsible one. I am too. Stop thinking of yourself and think of Viv. They want us to choose an aegis for her—does it have to be a specific one?"

Jeremiah sighed. "The aegis is supposed to be something

you have an affinity for. Like how front line fighters with the wood or steel aegis are usually the type of people who have a strong urge to fight evil. The sort of people who'd be police officers or soldiers under other circumstances. But Viv isn't awake to make that decision."

"So it's up to us."

Malcolm said, "You should consider Viv's personality and desires. Often the choice of aegis is obvious."

I thought about it. Not wood or steel. Viv was squeamish, so not bone. Malcolm was right, the choice was obvious. "Glass," I said. "She's perceptive and good at seeing to the heart of things."

Jeremiah's face cleared. "That's what I was about to say."

"Which means good things, right? That it was obvious to both of us?" I squeezed Viv's hand, which was cold and once again limp. "Just think how excited she'll be to be a magus."

A smile touched Jeremiah's lips. "True. I don't think it's anything she ever considered seriously, but she's griped so much about not having telekinesis whenever the remote is too far away, I think…I think she'll love it."

The door opened, and Ruby Wallach walked in. "So, we have a plan," she said with a smile. "This must be what Grandpa felt like all the time."

"We think it should be a glass aegis," Jeremiah said.

"That should be fairly simple to produce." Ruby checked Viv's vital signs. A cloud passed over her face briefly. "Good thing, because we have less time than I thought. No, don't worry, it's not urgent," she said, forestalling Jeremiah's protest, "it's just that the lower her magical reserves during Damerel, the less time we'll have for implantation. So the sooner we can do this, the better."

"How soon?" Malcolm asked.

Ruby's eyes went distant with calculation. "Tomorrow at seven a.m. Excuse me, I need to get someone working on that aegis. Go home and get some sleep, all of you. I'm sure you'll want to be here for this."

Jeremiah and I looked at each other. It was the understatement of the century.

AT 6:15 the following morning, Malcolm and I were on the freeway headed for the Gunther Node. We'd said goodbye to Claude earlier as he prepared to return to Switzerland. "It is all right, yes, to use your wardstone?" he'd said. "I have appreciated your hospitality."

"Of course," I'd replied. "I'm so glad we could put you up —and that you survived."

"I will contact you later, when I know the status of the Athenaeum," he'd said. "But if we are to restore it, it will be many months, perhaps years. It is better than 'never,' but I fear the Athenaeum will be of no immediate use in the fight. Again, I am angry, but there is nothing else I can do."

It made me angry, too, angry and worried. As each named Neutrality slipped away from us, it felt even more like we were headed for disaster. Whatever might happen if they all were destroyed didn't bear thinking about.

I tucked my hand under my leg—the dawn light was pale and slanted toward us from the east, but I was superstitious that if I exposed my hand to any sunlight, it would stay yellow forever—and traced the line of the door handle. "How many of these have you seen? Aside from the two you were in?"

Malcolm glanced my way. "Of the Damerel rites? Ah…

ten, I think. No, nine. The tenth was aborted by the partici-
pant, who changed his mind before it began. So, nine."

"And were they all successful?"

Malcolm's peaceful expression gave way to a frown. "Two
of them failed. One was someone who should never have
undertaken Damerel, but we couldn't convince her of that.
The other...just failed. Occasionally that happens."

"Oh."

"Don't let that upset you, Helena. Viv has as good a
chance as anyone. Maybe better, because she's a survivor, and
that matters." He took the freeway exit and turned right.
"Have faith."

Faith. I clung to that. It was all that was left to me.

Someone was waiting at the teleportation circle that served
as the entrance to the Gunther Node. He nodded to us as we
joined him inside the circle. Holding a plastic card attached to
a lanyard around his neck, he knelt and dipped the card into a
thin slit like running a credit card. "Three," he said, and in an
instant we were in the great central hub. This morning, it
smelled like maple syrup overlaying the usual gardenia scent.
"Waffle Wednesday," the tech explained, and shooed us out of
the circle before disappearing.

I took Malcolm's hand, and we followed the green line
down the infirmary corridor all the way to Green 1. We saw
Rick there, talking to a large man in teal scrubs whose tidy
blond beard made him look like a well-groomed Viking. Rick
waved us over. "This is Earl Kirschbaum," he said. "He's a
bone magus from Yakima who's done a lot of work in sports
medicine. I asked him to assist in rousing Viv because he
understands head trauma, which has some similarities to her
condition."

Malcolm and I introduced ourselves. Kirschbaum shook

hands politely. "Friends of Ms. Haley?" he said. "I have to warn you, this is not going to be pretty. She'd be disoriented even if all we did was wake her, but the amount of information we have to throw at her…you need to be prepared to be a calming influence."

"We understand," Malcolm said. "Is there anything in particular we need to be aware of? Anything to do?"

Kirschbaum scratched his beard. "Usually, rousing someone who's unconscious is a simple matter of goosing the autonomic system. It's confusing as hell to the patient, but sometimes it's necessary. The problem here is that Ms. Haley needs to be clear-headed for Damerel, and she hasn't responded to that intervention anyway. So that method is useless."

"Earl has something different he's tried in the past," Rick said. "We're going to shock her system with an influx of *sanguinis sapiens*. Processed, of course, but a concentrated dose."

"Isn't that dangerous?" I said. "It sounds like what caused the damage in the first place, being hit by a high dose of magical energy."

"That was raw, unprocessed magic," Rick said. "This is distilled, refined…you might think of it as magic with the rough edges filed off. It's true too much of it could be dangerous, but only in the sense that any drug is dangerous in high enough doses. We propose to give her just enough to wake her. But there is a different kind of danger involved."

Kirschbaum said, "The danger is combining this treatment with Damerel. She's going to have a lot of magical energy flooding her system, which could interfere with implantation of the aegis. With Mr. Wallach not here to supervise her body's resonance, we have to wait a while for that magical energy to work its way through her to a manageable level. And I'm told, with her own magic draining away, time is not something we have a lot of."

I realized I was clutching Malcolm's hand hard and released him only to have him grip my hand in turn. "But won't that magical boost increase her body's magic?"

"Not by as much as you'd think," Rick said. "It might give us a few extra minutes. Of course, even a few minutes could make a difference." He tapped the Fitbit he wore on his right wrist and checked the time. "Let's go in. Jeremiah and Judy Rasmussen are already here, and we need to discuss what will happen once Viv wakes."

He led us out of Green 1 and down two levels along the red line to a door labeled 36. I'd been here before, when Malcolm received his second aegis. It looked just as it had the other times I'd been there: bright, soft-edged LED lighting, cabinets along the far wall, a padded operating table in the center of the room. It gleamed with whiteness and resembled a film set for a science fiction movie about abnormally hygienic aliens. Jeremiah leaned against the wall, staring at nothing. His hard, emotionless look frightened me. I hoped he hadn't changed his mind. Judy stood beside him, looking as if she'd tried to make conversation and failed.

I eyed the table, which had white leather straps with buckles dangling from it on all sides. "You're not going to strap her down before you wake her, are you?" I said. "Because if it were me, I'd be freaked out if I woke up bound."

"No, you're right," Rick said. "It would save time in one respect, but we'd lose time calming her down, so it's a wash."

"Just tell us what to do," Jeremiah said. His voice, by contrast to his face, was calm, which relieved me somewhat.

Rick nodded. "Here's what will happen. We'll bring Viv in

and get her settled on the table. Earl will then boost the magic going into her system."

"There's no way to know how soon that will wake her," Kirschbaum said. "But when she wakes, she'll be a little disoriented. Jeremiah, you'll need to be the first thing she sees. You'll tell her everything we discussed."

Jeremiah nodded.

"Helena, when Jeremiah finishes, you'll talk to her," Kirschbaum went on. "Reassure her that she can do this. Tell her about seeing Damerel before and be honest with her that it's going to hurt. She needs to hear this from people she trusts instead of strangers."

"I understand," I said.

Kirschbaum looked at Rick. "That's it," he said. "Nothing left but to go for it."

"Just remember," Rick said, "we don't have a ton of time. Be thorough, but be concise. I realize that's asking a lot."

"Just…let's get this over with," Jeremiah said.

Rick raised his Fitbit to his lips and murmured something into it. So it wasn't just for tracking his movement. I made Jeremiah look at me. "This will work," I said.

Jeremiah's expression was bleak. "I hope so."

"If you are not convinced, Viv will know," Malcolm said. "You need to be optimistic for her sake."

"Please don't let Viv see how worried you are," Judy said. "It could be fatal."

Jeremiah nodded again, took a deep breath, and let it out slowly. "I survived this," he said, "and she's tougher than I am. It will work."

The door opened, and a handful of people in scrubs filed in, including… "Harriet!" I exclaimed, and went forward to hug her. "I didn't know you'd be here."

"I thought it might help," Harriet Keller said. "I created Viv's aegis, so it was reasonable to have me on the Damerel team."

I suddenly felt about ten pounds lighter. "I know she'll appreciate having a friend involved."

Harriet held up a Plexiglas ball about two inches in diameter. "Take a look."

The aegis floated on end inside, a needle less than an inch long and glittering like a diamond. It was so beautiful I forgot that it was going to be inserted into my best friend's heart. "I didn't know you could do that."

"It was what I did for many years once I started having children and left the front lines." Harriet tucked the ball into her pocket. "Poor Viv. This isn't anything I ever imagined for her."

"Me neither."

We stepped back from the table as a pair of orderlies pushed another hospital bed into the room, making it extremely crowded. Viv lay as still as when I'd seen her last, her arm still connected to the IV bags. She was naked from the waist up, with a blanket covering her breasts, though I was sure under these circumstances she wouldn't care about modesty. The orderlies didn't touch her, but as soon as the bed came to a stop next to the operating table, Viv floated off it and swiftly came to lie on the table without disturbing the blanket. The orderlies arranged the IV bags and wheeled the bed out.

"Everyone, stand back," Rick said. "Ruby?"

"Remember how we practiced this," Ruby said. "Rick will give the word when it's time to begin. We're short on time, but don't let that turn into sloppiness. I will count off the time. Any questions?" She looked in my direction. "From anyone?"

I shook my head. I couldn't think of anything to say.

"Then…good fortune to us, and God bless," Ruby said.

The magi in scrubs, six in lavender, two in pure white, stepped back from the table all the way to the walls. Kirschbaum crossed the room to the cabinets and withdrew an IV bag. It glittered like the one already attached to Viv, but with the purplish-blue tinge of *sanguinis sapiens*. I'd seen *sanguinis sapiens* in liquid form many times, but never like this.

Rick was already removing the other IV bags. Kirschbaum carried the bag like it was an unexploded grenade and hooked it up, uncurling the plastic tube that fed off it and connecting it to the valve in Viv's arm. Nothing happened. Kirschbaum checked the connection, waited for Rick to take Viv's other hand, then did something to the bag that turned the plastic piping purple-blue.

Still nothing happened. Viv didn't move. Rick's expression was remote, as if he was listening to faint music and needed all his concentration to make it out. My chest ached from me holding my breath.

Viv twitched. Her hand closed slowly, then opened again. Her eyelids fluttered open. Her body tensed like she'd tried to sit up, and her right hand went to the place where the IV entered her left arm. Rick grabbed her hand and nodded to Jeremiah, who left his place beside me and crossed the room to take Viv's hand from Rick.

"Sweetheart, it's all right," he said. "What do you remember?"

Viv blinked again. "I—the magic failed," she said. "The anchors vanished too quickly." Her voice was quiet, dry and scratchy like a rasp.

"That's right." Jeremiah drew a deep breath. "You broke

the fulcrum, and it knocked you unconscious. You've been unconscious for several days."

Viv coughed. "Several days?"

"Yes, and there's more." He kissed the back of her hand. "You were injured. The part of you that regulates your magic is broken. It can't be repaired."

"Oh," Viv said. "It...I don't understand. Am I dying? I need magic to live, right?"

"That's right. But we have a solution. If you receive an aegis, it will take over the job of regulating your magic. It will save your life."

Viv licked her dry lips and whispered, "I can't be a magus. That's not possible."

"It's possible," Jeremiah said. "But you have to make the decision yourself, and you have to make it soon. Every moment you're awake, more of your magic drains away."

Rick beckoned to me. "Helena. Judy."

I jerked upright and hurried to the other side of the table, followed by Judy. "You can do this," I said. "You just have to want it more than anything, and for you, that means wanting to live."

"Helena," Viv said, turning her gaze on me. Her eyes were deeply shadowed and gleaming with tears, sure sign that she was about to break down. "What do I do?"

I took her other hand. "It's painful," I said. "I won't lie to you. You have to be strapped down so you don't hurt yourself. When Malcolm went through it, he was in so much pain, and he nearly didn't recover. But you're strong, and I know you can endure this. Please, Viv. We don't want to lose you."

Viv looked from me to Jeremiah, who actually was crying. Her jaw firmed. "If it's my only chance at life, I'll take it."

I bowed my head in relief. "We'll be here the whole time."

I went back to stand by Malcolm, who put his arm around my shoulder. Judy resumed her place holding up the wall, but I saw her rub her eyes and knew she wasn't as calm as she seemed. Jeremiah was talking to Viv in a low voice, words I couldn't make out, but she smiled. He kissed her, nodded to Rick, and stepped away.

"That's it, people, let's do this," Ruby said. The lavender- and white-suited magi surrounded the table, all of them working the leather straps to hold Viv down. The magi on my side of the table pulled out an extension and strapped Viv's arm to it, swiftly removing the IV and making Viv cry out weakly. Jeremiah twitched as if he wanted to go to her, but stayed put. All I could see of her was that arm, buckled down securely, her skin nearly as pale as the leather.

Then they were done, and all movement ceased. For the longest time, nothing happened except Ruby, who stood by Viv's head, stared at her enormous diver's watch. Finally, she looked up. "Twenty-two minutes," she said. "Begin now."

It didn't look like they were doing anything. The two white-suited magi flanking Ruby put their hands on Viv's shoulders. The other magi just stood there. Harriet, next to one of the white magi, had her back to me. The back of her light gray hair was flattened as if she'd just gotten out of bed for this. I took Malcolm's hand and crushed it in mine. He hugged me closer. His warm, strong presence reassured me. I closed my eyes and prayed more fervently than I ever had before.

A low moan broke me out of my devotions. Viv's hand was clenched tight, and as I watched, she let out another moan. "It's all right, Viv, don't hold back," Ruby said.

The air around the table wavered like heat haze and stank of ozone and the sharp smell of magic. Viv moaned again, louder this time, and her arm strained helplessly against the leather straps.

"Fifteen minutes," Ruby said. "Step it up, people."

The ozone smell grew stronger until I felt I might choke on it. Viv began screaming, a garbled sound as if she were gagged —which she was; they would have given her a mouth guard as Malcolm had had. I closed my eyes again and buried my face in Malcolm's shoulder.

Then the screaming cut off, and Viv's hand relaxed. A low murmur went up from around the table. "Keep going," Ruby said, and put both her hands on Viv's forehead. I didn't see what happened next, but Ruby threw back her head and closed her eyes like an ancient priestess performing a sacrifice. Viv's hand flexed, closed tight, and once again she strained against her restraints. Ruby was sweating and her eyes were still closed. "We should have kept that infusion going," she muttered to Rick.

"It would have interfered with Damerel," Rick said. "Keep her awake. Just a few more minutes."

Ruby nodded and craned her head to see her watch without removing her hands from Viv's forehead. "Twelve minutes."

Viv screamed again, then sobbed as if the tears were being wrung out of her. Jeremiah's face was a mask of anguish. I was sure I looked the same. All that kept me from tearing those magi away from my friend was my knowledge that she would die if this failed. And if she could bear it, I could.

"Ten—"

"It's time," Harriet said. She took the Plexiglas ball out of her pocket and cracked it open one-handed. "Open the passage."

The two white-suited magi each took a step forward. Viv

made another strangled sound. The aegis drifted out of the ball and descended beyond my sight. There was a moment of total silence that made me feel I'd gone deaf. Then Viv screamed and bucked against the straps. Something broke, and her arm was free, allowing her to claw at her chest. Two magi swore and grabbed her arm, pulling it back down.

"Damn it, it's draining faster," Ruby exclaimed just as Viv went completely limp. "Four minutes. Jeremiah—"

Jeremiah and I shoved past the magi unfastening Viv's restraints. "Viv," Jeremiah said, "now you have to accept the aegis. It's trying to transform you, but you have to agree to it. Viv!"

I snatched up Viv's hand and gripped it in both of mine. "It's okay," I said. "Wake up, Viv. It's okay." Judy hovered at my shoulder, gripping the edge of the bed like she wanted to break a piece off.

"Two minutes," Ruby said. Jeremiah glared at her, and she backed away.

"Listen to me, Genevieve Haley," he said, "if you don't come back from this, I'm giving your drum kit to Goodwill. Think about that. Some pimply adolescent banging away like a monkey on *your* drums. Wake up!"

"That's good," I said, wiping away tears. "Viv, you have to come back, because Judy and I will drive each other nuts without you to get in the way." Judy choked on a laugh.

Jeremiah smiled. He leaned way over and whispered something in Viv's ear.

Viv blinked. "You would not," she said in a clear, strong voice. "You know how I feel about marriage."

I cried out and dove on her as Jeremiah did the same. Viv put her arms around both of us. "I feel so dizzy," she said. "And hungry."

Ruby put her hand on Viv's forehead again. "The dizziness is because your levels of magic are still dangerously low. It will take a few days for them to regenerate. And you're hungry because you haven't eaten for several days."

Viv touched the small white scar on her chest in wonder. Deep red scratches scored her skin around it. "So when do I get to use magic?"

"That will take some training, too. We'll get you set up for that as soon as you're able to walk without falling over."

"I look forward to teaching you my magic," Harriet said with a smile. "Welcome to the family, so to speak."

Viv nodded. "I'm sorry I scared everyone," she said, brushing her hair back from her face. "I didn't know breaking the fulcrum would do that."

"It was insanity," I said. "Why on earth did you do it? It should have been impossible."

A look of confusion crossed Viv's face. "Because you told me to," she said.

25

"I ...what?" I said.

"You were trying to reach Mr. Wallach," Viv said, "and you shouted at me to smash the fulcrum. I thought it was crazy, but that maybe you knew something I didn't. So I hit it with the toolbox, and that's all I remember before waking up here." She sat up, clutching the blanket around her chest, wobbled in a slow circle, and lay back down.

"I didn't say anything," I said. "Well, I guess I told Mr. Wallach not to touch the anchor—" I remember Viv wouldn't know Wallach was dead.

"Did it work?" Viv asked.

I glanced at Ruby, whose lips compressed in a tight line. "No," I said. "The anchors disappeared too quickly, and...Mr. Wallach is dead."

Viv gasped. "No."

I nodded.

Viv closed her eyes. "That's the end of the project," she

said. "If he couldn't make it work, and he's—gone, we can't shut our reality off from the invaders'."

"It's not so awful," I said. "You saved everyone by breaking the fulcrum."

"Not everyone," Viv said, and began to cry.

Jeremiah put his arms around her again. "I think she needs some quiet rest. When can she come home?"

"It's going to be another few days," Ruby said. "This is still an untested theory. We'll need to verify that her magic is regenerating as it should. But we can move you both into a suite outside the infirmary, which will be more comfortable in her recovery."

"I *am* sitting right here," Viv said, sniffling. "I need food. Macaroni and cheese. It's what I eat when things look bleak."

"I'm sure the cafeteria can handle that," Rick said.

The door opened, and a woman in teal scrubs entered, pushing a wheelchair. Jeremiah helped Viv get into the chair and tucked the blanket securely around her. "I also want clothes," Viv complained. "I feel so exposed."

Malcolm, Judy and I followed the wheelchair into the corridor. Harriet, with a final hug for each of us, went with the lavender-suited magi in the other direction. I checked the time on my phone. It wasn't even eight o'clock. "We won't be late for work," I said.

"What time is it?" Viv asked. "What *day* is it?"

"Let's just say it's a good thing your job is here," Jeremiah said.

"I guess." Viv craned her neck so she could look at me. "Helena, I swear it was you that told me to break the diamond. It's not like I don't recognize your voice."

"I believe you, but I also know I didn't say anything to you. But that can't be the weirdest thing that happened that day." I absently ran my fingers over my left hand and twisted my wedding ring back and forth.

"Yeah." Viv sounded suddenly down. "I can't believe Mr. Wallach is gone. What happened?"

"The anchors activated, and he was caught in their field."

"That's terrible. I wish—" Viv glanced swiftly at Ruby, walking beside her, and shut up.

"You wish he hadn't been so stubborn?" Ruby said. "So do I. I hate to speak ill of the dead, especially since it's Grandpa, but if he'd just let it collapse, surely he could have tried again."

"Not really," Rick said. "Those anchors took a lot of time and effort to create, and they each had to be unique. Meaning that if we'd had to repeat the experiment, we'd need a whole new set of anchors—no duplication. And we were running out of viable forms. I can't say, if I'd been in Darius's place, that I would have done something different."

We walked in silence to the elevator, which took us back to the main level. "I have to report to Lucia," Rick said. "She's been in meetings since six o'clock this morning, going over the Toronto incident, so this will be happy news."

"I'll get you settled and started on a new round of transfusions, see if we can't speed up your recovery," Ruby told Viv. "The rest of you...thanks. We did something no one's ever done before."

"I guess there are worse things to be a guinea pig for," Viv said with a smile.

Back in the car headed south, I leaned against the window and sighed. "I don't want to go to work. Everything feels so...anticlimactic."

"I understand," Malcolm said. "You get keyed up over something big that has to happen, and when it's over, all that energy and pressure has to go somewhere."

"Exactly." I looked at him. "Why do you think Viv heard me tell her to smash the fulcrum?"

"I have no idea. She might have been confused. That amount of magic, all in one place…it was contained, but suppose there was leakage? Or the field surrounding it expanded to encompass her? But if she heard someone and believed it was you, that doesn't answer the question of who actually said it."

"Maybe I'm the one that's confused, and I told her to do it and don't remember. My hand hurt so much, I might have blocked the memory."

"That's possible too. I don't suppose it matters, though, not at this point. Something warned her to do it, and Viv's actions saved almost all the people in the store."

"I choose to be grateful and not worry about it." That was only partly true. I felt it was a mystery that should be solved. But since I had no idea how to do that, I decided to set it aside for now.

Malcolm's phone buzzed with an incoming text. "You want me to get that?" I asked.

"Please. I'm expecting word from Tinsley about whether we're wanted for follow-up in Toronto."

I grimaced. "That sounds unpleasant." I swiped past his lock screen and tapped the display. "It's from Lucia, not Derrick," I said. That wasn't an improvement so far as Malcolm going into danger went. I read the few lines and felt numb. "She says a team in Baghdad went into the Well ten minutes ago. No news yet."

"That's suicidal," Malcolm said. "I hope al-Hussein knows what he's doing."

"Do you know him? Personally, I mean?" I'd been intro-duced to him at the Conference of Neutralities, but we never had the opportunity to talk. I remembered him as a tall, intense man with dark eyes and a friendly smile.

"We've met a few times. He's not careless, I suppose, but he takes risks I wouldn't. Like, for example, sending a team into the Well. But maybe now is the time for risk-taking."

"I think so." The phone buzzed in my hand, and I read the new text. "She says...al-Hussein is in touch with the team. That makes sense."

"It's actually remarkable," Malcolm said. "Everyone who's gone into the Well in the past fifty years has almost immediately been cut off from the outside world, regardless of their method of communication. Maybe al-Hussein isn't as careless as I thought."

I put the phone into the cup holder. "If they could regain the Well—"

"What a boost to morale that would be," Malcolm agreed.

"Who would be its custodian? It would need a custodian to be useful, right?" That sentence stirred distant memories I couldn't quite place. I grasped at them, but they slipped away.

"I don't know. The Board would appoint someone. Quickly, too." Malcolm glanced my way. "Something troubling you?"

"No. I don't know. It's just, when I thought about a Neutrality needing a custodian to be useful, I thought I remembered something. But it's gone."

"It will come to you."

We were almost to Abernathy's when Malcolm's phone buzzed again. I snatched it up. "The team returned from the Well," I said, feeling unexpected relief for a handful of men and women I didn't even know. "All of them. Lucia doesn't know any more than that."

"If they succeeded, the world will know soon." Malcolm

pulled into the rear parking lot and kissed me goodbye. "I'll be back at six."

I waved as the car drove away, then unlocked the back door and let myself in. Judy wasn't back yet, so I went out front in time to accept a bundle of mail from the mail carrier. Standing at the counter, I sorted the letters, rejoicing in how much easier this was with two hands, even if one of them was still stiff. I wasn't going to forget that injury for a long time.

Distantly, I heard the back door open and close. Soon Judy emerged from the stacks. "Did you hear about Baghdad?"

"Only that the team got out with no casualties. Why, what have you heard?"

"Just that. It's exciting, don't you think? The lost Wishing Well, recovered in time to help us defeat the invaders."

"It would be a relief to me." I gathered up the augury requests and slit the first one open. "But for now, I have work to do."

But once I was inside the oracle, I paused, tapping the folded paper against my palm. "Did it work?" I asked. "Can the Well be recovered?"

The oracle's attention shifted to me, then away again. **The guardians fall,** I thought. **Four are gone, two remain. Seal the cracks.**

That discouraged me. "I hoped it might make a difference. Them not dying, or whatever, inside the Well. Maybe that means the Well really is gone, if it doesn't have the power to affect reality to the extent of killing people." I walked down the aisles, looking for the augury. "And I don't know how they'd...I don't know. Purify it? If it was contaminated by its custodian's body?"

Frozen. It stands still. Outside time.

"That's an interesting concept, though I don't understand how it would work. Do you mean the Well is in stasis?"

Stasis. Yes. Waiting outside time.

"Huh. I think I should tell Lucia. Though probably she already knows."

I found the augury and set it on the counter, tucking the folded request between its pages. My phone rang as I was pulling it out to call Lucia. "There's been an explosion," Malcolm said. "In Baghdad. I'm sure you can guess where."

My chest felt tight with fear. "The Well?"

"The news is calling it a terrorist attack," Malcolm said. "We have had no contact with al-Hussein or the members of his team. For all we know, it *was* a terrorist attack, a horrible coincidence, and nothing to do with Wardens. But that seems unlikely."

"But they got out safely. Why would it explode after and not while they were in there?"

"I have no idea. I have to go, but I thought you should know. I understand how much it would mean to you to regain a named Neutrality."

"Thanks. I'm calling Lucia. The oracle told me something about the Well I think she should know."

"Be prepared to wait for a response. She's very busy." He hung up.

I called Lucia and waited for her voice mail to pick up. Instead, I heard, "Davies? Do you know something I don't?"

"Um…maybe? Were you waiting for this call?"

Lucia snorted. "We're dealing with a named Neutrality that's been corrupted for fifty years. If anyone's going to know if that's changed, it will be another custodian."

"Oh. Well, the oracle told me—I don't know if you already know this, but it said the Wishing Well was in stasis. Specifically, that it was 'waiting outside time.' Does that mean anything to you?"

Lucia was silent. Finally, she said, "It might. Al-Hussein's team didn't see any remnants of a body, not even scraps of cloth. While it's true the Well has a history of consuming things thrown down it, that was always offerings, money or whatever. Until the murder, its custodians entered it often with no side effects. And no one except the Well's custodians have known what goes on inside it. If it's holding the body in stasis somewhere, that could explain the curses."

"I don't understand how that works in practical terms."

"Neither do I, Davies. It's a piece of information I'll pass on to people who do. But it implies that the Well might be waiting for a new custodian."

I sat on the metal stool behind the counter and shuffled the remaining augury requests. "Wouldn't the Board have tried that before?"

"They didn't at first because the fighting was so intense. Once the warring families were wiped out, the Board used the oracle to request the identity of the new custodian. The oracle refused to help. Or so I've heard. It was before my time. The Board interpreted that to mean the Well shouldn't have a new custodian." Lucia sighed. "Not the reaction I would have had, but that's above my pay grade."

"So maybe it's time."

"Assuming the Well hasn't been destroyed, yes. Look, I'm sending Henry over later today, but I'll let Campbell know when anything happens. You should be aware...he's likely to have to go to Baghdad if the Well is intact. Al-Hussein sent a message, before we lost contact, that he needed some of the new steel magi for the second part of his plan. Not that he could be bothered to tell me what his plan was."

A chill rushed through me. "I thought——"

"The Middle East isn't deadly, just not always safe for American magi. Campbell will be fine." Lucia sounded grumpy, which frightened me further; she always sounded grumpy when she had to lie. "Later, Davies."

I put my phone away and closed my eyes. I wanted Malcolm to be safe, but even more I wanted the comfort of knowing a named Neutrality had been restored. I couldn't keep him safe if it meant losing that.

I did a handful of auguries before ten o'clock. The Nicol-liens kept me busy until almost noon, by which time I was hungry from having eaten breakfast before 5:30 and tired from having woken half an hour before that. When the last Nicol-lien was gone, I said, "I forgot to bring lunch."

"I'll run to the market," Judy said. "Do you want anything in particular?"

"Something substantial. A roast beef sandwich. And a pickle. And more Diet Coke. It's going to be——"

I felt dizziness pass over me. **They fall**, the oracle said. Its voice reverberated through me.

"Another attack," I managed. My tongue felt thick and choked my words. "I need to go." I turned and ran for the oracle. If the Sanctuary was under attack, I needed to be close to the oracle even if it was capable of communicating from anywhere.

The dizziness passed the moment I stepped into the oracle's space. "Who is it?" I demanded. "Is it the Sanctuary?"

He falls. It is gone. Danger. Seal the cracks.

I pulled out my phone, remembered there were no bars in the oracle, and shoved it back into my pocket. "Can we save Samudra the way we did Claude?"

Gone. He falls. See, the oracle said——

—and instantly I was elsewhere. The air was frigid and smelled of dust that made me sneeze. Tremors shook the earth, not little shivers but full-on quakes, and after the second one I fell to the ground, which was hard stone and not the cream linoleum of Abernathy's. Screams filled the air, the ground tilted, and I was falling, flailing to stop myself and not catching hold of anything. Through the dust, I saw other falling figures. I rotated helplessly in the air, saw the ground rushing toward me at a frightening speed—

I blinked. I was back in Abernathy's, on my knees and leaning against a bookcase for support. My throat felt as raw as if I'd screamed, but the air was clear of dust and smelled like raspberries. I sucked in air desperately until my heart rate slowed. "Was that...was I there?" I asked.

He falls. Helena falls. Five are gone, one remains.

I pressed my face against the smooth yellow wood of the bookcase and wept.

26

E ventually my tears ran dry, and I dragged myself to my feet, then clung to the bookcase to keep myself upright. My knees wobbled and I ached as if I'd been pummeled by the rocks in my vision, if that's what it was. I couldn't stop seeing the ground accelerating toward me at a terrifying rate. It made me wonder if I'd been in Samudra's head, right up until just before the end. The thought sickened me, and I clenched my teeth hard and swallowed to keep from vomiting.

When my legs felt less like cooked pasta, I walked slowly through the aisles until I emerged from the oracle's space. Judy waited there, her eyes wide and her phone in her hand. "What happened?"

"The Sanctuary is gone," I said, and found I was trying to shed more tears. "I think they…I don't know. It was physically destroyed, like by a bomb or something. They fell…fell off the side of the mountain. I saw it at the end."

Judy closed her eyes and bowed her head. Then she looked at me with the bleakest expression I'd ever seen on her. "And now it's just Abernathy's," she said. "What are we going to do? The invaders keep getting cleverer."

"I don't know. If they can restore the Well——"

"Mike texted me about the explosion. How likely is restoring it now?"

"I don't know," I repeated. "Judy, I've never felt this discouraged in my life."

Judy let out a deep breath. "I'm getting lunch," she said. "We need food before we face whatever disaster strikes next. Go get a Diet Coke and sit for a while. It's already been a long day."

I nodded. "Thanks."

When Judy was gone, I did as she'd suggested and went to the break room for a drink. I sat at the little table and sipped my Diet Coke and let my mind wander. Positive things: Viv was alive and looked likely to stay that way. The magi had gone into the Well and come back out unharmed. Claude hadn't been killed. I clung to those thoughts and refused to dwell on anything else.

My phone rang. It was Lucia. "What happened to the Sanctuary?" I asked before she could speak.

"Don't know yet," Lucia said. She didn't sound fazed by my abruptness. "That is, we know the outcropping it was built on cracked and fell off the mountain. No survivors—unless you pulled off another miracle?"

"No." I wiped my eyes. "Not this time."

"At any rate, we don't know how the invaders got past the wards, but my theory is that they tunneled through the outcropping outside the wards and let gravity do the rest. Which is a sickening thought, and I've got stone magi reevaluating Abernathy's wards so it doesn't collapse into a sinkhole."

That frightened me, but in a distant way, something I was

already too overwhelmed to worry about. "So the Sanctuary is gone."

"Sort of. Reports from Chowdhury say the node is still there, but it's hovering about a mile off the ground and is no use to anyone. But the invaders may have drained it by the time Chowdhury can get a team in place. So I'm not counting on that."

It was like the universe was conspiring against me. One piece of bad news after another. "Please tell me everything is all right with Khalil al-Hussein's team?"

Lucia sighed. "Still no word, but I'm not worried. Al-Hussein is the independent type who's likely not to call until he knows every last detail of the solution to his problem. Look, are you going to be all right? This is a lot to take in."

"I'm not all right, but I refuse to be afraid. I'm sure the oracle will warn me if anything else happens."

"That sounds like bravado, but I'll take it." Lucia sighed again. "Don't hesitate to call if something else comes up. Henry left here about five minutes ago, so expect him soon."

I said goodbye and hung up. The bells over the front door jingled, and shortly Judy appeared with a plastic bag. "Roast beef, pickle, and a slab of carrot cake," she said. "Not as good as homemade, but it smelled good enough, and you could use the carbs."

"I'm not sure that's true, but thanks." I took a bite of my sandwich and inhaled deeply the mingled scents of rich meat, sharp pickle, and sweet and tangy cream cheese frosting.

Judy divided her attention between her pastrami sandwich and her phone. "Mike again," she said. "We're making plans for when I move in tonight. I don't have any furniture except that cabinet in the bathroom, so it won't take long. Unless…

would you mind if I took the dishes? You paid for them, after all."

"I don't mind. I'd rather someone used them." I took a bite of my pickle, which was crisp and sour and delicious. "I'm a little sad thinking of Silas's apartment not being occupied anymore. It's so beautiful."

"Life goes on. Besides, if I'm wrong and Mike and I can't make this work, I'll move back in."

"Oh, I hope it works."

"Me too." Judy smiled at something she read on her phone, an unexpectedly tender expression that made me feel odd about having seen it. Judy was so private, it felt like an invasion.

We ate in silence, Judy tapping out messages, me letting my thoughts wander again. I didn't feel like cooking, so maybe Malcolm and I could go out to dinner to celebrate anything I could think of. Unless he had to go to Baghdad, which was a less pleasant thought. On the other hand, if he could make a difference there…that was a positive thought that almost outweighed my fear for him.

My phone buzzed with an incoming text. I swallowed a bite of cake—Judy was right, it wasn't bad—and checked the display. HEARD FROM AL-HUSSEIN, Malcolm wrote. THEY FOUGHT OFF INVADERS. WELL INTACT.

Relief flooded through me, making my joints weak again. "The Well is still there," I said.

Judy looked up. "That's wonderful news! What happened with the explosion?"

"I guess that was an invader tactic, because Malcolm said they fought them off." I tapped out BUT IS THE WELL ACTIVE?

It took a minute for the reply to come. NOT YET. TALKING TO AL-HUSSEIN NOW.

I took another bite of cake to calm myself. "More news soon," I said when I'd swallowed. "I could really use some good news."

"Yeah. Like that the Wishing Well has been purified, and it's giving out invader-fighting weapons that predict where they'll strike next." Judy swiped across her display. "Looks like Mike is coming over at six to help me load up my things. He says if Malcolm goes to Baghdad, their team won't be hunting tonight."

"That's true." I'd forgotten, for the moment, what Lucia had said about only the new steel magi being needed for the next stage of al-Hussein's plan. Impatiently I checked my phone, though I knew no new messages had come through. I threw away my trash and gathered up the phone. "I feel better now."

"No more low blood sugar," Judy said.

"I'll see if I can finish the mail-in auguries before two." I left Judy tapping rapidly and took my time passing through the stacks to the front of the store. I did feel better. Maybe it was just the effects of a good meal, but I felt more positive than I had since witnessing Samudra's death.

I did a few more mail-in auguries with no communication from the oracle. That was fine by me, given that all its recent communications had been of disasters. As grateful as I was to have warning of the invaders' attacks, those warnings wore on me. "It would be nice if, just once, your communication was of something positive," I said as I searched for the fourth augury. "Like…telling me that Mike and Judy are going to work out. Or giving me a winning lottery number. I mean, not the last one, because I don't need to win the lottery, but that's the sort of thing that makes people cheerful."

I will end. Helena will end.

I stopped mid-step. "See, that's the exact opposite of what I asked for," I said. The day's events had left me too numb to be distraught over the now-familiar warning. "Do you not understand human desires? You must understand, because you gave me my honeymoon." Another thought struck me. "You can't possibly mean that our ending is a positive thing?"

No. I will end. Helena will end. There was a pause that felt like the oracle was searching for words. **Life is. The enemy falls. We fall. Life is.**

"I have no idea what that means." I continued searching for the augury. "But life seems like a very positive thing. So… thank you, I guess."

Seal the cracks.

That one, I didn't understand either. We'd had our chance to seal the cracks and lost it. "I don't know how to do that, but maybe it will become obvious sometime," I said.

The augury was a paperback titled *I am the Messenger*, its cover disfigured by a dirty boot print. I brushed at it to no effect. Well, condition didn't matter to the oracle.

When I emerged, Dave Henry was leaning against the counter, his familiar aluminum briefcase beside him. "Four requests," he said by way of replying to my greeting. "How are you holding up?"

"Fine, I guess." I waved at him with my left hand. "I have two hands again, so I feel more positive."

"I heard they worked a miracle. Congratulations."

"I'm grateful." I accepted the first slip—*What is wrong with the Well?*—and disappeared into the stacks.

The oracle's attention was instantly on me, pressing down

like a soft but inexorable weight. "I guess it's not so strange that you'd care about this one," I said. I found the augury, a fat little paperback called *The Tin Roof Blowdown,* and examined it for a minute before remembering I wasn't allowed. "I hope this works. Though I don't know why people didn't try to figure this out fifty years ago, or any time in the years since. Maybe they did, and I just don't know about it. I guess it doesn't matter, so long as they're trying now."

I handed Dave the paperback. "$4000. That's good. Usually it means there's a lot of information in the augury."

"I hope you're right."

I filled the rest of the augury requests—*How do we defend the Well against invaders? Where will the invaders strike next?* and *Where is the custodian's body?*—with the oracle essentially breathing down my neck. I'd expected it to refuse to answer the question about where the invaders would attack next, because it had refused so many others along those lines, but the light never changed. Well, Lucia was in a position to get the augury immediately and act on it right away, so maybe that made a difference.

"I really hope those help," I told Dave as Judy wrote out his receipt. "It's not a good feeling, being the only named Neutrality left."

"We've got security surrounding this place, and stone magi monitoring the wards," Dave said. "There's no way we'll let invaders get to you."

"I didn't remember about the security."

"Lucia didn't want to make a big deal about it. She said it wouldn't help you do your job better, knowing about it. But you should know you're protected."

I almost wished I didn't know, as it reminded me that Abernathy's was almost certainly the invaders' next target. But it was sort of comforting. "Thanks. I'm sure everything will be fine. They tried an attack once already and failed, so they have to think twice about trying again."

"Right." Dave put the books into the briefcase and saluted me with it. "Hang in there."

He meant well, so I suppressed a feeling of irritation at his air of breezy confidence and went back to work.

The rest of the afternoon was quiet. Only a few Ambrosites showed up at two. "Everyone's waiting to see what happens in Baghdad," one woman confided in me. "As soon as we know if the Well is active again, you'll see a deluge of questions about what wishes to ask for."

That made sense. None of the Ambrosites' requests drew the oracle's attention; none were rejected. By 3:30, the store was empty again. Judy leaned against the counter as the bells jingled, saying goodbye to our last customer, and pulled out her phone. "Do you mind if I go upstairs and pack?" she said, reading something on her screen. "Mike will be here right at six, and I'd like to be able to load up and go."

"Sure. I'll text you if a big rush happens."

I crossed the room to stand in front of the crystal door. The afternoon was sunnier than it had been yesterday, and tiny rainbows danced across the surface. I wondered why the light didn't cast rainbows on the walls, like a prism. It made me realize I didn't really understand how illusions worked, despite my reading up on them back when the oracle was under attack by the Mercy's paper magi. If it fooled the brain, then it shouldn't stop the door from shedding rainbow light all over the place, and only I would be able to see it. Or maybe I was wrong, and the illusion on the door altered its nature. It was a fun distraction because it didn't matter if I figured it out.

My phone rang. I took it out and saw Malcolm's name. "Hi. Is everything all right?"

"Yes, and no," Malcolm said. "I'm afraid I have to go to Baghdad in two hours."

"I hope that's the good news."

Malcolm laughed. "I know you worry when I go into danger. This is…it's a tricky situation. The Well is inactive, but it hasn't aggressed on al-Hussein's people, and he thinks that means we have a chance of retrieving the former custodian's body and cleansing the Well."

"That *is* good news."

"You may not think so when you hear the rest. Al-Hussein needs glass magi to locate the body, and steel magi to go in after it. But the protections on the Well are similar to an invader's attack. When they tried to break through—not even to get the body, just to see if it was possible—it nearly killed the steel magi who tried. So al-Hussein wants to use the new steel magi to see if the alloy aegis is a more effective protection."

I sat on the stool, feeling the need for its support. "Meaning he doesn't know if it will work."

"No. The odds are good, though, and we won't take chances."

"I know. The truth is, Malcolm, I really want not to be the only named Neutrality. That outweighs my fear for you. And I have faith in your abilities."

"That's reassuring. What I did not want was to leave knowing that you were miserable."

"I won't be miserable. Worried, yes, but I always worry, and that shouldn't stop you."

"You're the strongest woman I know, love. We will survive this. With the Well and Abernathy's…they're the two most powerful named Neutralities, and they will make a difference."

Surprisingly, I felt better. "I'm glad you're able to do this. Al-Hussein couldn't have a better partner."

Malcolm laughed. "We'll see if he still thinks so when this is all over. We're both strong personalities who like being in charge. I'm steeling myself to be a helpful subordinate."

That made me laugh. "I wish I could see it."

"I'd say the same, but I'm relieved there's no reason to bring you with me. This will be dangerous."

"I know. I'll be fine here. I miss you. I don't suppose I'll see you before you leave?"

"Unfortunately, no. I'm pushing it to be ready in two hours. But I'll call you the moment it's over. I'm having someone drop your car off at the store so you can get home."

"Thanks. I love you, you know."

"And I love you. Take care."

Malcolm hung up, and I sat staring at my phone for a few moments. I'd been telling the truth; my fears about being the last named Neutrality standing were greater than my fears for Malcolm. Maybe some of that was not knowing the details of his mission, and maybe some of it was the numbness that still hovered nearby after witnessing the destruction of the Sanctuary. But I had faith in Malcolm's abilities, and it relieved my mind to know that he would be one of those tackling what might be the biggest challenge to the Wardens in modern times.

The day wore on—almost literally, since it felt time had slowed to a crawl. I managed not to check my watch every two minutes, counting down the time to when Malcolm would leave. I cleaned every surface of the store's front, starting with squeegeeing the windows and ending with mopping the floor. I polished the crystal door and regretted that no one but me would appreciate it. I dusted the bookshelves and moved a few piles from the floor to the empty spaces on the shelves.

That took forty-two minutes.

Inspired, I took my cleaning show into the break room, scrubbed the microwave, wiped down the refrigerator, and mopped that floor too. I didn't mop the office, just swept it, but polished Silas's picture and then removed it and scrubbed the front of the wall safe. As I replaced the picture, Judy came in from the back and said, "I'm about finished packing. I was going to offer to clean, but it looks like you've already done more of that than any sane person should do."

"I'm tackling the basement next."

"Oh, I can do that."

I set down my bottle of cleaner. "Malcolm's going to Baghdad in less than an hour. I need something to distract me."

"Oh." Judy nodded. "I'll sit up front and holler if someone comes in."

There really wasn't much to clean in the basement. The wooden file cabinets needed dusting, as did the metal safe deposit boxes, but we never did more than dry-mop the floor so the file cabinets wouldn't take water damage. I'd always wondered why someone, maybe Silas, had opted for wood instead of metal, but it was one of those questions I would never have the answer to. I scrubbed the porcelain sink in the corner and put away all the cleaning supplies, feeling tired and satisfied. I might even be able to sleep tonight.

My watch told me it was 5:32. Less than half an hour before I could go home. I remembered I didn't want to cook and began going over options. Fast food? Leftovers? Could I drop in on Harry and Harriet without warning? Thinking of Harriet reminded me that she was a glass magus with experience in the Middle East. It wasn't impossible that al-Hussein might call on her to help, in which case Harry might want company.

I texted Harry as I went up the stairs: MALCOLM GOING TO BAGHDAD, HARRIET TOO? No response.

Judy was flipping idly through the pages of a Stephen King novel at the counter. "I'm so bored," she said. "Are you done cleaning? We should plan something to celebrate Viv's aegis. Oh, and how she's alive."

"They said it would be a few days before she's released. Saturday? We could do dinner and a movie." It felt so odd to be making ordinary plans when the world was in such turmoil.

"Sounds good." Judy closed the book and slapped it down on the counter. "Have you heard the conspiracy theory?"

"About what?"

"That reporter the invaders killed. There's a theory going around that he surprised a black ops group that has been spreading the bioweapon." Judy smirked. "They got part of it right, anyway."

"Interesting. Who's the black ops group supposed to work for?"

"I have no idea. There's lots of theories. I like the one that it's really our own government spreading discord so the President can take a hard stand against terrorism and look good."

"That's absurd."

"Is it?" Judy's phone buzzed. "Looks like Mike's here a little early. Mind if I—"

I shooed her away. "Go. Make his nest your own. Don't forget the dishes."

When she was gone, I looked at the Stephen King novel. 'Salem's Lot. I didn't read Stephen King because I was, frankly, a big fat chicken when it came to being scared, but Viv swore he was one of the great American masters. This one was an older book, very battered, with a scary-looking bald man poised to attack the reader. I picked it up and jammed it onto one of the shelves, maybe even in the place she'd taken it from, given that there was a gap the right size. These were not books that would ever be auguries, because they were outside the oracle's space, but I couldn't help wondering if they contributed to the oracle's body regardless. There was so much about it I didn't know.

I glanced at the rest of the books on the shelf. A title caught my eye: *Mr. Penumbra's 24-Hour Bookstore*. That sounded like it could be about Abernathy's. I pulled it off the shelf and flipped it open, intrigued by the cover flap copy. My watch said 5:42. I could read this while I waited for six o'clock to roll around, maybe even take it home with me.

I settled behind the counter and started reading. It was fascinating, and the first bit did remind me a little of my interview with Mr. Briggs, though Abernathy's concealed a different secret, naturally. It would be funny if Abernathy's only loaned out its auguries rather than selling them. We'd be so busy tracking down returns we'd never be bored.

Reading the book also made me wonder, not for the first time, how things would have been different if Mr. Briggs hadn't been murdered. He couldn't have kept the secret of the magical world long, and I would have had a much different reaction if I'd come to it slowly instead of in the aftermath of finding my boss's dead body.

I glanced at my watch. 6:14. Amazing that reading had distracted me to such a degree. I used the cover flap to mark my place and stretched. Outside, evening shoppers passed by, chatting or holding hands or pointing at things I couldn't see. It was a peaceful scene that relaxed me further.

A couple strolled past the door, which turned them into diffuse smears, and came to a stop beneath the ABER-NATHY'S sign painted on the plate glass window. Both of them were pointing at something down the street. Then they took a few tentative steps backward, and I heard their muffled voices raised in argument.

No—it was fear.

I stepped forward to look in the direction they were pointing just as they turned and ran, screaming. I couldn't see anything that might scare someone, but then some people across the street turned and did the same thing, and suddenly the street was full of terrified people, caroming off the few cars noodling down the narrow road and shouting warnings I could barely hear.

I hurried to the door, but paused with my hand on the knob. A terrible, uneasy feeling crept over me. I returned to the window and pressed my face against the glass, peering into the distance up my side of the street. The street looked unreal, like a painted backdrop for a play, with the light all wrong for early evening and the air thick with impossible fog. Dark figures moved within the fog, too angular to be human. I involuntarily clapped my hand over my mouth to stifle a shriek as the first invaders emerged.

They slipped through slits in reality, two-dimensional paper cutouts that expanded into fully-formed, horrible shapes made more horrible by the obscuring fog. It had to be real, I couldn't have seen it if it were an illusion, but it looked ridiculously fake, a bad special effect in a horror film with no budget. The invaders strolled or loped or flew along the street as if they had all the time in the world—but that was a different kind of illusion, one born of my fear, because even as they moved slowly, they caught up to the fleeing people, and then the screams turned agonized.

I stood frozen at the window, watching people die. Security. Dave had said Abernathy's had a security detail. So where were they? No fatigue-clad men and women challenged the nightmarish figures. Which meant the invaders had taken them out first. Aside from the wards, Abernathy's was defenseless.

But if the security force was dead, that meant no one was around to report the attack except me. I had to tell someone.

The Wardens needed to know Portland was under attack. The invaders couldn't touch me, not with the store as well warded as it was, but the Wardens could save everyone else. But I couldn't stop watching the carnage, was unable to even take the few steps to the counter where my phone lay.

The first people collapsed, drained completely, then others joined them. Soon the street looked like a scene out of a disaster movie, bodies lying everywhere, blood red or moss green or chitinous black invaders leaping on new victims. A screaming woman fled past the store and was pounced on right in front of me, and I screamed along with her, my heart trying to beat its way out of my body. The invader, its blue body glistening like a scarab, its eight legs gripping its victim and its terrible jaws clamped on her throat, ignored me. I backed away, fumbled for my phone, and tried to find Lucia's number without taking my eyes off the invader.

The call went straight to voice mail. "Lucia, invaders are attacking Portland—maybe you know—they are outside Abernathy's right now and I don't know where the security is—I need help!" I gasped in one long breath. I ended the call. The invader had finished draining the woman and was gone. I went back to the window and gazed helplessly at the carnage. Cars idled in the street, their drivers having abandoned them, and invaders crawled or hopped over them, scoring the paint with their claws.

In the middle of the road, between two cars, a vertical black line cut through reality as if it were the stage backdrop I'd imagined it as. The line glowed bright blue all down its center, like light leaking through it from the other side of the backdrop. And a *thing* slipped through it, flattened like paper. *Insert Tab A into Slot B,* I thought madly. Whatever the thing was, it fit the line perfectly.

Then it shook itself, and became three-dimensional. Numb horror struck me. I'd seen that thing before. Its clawed, multi-jointed legs scraped the asphalt as it walked with deliberation toward me. A dozen beady eyes like drops of fresh blood focused on me, and the tentacles in the place where its mouth should be undulated slowly, as if it were tasting the air with fat, sucker-coated tongues. One eye was a ruined mess, and I remembered jamming a broken baton into that eye and felt sick.

I took an involuntary step backward and ran into the counter. That startled me out of my horrified, frozen state. I raised my phone, not sure what else I could do. Knowing the wards were there was no comfort to my primal animal brain, which was screaming at me to flee.

It had no mouth, but its tentacles curled in what was nearly a smile. *"Custodian,"* it said in a voice that cranked my instinctual panic to eleven. *"This is the end."*

Its words were muted by the glass, but it was perfectly intelligible. "You can't get in here," I said, proud of how my voice didn't shake even though the rest of me wanted to. "The wards are too powerful."

The invader cocked its pointed black head to one side. It was such a human gesture I wanted to run—but I had nowhere to run to. *"Suppose I told you we will go on killing humans until you let us in,"* it said.

"In the first place, I wouldn't believe you, and in the second place, I can't take that offer."

"Oh? Not soft-hearted Helena Campbell? You'd let thousands die to save your own life?"

I swallowed. "It's not about my life. You can't be allowed to get at Abernathy's. Not even at that cost."

"Hmm. I suppose there was never any chance that appeal would

work. " Its tentacles caressed the glass window, leaving smeary streaks of blue ichor. *"But we had to give you the chance."*

"You...what?"

It ignored me and walked away. I pressed against the glass to watch it as it went to the nearest lamppost and uprooted it as easily as plucking a daisy. Mystified, I took a step back. The invader dragged the lamppost behind it, sending up the scraping, shrill noise of metal on concrete, until it once more stood in front of the window. *"Stand back,"* it said.

I realized what it had in mind just as it grabbed the lamppost with two sharp limbs and slammed it into the glass like a battering ram. I ducked behind the counter in time to avoid the shower of glass that sprayed the store's front with a tinkling crash. Shaking my head and shoulders to rid myself of the sharp splinters, I stood and glared at the invader. "That won't be enough," I said. "You can't get past the wards."

The sounds of screaming had grown distant. The invader turned its head as if it were listening to the cries of agony. *"I'm sure they believed that,"* it said. *"How unfortunate for you it's not true."*

"You're trying to frighten me into doing something stupid. It won't work."

The invader shook its head, another human gesture that made me feel sick. It held up one of its forelimbs and waved it slowly, moving as if the glass were still there and it was wiping it with a cloth. A red glow pulsed wherever its "hand" moved, like someone turning up an adjustable bulb. At first, it was nothing but a haze, like fog lit from within, but as the creature's forelimb continued to move, strands like fine wires, almost too thin to be seen, became visible. The wires stretched randomly in all directions as if they extended far beyond what I could see, weaving in and out of each other to form a heavy red mesh. Soon, the invader was hidden behind the wires of what must be the powerful wards Campbell Security had installed. It made me even more afraid, not being able to see the thing.

I became aware of a faint, thin whine at the limits of my hearing, like a distant wasp's nest or a power saw running far away. Right at the center of the mesh, a bright speck glowed, sickly green by contrast to the warm red light of the wires. I stepped closer, mesmerized. The glowing speck expanded until it was the size of a penny, then a quarter, and then the size of my fist.

The wires surrounding the horrible green light shifted as if something were trying to fit between their close weave. Something hard and black and pointed poked out of the circle of green light, shifting the wires further. Another tip of the invader's wickedly sharp forelimbs emerged right next to the first. They wiggled around for a few seconds, and then they separated, slowly, dragging the wires apart and leaving a gap in the middle. The gap grew as the green light did, until I could see the invader's horrible face through the hole.

I realized what it was doing at the same moment it said, *"Not what you expected, yes?"*

I turned and fled.

In fifteen seconds I was in the office and flinging open the door that led to the back hall and the stairs leading to the upstairs apartment. I hesitated at the exit. There were almost certainly invaders outside. But they couldn't drain my magic, and all I had to do was run to my car. I could get away and be safe.

I reached for the doorknob, and stopped with my hand inches from it. If I left, the invaders would destroy Abernathy's, and whatever catastrophe happened when there were no more guardians would occur. I shook my head violently to dispel those thoughts and gripped the knob tightly enough to hurt my skin. If I stayed, the invaders would kill me, and they'd still destroy Abernathy's. My death wouldn't make a difference.

It would need a custodian to be useful. The thought flickered across my mind. I'd said it in regards to the Well needing a custodian, but now I wondered—didn't it make a difference to the Neutrality that it had a custodian? I was the oracle's hands, after all, and it communicated through me. And I couldn't abandon it even if it meant my death. My end.

I released the knob and ran for the stacks. If I could get inside the oracle, maybe together we could fight the invader and whatever slavering hordes it brought with it.

The whining drone was louder now, and it had an edge to it that made my skin crawl. I slipped through the aisle and headed deeper into the stacks, hoping I wasn't too late. Then the oracle's presence rose up around me, reassuring me. I staggered to a halt in the heart of the oracle and inhaled deeply, trying to calm my racing heart. "What do we do?" I asked.

The guardians fall. Seal the cracks. I will end. Helena will end.

It was mostly what I'd expected, but it still sent fear coursing through me. I wasn't prepared to die even after almost five months of warnings. "How do we seal the cracks? What will that do?"

A wave of intense frustration swept over me, so intense I didn't at first realize it was not my own emotion. "There's something I'm not getting," I said. "I'm sorry I don't understand."

The frustration retreated a little. **Speak,** the oracle said. **You and I are one.**

"You want me to become you?" I would do anything to save us both.

The oracle's attention pressed down on me, but this time I felt its curiosity, like a dog sniffing a scent trail. It reminded me of the times I'd meditated to connect with the oracle. "All right, let's try it," I said. I closed my eyes and rested my left hand on the nearest bookshelf. The grainy wood pressed against my new skin. I let myself open to feeling it completely, relaxing even as I gave the sensation my full attention. A breeze brushed my cheeks, bringing with it the scent of fresh cherries, and I inhaled it and let it sink into my lungs and spread throughout my body.

An image came into focus behind my eyelids. It was of a plastic sieve, an ordinary purple plastic sieve. Water flowed through it, a steady stream pouring from an unseen source that turned into rainfall as the water found the many holes perforating the sieve. I watched, confused as to what the oracle meant.

The water stopped flowing. The sieve shivered, and some of its holes disappeared as if they'd been filled in with melted wax. The water flowed again, and this time the "rainfall" was heavier, the remaining holes wider somehow. Again the water dried away, and more holes vanished. Three more times the image repeated itself until the sieve had one hole the size of my fist, and the water flowed through that hole unimpeded.

Seal the cracks, the oracle said. **The guardians fall. Many, few, one. Power flows stronger as the guardians fall.**

My whole world rearranged itself so fast I felt I might fall down. My connection to the oracle shivered. "Seal the cracks," I said. "Not us. *Them.* They destroy the guardians, and that seals the cracks until—"

"You didn't understand that before?" a horrible voice said. *"I thought you were smarter than that."*

I couldn't see the invader through the bookcases and had no idea how I was able to hear it. I'd only rarely caught glimpses of the ordinary world while I was inside the oracle. "If you're stooping to taunting me, you're more pathetic than I thought," I shot back, certain it could hear me.

"True. We're both above pettiness." I heard it moving around in the narrow aisles. *"Isn't this the time when, if I were human, I'd reveal all the details of my master plan?"*

"I don't care about your plan. You can't drain my magic, and that means when I'm the oracle, you can't destroy it either." It was the only thing that made sense.

"You are *smarter than you seem. It's true we can't destroy this node the way we did the others."* It laughed, sending waves of horror rippling down my spine. *"Fortunately for us, we don't want to destroy the oracle. That really would ruin our plan."*

"I already know you want to destroy us. I don't know why it took you so long to decide we were never going to give in."

"We hoped you would see sense, for all our sakes. There's just so much waste this way. But it was always going to turn out this way."

"What are you talking about?"

It laughed again. *"Not going to monologue, remember? Besides, you'll be dead when it happens, so it's not like it will matter."*

It was trying to unnerve me, trick me into making a mistake. The trouble was, I had no idea what it intended, so anything I might do could be a mistake.

Except one thing.

I centered myself in the heart of the oracle and let out a deep breath, relaxing my shoulders so my arms drooped at my sides and my hands hung loosely. The oracle's attention instantly increased, becoming so painful I had to bite back a whimper. I'd only ever done this twice before, and never so deliberately. The pressure built until I felt swollen with power, like a balloon about to pop. I realized I'd fallen to my knees, and I ground my teeth and closed my eyes as a keening wail escaped my lips, just before I exploded.

The pressure vanished, and I felt as light as mist. I opened my eyes to a golden glow that drifted around me. I floated higher until I could see over the tallest bookcases, did a slow roll out of sheer pleasure of being free from a physical body, and took a deep breath only to remember I didn't have lungs.

The invader was a black blotch between the shelves at the edge of my space. It didn't seem aware of me. Beyond that, dozens, maybe hundreds of smaller invaders pressed in through the man-sized hole the intelligent invader had made in the wards. They filled the space outside the stacks, crawling over the counter and the stool. Some of them had knocked the antique cash register to the ground, which would have made me angry if I'd still been in my human body and capable of such a visceral emotion.

Let's see what we can do, I thought. Memories of an earlier time surfaced, of glowing golden letters making thick chains. I retreated deeper into my meditative state and let my awareness extend throughout the oracle's space, all the way to the walls and through every bookcase. The spines began glowing with a soft light that grew as the letters printed or impressed on their spines turned gold. They danced and flowed into the air, spinning gently and forming chains of letters spelling words in a language I couldn't read. Probably no one could.

The chains twined together, became thicker, and their light filled the room until it seemed to lie at the heart of the sun, but cool and comfortable instead of scorching hot. The invader looked up, finally aware of my presence. "We're not helpless,"

I said, and directed the chains to wrap around the creature's hideous body.

It didn't resist. *"You're fighting back. I knew you were strong. How sad."*

I tightened the chains and the invader gasped. "You're even more pathetic than I thought if you're going to pull that whole patronizing evil villain thing."

It tilted its head. *"Not at all,"* it said. *"You've given me far more than I hoped."*

Confused, I responded by making the chains constrict the thing further. And it laughed. Somewhat breathlessly, which surprised me because I didn't know its kind breathed, but a laugh of such deep amusement that even in this state, I felt angry.

A tug on the chains brought me back to myself. It wasn't a tug from the invader trying to free itself; the pull came from above. I looked up. The ceiling looked melted, like a pat of butter dropped into a hot pan, and globs of thick paint mixed with plaster dripped and fell to the floor. They sizzled when they touched the letter-chains. Then, with a groan, a chunk of ceiling about ten feet across sagged and fell. I threw up arms I didn't have to protect my face, but it passed through my immaterial body to splatter across three bookcases and the linoleum.

Where the ceiling had been was—nothing. Not the timbers of the roof or even the evening sky, and not the darkness of the space between ceiling and roof. Just a blank emptiness that sucked at me like a riptide. Things moved within it, impossibly, things that might have been a million miles away or at arm's length. It tugged at the chains, making them twitch. I asserted control over them, and the twitching stopped, but the pull still dragged at me.

"It will take you, in the end," the invader said. It stood just

below me and had shaken off the chains somehow. I brought more to encircle it, but it waved a clawed forelimb and they retreated despite all my urging. The pull grew stronger until I had to focus all my attention on not being dragged into the void.

"What is it?" I demanded, hating how my voice shook.

"*Our reality,*" the thing said. "*Preparing to drain the magic from yours.*"

The image of water pouring through a single hole in a sieve came to mind again. "You can't do that," I said stupidly. Chains flew upward, and I pulled them back with terrible effort.

It roared with laughter. "*So foolish,*" it said. "*Obviously we can. The fewer nodes, the greater the conduit. And it's fitting that Abernathy's and its custodian should be the site of our victory. You've thwarted us so many times.*"

I lashed out with my chains as if they were whips, cracking them across the creature's hard exoskeleton. It flinched, but didn't move. "You can't drain this place even with whatever that thing is," I said, "and I will fight you to the end."

"*Of course you will.*" The invader looked up at me, its beady eyes gleaming with malevolence. "*And it will not matter. But it doesn't have to be this way.*"

I whipped it again, this time catching one of its eyes with the tip of a chain and making it pop like a blood blister. "I suppose you're going to offer me a deal. Forget it."

"*You're barely holding on. Would you like to know what awaits you in our reality? Humans can't survive in it—no air, for one—and its miasma will strip the flesh from your bones as you suffocate to death. That's if my idiot cousins don't get to you first. They may not be able to drain you, but they can destroy you trying. Is that how you want to end?*"

I didn't respond. I couldn't. The pull had grown agonizingly sharp, and I was afraid if I spoke, I'd lose my grip on this reality.

"*But, as I said, it doesn't have to be this way.*" The invader shook its head, sending a spatter of black blood across the nearest row of books. "*I told you once you would have one last chance, when all hope was gone. Give us access to the oracle, and we'll withdraw. We'll control the idiots so they only take criminals and useless people—you proposed that, didn't you?*"

"I did not!" I shrieked, and the pull redoubled until I was stretched taut like a drumskin. I screamed in agony.

The invader chuckled. "*Think how many lives you could save, protecting this reality. Be sensible. One Neutrality balanced against the lives of an entire world. Your choice, custodian. Choose now.*"

I felt the entire store tugging at me as it strained to be sucked into the void. The creatures within it were drawing closer. *I can't,* I thought at the oracle. *It has to be lying.*

The oracle, which had been silent until now, said, **I will end. Helena will end.**

But it will be pointless! The invaders will destroy everything!

Its voice thundered through me: **Make an end.**

I released everything I was holding and let myself and all those golden chains be dragged into the void.

A flash of light blinded me momentarily, and I tried to blink and found whatever I was using to see with didn't work that way. The blindness passed as rapidly as it had come, and I was in darkness as complete as the light had been, darkness that smelled of mold and dead things. I strained to see anything, even horrible invaders, but I might as well have been blind again. The chains had either disappeared or were invisible. I suspected the latter, because I still felt them tug on my immaterial body. Everything was perfectly silent. That all should have terrified me, but I felt only the ghost of fear, trembling through my core.

We are one. This place is not. See and know.

I can't see, I thought, but even as I did I made myself relax into the meditative state I'd practiced all those times. Once again, webs of light uncurled before me, like undulating jellyfish radiant with red and purple and blue light. Then they faded, and I cried out and tried to make them stay. My cry was silent, and I couldn't even feel a vibration in my throat—the throat I didn't have.

See, the oracle said. There was no light, nothing to illuminate my surroundings, but impossibly the blackness lightened, became dull brown like dried mud. The dreary, bland color sharpened until it appeared to be brown hills I was floating high above. Immediately, my perspective changed, and they were a bumpy brown wall—changed again, and I was looking up at a ceiling that hung pendulous above me. I twisted and made a slow roll, with the unseen chains dragging behind me. The brown bumpy surface extended in all directions, like being inside a sphere with hills for walls. I couldn't tell how far away they were; they might have been a mile distant or a million miles. I rolled again and confirmed that I was surrounded.

I sniffed, and smelled peanut butter atop the stink of decay, the same thing I'd smelled during the realignment. At the time, I'd known it was a phantom smell, and now I wondered how much of what I was seeing was real and how much a product of my brain's effort to make sense of the truly alien. As I thought that, the brown hills wavered and vanished, replaced by shiny black spikes in random patterns. *Which of these is real?* I asked the oracle.

I do not know real here. They come.

I rolled again, looking for the portal we'd entered by, and found nothing. *This can't be right,* I said. *It said I would die here.*

Not human. Not oracle. I am myself.

I knew, when it started talking like that, it saw us as a unified being even though I still could distinguish between us. *So what happens now? We wait to be killed?* I hadn't seen any other creatures in this bizarre landscape.

Lose the battle. Win the war.

I think we've done that. Lost the battle, anyway.

I am myself. Fight.

The tugs on my body grew stronger. I envisioned the golden chains, but nothing happened. I willed them into existence harder and felt, again, nothing.

In the distance, something moved, black against black, like an insect skittering across the wall. Another, and another, until tiny creatures were swarming over the black spikes, making them appear to wave at me like seaweed fronds. I again felt a twinge of fear and was grateful I couldn't panic in this state. *They're coming for us,* I said. *Can they hurt us?*

I will end. Helena will end. I am myself.

It turned out I was perfectly capable of feeling frustration. *You have to tell me what to do,* I insisted. The swarm was growing larger, the specks becoming thumb-sized dots. The black spikes became charcoal gray blocks stacked irregularly atop each other. *I don't want to die.*

A tremor went through me. Pressure grew as if, impossibly, the oracle intended me to possess it more fully. I cried out silently. *You can't! There's no room!*

I

AM

MYSELF

My thoughts shook me to my core. And just like that, I knew what it meant.

I can't do it, I said.

The oracle said nothing, but I quivered with tension as it waited for me to accept the inevitable. We were not one. And could not be one so long as I clung to my own identity. My life.

I looked around again at the alien landscape, at the oncoming flood of invaders bent on destroying us. There was *no point* in doing what it wanted. I would die, and then we would die, and the world would follow soon after. No one would know what had happened to the oracle and its custodian because there would be no one left to care.

Malcolm, I thought.

Then I let myself fall more deeply into that meditative state. The oracle pressed down on me with such force I instinctively fought back. **No**, the oracle said. **I end. Helena ends. Now.**

With a scream of equal parts fear and pain, I stopped fighting and let the oracle fill me.

Even in my immaterial body, it hurt like nothing I'd ever experienced, worse than touching the anchor's field, worse than becoming the oracle. It felt like drowning in acid. I struggled to breathe despite having no lungs and wanted to flail and kick until I reached a place where there was air. Instead, I made myself hold still as the oracle scoured through me, tearing me apart.

Memories rose unbidden and dissolved, leaving only fragments. There went my high school stage crew experiences. The first time I rode a bike by myself. Fighting with my sister. Then people began disappearing. People I barely remembered meeting went first, followed by Wardens I'd helped with auguries. My ex-boyfriends Chet and Jason. Sydney the therapist. Rick and Ruby. The memories came faster and more painful now, as if they were being stripped away by a caustic substance.

Judy. Gone.

My parents.

Viv.

Malcolm.

The last thing I remembered was my final sight of the intelligent invader, its blood-red beady eyes fixed on me as I fell upward into its reality, and then my mind was blank nothing.

THE BLACK TIDE rushed toward her. It was composed of millions, maybe billions of creatures. She couldn't remember what they were or if she had ever seen anything like them before. They were still distant enough that she couldn't make out details.

Something filled up the corners of her empty mind, and she came alive. Color washed into the forbidding landscape, revealing it for what it was: clouds of unformed matter in every imaginable hue, gaudy and horrible. The oncoming tide never hesitated, but in an instant the creatures, too, were filled with color so profoundly wrong it made her want to end them.

Her body, immaterial and glowing, was a spot of purity within that horrible landscape, and she knew without looking at herself that she had grown—grown from what? She didn't belong here, and she wanted to return to the place where she did.

Something tugged at her in all directions. She spun and felt a pull as if things attached to her were dragging on her body. With a thought, she brought them into being: golden chains made up of billions of glowing letters. Suddenly she was the brightest thing in that wrong, awful place. The wave of creatures paused, rippling backward. As if in response to their reaction, she grew again, the chains becoming wrist-thick. She flicked those chains, and the creatures surged forward as if she had challenged them instead.

She remembered, then, what she had seen of these creatures before. They fed on other creatures, drained them of their magic, fed again, insatiable and pitiless. They would feed on her if she did nothing.

Whatever those chains were, she was sure they could lead her back where she belonged. She ignored the oncoming tide and focused on the chains. They seemed to float in midair, though there was no air, and she let them drift, hoping if this was like an airless, waterless sea, they might find a current to lead her home.

They rippled, shifted, and gradually pointed up and away. She let them draw her along after them. The creatures were close enough now that she could make out their features, angular or fleshy or round, all of them bent on tearing her apart. If the chains were leading to an escape, it would come too late.

A memory arose, one so clear it felt as if someone else had put it into her mind: a hand, cupping water from a pool to drink. The same hand, flailing from the surface of the pool as if its owner was drowning. The images repeated, drinking, drowning, drinking, drowning. The creatures were so close the reek of their bodies, the same rot that permeated this space, threatened to overwhelm her.

She was pure magic. Let them drown in it.

She faced the rushing tide and drew on all those golden chains. They flared into painful brilliance. A surge of power shot through her, and her body burned with the light of a thousand suns, a golden mirror shooting rays of light in every direction.

For the first time in this dead place, she heard sound, the death screams of a million creatures. As the light faded, she saw the onrushing tide had vanished. A few creatures remained, but they fled, disappearing as fast as they had come. She felt the power continue to pulse through her, filling her with light. The golden chains spun around her in a dizzying display, all of them tugging in one direction. It looked no different from anywhere else in this hellscape.

She gathered the chains into a single thick rope and flicked them like a whip in that direction, willing them to strike. Dizziness claimed her, and once again the chains flared so brightly she could not bear to look at them. They jerked her forward, and then the world spun and she was falling. She threw out her arms and rolled, felt something collide with her immaterial body, and looked in the direction she had fallen from. Blank nothingness met her eyes, a gaping void in an otherwise normal ceiling.

Ceiling?

She remembered ceilings, and floors, and bookcases. She remembered thousands of books. She remembered people, a long line of people who had brought her questions she answered, or not. Why had she done that? Because it had been what she was created for.

Then everything happened at once:

...she fit herself between bookcases arranged at random in a way that nevertheless made a pattern to her, and knew each book and its limitless possibilities...

...she saw a blonde woman sitting beside the door and whispered to her, but the woman didn't understand even though she had brought her here...

...she watched a bald man in a three-piece suit wander the aisles, touching the books as if looking for guidance, and she told him to change his destiny...

...she saw a woman in a long gown directing others in loading books onto shelves and felt the beginnings of a tug toward a new home...

...she felt the foundations of the store shake and shouted at a woman with vividly magenta hair to break the stone and save them all...

...she came face to face with a creature anathema to life on earth and—

—but that was here, now, and she lashed out with all her golden chains and bore the monster to the ground.

"*Impossible*," it said. "*It should have killed you.*"

Not impossible, she said. **It is what I was made to become. I see every possibility, even those about you and your kind.**

"*It doesn't matter. We have already begun draining your world. You can't stop us.*"

You're right. I can't stop you. Even if you beg me to.

The monster took a step backward. "*What?*"

You sealed the cracks. You made this the one point of contact between my reality and yours. You made a fatal mistake.

She tilted her head to look up at the void. Its edges trembled. More plaster and paint broke free, but instead of falling to the floor, it was sucked into the void. The air in front of the hole shimmered with heat haze, not invisible, but like a rainbow-tinted oil slick, as if the true nature of the place beyond the void shone through.

Do you know what a firehose is? she asked.

"*I'm not an idiot.*" The creature's voice trembled, giving the lie to its defiant words.

You wanted our magic. Take it. Drown in it. Then, when there is nothing left of you, I will seal your reality and you will drift forever, sterile and dead.

The monster snarled and leapt at her. Dozens of golden chains flew between them, binding it so it smacked into the floor, struggling and spitting vicious words in its own language.

She snapped those chains upward, and they flung the creature into the void, where it vanished in an instant.

Now, she said, and detached the rest of the chains from herself. They, too, flew upward, but instead of disappearing, they clung to the mouth of the void and made a golden curtain defining its edges. She drifted upward, creating more chains and bringing them with her until she and they filled the space with light. There was power here, not just her own power but a source almost as large as she, a source she recognized from having lived beside it and within it for almost a century. She reached out to it, and felt it reach back until immaterial hand touched inexorable force.

Power surged through her, making her cry out in mingled pleasure and astonishment. She tilted her head back as that power flowed through her and into the other reality. As it flowed, it became visible as waves of red and purple and blue light, powerful and clean and reassuringly of her reality, a wonderful contrast to the bizarre, alien landscape.

Half in and half out of the monsters' reality, she saw things impossible to perceive, as if some strange synesthesia worked its magic on her. She saw, in that dead, silent place, the screams of creatures tormented beyond bearing; she heard colors clashing and bleeding together as the landscape tore itself apart; she smelled peanut butter and had no idea what it really meant.

Then dizziness struck her again, and she fell, her immaterial body sinking into the floor. She dragged herself out of it and collapsed on the cream-pale linoleum, rolling onto her back. It wasn't finished. She had to finish it or everything would start all over again and there would never be an end to the war.

The golden chains still waved in the void. The hole in the

ceiling needed to be closed. With her last vestiges of power, she directed them to weave together. First one chain crossed the hole, then another, and then all of them wove a tight mat that quivered with golden light. Nothing would ever come through that hole again.

She lay back and examined the hole. The light was already fading, and the chains had taken on the appearance of painted plaster. She, too, was fading, her golden power dwindled to nothing. She rolled onto her side and came face to face with a dead woman. The woman's dark blonde hair was dusted with chunks and crumbs of ceiling, her eyes were open, and she wasn't breathing. She should know who the woman was, but her memory was fading as her light did.

The room went dim, and she saw nothing more.

I walked down a long hallway carpeted in plush red velvet, its bronze ceiling casting a wavery reflection of me with every step. Where my bare feet touched the carpet, the scent of lilacs wafted toward me. I couldn't see an end to the hallway, and I knew without turning around there would be no end behind me, either.

The wall to my left was a single sheet of mirrored glass. I glanced once again at what was reflected there and said, "Elizabeth Abernathy didn't know what she was creating. Though maybe that's wrong, because she did originally intend for the oracle to be within a person."

"So this really is what we were intended to be," Helena Campbell said—or, rather, the essence of Helena Campbell, a remnant of her. Though she was the reflection I cast, we looked nothing alike. Maybe *I* was the reflection *she* cast. It was as likely as anything else.

"The oracle grew and changed over the years," I said. "It had to reach a state where it could become human, or whatever it is that happened at the end." I, too, was a remnant, all that was left of Abernathy's after my—our—transformation. My memories of being the oracle had mostly faded, and it seemed as natural to refer to those memories in the third person as to think of myself as still the oracle.

Helena must have felt the same, because she said, "And Helena was the hands of the oracle. Why Helena? Because of her genetic difference?"

"Helena was an outsider to the magical world, and young enough to be mentally flexible. And she had a passion for justice. Anyone with those qualities would do. But the oracle... liked her. Maybe that was a cruelty, if it meant condemning her to that fate."

"She had to choose," Helena said. "I think, if she had been the wrong person, she would have chosen differently." She laughed. "I don't think she regretted it. And now, here we are, the two of us in one."

"Here we are," I agreed.

I walked a few more steps in silence. Helena said, "I see now why Wallach had to be allowed to try, even though you knew he would fail. Once you couldn't convince him to give it up, it was better he do it in Abernathy's, and make that crack even more appealing to the invaders."

"I wish things had gone otherwise. His plan was sound." My regret over Wallach's death was as distant as everything else, but still hurt.

Helena sounded less regretful than I felt. "But it would have left the invaders free to attack another reality. I prefer our solution."

I nodded. Helena did not. Even though I had foreseen this, even though I'd known what it meant that we would end, I hadn't been able to predict what it would be like when I was not the oracle, but a single entity with aspects of both myself and Helena. It was unsettling.

"So, what now?" Helena said. "Is there an afterlife for creatures like us?"

"I don't know any more than you do," I said. "I expect once we reach the end of this corridor, things will become clear."

"That could take a while."

I shrugged. "We don't have anything better to do, do we?"

Again I walked in silence beside my reflection. "I regret not being able to communicate better with Helena," I said. "Seeing into all times at once was hard to explain to someone who lived a linear life."

"You was as clear as you could be," Helena said, "and Helena did her best to understand. Besides, I think if I had understood better, I might not have made the right choice."

"Did you make the right choice?" I asked.

Helena stopped walking, forcing me to stop as well. "Of course. We could not have stopped the invaders if I'd chosen differently."

"The oracle only gave up its immortality," I said. "Helena gave up her whole life. Her friends, her family, her husband. Her chance at having children and gaining immortality that way."

"We owe her our existence."

I smiled bitterly. "That might not be worth it, given that we appear to be dead."

Helena sighed. "There's no way to change that. I wouldn't want our reality to die for the sake of one woman."

"Would it die? The sacrifice has already been made. No, that's not the death I'm talking about."

Helena shot me a sharp look. "You mean we should die."

I returned her look for look. "Are we any more deserving of life than she is? Considering, again, that we're probably already dead and can benefit no one?"

"I don't think it's possible. Even if we die, there's no guarantee Helena will live. She was killed by the oracle to make room for the two of us in one form. Our form." She gestured to herself and managed to encompass me in the movement.

I shook my head. "But we have all of Helena's memories in this form. She still exists, in a sense."

"All right," Helena said. "What are we going to do?"

"Something crazy," I said.

I drew back my fist and smashed the mirror between us.

I DREW in a deep breath and immediately started coughing and wheezing as I sucked about five pounds of plaster dust into my lungs. I pushed myself up on my hands, got to my knees, and forcibly tried to eject my lungs from my body. When I could finally breathe again, I wiped tears from my eyes, smearing more dust into paste across my cheeks, and sat with my back against the nearest bookcase.

Natural light filtered through the aisles, telling me it was still early evening even though with all I'd been through, it felt like it should have been later. I heard no distant screams and wondered if sealing off the invaders' reality had drawn all the remaining invaders into it, or if the Wardens would be playing cleanup for the next several months.

<The invaders are not gone, but they will be soon.>

It was a realization that came and went so swiftly my mind barely had time to put it into words. I just knew, deep in my bones, that this was the future. *A* future, maybe, but one I felt confident would not disappear. I got to my feet and clung to a bookcase as my knees shook. Dying had had more of an impact on me than I'd realized.

I closed my eyes and sorted through it all. I remembered everything. Being sucked into the invaders' reality. Having my memories scoured away so I was empty and capable of truly becoming the oracle. Using the power of the oracle and Abernathy's node to destroy all the invaders and seal off their reality. Walking down that corridor having a conversation with my reflection, who was also me. These were not memories that were likely to fade any time soon.

The door slammed open, and I heard running footsteps and a voice calling, "Ms. Campbell? Where are you?"

I staggered out of the stacks and once more had to hold onto a bookcase to support myself. Half a dozen Wardens in the bland fatigues that meant they were from the Gunther Node spread out through the store's front, their guns held at the ready. They tilted them away from me when I appeared.

"Are you all right? You look—" The man leading the force looked like he'd decided against saying *terrible*.

"I'm fine," I said. "Everything's fine. But I need to go to the Gunther Node immediately. Lucia's going to want to hear this."

———

Lucia stared at me from across her desk. "You have got to be kidding me," she said.

"Lucia—"

"All right, all right, I know you wouldn't make something like this up, but—" She pinched her lips tight and shook her head. "You have to admit it's unbelievable."

"That the oracle had that kind of power? Or that I died and came back? Or—"

"All of it, Davies, all of it." Lucia leaned back in her chair and put her hands behind her head. "And it's just...over."

"Not over. There are still a lot of invaders loose in our world that need to be destroyed. And..." Another flash of awareness struck me: <The Well will be cleansed and Lucia will be the first to wish on it.> "Um. When the Well is cleansed, you need to be the first to wish there."

"Excuse me?"

I had a feeling this would be the hardest thing for people to understand. "I'm the oracle now. We're the same person." That was more or less true. I still felt more like Helena Campbell than a dual persona, but the oracle no longer spoke to me through my thoughts, and it was the best I could do to explain those flashes of insight.

Lucia's jaw went slack. She recovered quickly and said, "That's going to drive the Board of Neutralities crazy."

I hadn't thought about that. "They can't control me, can they? I'm not a Neutrality, I'm a person!"

"I have no idea what they'll think. But you shouldn't fall in line if they want to order you around. I'll back you up if necessary, but I think you'll find they're intimidated enough not to behave as if everything is as it used to be." Lucia shoved back her chair and stood. "Go home. Shower. I'll send Campbell to you when the Well is secure. Let us take care of the rest—what the hell are we supposed to do about the store?"

There were a lot of things I hadn't considered yet. "In a sense, the oracle is lost. I don't think I can do what it did with choosing auguries, but I could be wrong about that. I guess, as soon as it's repaired, I'll go back and...see what happens."

"You have the strongest work ethic of anyone I know. Don't you ever get tired of it?"

I shrugged. "I plan to go home and sleep for a week. How's that for getting tired of it?"

I'd driven to the Gunther Node in my own car despite Lucia's commando insisting that I didn't look well enough to drive, and now I took myself home. I didn't know what I looked like, but I felt perfectly okay. I didn't even feel emotionally overwhelmed. That would probably hit me later that night. I didn't feel anything except hungry and in the mood for pasta.

When I got home and into the bathroom, though, I realized why I'd gotten all those strange looks. My hair looked like rats had nested in it, my face was white and streaky with plaster dust, my clothes looked like I'd rolled around on a dirty floor—not true; Abernathy's was always clean—and my eyes were red-rimmed like I'd been crying. They also looked strange beyond that, but I couldn't put my finger on what was different. I ran my fingers through my hair and shook about five ounces of dust onto the countertop. Time for a shower.

It took three shampoos and rinses to get all the dust out of my hair, but when that was done, I felt cleaner than I ever had. I examined my left hand, which wasn't as stiff as it had been. It was still faintly yellow. I couldn't tell if the color had faded at all, but I liked to think it had.

Downstairs, I set water on to boil for pasta and turned on the television. The news was still reporting on the attack on Portland, and it sent a chill through me—maybe I was wrong, and I hadn't stopped anything—until I remembered the finality of that golden attack, and my knowledge that there were still invaders in our reality. I felt the tiniest twinge of guilt that my solution hadn't saved everyone and mentally slapped myself. I'd sacrificed my own life for this, and I needed to be grateful for all the people it *had* saved.

I changed the channel to *Jeopardy!* and set the pasta to cooking. I didn't want anything more than noodles Romanoff, simple and delicious, and easy to make for one person—

I sank down onto a kitchen chair and put my face in my hands as the enormity of what had happened finally struck. I didn't feel like crying, but I shook as if the tears were pouring out of me. It was too big to comprehend. What I'd done…and the oracle had said it wasn't even because I was anything special, just a woman with certain qualities who the oracle had liked. That felt right. I certainly didn't want to be some superhero.

And yet, now that I was the oracle, wasn't that what it made me? A superhero? The shakes returned, double strength, and I wrapped my arms around myself and tried to breathe normally. I didn't even know how it worked, whether other people still had to ask me questions, or if prophecies would come to me at random, or something else I hadn't even considered.

I wished desperately that Malcolm was home so I could tell him everything and get his advice. I didn't dare text or call because I didn't know if that would disrupt whatever he was doing at the Well. And I wanted him to be the first to know— the first after Lucia—so I didn't want to call Judy or Viv, even though I was sure they'd be supportive.

I realized I'd let the pasta cook too long and hurried to drain it. It would be too soft, but I no longer cared.

When I finished eating, I put my dishes into the dishwasher and contemplated the sink. For once, the idea of cleaning didn't soothe me. What I wanted, I realized, was to read more of that book I'd been engaged with before the attack. Did I want to drive all the way back to poor, ruined Abernathy's just for one book? I realized the answer was Yes and got in my car.

I decided to enter from the street side, as I'd left the book on the front counter and going through the back meant passing the enormous mess the invader had made of the store. The street was crowded with National Guard forces helping to clear away bodies. I'd almost forgotten all the deaths that had preceded my destruction of the invaders. The cordon stretched well down the street, so I parked beyond it and walked the rest of the way. No one stopped me, either because the growing darkness obscured me from the busy people or because part of my transformation had given me a limited invisibility. Probably it was the former. I hoped it was the former. Invisibility was a pain.

I let myself in through the front door, marveling at how it transformed the light of the setting sun into a hundred tiny rainbows. The book had been knocked off the counter by the teeming mass of invaders that had destroyed the cash register, but it was unharmed. I picked it up and dusted it off carefully, shaking the glass shards from the broken window off it. I would have to tell Judy what had happened before she came in tomorrow morning and found out about the destruction the hard way.

Aside from the shattered window and the thick coating of plaster dust that covered the counter, the shelves, and the floor, the store looked remarkably intact. No bookcases had been knocked over, no books had fallen off the shelves. I tried to right the cash register and discovered it weighed about a ton. I'd leave it for the Wardens, assuming anyone wanted to rebuild Abernathy's.

I'd thought I only wanted the book, but something drew me into the maze of aisles. It felt so strange, wandering in the stacks without the oracle's presence. "We both changed, I think," I said quietly. "It sounds like we both died to become something new. And now that something new is…I don't know what we've become, but I'm grateful it let the Helena part have her life back. I'll miss talking to the oracle, though."

An image rose up before me, like a memory, but sharper and clearer. I recognized it as Mount Scott. <The invaders are moving south to Crater Lake.>

Again, it was like the knowledge simply appeared in my mind, and seconds later I translated it into words. I immediately pulled out my phone and called Lucia, who to my surprise picked up rather than letting my call go to voicemail. "The invaders are leaving the city and heading south to Crater Lake," I said.

"We'll surround them. Thanks," Lucia said. The phone went dead.

I shoved my phone into my stupidly shallow pocket and leaned against a bookcase, regretting it instantly when my shoulder picked up a line of white dust. "That was interesting," I said. "I wonder if I'll ever get to where I don't need to turn that knowledge into words? Though if I have to communicate those prophecies to other people, they'll have to be words sometime."

I walked through the stacks to the back hall and entered the office. That room didn't look as if anything had happened to the store. I looked at Silas's picture for a while. "So the oracle really did tell you to become a magus," I said. "I guess we won't ever know why. Maybe it liked you and wanted you to be happy."

After another moment's consideration, I took Silas's picture off the wall. It revealed the wall safe, but I found I didn't care whether anyone saw that or not. "You saw the beginnings of the store here," I told the picture, "and I saw its end. I think that means we should stick together."

I stacked the book on top of the picture and walked back to the front of the store, crunching glass shards underfoot as I neared the counter. The wards the intelligent invader had revealed had disappeared again. Whether they were destroyed or had reformed, I had no way to tell, though the way the invader had parted the threads without breaking them suggested that maybe the hole had sealed itself. It didn't matter. The invaders weren't coming back, and there was nothing mundane that would be interested in the store's contents, especially with the National Guard just outside.

I stood inside the broken window and watched the National Guard carry body after body to ambulances and trucks. The sight of so many bodies made me sick, and again I felt guilt that I couldn't save them. Misplaced guilt, since that would have been impossible, and what I really felt was sorrow and anger at their deaths. I wondered what the final death count had been. It didn't matter. Even one death at the claws of an invader was too many.

The sky grew darker, and street lights came on, making the horrifying scene less terrible. The pole halfway inside Abernathy's stayed dark, of course. I finally snapped out of my reverie and let myself out, locking the door behind me out of habit. I again walked unnoticed down the street to my car. The distant hum of the city comforted me. Life went on, even in the midst of tragedy.

When I was in my car and about to start the engine, my phone buzzed with an incoming text from Malcolm: WHY ARE YOU STILL AT THE STORE?

We had apps on our phones that let us see the other's location, something Malcolm had suggested a while back when he'd come home late from the hunt and I'd freaked out a little. LONG STORY. YOU COMING HOME SOON?

EVEN LONGER STORY. BACK IN AN HOUR. LOVE YOU.

I smiled and headed for home.

It was closer to an hour and a half before Malcolm returned, but I was engrossed in my book and hadn't noticed he was still gone until the patio door slid open. I ran to greet him and fell into his arms, welcoming his kiss that felt as if we hadn't seen each other for a year. "Sorry for the delay," he said. "It took longer than expected to retrieve the custodian's body."

"But you found it? Does that mean the Well is usable again?"

Malcolm took my hand and led me upstairs. His fatigues and his face were filthy, making him look like a coal miner after a long day in the mines. "What happened to your eyes?" he asked, peering into them. "They've changed color."

I remembered thinking something was different about them. "What color are they now?"

"Sort of brownish-blue. It's nothing I've ever seen before."

"Um…that's a long story." I wondered in passing why no one had told the teams in Iraq what had happened in Portland. Malcolm would still be gone if he knew that. I guessed Lucia had done as she'd promised. "But you didn't say if the Well is active now."

"Not yet. Al-Hussein thinks if the Board appoints a successor, and the Well receives the right kind of supplication, it will be restored in a few months. Not good news, but not the worst. We'll just have to hold out against the invaders without it."

Right. The Board of Neutralities. I'd need to tell them

what happened. "Get cleaned up," I said. "I have something to tell you."

Malcolm began taking off his clothes. "Something good? I could use some good news."

"Something...unexpected," I said.

WE LAY TOGETHER in bed while I told Malcolm the story. He became gradually stiller as I progressed, listening intently the way he always did when something awful happened to me. When I got to the part where I died, his arm around my shoulders tightened, but he made no sound. At the end, he said, "That seems so...anticlimactic, maybe? One person goes into the invaders' reality and destroys it. Not shuts it off from ours, destroys it."

"Not one person, the oracle with the power of Abernathy's' node. And the collusion of the invaders, apparently. They had to shut down all the other ways they were getting into our reality, or something like that."

"But they were slipping through all sorts of little cracks, all over the world."

I shrugged. "I didn't say I understood it."

Malcolm took my hand with his free one. "I can't believe the Long War is over. Mostly over."

"There's still a lot of loose invaders in our world, and probably some of the intelligent ones. But...yeah." I stretched and cuddled closer. "It still doesn't seem real. I wouldn't believe it myself if I didn't have such vivid memories."

"And now you are the oracle."

"I don't understand that either yet. Knowledge comes to

me without me asking for it. That seems not nearly so useful as the oracle was."

"Time enough to work that out." Malcolm squeezed my shoulder. "Does the Board know?"

"Not unless Lucia told them. I'm going to tell Viv and Judy first, and *then* I will call Ariadne. And after that, I'm going to sleep for a million years."

"I hope not," Malcolm said. "I had other plans for tonight."

I laughed, and kissed him, a casual gesture that turned into more kisses, warm and passionate kisses I craved. He drew me closer until I was pressed against his body, holding him tight. "You know I might be a powerful supernatural being now?"

"Even better," Malcolm said.

EPILOGUE

SEVEN YEARS LATER

Picnic day. I laid out slices of bread on the counter and slathered creamy peanut butter on half of them, wishing I'd thought to grab a stool. Standing at the counter made my back sore these days, but I never remembered that until I was there. The ache was motivation to work fast. I squirted honey from the plastic bear onto the peanut butter and slapped more bread atop that, finishing all the sandwiches in record time.

Xerxes shot through the kitchen, heading for the stairs, and then a streak of pink flashed past, laughing like crazy. I put my hand on my lower back and shouted, "*Malcolm!* Your son is naked again!"

Thumping came from the direction of the stairs. The laughter turned into a shriek and helpless giggles. Soon Malcolm came into the kitchen, holding Duncan upside down by his ankles. "Why is he always my son when he does this?"

"Because your mother told me you used to do it, and I blame your genetic contribution." Three-year-old Duncan reached for me, and I squeezed his hand before rubbing the curve of my enormous protruding belly. "Please dress him? And maybe convince him to stay dressed?"

Malcolm tossed the boy into the air, catching him in an upright position. "No park if you take off your clothes," he said in an exaggeratedly menacing voice.

Duncan giggled again. "I want to go to the park."

"Then let's put on some clothes," Malcolm replied, and put the boy under one arm like a football and charged out of the room. I sort of hoped Duncan would pee all over him at times like that. He'd certainly done it to me often enough before potty training set in.

I cut the sandwiches into triangles and inserted them into plastic baggies. "Alastair, come help Mommy," I called out.

My oldest son came in from the living room, his book in his hand. "I'm reading."

"You're always reading. The book isn't going anywhere. Why don't you pick out some fruit and put it in the basket?"

Alastair nodded and set the book on the counter. I eyed it suspiciously. *Harry Potter and the Goblet of Fire.* Not as heavy-going as his usual fare, but Alastair had been reading since before he was three, and five years old struck me as a little early for Harry Potter. He was so serious all the time, it was like having a tiny adult in the house. I wasn't sure I was up to being the mother of a genius, but he was also sweet and considerate and a huge help in keeping Duncan out of trouble.

My baby chose that moment to stretch painfully within me. I was so past ready for her to be born, even though I had another two weeks to go. Alastair looked from my belly to me. "Does it hurt?" he asked, for once sounding like a child.

"Only a little. It's more like someone pushing on my tummy." I took his hand and pressed it to where he could feel the baby move again. His eyes, the same brownish-blue as mine, lit up.

Duncan came running in again, this time clad in shorts and T-shirt with his little bare feet slapping the tile. "Mommy, can we have cookies? I want to choose the cookies!"

"All right, you can choose. Use a stool." It probably wasn't the best idea to encourage Duncan in reaching the upper shelves of the pantry, but he was remarkably well-behaved when it came to not taking food without permission and it beat having him climb them like a blond monkey. I suspected Alastair's example.

Alastair was putting bananas in the picnic basket. Duncan brought me an unopened package of Oreos, which I set beside the bananas. He watched me curiously with those same brownish-blue eyes as I moved the sandwiches so they wouldn't get squished. Suddenly, he laughed. "Mommy, you wet your pants!"

I looked at him in confusion. Then I bolted for the washroom. I made it as far as standing in front of the toilet when my abdomen lurched weirdly and a gush of fluid poured down my legs. For a moment, I stood still, shocked by the suddenness of it. Then I shouted for Malcolm.

"He's not naked anymore..." Malcolm came into sight of me. His smile fell away as he took in my shocked expression. "What—"

"My water broke," I said. "I need a towel."

Malcolm pulled a towel out of the cupboard and handed it to me. "Go get changed. I'll call Viv and tell the kids the picnic is on hold."

I mopped myself as dry as I could manage and went upstairs. About halfway up, a contraction gripped me, not a hard one, but enough to make me pause. There was no need to rush, but wasn't it true that labor got shorter with every child?

I hurried through giving myself a quick sponging down and changing into a new loose-fitting dress. Then I made my way back down the stairs and sat in the rarely-used front room.

Alastair peeked around the door frame. "Are you having the baby?"

"I will soon, yes. Don't worry, everything will be fine."

"Don't take the freeway."

"I—" He sounded just like he always did. "We won't."

"Good." He gave me a hug and ran off. I stared after him. Good warning. I could imagine being in active labor, stuck on the freeway and giving birth in the car.

Someone knocked on the front door and opened it without waiting for an invitation. "I hear someone is in need of a babysitter," Viv said. "You all right?"

"That was fast," I said, rising to greet her and Jeremiah. "Malcolm called you just minutes ago."

"I had a feeling we would be needed." Viv hugged me. Ever since receiving her aegis, she'd started having premonitions—nothing as specific as what Victor Crowson saw, but in combination with the perceptive powers of the glass aegis, they were unambiguous and one hundred percent accurate. Viv had taken it in stride the way she'd accepted everything about becoming a magus. It almost made me forget that she hadn't been one her whole life.

Another contraction hit just then. It still wasn't as strong as they would become, but it was closer to the previous one than I liked. "We were going on a picnic," I said.

"We can handle that," Jeremiah said. He called out, "Alastair, I brought you and Duncan something."

Alastair shouted something in the distance, once more

sounding like a five year old, and he and Duncan ran into the entryway and threw themselves at Jeremiah, who laughed. You'd never know he disliked children by the way he treated mine, but then he also always treated them like adults, and to my surprise, they responded well to that.

Malcolm appeared behind the boys, toting my bag. "Time to go," he said. "You know where everything is?"

"Someone will," Viv said. "Hurry. I'm looking forward to meeting my namesake."

Malcolm helped me into the car, the Honda Accord he'd bought the minute he found out I was pregnant with Alastair. I didn't think he missed the Mustang much. "Alastair said to avoid the freeway," I told him as we backed down the driveway.

Malcolm shot me a look I had no trouble interpreting. "Just like that?"

"Malcolm—"

"Helena, we have to figure this out soon. He'll be starting kindergarten in the fall. Bad enough he's a genius, what happens when he starts prophesying on the playground?"

"I've taught them both to identify thoughts that are actually prophecies, and we're working on learning what to do about them. He knows not to mention them to anyone. He can keep the secret."

"And if the prophecy is to save someone's life? Some other child?"

I sighed. The sigh turned into a gasp as a contraction hit. It took me a second or two to regain my breath to respond. "I don't know the answer, Malcolm. I have a hard time figuring out what to do with spontaneous prophecies for non-Wardens myself. You know the alternative."

Malcolm's hands tightened on the steering wheel. "I don't

want him homeschooled. You have enough to deal with without adding that burden. And a tutor is almost as bad. He needs to learn how to get along with other kids."

"You know all the research says kids are better socialized when they're around adults than other kids."

Malcolm shook his head. "I'm not worried about his socialization. He's like a tiny adult. That makes it even more important that he understands the way ordinary people his own age behave."

Another contraction gripped me. "I don't want to tell you to speed," I said through gritted teeth, "but sooner is better."

"We're almost there."

We pulled up under the hospital portico, and Malcolm got out and ran inside to find someone with a wheelchair. The contractions were hard enough now I didn't think I could make it under my own power. Men and women passed our car and glanced at me incuriously. I didn't try to smile. It would have come out as a grimace.

Malcolm returned, trotting beside an orderly pushing a wheelchair. "All right, let's get you inside," the man said with a cheery smile. I nodded, unable to speak as the biggest contraction so far hit me.

The rest of the time passed in a haze of pain. I remembered my doctor saying, "No epidural, Helena, you'll give birth before it has time to kick in," and then a lot of moaning, probably from me. Then Malcolm was gripping my hand and telling me to push, and I pushed, once, twice, and on the third time felt my belly go slack as the baby slipped out of me. I gasped with relief. Malcolm kissed my forehead. "She's perfect," he said.

He left me to help bathe her, and soon they brought her to

me and tucked her into my arms. "Genevieve," I whispered. "Little Jenny."

She opened her eyes and looked at me. They were the same brownish-blue as my own. *It breeds true,* I thought, and cuddled her close to my heart.

MALCOLM BROUGHT the boys to see their sister that evening, shortly after my mother and father stopped by. Duncan bounced until I reminded him he had to sit still if he wanted to hold her. Even so, Malcolm hovered nearby. Alastair watched everything in wide-eyed silence and held his sister gently when it was his turn. "She's so small," he said.

"You were even smaller than that when you were born," I said.

"I spoke with Mother this afternoon," Malcolm said. "She won't be back from Vancouver for a few days, but I told her it would be all right for her to visit after that."

"Send her lots of pictures," I said. Sometimes it still struck me as strange that Madeleine and I weren't at each other's throats anymore. We would never be close, but she wasn't my enemy.

Someone rapped on the door, and Judy poked her head inside. "We're not intruding, are we?" she asked.

"No, come in. You didn't bring Sophia, did you?"

Judy entered, followed by Mike. "She's with Father," Judy said. "I think he likes the excuse to eat fast food."

"I don't like Sophia," Duncan said.

"Duncan, don't be rude," I warned him.

"You like Sophia," Malcolm said, "right up until she outraces you."

Duncan scowled. He and Judy's daughter were the same age, and they were either going to kill each other or end up married.

Judy glanced at me for permission, then took Jenny into her arms. "She's precious. And…she has the eyes."

"All babies have eyes of an indeterminate color," I said.

Judy shot me a narrow-eyed look. "You know better, though."

"I know better." I sighed. "Sometimes I wonder if I don't have a duty to the world to bear as many oracles as I can."

"You know better than *that*, too." Judy's expression went distant, and I felt like a jerk. Sophia had come along after seven miscarriages, and Judy and Mike had decided not to risk Judy's health further. Judy refused to talk about it, and I would never push, but the look in her eyes told me everything she wouldn't say.

"Yeah. Three is enough for me. We're officially outnumbered." I accepted Jenny from Judy and examined her, though I knew nothing bad had happened to her while she was away from me. The baby let out a tiny cry and waved a fist, tapping my nose and making me laugh.

"So are you taking a break?" Mike asked.

I nodded. "For a week. That's assuming I don't have any spontaneous revelations."

"A week isn't very long," Judy said with a frown.

"That's what I told her," Malcolm said. "She has a weird concept of maternity leave."

"It's not like my calling is a burden," I said. That wasn't precisely true. Being an oracle meant seeing things I wished I hadn't. But I'd never been able to explain to anyone, not Lucia, not my friends, not my husband, the swooping, beautiful feeling of a revelation unfolding inside me, even the devastating ones.

Just then, I felt it—a rush like diving into a deep pool, followed by bright images and knowledge I translated into words for the benefit of others. "Somebody tell Lucia her prey is holed up in the Bide-a-Wee Inn just outside Cardston," I said. "Room 208."

"He has a gun," Duncan said. "A big gun."

"And there's a lady with him," Alastair said.

Mike cleared his throat. Malcolm took out his phone and stepped into the hall. Judy said, "That never gets less disturbing."

"I wonder if Jenny saw it too?" I said, brushing a wisp of pale hair away from her forehead. Jenny burped. "We almost never all get the same revelation at the same time, or even related ones."

"Even so," Judy said. "The boys—" She shut up. I could guess what she was thinking.

"They'll learn," I said. "They all will."

―――――――

Eight days later, I sat down to the computer in the office and opened my message program. I'd switched to this dedicated computer years before, when the Board of Neutralities and I had worked out the details of how the new oracle would work. The office gave me more privacy. Now that there were no more factions in the aftermath of the invaders' attempted destruction of our reality, the Neutralities didn't need to be neutral anymore, but it comforted people to know that some things, at least, hadn't changed.

The oracle wasn't one of those things.

I checked my personal message box first. That was overflowing with congratulations from people all over the world. Claude had sent a letter and a baby blanket rather than a message, but Abdel Fayed, custodian of the Well, had messaged to let me know he had made a wish on our behalf. That warmed my heart.

I decided to leave answering those messages until later and changed to the oracle's box. That wasn't nearly so full, but the messages took longer to handle. I closed my eyes and centered myself, then turned to the message with the earliest time stamp:

I think my boyfriend is cheating on me. I don't know what to do.

No salutation, no signature. Not even really a question. The woman's pain, however, rang through those two sentences. Even now that the oracle was a person rather than a bookstore, the questions were always the same: Does he/she love me? Am I being played for a fool? How do I make this devastating choice? And the oracle still cared.

I let my knowledge of the answer fill me, and typed *You're afraid of being alone, but as long as you're with this cheating scumbag, you'll never find true love. Have the courage to confront him, and see what happens.*

I clicked Send, but didn't go on to the next message. I'd heard someone coming down the hall. Soon, the door opened, and Alastair came in. "What are you doing?"

"Oracle business." I hesitated, then said, "Do you want to watch?" Privacy was one thing, but my son was an oracle, too.

Alastair nodded and climbed into my lap. He had long, gawky legs that dangled and a very bony butt, but we found a comfortable position and I let him click open the next message.

I have the opportunity to take a new job, but it's risky and I have a young family who would bear the burden of that risk. I need to know where I'll be in five years if I take the new job.

Alastair reached the end of the message before I did. He ran his fingers along the frame of the keyboard.

"What do you think?" I said.

He turned his head to look at me. "Me?"

"This will be your job someday. Maybe someday soon. You already see the future...so what lies ahead for this woman?"

He turned back to regard the screen. "A big house, a nice car, but one of her children is gone," he said. "Should we tell her that?"

"What do you think?"

He shrugged one shoulder. "You said not to tell people scary things."

"That's for when you see their future and they didn't ask for it. This woman asked us a question. Don't you think she deserves the truth?"

Alastair thought about it for a minute. "Yeah. I think she wants her family more than the big house."

"Maybe. I agree. But the choice is up to her." I typed up a response and sent it.

Alastair put his hand on the mouse. "Can I do the next one?"

"Sweetheart," I said, "I know you can."

AUTHOR'S NOTE

How it all started:

This series began as a writing exercise in description. I had a couple of concepts in mind: the disorganized bookstore I'd seen in the French Quarter in New Orleans, the idea of books as prophecies, and my own superpower of being able to find random literary treasures when I'm not searching for them. I had no intention of writing a book; contemporary fantasy is not my usual thing, and all I really wanted was to practice writing deep description, something I felt inadequate at.

Then something strange happened. I couldn't find a stopping point, a place at which I was satisfied with the exercise. I wrote four chapters of *The Book of Secrets* before admitting to myself that I had at least a book in there somewhere, more likely a series.

This meant more serious planning. The original exercise was set in a generic city, but a real contemporary/urban fantasy needs a solid real-world anchor. Portland, Oregon is the only large city I both know well and was willing to set a story in—I was born in Gresham, and my grandparents still lived in Happy Valley (in a house that later became the model for Helena's parents' house). Helena, who had been a nebulous figure in the exercise, needed to be fleshed out. And I needed both a magic system and a conflict to provide a framework to hang a story on.

I'd written the first chapters while on vacation in Washington State, and on the drive back to Utah I asked my family for ideas about magic. It was my husband who came up with the idea for the aegis; the rest of us all said, "Ew, gross," and then set about making it work. I can't remember where the idea of invaders came from, but I know the factions were all mine. I loved the idea of pitting humans not only against monsters, but against each other.

I have a history of spitballing details that I later have to live with. Lucia Pontarelli's habit of referring to people by surname came *after* I'd named her aides, for example, leading to poor Dave Henry and Martin Maxwell being the guys with two first names. (Martin was not meant to be a traitor; that was more spitballing in book five, because I didn't know about the Mercy until I started writing book four.) Helena's fondness for lasagna. Absolutely everything about glass magic—I think glass magic was my favorite thing to invent. It is a minor miracle that I managed never to contradict myself—or at least was able to cover up inconsistencies. I hope. I'm sure fans will be quick to correct me if I'm wrong.

Before the end of *The Book of Secrets*, I had a plan for much of what the series would cover that amounted to some details about each of the series arcs, specifically the end of the Long War and the way Malcolm and Helena's relationship would play out. That left so much room for invention. Jeremiah Washburn, for example, was just a throwaway character in *The*

Book of Mayhem, someone who could wear funny T-shirts and appear to be a stereotypical geek while actually being a badass fighter. That he would stick around never occurred to me. It's thanks to Hallie O'Donovan that he is a reformed traitor and not an actual one. I think she said it would look bad to give Viv a serious boyfriend and then have him turn out to be evil. I like how it actually worked out way better.

Another thing that constantly surprises me is having the ability to accurately estimate how much space I'll need to tell a story, or in this case, a series. I originally thought it would take ten books, but I hadn't realized how compact the events of putative books eight and nine really were. So I guessed pretty close to what it ended up being. (And *The Book of War* remains one of my favorites of the series, so I feel combining the two potential books worked out great.)

It is always bittersweet, coming to the end of a long series. I remain deeply satisfied with how the whole thing worked out, and it's wonderful to let the final book out into the world for others to read. But I was immersed in the world of The Last Oracle for what works out to just over a year of writing (spread out over a couple of years) and then three years of publication, and that's a lot of time to be absorbed in anything.

I feel extraordinarily grateful that the series' rocky start with my former publisher, and the difficulties I had in getting the series re-released, did not result in the series disappearing. My thanks go out to all the readers who remained fans through the months during which *The Book of Mayhem*'s publication was repeatedly delayed for one thing and another.

I would also like to thank the many people who supported me and this unexpected series throughout its genesis and release. Alexandra Brandt did fantastic work not only with creating the covers, but researching other works in my odd genre before telling me that no, my idea was not crazy. We took a chance on not using people on the covers, and I think it paid off. (Anyone who remembers the original covers for the first two books—that was the same woman. Yes, I know she looks completely different in each. That inspired me to look for a different solution.)

First readers Jana Brown and Hallie O'Donovan patiently read each installment as I produced it and gave wonderful feedback. And, most importantly, my husband Jacob Proffitt was and is my greatest support and biggest fan, quick to laugh and quick to cry over Helena's adventures. Thank you all.

And, finally, thanks again to you, the reader. Writers work more or less in isolation, and it isn't until a book gets out into the world that we know if other people will love it like we do. You readers have made this series a tremendous success, and I cannot express how grateful and thrilled I am that you've embraced it. Thank you for giving me the opportunity to share my imagination with you.

ABOUT THE AUTHOR

In addition to The Last Oracle series, Melissa McShane is the author of The Extraordinaries series, beginning with BURNING BRIGHT, the Crown of Tremontane series, beginning with SERVANT OF THE CROWN, as well as COMPANY OF STRANGERS and many others.

After a childhood spent roaming the United States, she settled in Utah with her husband, four children and a niece, four very needy cats, and a library that continues to grow out of control. She wrote reviews and critical essays for many years before turning to fiction, which is much more fun than anyone ought to be allowed to have.

You can visit her at her website www.melissamcshanewrites.com for more information on other books.

For information on new releases, fun extras, and more, sign up for Melissa's newsletter: http://eepurl.com/brannP

If you enjoyed this book, please consider leaving a review at your favorite online retailer or Goodreads!

ALSO BY MELISSA MCSHANE

THE CROWN OF TREMONTANE

Servant of the Crown

Exile of the Crown

Rider of the Crown

Agent of the Crown

Voyager of the Crown

Tales of the Crown

THE SAGA OF WILLOW NORTH

Pretender to the Crown

Guardian of the Crown

Champion of the Crown

THE HEIRS OF WILLOW NORTH

Ally of the Crown

Stranger to the Crown (forthcoming)

THE EXTRAORDINARIES

Burning Bright

Wondering Sight

Abounding Might

Whispering Twilight (forthcoming)

THE LAST ORACLE

The Book of Secrets

The Book of Peril

The Book of Mayhem

The Book of Lies

The Book of Betrayal

The Book of Havoc

The Book of Harmony

The Book of War

The Book of Destiny

COMPANY OF STRANGERS

Company of Strangers

Stone of Inheritance

Mortal Rites

Shifting Loyalties

Sands of Memory

Call of Wizardry

THE CONVERGENCE TRILOGY

The Summoned Mage

The Wandering Mage

The Unconquered Mage

THE BOOKS OF DALANINE

The Smoke-Scented Girl

The God-Touched Man

Emissary

Warts and All: A Fairy Tale Collection

The View from Castle Always

Printed in Great Britain
by Amazon

24442768R00225